FOREIGN
GODS,
INC.

FOREIGN GODS, INC.

OKEY NDIBE

SOHO

For Chibu, Chiamaka, and Chidebe—the best stories Sheri and I will ever tell.

Published by

Soho Press, Inc.

853 Broadway

New York, NY 10003

Library of Congress Cataloging-in-Publication Data

Ndibe, Okey, 1960–
Foreign Gods, Inc. / Okey Ndibe.
p. cm
ISBN 978-1-61695-313-3
eISBN 978-1-61695-314-0

1. Taxicab drivers—Fiction. 2. Nigerian Americans—Fiction. 3. Artthefts—New York (State)—New York. 4. Arts, Nigerian—New York (State)—New York.
I. Title.
PR9387.9.N358F67 2014
823'.92—dc23   2013025995

Interior design by Janine Agro, Soho Press, Inc.

Printed in the United States of America

10 9 8 7 6 5 4 3 2 1

CHAPTER ONE

kechukwu Uzondu, "Ike for short," parked his Lincoln Continental cab at a garage that charged twelve dollars per hour. Before shutting off the engine, he looked at the car's electronic clock. Nine forty-seven A.M.: it meant the gallery would have been open for a little less than an hour. *Perfect,* Ike thought, for he wished to be done transacting his business before the place started buzzing.

He walked a block and a half to 19 Vance Street. Had a small animal been wedged in his throat, his heart could not have pounded more violently.

The eave over the door bore a sign etched in black over a bluish background: FOREIGN GODS, INC. It was written in tiny, stylized lettering, as if intended to create a tactful anonymity. Few would stumble upon a store like this; it would be found, it seemed, only by habitués and devotees.

Across the street was a bar. Ike contemplated a quick drink or two to calm his nerves. How odd to vend a war god while jittery. Yet, to go in smelling of alcohol might also be a costly mistake.

The gallery door clicked, and a tanned woman walked out. A squat carved statue was clutched close to her breast, held in a suckling posture. At the curb, a gleaming black BMW pulled up. She opened the rear door and leaned in, arched backside revealing the outline of her underwear. Her black high-heeled shoes were riveted with nodes of diamond. She strapped the deity in place with the seat belt and then straightened. The car's front door was opened from inside. She lowered herself in, and the car sped off.

Ike pulled at the gallery door—surprisingly light. A wide, sprawling space unfurled itself: gray marble floors, turquoise walls, and glass-paneled showcases. A multitude of soft, recessed lights accentuated the gallery's dim, spectral atmosphere. In the middle of the room, slightly to the left of the door, a spiral staircase with two grille-work banisters rose to an upper floor. Ike knew from the *New York* magazine piece that people went upstairs only by invitation. And that those invitations went only to a small circle of long-term collectors or their designated dealers.

There was an otherworldly chill in the air. There was also a smell about the place, unsettling and hard to name. Ike froze at the edge of the run of stairs that led down to the floor of the gallery. From the elevation, he commanded a view. The space was busy but not cluttered. Clusters of short, squat showcases were interspersed with long and deep ones. Here and there, some customers peered into the glass cases or pored over catalogs.

In a matter of two, three weeks, his people's ancient deity, Ngene, would be here, too. And it would enjoy pride of place, not on this floor, with the all-comers and nondescripts, but upstairs, in the section called Heaven. Ngene was a majestic god with a rich legend and history. How many other gods could boast of dooming Walter Stanton, that famed English missionary whose name, in the syllable-stretching mouths of the people of Utonki, became *Su-tan-tee-ny?*

The thought gave him a gutsy boost. He trotted down the steps to the floor of the gallery. Walking unhurriedly, he cast deliberate glances about him, so that an observer might mistake him for a veteran player in the rare sport where gods and sacred curios were bought and sold. He paused near the spiral staircase. A sign warned PLEASE DO NOT ASCEND UNLESS ESCORTED. He walked on to a chest-high showcase. A hefty wooden head stared at him from atop a rectangular stump. The face was pitched forward, like a tortoise's head poking out of a shell. On closer inspection, Ike saw that the carved head was deformed by a chipped, flattened nose and large, bulgy eyes. Inside the case, four fluorescent puck lights washed the statue with crisscross patterns of luminescence and shadows. A fork-tongued serpent coiled itself round the statue's neck.

There was an electronic key code for the showcase's twin-winged door, and several perforations in the glass, small and circular, as if designed to let in and let out just enough air to keep the glum, rigid statue from suffocating. A strip tag glued to the glass cage identified the deity as C1760. Ike picked up a glossy catalog and thumbed to the C section. Each page was columned, with sections marked "inventory code," "name," "brief history," and "price." He ran his finger down the line until he saw the tag number. Then he drew his finger across to the price column: $29,655.

He flipped the pages to the catalog's last section, marked "Heavenly Inventory." The lowest price in the section was $171,455; the highest $1.13 million. He studied the image of one of the deities in that section. Carved from soot-black wood, it had two fused figures, one female, and the other male. The figures backed each other. The female was big breasted and boasted a swollen belly. The male figure held a hoe in one hand, a gun in the other, its grotesque phallus extending all the way to its feet. They shared the same androgynous head, turned neither left nor right but forward. A pair of deep-set eyes seemed to return Ike's stare. It was listed for $325,630. Ike read the short italicized description: *A god of the crossroads, originally from Papua New Guinea.*

"Wait until they see Ngene," he said under his breath, a flush of excitement washing over him. Surely, a legendary god of war would command a higher price than a two-faced crossroads idler.

At the thought, the catalog slipped from his hands and thudded on the floor. He hastily picked it up, glancing all around. Perhaps the gallery's surveillance camera was beamed on him, trailing his every movement?

He moved to another showcase. He squatted, bit his lip, and peered intensely at the encased quarry, nodding like a connoisseur. From nowhere some foul whiff brushed his nose and he recoiled.

He heard a woman's low voice and stood to look, but two show-cases blocked his view.

"Have I ever—ever—been too busy for you?" a man answered in a stentorian voice.

A pair of sequined magenta shoes descended the staircase. These yielded toned calves, then sturdy thighs that disappeared beneath a tight purplish skirt, and then the tanned, tight upper body of a blonde. Then, behind her, the man appeared.

Ike recognized Mark Gruels, the owner of the gallery. He did not panic, his poise a remarkable feat, considering what was at stake. Neither the woman nor Gruels looked Ike's way. Her right arm was around his waist, his left arm draped over her shoulder. They circled the staircase and walked down another aisle, toward the far wall.

Ike watched them but pretended to be riveted by the catalog. Gruels was a head taller than the woman, even though she looked at least five nine. Cerise pearls adorned the woman's neck. Gruels's groomed appearance seemed to leave some room for cultivated ruggedness. He had a full head of black hair, garnished with dots of gray. He wore a dark green down vest over a bleached green shirt, one sleeve rolled up to the elbow, the other left unrolled.

Gruels and the woman spoke inaudibly for a moment, entranced by the same object: a mammoth, snout-faced statue in a showcase.

"So?" the woman finally asked.

Gruels swayed side to side, as if in deep thought. Then he shook his head doubtfully.

"Why not?" she asked.

"Not that one," he said in the tone of a man accustomed to confident judgments. His voice was deep, even a little gravelly. "You're looking at a goddess. She's definitely not a good fit. Not for you. You do better with strong male gods. You'd find her—shall I say—a bit too feisty. Too cranky."

"She's quite the cutie," the woman said, leaning into Gruels.

"No question, but she's not your type. Trust me." He pressed her closer to him. "You don't want a goddess that clashes with your personality. Plus, it doesn't jibe with your other acquisitions."

"It's actually not for me. I'd like something amazing for my brother. And this should do."

"Birthday?" Gruels asked.

"No, he's never been big on birthdays. He's just having a tough time rebounding."

"Has he been sick?"

"No, divorced."

"Josh?" Gruels sounded incredulous.

"Yes, darling—you know I have only the one brother."

"He and Heather parted ways?"

"Oh, Mark, have you been living in a cave again?"

"No, really," said Gruels. "I'm sorry to hear it."

She turned sideways and rested her body against his. Gruels rubbed and kneaded her shoulders. Ike felt a tug in the crotch.

She related how Heather had run away with another woman, leaving Josh crushed.

Finally, Gruels said, "A man dumped by his wife for another woman deserves some spectacular gift. You can't get better than this." He glanced up at the deity. "This, here, is a Mayan marvel."

"And what are you asking for her?"

"Twenty thousand—eighteen thousand for you."

"Sir, can I help you with anything?"

Ike turned, startled. A petite woman stood behind him.

"How may I help you?" she asked again.

Her nose was pierced midridge with a toothpick-sized coppery crossbar. Her head was shaved close to the scalp. A whorl of tattoos ran all over her arms and neck.

"I came to see—"

"Mark?" she interjected.

"Mr. Gruels," he said. Despite all his years in America, he'd never become comfortable with the idea of calling strangers by their given name. "Yes."

Her eyes lit up. "Did you call two days ago?"

"Three. Yes."

"I recognized that accent!" Ike stiffened at the word "accent," and his eyes blazed. Oblivious, she continued: "Listen, Mark's busy with a customer right now. You can wait for him right here. Unless it's something I can help you with. My name is Stacy."

"I'll wait," he said, still vexed by that reference to his accent.

He turned and nearly bumped into Gruels. The gallery owner held the blonde with one hand, the Mayan deity with the other.

"Mark, this gentleman wants to see you," Stacy announced.

Letting go of the blonde's hand, Gruels seemed to whirl around to Ike.

"You want to see me?"

Not in everybody's presence, Ike thought. "I'll wait until you finish. With her." He pointed at the blonde.

Gruels smirked and then retook the woman's hand. "Until I finish with her? What makes you think I want to *ever* be finished with her?"

Gruels laughed, and the woman followed suit, her head thrown back. Gruels whispered into her ear, released her, and circled back to Ike. "Yes, I'm listening," he said.

Ike's tongue felt coated. Why didn't Gruels invite him to an office or some secluded corner?

Gruels folded his arms. "Yes?"

"I have—"

"Yes, you have what?"

"A business proposal."

Gruels slapped both hands, bemused. "You want to invest in my business? Great! How much are we talking here?"

Ike gave a short, awkward chuckle.

"It's a busy morning for me," Gruels said. "Business proposal. You've got to spell out what you mean. And you've got to do it quick." He glanced at his wristwatch. "I have a meeting to run to—in, like, *now*! So?"

"I have a god I can bring," he said.

"You have a god?"

"Yes."

"Great. Let's see it."

"I'm traveling to bring it."

"You don't have it?"

"Not yet."

"So what's the point of this discussion?"

Ike swallowed hard. "I want you to buy it."

"Buy what? I can't buy what doesn't exist." Gruels glanced at Stacy, who tightened her lips and shrugged.

"It exists," Ike cried, his voice close to combative. Then, checking himself, he added, "It's a powerful deity, too."

Gruels regarded him with intense eyes. "I don't buy stories; I buy *things*. You see what I mean?" He glanced at his watch again and turned sharply sideways, as if to walk away. Instead, he tarried and addressed Ike. "Bottom line, you have nothing to show me."

"In less than three weeks, I will have it."

"So why are we holding this discussion *now*? Why don't we have it in three weeks—or whenever you've got something to show?"

Ike said, "It's a god of war."

"It could be a god of shit for all I care." Gruels paused, his eyes danced, taking in Ike with curious interest. He put a left hand on Ike's shoulder. "I don't mean to insult you. That's not what I'm about."

"It used to lead our people to war," Ike explained, determined to capitalize on the indirect apology.

"That's great," Gruels said, his tone flavored anew with sarcasm. "Great for your people."

Thoughts tossed about in Ike's mind. He foraged for the magic words that would kindle the other's interest. He saw Gruels's lips quiver, about to speak. Anxiety overcame him.

"Trust me," he said. "It's a very, very ancient deity. A very powerful god."

"So you say. Great! Nobody ever sold me a shitty god. And nobody ever bought one from me. Every god I ever bought or sold had the greatest mojo in all of time. So, what's new?" He took another look at his watch.

"How much are you willing to pay for it?"

Gruels scratched his forehead and then gazed at Ike, silent.

"Trust me," Ike said, unable to bear the silent exchange of stares.

Gruels spread his arms in a sweeping gesture. "This store has great inventory. Look around, see for yourself." He paused, as if to permit Ike to take a look. "You don't seriously expect me to discuss the buying of—*nothing*! It doesn't even make sense."

"I told you about the—"

"Yes, you've told me a lot. You've said how powerful this god is. You've said it's ancient. You've said blah blah blah." He spread his arms again. "Well, guess what? My entire inventory is made up of powerful, ancient deities. I ask again, what's new?"

"In olden days, this god—it's called Ngene—led our warriors to wars. And they never lost one."

"Ngina—that's the name?"

"Ngene." Ike spelled the word.

"Are there written accounts of these wars?"

"My uncle told me."

"You expect me to do a deal—based on something your uncle told you?"

"He's the deity's chief priest. He knows everything about Ngene."

Gruels crinkled his brow. "Did you say your uncle is the chief priest of this same god?"

Ike nodded and looked away.

"So, is he offering to sell this—what's its name again?"

"Ngene."

"Is the priest offering to sell this god?"

Ike shook his head.

"So, you're not acting as your uncle's agent?"

"No."

"Let me ask a different way. Do you have your uncle's permission to do this deal?"

"No."

Gruels gave a mirthless smile. "Listen, don't think I'm judging you; that's not my thing. I'd love to do business with you—and I mean it. But you've got to show me something. Not just stories your uncle told you, *something*. We have a process of authentication, and it's fairly rigorous. The gallery's policy is to insist on things that are written down."

"I know," Ike said. "There's a story about the first British missionary who arrived in Utonki."

"What about him?"

"He threatened to destroy Ngene but drowned in a river owned by the god."

"Your uncle told you this?"

"Everybody in Utonki knows the story. But it's also in a booklet."

Gruels nodded eagerly. "Great! Now, if that booklet exists, bring it along with the inventory."

"Mark, remember your meeting at Elbow Room," Stacy shouted.

"Thanks, Stace," Gruels said. Then to Ike: "We'll see you when you've got the stuff in your hands."

Ike raised a hand frantically.

"Yes?" Gruels said.

"We haven't discussed the price. Could you tell me the range?"

Gruels's brow became furrowed in exasperation. "No, really," he said, slowly. "I discuss prices only when the inventory is in front of me. That's policy here at Foreign Gods. But you can be sure of one thing—no dealer tops our offer. You said you've got great merchandise. You get me a great item, you can count on getting a great offer. That's a promise."

He extended a hand. More out of confusion than design, Ike hesitated for a moment and then took it. Again Gruels placed his left hand on Ike's shoulder.

"Don't think I doubt that this is a great god. But this gallery is huge on authentication. Remember that. Nothing beats seeing things on paper—photographs, books, documents. If there are mentions in one or two scholarly texts, that's terrific."

Ike's heart chugged as he headed for the exit. Once outside, he drew deep drafts of air until he felt steadied. And then, in quick, springy strides, he hastened back to the garage.

CHAPTER TWO

Ike's body was belted to the car seat, but his spirits soared. For a moment, it seemed unreal that this was his last day as a cabdriver. His meeting with Gruels had not gone quite as well as he had hoped, but it was far from woeful. The man had said he'd love to do business with him. That, in the end, was what counted. All Gruels asked for was to see Ngene—to see *something*. *Fair enough,* Ike thought. After all, everything was set for his journey to scoop up the wooden statue of that ancient god of war named after a moody, mud-colored river.

It was already 11:36 A.M. There was the option of retiring to his apartment, but Ike dismissed the urge. At all hours, the noisy street intruded into the apartment, breached his solitude. It was better to roam the streets awhile, perhaps pick up a few last passengers, and trust the accustomed routines of work to contain the thoughts that sawed through his mind.

He'd worked as a driver for thirteen years, ever since graduating from Amherst College, cum laude, in economics. Now, it would be over. He had a confirmed seat on a KLM flight bound for Lagos, with a stopover in Amsterdam. From Lagos, he would travel east to

Utonki, the riverine town where he was born and had lived through secondary school. He'd wait for the perfect accomplice: a dark, moonless night. Then he'd tiptoe into the doorless, rectangular shrine. He'd sneak away with the war deity and be on his merry way back to New York City, where he would sell it to Foreign Gods, Inc. Gruels had refused to name a price, but Ike expected the gallery to offer far more cash than he ever made in any two or even three years he worked as a cabdriver, first in Springfield, Massachusetts, then Philadelphia, Atlanta, Baltimore, and now, New York.

After driving past several passengers, he finally stopped for two young women who hailed him on Chambers Street. They were headed for Mansoory Deli on East Fortieth Street. Settled in the backseat, they chattered. One had pale skin, a freckled nose, and dimpled cheeks. She prattled about visiting the Alps with two Norwegian friends but failing to ski even once; about different pubs in London; and about "making out with this mad cute guy" at a nightclub in Amsterdam.

Whenever she paused, the other—tanned and big boned—filled the silence with pieces of an extended story about private tango lessons she'd taken in Buenos Aires with one of the city's most famous dancers. The lesson was a birthday present from her grandmother.

When they got out, the tanned girl handed Ike a twenty-dollar bill for a fare of eighteen dollars and seventy-five cents. "You too," he muttered, in response to the freckled one's spirited wish of a great day.

For a moment, he again entertained the idea of heading for his apartment. He intended to turn right on Second Avenue. Instead, he turned left, toward United Nations Plaza. Nearing the plaza, he fixed on a man who seemed at once part of the familiar bustle and outside of it. The man, in turn, sought him. There was a certain air about the man, the more powerful for its oblique quality.

A *diplomat,* Ike thought, *most likely European.* The man seemed to possess an inbred, controlled charm. He was tall but with the suggestion of a stooped shoulder. In Ike's eye, the shoulder's slight curvature was a flattering feature; it hinted at personal gravity and the shouldering of diplomatic burdens.

He would make the perfect last passenger.

"Columbus Ave." the man said. "Three twenty-two." His voice was so soft and muffled that Ike couldn't tell whether his accent had a trace of foreignness. He trailed a rich, spicy fragrance into the cab.

"Hello," Ike said. When he heard no response, he added, "Good afternoon." Then, "Welcome, sir."

Not even a cough came in acknowledgment. The passenger held open a paperback book, hands raised in a boxer's defensive stance, a sparkling golden watch at his wrist.

Ike released his foot from the brake, and the car jerked forward, rolling up First Avenue. He had only gone a block when he was forced to stop. Ahead, a long line of cars shat a smashed omelet of red brake lights.

For the next ten minutes, the car did little but idle.

The passenger turned on the overhead light. The sun had vanished. Dense, lumbering clouds loomed. Lightning signed the sky. There followed a slow, liquid growl, a sky-sized monster's after-meal belch. Ike wanted to fight off the word *rainstorm,* but couldn't.

He sat up from his slouched position. Something vibrated against his left thigh. He shuddered. Then, pulling a cell phone out of his pocket, he saw notification of a text message. He studied the phone with irritation, certain that the message was from Big Ed Thelwell, his Jamaican neighbor and fellow cab driver. It was Big Ed who had pressured him to get the phone. For two or so years, Ike had defied all taunts about living in the past. He rather liked his antiquated, cordless landline. He abhorred the idea of other people being able to reach him at all hours, wherever he was. He slid the phone back in his pocket, uninterested in the message. Spine straightened, he pulled forward, as if hugging the steering wheel. The sky unleashed its torrent. The first sheets lashed against the car's roof and windshield. Then, as if some invisible conductor had given a cue, the storm ceased, leaving a mizzle of long, tiny darts.

IKE FEARED STORMS.

He was a second-year student in secondary school when the first assault happened. He was in the school's crowded cafeteria. A rainstorm began. Its *doowah*, *doowah* made him groggy, turned his limbs weak. Before shocked onlookers, he staggered this way and that, like a senseless drunk, and then fainted dead away. "You seemed to be sleeping," a friend told him later. "You even had a smile, as if you were having a sweet dream. Or just playing a game."

Ike remembered the sensation of absolute calm. That, and a feeling of being carried on something soft like a cloud, calm as a lake's surface on a windless day. And he remembered seeing many things that shimmered with such heartbreaking beauty there was no language to describe them.

The next time it happened, four storms later, he was in the classroom, taking French. Later, a classmate told him that the irate French teacher, Robertson Iwu (Monsieur Iwulili Iwuliti, the students named him) had rushed at him, trademark cane at the ready. The teacher was certain that Ike was up to some folly. He released two or three strokes on Ike, who lay there, motionless. His body absorbed the lashes without as much as a twitch. The furious teacher fled the classroom, convinced that his famous cane had flogged a corpse.

It was after this episode that the principal sent Ike home to seek medical treatment. His parents took him to a doctor. Numerous tests later, the baffled doctor said he had found no explanation.

One day, Ike went to visit his paternal grandmother, Nne. He told her about the strange force that snatched him away sometimes during rainstorms, and about the indescribably beautiful things he would see during his raptures.

"Ngene has favored you," Nne said.

Taken aback, Ike asked, "What does that mean?"

"You'll find out once you're old enough to understand. The same thing happened to your uncle, Osuakwu. Be patient."

"Are you saying I'll be the chief priest, like my uncle?"

"I don't speak for Ngene," said Nne.

Ike never shared her words: not with his parents or anybody else.

In the intervening years, the storm-triggered spells happened less frequently. Sometimes, a few years went by without one episode.

There had been only a few public incidents in the United States. After each episode, he awoke in a white room filled with bright lights and to questions about illicit drug use. While a seizure happened, it was close to rapturous release. Fear was in the anticipation. And then shame followed, when he noticed the curious glances of witnesses, their fear-filled whispers. It was that shame that made the experience anguished, impossible to forget.

That was why Ike never worked any day a storm was in the forecast.

He remembered the anchor saying last night, "Keep it right here and stay tuned for pinpoint weather, coming up next." And then there was Derek Jeter pitching some credit card. Ike had dozed off. He startled awake as a sports reporter screeched about the Yankees' tie-breaking home run in the second game of a split doubleheader against the Boston Red Sox at Fenway Park.

IKE'S HEART BEAT VIOLENTLY. His hands shook. Sweat pooled in his armpits, and then licked his sides. If only the passenger would hold a conversation, he might be able to keep his focus off the storm, and fight off an attack.

The cab's electronic clock blinked 1:32 and then changed to 1:33. A frantic idea chimed in his mind. Music! He would use music to hold off the storm's paralyzing *doowah*, *doowah*. He clicked open the glove compartment, shuffled through several CDs, then put one in. The sound deafened. In the haste to turn down the volume, he mistakenly raised it.

The passenger banged. "What's that?" he cried over the amp of the music.

"Music." Ike twisted the knob sharply left. Then, in a calmer voice, he said, "Shakara."

"Chaka what?" the man asked hotly.

"*Ra.*"

"I don't care for it."

"It's by Fela," Ike said.

"I don't care for the fella."

"Fela Anikulapo-Kuti. That's the musician's name."

"Turn the damn thing down," the man said. "I'm reading."

Ike's foot beat a *tam tam* on the accelerator, in time with the music. The traffic eased slowly forward. Ike switched off the CD and rolled down the front windows.

A blustering breeze whistled. The scent of rain on sun-baked asphalt swelled his lungs. He marveled at the storm's tease, how it started and ended with equal suddenness.

In the midst of his thoughts, a bolt of lightning flashed, followed by a slow belch of thunder. Then the storm resumed, fiercer. Soaked pedestrians dashed for shelter. Ike's windshield and windows turned blurry with vapor. He clicked on the cab's headlights. He wiped the windshield in large, circular motions.

A blind woman walked across the street, led by a Seeing Eye

dog. First dog, then woman, stopped at Ike's car. Skirt and gray
sweater drenched, she tapped her stick on his fender. Then she used
the stick to prod the dog. Tongue lolling, the dog feinted left, then
right. It was all futile—Ike was bumper to bumper with the next
car. He felt stirred to hop out and help the woman across. But he
was sure that if he stood, he'd pass out.

In a fit of desperation, she hit the fender harder. Then, her hol-
low gaze in his direction, she raised a finger, her lips formed to
deliver a curse. Ike drew the gear up to reverse. From behind, a
long blast of horn rasped. He lowered the gear once again to drive,
foot firmly held to the brake. She delivered another curse. Then she
turned the same direction as her dog and let herself be led back the
way she came.

"Is it good?" Ike asked.

"What?" The response came after a moment's silence.

"I mean the book," Ike said.

The passenger muttered inaudibly.

The rain beat against the cab's windows. Ike would not stand for
the looming spell of silence. He'd talk and talk, do whatever it took
to draw the man out. Even if all he got in exchange were listless
grunts or bored silence.

"I will write a book someday," he said.

"You will?" the passenger asked quickly. "What about?"

"About Foreign Gods."

"Foreign, did you say? Foreign what? It's hard to understand
your accent."

Ike brushed off the hurt. "There's a gallery called Foreign Gods,
Inc. They buy and sell gods. That's what I plan to write about."

The passenger guffawed. "Why, that's a neat idea."

Ike felt elated, awake. "It's going to be interesting."

"Where?"

Confused, Ike gave no response.

"Where's the gallery?" the man elaborated.

"Oh, here in New York. On Vance Street, number nineteen."

"You don't say," the man said. Then he coughed, eyes fixed on his book.

Ike felt let down. He wanted to keep talking, to keep the conversation going. In fact, it didn't matter whether the passenger spoke back or not. Let the man just listen: that would do do do. *Doowah, doowah,* sang the rain. From somewhere deep inside of Ike, tales surged to the surface, weaving in and out of the storm's refrain. A torrent of words to repel the storm's *doowah*. The words spun, chasing down several stories that, in midstride, suddenly changed contours. He had many stories to share, too little time. There was his former wife, Bernita Gorbea; he recalled how he could never equal her lacerating tongue, his dread of her fiendish lovemaking, the sheer nastiness of their divorce. There was his friend, Jonathan Falla. It was Falla who, back in college, first sowed in him the idea of looting his people's ancient god, a war deity at a time bereft of wars. There were a lot of wars it could fight for us here, Falla had told him. Think of all the shit it could do for black folks in the States. How it could sneak into the White House or Wall Street. Cause mayhem and shit. Help overthrow this whole unjust system and shit. And it was Falla, too, who had sent him the copy of *New York* magazine that profiled Mark Gruels, the owner of Foreign Gods, Inc.

Ike found himself telling all these things and more to his passenger—whatever came into his mind, no matter how inappropriate or fragmentary. Anything to fight back the power of the storm pelting his windshield.

He talked about old friends and classmates back in Nigeria. About his mother who bombarded his e-mail. Each new e-mail bore the same message as the preceding ones: it reminded him of a promise he had failed to keep. And there were his forays into gambling, a venture driven by dreams of great fortunes that always ended in huge losses.

"You gamble?"

Ike started at the man's voice. "Yes," he said. His voice sounded weary, distant, and unfamiliar.

"And you blame your mother for your gambling?"

Ike's eyelids blinked uncontrollably. Fingers entwined, he raised his hands behind his head, thrust out his chest in a fatigued stretch, and yawned.

"You gamble, you gamble. To blame your mother . . ."

Doowah, doowah, raged the storm. Ike reeled, as if struggling to jiggle free of the seat belt. His body settled into a sweet laggardness.

"To blame your mother for your choice is foolish," the passenger said.

Ike was helpless. He tried to raise his eyes to the rearview mirror but failed.

He heard his passenger ask if he was all right. But the storm's wild, whirring music was already sweeping him up to that terrain of enchantment, up in the cloud, way beyond the wet, weeping skies.

A sharp metallic blare sounded. It was not just one driver honking; there were three or four.

And it was over: the storm had calmed, and a faint, vague light hovered in the sky.

It seemed he had been driving on autopilot.

"I'm going to guess," he heard his passenger say. "Jamaican, right?"

"Nigerian," Ike replied, surprised by the calmness in his voice.

"Nigerian!" the passenger exclaimed, filliping his fingers at the same time. "One of our smartest attorneys is from there. His name escapes me, but he's a smart, smart kid. Not a bit of an accent." He slapped his palms. "None at all."

The sky glowed, its vast dome tinged with turquoise. Now that it no longer mattered, the man seemed interested in talking. He said his name was Giles Karefelis.

"Ikechukwu Uzondu," Ike responded.

Three times Karefelis tried to pronounce the name. Then he protested, "It's too hard to say!"

"It's Ike for short."

"Eekay," Karefelis said, mangling the pronunciation. "How do you spell that?"

"I-K-E. *Ee-kay.*"

"That's Ike," the passenger said in an excited tone.

"It's the same spelling," Ike explained. "But mine is pronounced *Ee-kay.*"

"Eekay," the man repeated, omitting the hyphen.

Ike winced. "Your way of saying it means 'buttocks' in my language."

Karefelis roared with laughter.

"But my name means strength," Ike said. "*Ee*-kay, not Eekay. It's short for Ikechukwu—God's strength."

"Ike's a proud American name, too. It was Eisenhower's name. He was a great American general and president."

Ike eased forward and pulled up outside 322 Columbus Avenue.

"Here," said Mr. Karefelis, holding out two crisp bills. "You've been a great sport, Ike." He strode away in a brisk gait, leaving Ike with two $50 bills—and a venerable American name.

CHAPTER THREE

Ike drove as if in a daze, then parked when he arrived at Saint Stephen's Church, a few blocks from his home. He loved sneaking into that church during quiet times, when nobody else was around and he could sit in solitude and let the silence swirl around him. Stealing away, sneaking into the church, was often what he did after fights with Bernita. But today, with the lights dimmed, the stained glass seemed too dusky, more stained than lustrous, the series of saints' images too sad and spectral. And then he wondered whether the sadness had sprung from his own heart, discoloring his eyes. He fixed on a large wooden crucifix that seemed to dangle from above the altar, surveying everything under. After a while, he felt himself the focus of its expressionless stare. He gazed back, disquieted.

Deep down, he knew it was unjust to blame Bernita Gorbea, aka Queen B, aka Queen Bee, for his recourse to Foreign Gods, Inc. Yet, he often wondered how his life might have turned out if he had not married her. Sometimes he bemoaned their marriage, holding himself out as a victim of a large, sinister plot by Fate herself. But he was also honest enough to admit that, in some respects, she had done him a marvelous turn. Without her, he might well have fared far worse.

They had met five years ago in Baltimore. The venue was a hall where a Mexican cabdriver, a mestizo, and his African American wife celebrated their wedding reception.

It was easy to notice Bernita. She was tall and light skinned, with shapely legs and large, firm breasts. In sheer physique, she reminded him of Penny Rose, a girlfriend from his college days—perhaps the only woman he ever fell in love with in America. But the differences were just as significant. Penny was dark toned, managed to convey an impression of eloquence even when she was silent, and dazzled with something deeper, more interior, than her body. By contrast, Bernita came across as reckless. And on their first meeting—and for the years they lived together—he remembered her as oozing sex. He would discover that she had two small roses tattooed on the skin underneath each breast's tuck. On her right inner thigh, inches from the V of pubic hair, was tattooed the name DONNELLE, a mystery lover she never agreed to speak about.

At first sight, Ike had not cared for Bernita's talent for self-display. Her gait comprised a jerking of the shoulders and an exaggerated swaying of her hips. Yet, despite his first impressions—or, perhaps, because of them—he and Bernita were married a couple of months after that first meeting. He moved from Baltimore, Maryland, where he eked out a living as a single cabdriver, to join her in Brooklyn, New York.

Two distinct, different dreams had driven them into marriage. Ike was desperate to obtain a green card. It seemed that Bernita wanted to acquire her own in-house sex service.

Had Ike not let pride deprive him of the woman he loved—and who loved him—in college, he might have ended up in blissful marriage, his green card long taken care of. But things changed after he'd stolen a peek into a letter Penny's father, an Atlanta-based medical doctor, had written to her. The message was blunt. Penny needed to know, Dr. Earl Rose wrote, that he and his wife were terrified of one day learning that their only child "had run off with an African to some remote African village." And then, in an exasperated tone, he'd added: "I don't understand why you refuse to find a nice fellow African American man." He underlined the word "refuse."

Penny had done her best to assure Ike of her love. In his presence, she had even telephoned her father to say that she, and she alone, must decide whom she wanted to be with. Still, Ike had recoiled, wounded by words of rejection. Months later, unable to coax him out of a cold, whining resentment, Penny moved on. She began to date a Senegalese engineering student named Diallo Dieng. One day, two years after they all graduated, Ike received a letter from Jonathan Falla with the news that Penny and Diallo had married.

It was then that the finality of losing her dawned on him, leaving a bitterness that made him shiver. It was all the sadder when he considered all the trouble he'd been through for the sake of a green card.

HIS QUEST HAD STARTED in 1997, a few months before graduation. He had applied for a job at two banks, but when he phoned one bank's human resources department, a female employee called back and left a terse message on his voice mail. "Sir," the woman said, "BayBank does not interview aliens unless they produce evidence of authorization to work in the US."

Later that day, Ike went to visit Harrison Amadu, a Nigerian acquaintance who lived in Springfield, Massachusetts. Harrison was a cabdriver, but also knew his way around immigration problems faced by Africans.

Through him, Ike contacted a Puerto Rican broker named Ricardo Otis who in turn produced a twenty-two-year-old woman named Yesenia Diaz to be Ike's "green card" bride. The broker demanded a fee of five thousand dollars before Yesenia would pose as Ike's bride. With Harrison's help, Ike negotiated the fee down to thirty-five hundred dollars. And then he borrowed fifteen hundred dollars from Harrison to make the down payment.

Ike and Yesenia Diaz were to meet at the office of a justice of the peace to exchange marital vows. They held a rehearsal, Yesenia's face bearing a sneer through it all. Came the appointed date, and Yesenia was nowhere in sight. Ricardo showed up alone with the news that Yesenia's grandmother had taken ill in Puerto Rico, and the would-be bride had traveled to be at the matriarch's bedside. "She coming back soon," Ricardo assured, "and then the wedding, it gonna happen."

For the next three months, there was no Yesenia. Yet, at the end of each month Ricardo appeared at Ike's door and demanded the due installment of two hundred dollars. Ike, who combined his studies with a menial job—cleaning several movie theaters, restaurants, and offices at night—chafed at the unfair arrangement. Why did he have to scrape from his meager earnings to make monthly payments for a fugitive bride? Grudge notwithstanding, Ike had little or no negotiating room.

Then came the fourth month when, felled by the flu, he couldn't work for close to two weeks. He had no cash to pay the installment. He dialed Harrison Amadu, hoping to be bailed out with a small loan.

"You should start driving a cab," Harrison said in a tone drained of sympathy. "The job brings steady money."

The next day Ike presented himself to Harrison who introduced him to the office manager of Triple E Taxi Company.

With his boosted income, he paid off the bride fee in three months. To his dismay, Yesenia remained missing. Even so, Ricardo showed up once or twice each week asking for various sums. "Is a loan," he'd say. "Soon I pay you back."

One day, Ike refused any longer to be duped. That night, just past midnight, he was jerked awake by the ring of his phone. He was in the middle of a terrible dream.

"My cousin, he say you playing stubborn," said a woman's voice.

Confused and agitated, he slurred, "You have the wrong number."

"Oh yeah?" said the female voice in a fighting tone. "You gonna play the *wrong number* game now?"

"Who is this?" he asked, sitting up in bed, perplexed.

"Is me, Yese. Ricardo cousin. Yesenia."

Recognition hit, accompanied by a flurry of confused, stuttering statements. "I have been . . . We need . . . Ricardo said you . . . I've been looking for you. We need to meet. We have to file a marriage petition."

"Oh yeah? I not marrying you. My cousin say you proving difficult."

"He kept asking to borrow money and he never paid back," Ike said. "And he was supposed to bring you."

"Bring me? I ain't bringing unless you pay Ricardo."

Ike sulked for a few weeks. Then he gathered himself up and relocated to Philadelphia where he continued to work as a cabdriver. From there, he moved to Atlanta, and then to Baltimore. Wherever he moved, he brought along that stubborn dream for a green card. The card was the open sesame to a corporate job befitting his education. Often, when he met a woman, he calibrated his interest to the likelihood that she would consent to marry him. Until he met Bernita, he had had a streak of failures.

At their first meeting, Ike sensed that Bernita was trouble on two legs. She walked up to him like an old acquaintance. Without saying a word, she gathered up the folds of his *agbada* made of white brocade and lavishly embroidered. She turned the fabric this way and that, trying to hold it to what light there was in the dully lit hall. Then, after close to a minute, she finally looked up at him. Her eyes, guileless and frolicsome, dissolved his half-puzzled, half-consternated expression.

"Where the brother from?" she asked, in a tone that was innocent and tactless. "You from the same town as the dude in *Coming to America?*"

He couldn't help smiling. Then he said, "I'm from Nigeria. I don't know the dude's town."

"*Ni* what?" she said. "Never heard of it."

"N-I-G-E-R-I-A," he spelled out.

"It's where?"

"West Africa."

"Neat." She regarded him with blithe curiosity. "So you's a king or what?"

He wanted to say, *No, a plebeian, a cipher, and a certified member of the lumpen proletariat,* just to fashion a language that would deter her. But he suspected that nothing would shake her. Instead, he laughed.

"I knew you was large," she said, pulling at his outfit. "Your costume be swinging and shit."

Her hair, cut low, dripped with oil. A cowl covered her bosom but sat on her like an incongruous item of modesty. Perhaps, Ike thought, the cowl was a necessary part of a calculated provocation—a way to guide the prying eye to her full, braless breasts. Her toothy smile and overeager eyes conveyed a beseeching air.

"Thank you," he said, aware that she had stirred something within him, a lust he loathed.

"Name's Bernita," she said.

"Nice to meet you, Bernita," he said. An unbidden smile softened his formal stance. He didn't say his name.

"Folks call me Queen Bernita."

He nodded.

She swept an arm to indicate his outfit. "It's what Jesse Jackson and Farrakhan and dem other folk supposed to be wearing. The shit is great."

She saw a woman walking past in slow, gingerly steps, her glass filled to the brim with some colorless drink.

"Hey, galfriend," she hailed, waving spiritedly. The woman halted. Bernita ran off to her without excusing herself.

She was too crass for his taste, yet his eyes followed her. She tippled glass after glass of iceless gin and tonic. She seemed to stay sober—or, as Ike saw it, to get drunk too slowly.

Soon, Ike struck up a conversation with a keen-eyed, dimple-faced Hispanic woman. Her name was Rosita Ramos, and she was a political science major at American University. She spoke in a low, lisping tone that resembled a whisper, her body inclined toward him, her floral perfume brushing his nostrils. Speaking or listening, she held a steady, eager smile. Overpowered by her presence, Ike lost track of Bernita.

"Do you know a writer called Ama Ata Aidoo?" Rosita asked.

Ike didn't.

"You have to read her. She's a powerful writer, from Ghana. I read one of her books, *Our Sister Killjoy,* in a class I took in African feminist politics."

Ike leaned forward, wearing a wide smile. "You've taken a class in African politics?"

"*Feminist* African politics," she corrected.

"Oh yes. So, what's the *Killjoy* book about?"

That instant, Ike sensed a presence swooping in. He looked up. Bernita stood over them, right hand on her hip, head slightly thrown back, her eyes narrowed. Then a cold calm came over her face. She began to address Ike, as if there had never been any break since their last interaction. He wanted to protest that he was in the middle of another conversation but felt powerless. Rosita sat pat for a minute or two, as if intent on waiting out an impostor. Once she rose to leave, Ike wanted to tell Bernita the obvious: that he was in the middle of a conversation with somebody else. But he failed to speak.

Bernita took the vacated seat, then flashed a mischievous smile.

She stuck to him the rest of the evening. One moment, she described the bride as some sort of cousin; another moment, she called the woman a friend. Out of pique, Ike asked which it was. "Me and her are tight," she said, and twined her fingers.

She made two or three more trips to the bar. The details of her life spooled out of her mouth in a jabbering, skipping fashion. She was born in Augusta, Georgia, but grew up, and still lived, in Brooklyn, New York. She had lots of family all over the city. Her mother had had seven children with three men, but she was one of two females. She loved her sister but didn't care much for her brothers. She spoke with a mixture of pride and contempt about one particular brother. She described him as "kinda strange, kinda crazy." A smart ass, he'd won a scholarship to Tulane. And then he "got another what-a-ma-call-it degree from Emory. MBA, I think it is." This brother took a huge job and settled in Peoria, Georgia. "It's some lily-white hood he's living in. The burb's so white, folks used to call the police some days when my brother be driving home in his nice BeMa. Of everywhere in the world, it's that kinda place he see fit to get his pad. Far from folk who look and talk like him. Strange and crazy."

Worse, the lost sheep of a brother was not married, but dated only white bitches.

The more she drank, the more her stories loped, spilled in all directions. Soon her voice was a drone in his ears: a strangely melodious sound that made him warm and droopy with sleep.

He didn't remember whose idea it was, but she went home with him. After the sort of evening they had had, it seemed an inevitable culmination. Between rounds of frenzied, tossing lovemaking, she broached the idea of his moving to New York City.

At first, he found the idea ridiculous. She physically resembled Penny Rose, true. She had a quaint sort of charm as well—a gift for spinning stories, to say nothing of her vehement manner of making love that both gratified and flattered him. But all that would quickly lose their novelty—and then what would there be to build on? Besides, he'd been to New York once, years ago now, when he was still at Amherst College. He had found the city menacing. Some of the things that made the city vital— its horde of ceaseless, fast-moving pedestrians, its traffic, its litter of skyscrapers—unnerved him. He remembered looking up at the Empire State Building and being seized by a sensation that the building had shuddered ever so imperceptibly. It was going to topple, like a rotted iroko tree, and mash him into a flat crust. Cramped with cars, clogged with people, the streets of Manhattan had pronounced his own terrible smallness, his anonymity.

Bernita stayed with him for one-and-a half weeks. Ike had dated other women, all of them more educated, Africans and African Americans—even a smattering of Caucasians. He would gladly have married two or three of them, but it never ever came to that point before each woman, it seemed to him, fled. The experience had taught him one lesson: that a man chasing simultaneously after love and a green card had to contend with the elusiveness of the ideal spouse.

Marriage to Bernita struck him as a huge risk. All told, a risk worth taking. With a green card in his possession, he would be in line for a good corporate job. The day before she left for New York, he brought up the subject of marriage. They had just finished a long, tossing bout of sex, and lay in bed, wasted. Having decided he had nothing to lose, he spoke directly, offering to pay if she'd marry him.

"What?" she said, then sat up. Head cast back, the sides of her lips drawn down, she regarded him with an indignant expression. He was about to wave off the idea, but she spoke first. "Take cash to help a brother out? Why?" Her expression softened, as if encouraging him to fumble for an answer. Then she smiled. "I'm gonna help you out."

By the time Bernita left, he had agreed to join her, in two months, in what she called Da City. At least initially, he did not regret the move. In short order, he received his work authorization and began to apply for jobs. It was then that frustration set in. He attended five interviews at banks and investment firms, but the expected job offer never came. And then he had an interview for a job at Frisch Investments, Inc. After just five or so minutes, the interviewer swept up a sheaf of papers on the desk that included Ike's transcripts, letters of recommendation from two of his professors, and application form.

Eyes fixed on Ike, the man clasped his fingers together and leaned forward.

"Your credentials are excellent, but the accent is crappy." He said the words with the blasé directness that Ike associated with the city.

There was a time when the word "accent" did not bring Ike pain, only a certain kind of pleasure. In his college days, before he met Penny and after their breakup, he'd scored with several women who confessed to adoring his accent. In fact, his accent was the spark for his relationship with Jill Goldstein, which lasted three semesters. They met in Professor Kevin Greene's popular Intro to

Econometrics course. One day, Professor Greene had called on Ike to read a paragraph from the textbook.

Jill caught up to Ike at the end of class. "I want you to know that I really, really, really *love* your accent," she said, keeping pace with his stride.

But now he sat opposite a man telling him that if he wanted a job in the corporate world, he'd have to learn how to speak English. The man unclasped his fingers. He permitted a perverse gentleness to possess his face.

"I speak English," Ike said. "I took English courses at Amherst— and made straight A's. You can look at my transcript."

"It is what it is. The accent isn't right. I can't hire you."

Ike did not submit any job applications for the next six months. He settled into his cab business. Luckily, the city teemed with passengers. Some could be generous-enough tippers. A steady, low-grade anger burned inside him, but he often judged his life better than tolerable.

His hardest times came from Bernita. Sometimes he recalled the four years of their marriage as a period of persistent nagging. She demanded more and more money for her shopping sprees. To meet those demands, he stopped sending "food money" to his mother. When his neglected mother peppered him with remonstrances, he couldn't point a finger at the culprit. He had not told his mother about his marriage. Nor had he confided in her about his long, anguished quest for a green card or his woes in searching for a job.

Bernita carped at him about sex. She was enraged when, fatigued after long hours behind the wheel, he made a quick job of it. If he ever said he wasn't up to it, she became even more furious. She harangued him with charges of infidelity. "You's chasing after bitches," she'd rail each time he was tired. "'Cause I don't holler don't mean I don't know. Some white bitch got you all crazy and lost."

He had made the mistake of telling her about the executive who commented on his accent. Thereafter, whenever she had a grouse or bore a grudge, she drew out the word "accent" like a sword from its scabbard. She did merciless mimicries of his speech. He dreaded her flair for fashioning otherwise-innocent words into swords. One day, just after making love, they lay in bed watching a documentary on South Africa's anti-apartheid struggle. The presenter said something about a Zulu chief. She suddenly hoisted herself on her elbow and scanned his face, her eyes twinkling with mischief.

"That's who you are, a Zulu chief, right?" she asked. In her singsong accent, she made the word sound like *Zoo-loo*. "That costume you was wearing in Baltimore, it gotta be Zulu."

"Zulus live in South Africa," he said, hardly hiding his vexation.

He had inadvertently handed her another sword. Thenceforth, whenever she worked herself into a rage, she'd use that sword to slash him. *Your Zulu dick be running around, looking for some white ho,* she'd accuse. *Fuck you and fuck your Zulu shit,* she'd curse. Or she'd berate: *Why you always speak English with that Zulu accent?*

But it was her affair with Cadilla that delivered the deepest, most merciless cut of all. He had walked the seven blocks to Saint Stephen's Church the day he'd found out and sat in a pew, helpless against the tears that rolled down his face.

It was the same pew that Ike was sitting in today, though he wasn't crying now. He wasn't sure how he felt. A part of him wondered where Bernita was but without figuring out how such knowledge would serve him. Staring at the crucifix, he wondered if Gruels and his crowd of collectors ever saw fit to poach a god from a church like Saint Stephen's.

He thumbed to a random page of the missal. Then he began to read from Ecclesiastes: "Vanity of vanities, says Qoheleth, vanity of vanities! All things are vanity! What profit has man from all the labor which he toils at under the sun? One generation passes and another comes, but the world forever stays . . . All rivers go to the sea, yet never does the sea become full. To the place where they go, the rivers keep on going."

IT WAS 6:27 P.M. when Ike pulled up outside 99 Flatbush Avenue. It was rather early for him. Since the marriage ended, he had taken to working until 11:00 P.M., often till midnight or even later. There was a parking spot right in front of Cadilla's store. He exhaled through gritted teeth and cut off the ignition but remained in the car. His shattered nerves would need to be pepped up. Curry goat at Big Ed's apartment would help. But he'd need a few bottles of Guinness before that.

He considered driving out to the package store on Avenue U, but he was in no mood to spend more time in traffic. And he was pressed for time.

Outside Cadilla's was the usual rowdy scene. The store was directly underneath Ike's second-floor one-bedroom space. Still, he rarely shopped there. In fact, once he sold Ngene, one of his first priorities would be to relocate.

It wasn't just Bernita's confession to two flings with the man she called Cad that made him hate the place, though that aggravation was there, a constant pain. He also detested the store owner's brand of gregariousness. Cad's idea of a handshake was to raise his hand high and then bring it smashing down with full force. And the man loved long, loud conversations.

Bernita had sworn that her trysts with Cad happened only twice, once before Ike moved to New York and once after. She had volunteered the confession, with no prodding. Even so, he suspected at the time that this was not the whole truth.

Ike walked past a haphazard circle of spectators gathered around two men who hunched over a game of chess. Both the players and many of their observers held bottles wrapped in small wrinkled brown bags. Beyond the circle of spectators, other men and a few women milled about. This hubbub had kept Ike awake through much of the night.

Six or seven youngsters, boys and girls, rollicked around the store's swinging door.

"Excuse me," he said.

They ignored him.

"I said, excuse me!" he said in a raised voice.

They snickered and then slowly parted.

He padded to a back aisle and grabbed a six-pack of Guinness. Then he took his place behind six customers.

Cadilla was as high-spirited as ever. A stodgy, middle-aged man stepped up to the counter. His red hair was dirty, tousled and gray, his hardy skin tanned a tarnished red. Ike recognized him. He was a fixture in the neighborhood. He often held court at street corners, an aficionado of baseball, movies, and international affairs. Ike had overheard snippets of neighborhood gossip—about the man's roots in southern Virginia, his stint in the navy, and his arrival in the city on the trail of a capricious Creole woman named Lady Matilda, a woman who shattered his spirits when she took off with another man and left him, for some years, a yarn-spinning wreck.

Red Ray bought eighty-eight Mega Millions lottery tickets for the jackpot of $88 million. He said his pastor—a well-known former jailbird—had prayed over each dollar. He was sure of winning: heaven had decreed it, and he had claimed it. When he won, he said, he would get himself a Hollywood lady, buy a Cadillac with leather upholstery, purchase a grand mansion some place super nice—"and then leave town, fast as I can."

Cadilla asked which Hollywood ladies he had his eyes on.

Red Ray said, "If I fancy, I take me Julia. Julia Roberts. Or Halle Berry. Depends on who I like better."

Everybody laughed, except Ike. His irritation grew with each second.

"My man!" Cadilla exulted when Ike stood before the counter. He raised his hand for his usual hard slap. Ike plumped down the six-pack on the counter and extended a hand. "Haven't seen you in like three months or something."

"Two weeks."

Cadilla grabbed Ike's outstretched hand, tightened his grip, then pushed and pulled in a sawing motion. "What you been up to?"

"Nothing," Ike said.

"I saw your former lady last week. Went to see my Mets rip the Marlins. Me and her ran into each other at Shea."

"You and *who*?"

Cadilla frowned up a little. "You know who I'm talking about. Your old lady, Queen."

Ike wished he had driven to Avenue U after all.

"Queen was looking good," Cadilla said. A sly smile spread on his face. "She asked about you and all."

"Good." Ike put down a ten-dollar bill on the counter.

Cadilla ignored the cash. "She's an amazing lady, Queen. She's good people—*real!*" He stamped his feet to express enthusiasm.

"Good," Ike said again.

"I thought y'all was gonna hit it off big time. But marriage is like that. Sometimes it works, sometimes it don't."

"I must go," Ike said. "I have an important call to make."

"A'right, man." Cadilla raised his hand for another handshake. Ike grabbed the six-pack with two hands. For a moment, Cadilla seemed offended. Then he said, "You go on. The drink's on the house."

"I will pay," Ike said agitatedly.

"No, Queen said to be nice to you. It's on me."

Ike slapped the ten-dollar bill on the counter, turned swiftly, and walked toward the exit. His path was blocked. A boy clasped a girl in an embrace, and she playfully clawed at him, threatening to bite his arm. Other youngsters egged them on, laughing.

"Make way!" Ike barked.

They maintained their wall.

"Heh!" he said, so angry he was stumped for words.

He felt Cadilla's hand slip into the pocket of his pants. Then the storekeeper's voice: "Man, you gotta let me treat. Me and you are supposed to be tight."

Ike froze, filled with rage. He heard Cadilla's footsteps retreating to the counter. Two customers asked why Cadilla never treated them to drinks.

"Can assure you I ain't about to say no if you offer," said a male voice.

"Me neither," said the other, a woman. "Matter of fact, I ain't got *no* nowhere on my lip."

"You don't, that's for sure," Cadilla retorted, laughing.

"You the only man I ever said no to. Don't never forget that." The woman took her turn laughing.

"That 'no' cost you. You both want beer, you paying for your damn selves."

Without looking back, Ike pulled the money out of his pocket and flung it down.

As Ike pushed out the door, he heard Cadilla scream at the youngsters to get the hell out, or they'd get their behinds whopped by their sorry mamas. They streamed out past Ike, one of them slamming into him.

Ike cursed in Igbo.

"Zulu!" the young man riposted, without looking back.

CHAPTER FOUR

Ike was so livid that he bounded up the first flight of stairs before he remembered the mailbox. He had, by design, not checked it for more than a week. What mail he received was—almost without exception—bills. Bills he had little cash to pay. So, in the eleven months since his divorce was finalized, he had taken to picking up his mail only once a week. He'd figured out that a week and a half into a new month was when creditors sent out all the disconcerting mail: late-payment reminders, disconnection warnings, cancellation threats, repossession notices, eviction slips.

Ike descended to the landing where tenants' mailboxes were located. Though unable to read his name in the pale light, he instinctively knew where the box for 2F was. The box was fuller than usual, just as he expected. He retrieved the mail and then began to climb the dank, poorly lit stairway. There was an ever-present frowsy smell. It was a commingling of spilled liquor, urine, cigarette smoke, perfumes, and the rich, leafy scent of marijuana. He stepped carefully to avoid the chewing gum stuck here and there on the stairs.

His living room sizzled with heat. He kicked off his shoes and flicked on the light. Instantly, a fly began to buzz about as if startled. He put the six-pack in the fridge. As he passed to the leather couch that Bernita had left behind when she carted away the rest of the furniture, he stopped and put on a CD. Brenda Fassie's plangent voice filled the room, singing "Vulindlela." He lowered himself onto the couch. Its caving softness reminded him of the time when he and Bernita had nightly bouts of turbulent sex. Fassie's song had often served as the raunchy anthem, goading his body and Bernita's to higher plateaus of pleasure.

HIS EX-WIFE HAD CRAVED sex with a voraciousness that at first flattered him. Her breasts seemed wired with some hypersensitive antennae. He had only to give her a long, tight hug, and her nipples would harden, her body quaking uncontrollably. If he cupped a hand over her breasts, or bit her nipples with chattering teeth, she went wild, croaked, groaned, and writhed. She dug her nails into his flesh, crooning, *I'm your queen, Queen B, your Queen Bernita.*

At the time of their marriage, he had not had any steady relationship for close to two years. His sexual appetite high, he welcomed their nightly romps. Each night, as he walked into the apartment, his heart quickened with anticipation of some amorous surprise. Bernita's favorite maneuver was to sally to the door the instant she heard him fiddling with the key from outside. She'd then jump into his arms, her breasts positioned near his lips. When he took the bait and sucked at the swollen nipple, she'd let out a choked cry and fling her body back, forcing him to hold tight or risk both of them tumbling to the floor. Then, holding tight, he'd carry her to the couch.

Their first serious fight came the third week after his relocation to New York. It was triggered by his plea that he had a headache and was in no shape to make love.

"You been hanging with some bitch?" she railed.

"I'm just coming back from work. I wasn't running around look-ing for—" He paused, the word "bitch" too heavy to pass his lips. She glowered at him, her lips twitching. "I've not been looking for women," he said.

"You was, too!" she bickered. She stood akimbo, her breasts swelling and falling, her eyes fierce. "What kind of Zulu shit is you're tired, Zulu?"

It was the first time she called him Zulu. That day, it dawned on him that she regarded the word as a pejorative in its verb, adjec-tive, and noun forms. Her favorite curse—and the one that stung most—was "Don't Zulu me your Zulu shit, Zulu!"

In retaliation, he began to call her Queen Bee.

IKE NEEDED SOME TRANQUILLITY to plan the next day's errands, but the touch of the sunken couch scraped a raw sore. He'd long suspected that the same couch had hosted Cadilla and Queen Bee's trysts.

As he lay on the couch, face up, he became impatient for the bottles of Guinness to turn cold. His thoughts roamed to Foreign Gods, Inc. He envisaged his next meeting with Mark Gruels. It would be a different encounter. He would have Ngene in his hand, and his voice would be strong and confident—even a bit command-ing. He pictured Gruels gazing at the statue, sniffing it, fawning over it. Thoroughly fascinated, the man would make a solid first bid. He, Ike, would balk. And then Gruels would go higher and higher, jacking up his offer. And then, once they agreed on a price, Gruels would reach for his checkbook and Ike—overcome with euphoria—would faint dead away.

He even imagined the shape of Gruels's handwriting on the check: strong lines, straight and prim like soldiers at a parade, smooth and unbroken, devoid of squiggles. He pulled back only when his mind sought to snoop around Gruels's imaginary shoulder to peek at the amount scribbled on the check. He was content to savor the eerie joy yielded by expectancy and sweet, lingering mystery.

He sprang up and fetched a bottle of stout and a glass. With his teeth, he pried off the cap of the bottle. As he poured, a fly zipped past, barely missing the glass. Years ago, there was a drunkard in Utonki who was fond of saying, "A fly in beer is meat for the mouth." Ike once saw the man throw his head back and down a glass of beer with two dead, bloated flies.

Fly that craves beer, know that you court death!

The thought of flies in beer disgusted Ike.

After several swigs, he found the heat oppressive. He unbuttoned his shirt and then raised the latch of the window that overlooked the street. Clamorous sounds flooded in.

He switched on the standing fan and turned on the computer, his shirt fluttering from the steady breeze.

He had not checked his e-mail for three days. His Internet service was disconnected, but he poached somebody's open wireless connection. As the Internet loaded, he went to the fridge for another bottle. This time he drank straight from the bottle. Flapping his shirt, he bared his chest to the gush of warmish air.

There were eleven new messages in his in-box. Five of them were from his sister, Nkiru—and each had the subject line, "Mama's Message."

He clicked open the most recent one.

Mama asked me to remind you, that you're your late father's only son, that your sister has gone away to her husband, and Mama doesn't know when the good Lord might call her to His glorious kingdom. Mama is sad that, at your age, you have no wife and no son to take your place if anything should happen (God forbid!). Since you don't seem to be concerned, Mama is looking into it for you (a wife). So make arrangements to come home soon, unless you don't care what happens to your father's compound and to the poor woman who gave birth to you. For a few years now you haven't sent Mama (or me, your only sister) any money. Mama wonders if you want us to eat sand. Also, Mama says she has been telling you that there's an important spiritual matter she must discuss with you in person, face-to-face. It's about satanic Uncle Osuakwu. After killing Papa, he is now making diabolical plans against all of us, but especially you. Mama says it's urgent that you come home as soon as possible. Then you will be fully informed of this demonic plot, and how to cancel it in the mighty name of Jesus. Every day I go to a cyber café to check for your reply, but you don't write. Please don't fail to respond this time. Mama's prayer is that you may be covered by the blood of our Lord and Savior. Your sister, Nkiru.

He opened his older sister's other e-mails. They were variations on the same message. Each ended with a plea for his reply in order to put their mother at ease.

Suddenly, an ache flared up on the right side of his head. With one thumb he pressed hard at the spot where the pain was sharpest. It hurt to read the e-mails. He didn't reply because he couldn't say a thing that would make sense to them. How could he explain that the "food money" he once sent each month had dried up because a woman named Queen Bee, whom he had married in order to get something called a green card, had developed an ever-insatiable appetite for shopping? And how to explain his gambling to them?

A year after arriving in the city, he'd taken to gambling. He had wanted quick cash to replenish some of the money Queen Bee lavished on expensive clothes and jewelry. And he had wanted extra cash to send to his mother and sister, to keep them quiet. But gambling brought him nothing but sorrow. No, his mother would never understand why her messages, sent in e-mails his sister wrote, went unanswered. He regretted having ever given his e-mail address to

Nkiru, his only sibling, three years older than him. Over the last year, her e-mails came, by his rough calculation, at the rate of six or more per week. Some days, as if in the grip of malarial urgency, she sent two or three at once. Each one belabored the same point: Mama's demand that he visit home "as soon as possible," "without further ado," "without any further unnecessary delay," "in due haste." And the come-home entreaties often addressed the need for him to take a wife and begin the race to produce an heir. Or they had to do with some "urgent spiritual matter," to neutralize nameless persons plotting diabolical mayhem or combat others scheming to steal his inheritance. The specificities of the plots and the alleged schemers' names remained stubbornly cloaked in secrecy. It was only the latest batch of e-mails that finally linked it all to Uncle Osuakwu.

His mother and sister could never know how their barrage of e-mails tormented him. They accused him of shirking his duty to provide for his widowed mother. Yet, he had spelled out his acceptance of that responsibility in a long, earnest letter to his mother after his father's sudden death a month into his sophomore year at Amherst. He had beseeched her to harbor no fears but to remain confident that he would secure a good job after graduation. And that having done so, he would take care of all her needs. It was perhaps the hardest letter he'd ever written. The words poured out of him through spasms and tears. As he wrote, he was haunted by the image of his father, gaunt and inert in a coffin, and of his mother gazing at what remained of her husband, too stunned to wail her grief, her eyes drained of life, forlorn.

Having made that promise, Ike pushed himself at Amherst College as hard as he could. And when he earned a cum laude in economics, he trusted that he'd made himself an attractive hire for any Fortune 500 company. He had hardly anticipated any of the adversities that stood in his way, up to and including the moment the judge in his divorce case allowed Queen Bee to cart away his little savings and any of his possessions she fancied.

There were times when he regretted failing to confide his woes in his mother or sister. He had tried once or twice, alternating between anger at his situation and a tenderness for his mother, fed by memories of the nights during childhood when he could not sleep unless cuddled up against her body, which reeked of smoky wood, warm like sun-baked clay. But what end would confiding have served? Would the knowledge that he too had suffered reduce their own pain and hunger?

He read Nkiru's latest e-mail again. This time, he felt not the old indignation, but a sense of mellowness. He smiled. His plan had been to surprise his mother by showing up in Utonki, unannounced. He took another long gulp, emptying the bottle. Then he composed a reply to his sister: *Dear Nkiru, Tell Mama that I will come home within a week. Love, Ikechukwu.*

As he poured from another bottle, squeals broke into his reverie. He placed the bottle and half-filled glass on a small side table and dashed toward the window. He glared down at the youngsters hard at their nettlesome game right in front of Cadilla's store. As he cupped his mouth to scream at them, he heard three sharp knocks on his door.

"Who's that?" he barked.

"Is me, Big Ed," came the response in a familiar Jamaican lilt. "You didn't see my text, man? Janet finished cooking, you know. You come quick, you still find some curry goat. You come late, I'm eating fast."

Ike gathered two bottles of Guinness and headed out to Big Ed's apartment, 2C. As usual, the two huge color posters that dominated the left wall of Big Ed's living room caught his eyes. One was

of Bob Marley chasing down a soccer ball, the locks of his Rastafar-
ian hair stretched backward as if in flight. The other was of Jimmy
Cliff, arms spread out, head raised to an endless, blue sky, mouth
wide open, seduced by a song.

As they settled to their drinks, Ike spoke about being mad at a
passenger who had ignored his greetings.

Big Ed stared at him as one might a puzzling object. He had
this way of fixing his face into a blank plasticity, so that his restless,
roving eyes seemed hyper-animated.

Disquieted, Ike spoke again. "I was tempted to stop the car and
order the man out. That's how angry I was."

Big Ed perked up, threw his head back, upended a bottle, and
drained its contents. Ike was riveted by the push and pull of the
man's Adam's apple, the gurgling sounds emitted by his throat.
Putting down the bottle, Big Ed broke into his signature laughter,
a carefree boom accompanied by stamping of feet and clapping. Ike
wore an expectant smile, for he knew that Big Ed's eruption was a
prelude to some captivating anecdote.

After a moment, Big Ed's laughter ceased. Sharp, inquisitive
eyes fixed on Ike, he asked, "Why you even worry about that, man?
What you seeking the passenger face for?" His face took on an
expression of avuncular patience as he awaited Ike's explanation.

"I just think—" Ike began.

"You think?" Big Ed interrupted. "What you think?" His eyes
roved, now settling on Ike, now on his wife Janet, who sat on a
wooden chair near the living room door, a bemused grin on her
face. "Listen, man, you ever seen a one-legged man winning an
arse-kicking match? I turn gray doing cab. I loss half my hair
doing it. I send two daughters and a son to college, and I bury my
first wife, Martha, and marry this puppy of a gal here who don't
know half the time whether she's my daughter or my wife." Janet

laughed, and Big Ed paused and fixed her with an endearing gaze. She was petite, with a youngster's tight, defined arms, hair done up in tiny, shoulder-length braids, their tips decorated with beads of different colors. The first time Ike met her, he mistook her for Big Ed's daughter. Even now, he found it hard to believe she had given birth to two girls, eight and five. Big Ed waited until she quieted down, then he addressed Ike. "I have done low and mighty things, my brother, driving cab. So, therefore, I can tell you this one truth: It's not how many dogs you have in the fight; it's how much fight your dogs have in them. So, tell me now, what you say you thinking?"

Silent, Ike followed the darting dance of Big Ed's eyes. Then he said, "In my culture, people always exchange greetings—"

Big Ed cut him off again. "Your culture got nothing to do with it. This ain't your culture. It's NYC. Let me tell you some'in, bro." He lifted another bottle to his lips and drained its content. He turned to his wife. "I loss me leg, Janet. Look in the fridge and grab me another beer." He took a sip from the new bottle, then took up the thread of his talk. "Whether a passenger says hi or no hi to me don't bother me none. Listen now: so long as the passenger pay, I could care less." He paused, delivered himself of a quick guffaw, and used a finger to pry a strip of meat caught between his teeth. He slurped more beer. Ike knew that as Big Ed became tipsy, his speech was apt to drift deeper and deeper into Jamaican cadence.

"Cabdrivers, we are two kinds, you know," Big Ed continued. "One kind likes to grovel and search for the passenger's face. But why do I have to look the passenger face for? Is the same mother born both of we? A cabdriver looking for passenger face is hoping for a big, big tip. Then it's another kind of driver, my kind. I tell you, bro, my kind don't give a shit about tips and all that. My job is to do my job, which is to get the passenger from point A to point B—end of matter." He permitted himself another interlude, to accommodate his wife's laughter. Then, after a quick sip, he said, "Is the same two kinds of people in the world. There's the lawyer who is holding you by the shoulder and squeezing like he's your best buddy. But he's billing you merciless by the hour all the same. And he is expecting you to pay every last cent. You don't pay, he is dragging you out to magistrate to be judged. Or the doctor who is smiling and making jokes when it's you lying and dying in his hospital bed. Lying and dying and still yet paying that bill. Look man, some people trying to tell you it's a sunny day, have a great day, even though life got you down in the dirt and thrashing the hell out of you. Why you wanna dabble in converse with a passenger, like he is a friend of you? A man doesn't stop your cab 'cause he wanna jump into friendship with you. Passengers don't care whether you say good afternoon or bad afternoon, so long as you getting them to their destination. Me, it's my friends I do the saluting shit with. As for my passengers, they wanna greet, fine; they start and it's I who answer. They don't wanna greet, fine with me, too. I ain't fussing. I ain't even expecting no shitty tips. Just pay me what the bloody meter say, go your bloody way."

Big Ed shrugged and grabbed his beer.

"Anyway," Ike said, "today's my last day."

Big Ed laughed. "You're fixing to die, my friend?"

"Last day as a cabdriver. No more insults from passengers."

"You've finally got a big man's office job?" Big Ed's tone was excited.

"I'm traveling to Nigeria."

"You're going to the continent! When?"

"In two days."

"Two days! And you're just telling? You're taking a job there?"

"No."

"So how you going to do to pay the white man's bills?"

"I'm going into business."

"Oh, business?" Surprise and disappointment rang through in the words. "What kind of business you fixing to do?"

"Buying and selling." Ike lifted a bottle to his lips. As he drank, he thought, *Snatching and selling*.

Big Ed belched. His wife sneered at him.

"You not going to bed, little gal?" he teased. Then he looked at Ike with dulled eyes. "This thing you're buying and selling—it have a name or not?"

"Anything that people would pay me good money for," Ike said, letting out a nervous laugh.

"Fine with me—so long you're not selling people for make the money."

"No!"

"And so long you're not selling the ancestors."

"No," Ike said in a subdued, tired voice. Then he announced that he had to leave to get started with packing.

"Take two Red Stripe for drink in your pad," Big Ed offered. "When you fixing to return from Africa?"

"Less than two weeks."

"Get me a danshiki from the continent. Janet see me wear the danshiki, she learn to respect me."

Janet walked up to him, stuck her tongue out, and playfully smacked his arm. She fled, shrieking, as Big Ed pretended to rise from his seat.

CHAPTER FIVE

As Ike walked into his apartment, the phone began to ring. He paused, poised between irritation and curiosity. His voice came alive on the answering message, inviting the caller to leave a message. Then he heard: "Ike, Usman Wai here. Long time. Well, nothing important as such, just touching base. Give me a call tonight when you get in—however late. Actually, I'm going to be up till midnight or twelve thirty. If I don't hear from you today—"

Ike lurched and snatched up the handset.

"Hello, Usman!" he shouted into the phone.

"You little rascal," Usman teased. "You're now screening calls?"

"Actually I was in the middle of something."

"Oh yeah?" Usman said, chuckling. "You just got divorced, and you're already getting into another *middle*."

"Dirty mind! Who told you I was in that line of activity?"

"I don't trust you Nigerians with middle affairs."

"Oh, so you little Sierra Leoneans have now picked up the habit of insulting your Nigerian masters?"

Usman roared in his shuddering laughter. "You Nigerians always confuse size with seniority."

They had not spoken for close to three years. Usman was the first
African Ike met after moving to New York. They used to exchange
visits and hold long telephone conversations, at least twice a week.
Then Usman had called one day when Ike wasn't at home. Ike and
Bernita had had one of their incessant, senseless fights. He had
stormed off to the quietude of Saint Stephen's and from there to a
bar. Bernita had answered the call. As Usman expressed pleasantries, she cut him short.

"I ain't interested in none of your Zulu greetings," she
screamed. Usman laughed nervously, thinking she was joking. He
froze when Bernita huffed, "And I ain't laughing with your Zulu
ass needa." Stunned silent, he listened as she outlined his offenses.
In essence, he was accused of procuring "wide-ass Zulu bitches"
for Ike.

Ike had apologized profusely to Usman, but the wound was
hard to heal. Their friendship had seemed to cease. And now came
Usman's surprise call.

Usman was in his late sixties but had stern eyes that belied
a genial nature. He spoke with a broadcaster's baritone. And
he had enjoyed a bright career as a young broadcaster with the
Ghana Broadcasting Corporation. The coup that ended Kwame
Nkrumah's reign also swept away a corps of idealistic profession-
als who'd meandered their way to Ghana, drawn by Nkrumah's
Pan-African vision.

"What a surprise, Usman. You just cut off and went under-
ground," Ike said.

"Your bee stung me," Usman teased. "I had to run for cover."

"And you left me to battle the bee all alone." Ike snickered.
"Some brother you are!"

"My mother didn't raise a man who would stand up to a bee. I
know when to run four forty."

Again, the sound of deafening commotion outside Cadilla's store flooded Ike's apartment. As Usman spoke, Ike's antennae were tuned to the irksome racket.

"Hello?" Usman shouted. "Are you upset I called?"

"Why would you even think it?" Ike asked.

"You just sighed."

"I did? Well, there's this bunch of kids down at the store . . ."

"What about them?" Usman asked.

"Well, day or night, they gather outside the store. They're there, rapping and screaming. I'm going to shout down and tell them to go home and sleep."

"You're out of your mind, you funny fellow," Usman said between spasms of laughter. "Who do you fancy yourself to be, a village headmaster?"

"I'm tired of their rowdiness."

"My friend, don't mess with these American kids. You're looking at the freest kids in the whole world. They can curse you out real bad. And they have the law on their side, too."

"It's not funny," Ike said severely.

"You think I was testing out some comedy sketch here? I've lived in this country long enough to know that you leave kids alone. They could kick your ass, too."

Ike stayed silent, seething.

"So, tell me about Queen," Usman demanded.

"It's over. We're divorced."

"What kind of divorce did you have?"

"Are there varieties? A menu list?"

"I mean, was it contentious and protracted?"

"Short and bitter."

"Acrimonious?"

"You're just in love with big words, Usman. You know Queen.

Do you think she would care for an amicable way of doing anything? For her, even sex was like waging a war!"

"Leave out the pornographic asides," Usman teased. "I'm not interested in those."

"Instruction taken. So, Bee hired an attack dog for an attorney. Her attorney was this short woman with a quiet face. But when she opened her mouth—*phew*! It was fire, Usman! The way she came after me, you would think I was a Manhattan millionaire."

"How was your own lawyer?"

"Terrible! A wimp! She behaved as if her job was to worship Queen Bee's lawyer. And I was paying her!"

"Did Bernita gun for money?"

"*Gun?*" Ike echoed as sadness descended on his mood. "She gunned and got! I think the judge found her lawyer intimidating. Basically, the judge ruled that Bee should walk away with my savings."

"Listen," Usman said, "you'll rise again."

Ike thought, *Rise again?* Had he, he wondered, really risen before? The idea perplexed him. But his mind soon fastened on the coming trip. His spirits rose. He looked about the room until he caught his image in the mirror. Dark circles ringed his eyes. He leaned close to the mirror and peered at the mild devastation his face had become. Then, recalling Usman's words, he smiled at the mirror.

"I will rise," he said, fondling a bottle of Red Stripe. Quite unexpectedly, Bernita scooted into his mind. For how could his rise be complete or confirmed if she did not stalk him again, as on the day of their meeting at that wedding in Baltimore? Buoyed by the vision, he raised the bottle to his lips, sucked, and rinsed his mouth with the swill. Then, slowly, he swallowed.

"The good thing is, you're a talented young man. America offers great opportunities."

"I used to think so, too," Ike said wearily. "But now I know better."

"Don't tell me you've become one of those who bash this country. I've lived here twice as long as you. There's no place in the world where people like us have it better."

"You could be an American Methuselah, if you wish. But I also know what I know. With a cum laude in economics, I have been driving taxis for thirteen years. Do you know why?"

" You told me before."

"Yes, it's all about my accent! So the talk about opportunities— it's ridiculous."

"You hate it here? My friend, try Europe. Or Asia."

"Well, I'm here for now, not in Europe. We're supposed to be living in this new global setting—a village, many call it. In college, I took classes where the buzzwords were 'synergy,' 'hybridity,' 'affinities,' 'multivalency,' 'borderlessness,' 'transnationality,' whatnot. My sister lives in Onitsha, near my village, but she has Internet access. A gallery somewhere in this city buys and sells deities from Africa and other parts of the world. Many American companies are selling stuff to people in my village. They're certainly selling stuff to me, to lots of people who speak the way I do. But I apply for a job and I'm excluded because of 'my accent,' quote, unquote. It's worse than telling me outright I'm a foreigner, I don't belong. Then academics rush in to theorize me into an exile. That's why *I* refuse to wear that tag."

"I'm not going to argue with you. You feel quarantined because of your accent, and you're a bitter kid. I would be, too, if employers treated the way I speak as a terrible disease. I'd be hopping mad, as a matter of fact. But why am I even discussing accents with you? I called to see how you were doing."

"After the human hurricane swept over me?"

"Exactly! So, what are your immediate plans?"

"Up in the air, literally."

"Why don't we plan to meet next week, for lunch or something? My treat."

"I will be in Nigeria next week. In my village, in fact."

"Is everything okay?"

"My mother summoned me home ASAP. My sister has cluttered my in-box with e-mails demanding I come home to take care of some business. She writes on my mother's behalf. I wish they had just sent me the ticket."

"You really have to go, it sounds like."

"Sounds like? I've booked a solid seat on KLM. I've also found a great business opportunity."

Usman asked, "Sounds like you're about to make some good money?"

"Serious money, yes."

Usman laughed. Infected, Ike laughed, too.

"Doing what, exactly?" Usman asked. "Gambling?"

Ike chortled and then collected himself. "A trade secret! If I tell you, I have to kill you."

"Don't get into drugs, my friend." Usman's tone was devoid of joviality. "These American chaps have no mercy in their dictionary. They can throw your ass in the slammer—and let you rot there."

"I won't touch drugs, am I crazy?" Ike protested.

"You got me scared for a moment."

"No, my deal is clean. It's the main reason I'm making this trip, even though it's costing me lots of money I don't have."

"You're the first African cabdriver I know to ever complain about lack of cash. The others roll in lots of cash."

"They didn't marry Queen Bee!"

They succumbed to long, hard laughter. Then Usman spoke with his characteristic humor.

"Listen, I have a little bit of cash lying around. I can put two thousand dollars in your pocket. Half of it is a gift; let's call it my contribution to your post-Bee survival fund. The other half is a loan."

"Are you sure?" Ike asked, stunned.

"No," Usman said. Then, feigning a child's voice, he added, "Let me go and ask my mommy."

Ike said he'd repay the full amount. Usman insisted on giving him half as a gift. He said he would drop off the cash at Ike's apartment the next day, around seven in the evening.

CHAPTER SIX

It was in August 2005 that Ike Uzondu first read about Mark Gruels in an edition of *New York* magazine. His friend, Jonathan Falla, had filched the magazine from a dentist's office and mailed it to him. By the end of December, Ike had made up his mind to travel to Nigeria, snatch the war deity his people called Ngene, and sell it to Gruels's gallery.

He had come to that decision after weeks of agonized indecisiveness. He'd been disgusted the first time he read Gruels's story. The idea of a few wealthy individuals buying up so-called Foreign Gods and sacred objects just didn't sit well with him. The sport struck him as the height of arrogance. If you had loads of cash, you could purchase deities torn away from their shrines in remote corners of the world. You could install these displaced, forlorn gods in your expensive city apartments or country mansions. And then you could invite friends and relatives over to gaze, in astonishment, admiration, or awe, at your odd acquisitions. What did it all prove? It was sheer decadence. When Ike read in the magazine that anybody who acquired a deity was known as the god's "parent," he paused and suppressed a rueful laugh.

The *New York* magazine piece reminded Ike of that derisive name Nigerians had for anybody with too much money and too little sense: money-miss-road. He remembered the classic case of a vain, wealthy man. As the man neared death, he had gathered his family to give instructions for his burial and funeral. He instructed that a huge, wide grave be dug when he died, enough to swallow a wide car. "I have driven a Rolls-Royce for much of my life," the man said. "Death should not end my splendor. When I die, I must continue to drive the same car in the spirit-world. I order you to lower a Rolls-Royce inside my grave, right next to my casket. I should not be mistaken for a wretched man when I arrive in the land of the dead."

Those who collected high-priced deities shared something with that Nigerian money-miss-road. In a fit of outrage, Ike had flung the magazine across the room.

The next day, he dialed Jonathan Falla.

"You got it, right?" Jonathan said in accustomed ebullience. "Didn't the story blow your mind?"

"There are too many crazy people with too much money around here," Ike replied.

"I agree! That's why you need to go get that god of war from your village."

Ike, shocked, asked, "Why, exactly?"

"Why, you ask? We need a revolution around here."

"You're always talking revolution, but you're a child of privilege. You're part of the enemy."

"Nope, I already committed class suicide, my man. I'm ready for the revolution."

Ike laughed. He'd known Jonathan for many years, and yet it was impossible to know when his friend was speaking in jest.

"So your revolution requires that I steal my people's old deity and sell it to some rich fool?"

"You've got a goddamn war god, don't you? And it's sitting pretty in your village, not fighting any wars. What use is it to your people? Nil! But you bring it over here, it'll enter the oppressive system and fight the power. Lead the revolution from the inside."

"Jay, you still come up with these crazy ideas!"

"Crazy to you, but it's strategic thinking."

"Well, I'm not touching Ngene."

"Okay, be on the side of the oppressors!" Jonathan quaked with laughter.

Ike seemed to forget the magazine where he tossed it. One fateful night, two or three weeks later, it crossed his mind again. He had just taken a long shower to shake off the languor of hours spent in traffic. As he sat moping at the TV and sipping from a mug of Guinness, he suddenly began to wonder where he had seen one of the actors before. Then it dawned on him: the man strongly resembled Mark Gruels. He sat up and searched for the magazine, already lightly coated with dust. Back on the sofa, he read the story again. To his amazement, the initial disgust had disappeared.

Over the next few weeks, he read it again and again. Sometimes he read slowly and closely, pausing to reflect on one sentence or another. Other times, he read fast, skipping sentences or even whole paragraphs. He'd become obsessed. In some curious way, the story transported him, kept him spellbound. It became an eerie reminder of the sense of wonder he felt as a history student in secondary school, when he first learned about some of Africa's ancient kingdoms— Mali, Songhai, Ghana, and Kanem Bornu—and encountered their great heroes and warriors, names like Mansa Musa, Askia the Great, Osei Tutu, Queen Amina of Zaria. Each new reading of the magazine drew him ever closer, fearfully, to the edge of fascination and temptation.

There came a weekend when he could neither work nor escape

to a casino to gamble. An ice-tinged snowstorm had come on the heels of a blitz of powdery flakes that left banks and banks of snow.

Trapped in his apartment during those wintry doldrums, Ike had eaten little food. He mostly nibbled on potato chips, cookies, and buttered bread. But he drank swill after swill of Guinness. With little else to occupy him, he used some of his empty time to reread the *New York* magazine. And then he spent long hours in agonized self-examination. The major question he considered was this: Did he have the guts to snatch the statue of Ngene and sell it?

At first, his mind seesawed, leaned this way, then that. The torturous exercise racked his nerves and left him fatigued and mentally exhausted. Yet, he ultimately decided that the answer was—yes! The date was December 29, 2005.

Having reached that decision, he realized that it would be best to make an urgent job of it. He wanted to set an early date for his trip. He had close to three thousand dollars on hand, but the sum was far from enough to pay his rent and other bills and buy a flight ticket. By acting quick, he would reduce the emotional cost to himself. Already, he felt an ache in his heart. It came from a nagging sense that he was about to betray his uncle Osuakwu—his father's only brother and the chief priest of Ngene. There was no satisfactory way around the shame and guilt. In the end, Ike settled for Mark Gruels's argument in the magazine. It was this: that, in a postmodern world, even gods and sacred objects must travel or lose their vitality; any deity that remained stuck in its place and original purpose would soon become moribund. Deep down, Ike felt it was a lot of mumbo jumbo, fanciful but meaningless. No, he was not himself convinced of its soundness. Still, he made it serve.

Ike realized the advantage of moving fast. He considered asking Jonathan for a loan but decided against it. Instead, the following weekend, he took off on a gambling junket, not to Atlantic

City, this time, but to Foxwoods Resort Casino in Connecticut. He couldn't resist the casino's special offer of double-bed rooms for twenty-three dollars (plus tax), complimentary drinks thrown in. After a weekend of binged gambling, he left the casino in sour spirits, dazed, and broke.

He ceased reading the magazine, which he tossed underneath his bed. Ike's plans to transplant and sell Ngene might have stayed on hold had he not received an e-mail from his sister that jolted him. Part of the e-mail read: *God has told Pastor Uka that it is time to destroy Ngene. God revealed that the deity is demonic. It is the cause of barrenness in our married women. It's the reason sickness and disease have entered Utonki. Its shrine is the headquarters of witchcraft in our area. God gave the pastor a special message for you. You're divinely favored to be a millionaire, but Osuakwu and Ngene have been closing your doors. Osuakwu and Ngene caused you never to get married. God told Pastor Uka that you must send 1,000 dollars immediately. The money is to help the pastor to destroy Ngene. Once you send it, God will unleash blessings in your life. You will find a wife and millions of dollars will find you. God told the pastor that Ngene must be destroyed in the month of May. The statue will be thrown into a huge fire. Mother asked me to tell you not to joke with this message. You must act immediately.*

The e-mail was sent on April 2, 2006. Ike wasn't sure whether Pastor Uka was bluffing, but he couldn't afford to wait and see. Suddenly, he had a new impetus to save Ngene, even if he didn't have to sell it. The thought of the statue smoldering in a fire was too jarring to imagine.

Ike's financial state was dismal. He had less than thirteen hundred dollars saved. His March rent of fifteen hundred dollars was long overdue, the April rent was due. Yet, none of that mattered. He had to move, and fast. His rent and other bills, he decided, must wait until he returned from the trip. Then, with the windfall reaped from the sale of the deity, he would clear all his debts. And he would have lots of cash to start any life he wished.

Four days after reading the e-mail, he had set a date for the trip. And then he drove to a travel agency on Hoyt Street in Brooklyn and charged the fare of $1,583 on a Visa card activated that same day. The card had arrived in the mail a month ago. He'd seen that it carried a usurious interest rate of 28.9 percent and had meant to cut it up. It was only his habitual hesitancy that stood in the way. He had inserted the card in his wallet and forgotten about it—until now.

Having settled the matter of a ticket, Ike had to think about cash for expenses. There would be expenses, a lot of them, once he arrived in Nigeria. He would make a stopover in Lagos for a night or two. He'd need a place to stay in the city. He'd need money for eating, for moving about. Then there was the domestic flight from Lagos to Enugu. There was the cost of hiring a taxi from the Enugu Airport to his hometown. Once he grabbed the deity, he could not afford the risk of a customs officer prying into his bag. It would take doling out a handsome bribe to persuade customs officers to— as Nigerians said—go blind small. The thought unsettled him, but he knew that his mother and sister would expect some cash.

Ike had two or three good friends who lived in Lagos. He had only to ask, and they would graciously pick him up or drop him off at the airport. He could easily ask any of them to host him in their homes. But he had decided not to make contact, for the nature of his trip required that he operate with extreme caution and tact. The company of friends, he feared, might stimulate nervousness. He was better off isolating himself as much as possible. He would be the master of his own fate: see to his own accommodations and care in Lagos and make arrangements for his movements once he touched down in Nigeria.

Ike's credit card came with a cash limit of twenty-five hundred dollars. He withdrew it all, unperturbed by the high interest rate. He had a beloved deity to rescue. And he stood to make a great fortune doing it.

The trouble was that twenty-five hundred dollars was not enough for the expenses that Ike envisaged. He had worried himself sick about where to get some more cash. If he had had time, he might have been tempted to make a quick dash to Atlantic City or Foxwoods. The more he thought back on all his gambling losses, the more convinced he was that luck lurked around the corner, finally ready for him.

And then Usman stepped out of the shadows with his largesse.

Ike glanced up at the clock hung above the framed black-and-white photograph of his family and saw that the time was 11:53 P.M. Then he lowered his eyes and stared at the picture. He looked lingeringly on his parents. They sat side by side. His mother seemed somewhat uneasy. Hands folded on her lap, she stared straight, as if suspicious of the camera. His father was noticeably more relaxed. He leaned back in his chair, left hand thrown over the back of the chair, fingers clasping his wife's shoulder. Ike and his sister stood behind their parents. At the time, Ike was still slightly shorter than Nkiru. His head of bushy hair was cocked right, away from his sister, his lips parted in a hesitant muttering of *cheese.* His sister Nkiru's eyes were already branded by that appetite for rebellion and adventure that, at nineteen, would leave her carrying a baby for a police sergeant.

Looking at the photo, he wondered if he had not betrayed his mother and sister—and, in some vague way, his late father. Once he came back from his trip, he would have enough money to do a better job of taking care of his mother and sister. Guilt, grief, and penitence spun in a whorl inside of him. He turned away from the photo, but thoughts of his father, mother, and sister stayed with him.

Ike opened the last bottle of Red Stripe and emptied its contents into a large tumbler. He upended the tumbler, drained the beer, and licked his lips. He lay down on the couch, curled up in the fetal position. As his head snuggled on the armrest, his nostrils caught the scent of Queen Bee's hair spray. It turned his alcohol-filled stomach. He sat up, upset, but also astonished to find himself aroused. He thought: *She left a whiff of herself on the couch, and then left the couch behind to torment me.* He shut his eyes, not in submission to the lure of sleep, but to expel the thoughts of her.

It was 1:14 A.M. when he opened his eyes. Insomnia made him crave alcohol, but he had run out of beer. His only option was a bottle of Jack Daniel's whiskey he had hidden under the bed. Queen Bee had bought it—in all likelihood, Cadilla had given it to her. For months, the bottle had sat on the kitchen counter. After the divorce, she left without taking it. Ike had been tempted to throw it away or to hand it to some homeless man. But a deep fear of Queen Bee kept him from either action. He wouldn't put it past her to show up one day and demand that bottle of whiskey. He had rolled it underneath the bed to keep it out of sight.

CHAPTER SEVEN

Ike swept his hand under the bed until his fingers felt the bottle of whiskey. He used his shirt to wipe off its film of dust and then twisted off its cap. Its rich scent hit his nostrils and made his stomach heave slightly. He had never liked the smell of whiskey. If he could help it, he never drank it. When he did, he first killed the smell with a liberal spray of Coca-Cola. Nor did he care for its taste, unless it was mottled in chunks of ice and lemon juice.

Tonight, he was prepared to drink the whiskey straight, braving its reek and its strong, burning taste. He was having one of those desperate nights when sleep fled from his eyes.

He poured the drink into a glass, alert not to exceed the halfway mark. He brought the glass to his nostrils, testing out his abhorrence against his desperation. He flinched, surprised by the ease with which repulsion weakened his will. From the refrigerator he fetched three cubes of ice and a can of ginger ale. After throwing in the cubes and two dabs of ginger ale, he swilled the whiskey. It was far from a smooth affair, but neither was it as hard to swallow as he feared. The liquid slipped, scalding and cold, through the circuit of his belly. He felt a sharp pain in his guts, hunger flaring up. He immediately lifted the glass again to his lip. Another jet of liquid coursed down his throat.

He continued sipping until his tongue became accustomed to the taste. Then he once again found and opened the May 1, 2005, edition of the *New York* magazine.

He sat down and twisted the knob of a standing lamp. The bulb blinked, steadied itself, and bathed the room with a bright glare. He set the glass of whiskey on the floor. Then he spread the magazine on his lap. Having met Mark Gruels hours before, he studied the photo that dominated the first page of the profile. A beaming Gruels was dressed in a twilled blue T-shirt and a pair of black pants. In the crook of his left hand was a joss, in the other hand a statue of the Ewe god of rain. In bold red letters that grazed the hair of the smiling entrepreneur was the headline: "The Man Who Sells Gods."

An hour and six minutes later, he woke up to the pulse of a terrible pain in his neck. The couch was soaked with his sweat and reeked of whiskey. For a while he lay still, bedraggled. Eyes half shut, right hand cramped, his mind seemed vacant, unable to remember the last thing he did before he was swept off by sleep. He had slept deeply, dreamlessly, aroused finally by the throb of pain in his neck.

Eyes fully opened, Ike surveyed the room with the curiosity of a man transported in a dream to a strange room. Gradually, the shafts of light from the slatted window restored his sense of bearing. With his left hand he pulled out the cramped right hand from underneath his head. The rescued hand felt numb. He clenched and unclenched it to regain some sensation. Then, shifting his body, he felt the crinkle of paper.

He lifted himself and pulled out the wrinkled copy of the magazine. The slight movement gave him a feeling of nausea and made his headache flare up. He was familiar with the drinker's credo pertaining to a hangover: *Kill the pain with more of the same.* His fingers swept the floor until they touched the glass that held the remnant of whiskey. He took a sip and burped, convinced that the hangover was assuaged, even if slightly.

He lowered his legs to the floor, leaned his reeling head on the couch, and began to read, freeing himself to be absorbed.

This time, his eyes seemed to conjure up the very words of the profile. It began with the strange story of that eccentric and reclusive Japanese businessman named Ryoei Saito and the record-breaking $82.5 million he spent to purchase Vincent van Gogh's *Portrait of Dr. Gachet* and the princely $78.1 million that fetched a smaller version of Pierre-Auguste Renoir's *Au Moulin de la Galette*. Then the magazine dived into the new art of god collection, *"gaining ground as a new diversion for the wealthiest of the wealthy whose after-dinner drone is peppered with talk of million-dollar losses in capital ventures, the purchase of multimillion-dollar yachts, or splashes of excess on the island of Saint-Tropez, a haunt of Hollywood stars and well-heeled titans of the corporate world who think nothing of spending forty-five thousand dollars on a bottle of Dom Perignon."* Two pages described the growing exotic taste for primitive deities and sacred objects. After two decades of nurturing itself in the shadows, *"this passion for Foreign Gods has emerged as a visible and powerful cultural current and force."* It named some of *"the big-name, dazzling players in the trade, and its dark and not-so-dark secrets: jealousies, betrayals, cattiness, derring-do, and brinkmanship."*

Over the last ten years, major galleries had opened in such locations as Seattle, Napa Valley, Palm Beach, and Atlanta to cater to a rising appetite for foreign deities and sacred objects. But the oldest shop—and the acknowledged dean of them—was Foreign Gods, Inc., *"a gallery that occupies two floors, located on a quiet street corner in Greenwich Village, New York."* The rest of the piece focused on Mark Gruels, a Harvard Business School graduate who took over the running of the gallery after the 1996 death of his father and gallery founder, Stephen Gruels-Soto. Ike found Gruels's boast arresting: *"Yes, we're the world's oldest god shop."* Then he lingered over the section on the gallery's so-called Heaven:

"A summons to Heaven doesn't come easy or cheap," said Robert Pemberton III, *a collector of rare gods and ritual objects. "I waited three years to receive my first. It's to be treasured."*

Mr. Pemberton's use of the word "summons" is no idle quirk; it's the precise lingo for an invitation to view, and bid for, the fare tucked away on the gallery's upper floor.

Less lucky collectors may get their thrill on the first floor, open to all comers. It is here that the gallery stores what in the art world might be called the secondary market. Except that a lot of the items even on the first floor command dizzying prices.

Ike glossed over the section about Mr. Gruels, who described himself as *"a hands-on, hardnosed, intense, but forward-looking business executive with a modern outlook—and a zest for life."* Gruels's *"charm and infectious humor often persuade collectors to put down several hundred thousand dollars for a godhead from the Tiv pagans of Africa, or fork over a cool million for a sacred totem from a remote, often unpronounceable Southeast Asian tribe."*

Having read the piece numerous times, Ike had lost interest in the lush portrait of Mr. Gruels as *"a hard frolicker who had dated some of the city's most desirable women and been linked to a major Hollywood actress."* Nor did he care to go over the gallery owner's intellectual sophistication, his habit of quoting Derrida, Foucault, and Lacan, or his notorious misadventure in Morocco where he, his girlfriend, and two other friends landed in jail for flaunting their ill-clad bodies near a mosque during Friday prayers.

He stopped reading and then put the badly rumpled magazine in his carry-on bag. If he felt the urge, he would read it again—perhaps for the last time—during his flight.

CHAPTER EIGHT

Ike stayed awake for the New York to Amsterdam leg of the trip, his chest knotted tight with apprehension. His mind flitted from his mother to his uncle, obsessed with their physical scars. His mother's right thumb was shriveled from an attack of whitlow she suffered years ago, when Ike was in his first or second year of secondary school. He remembered the evening he'd surprised her in her bedroom. She sat in bed and stared at her disfigured thumb, tears trailing down her face. He'd hurried away to his own room to weep into his pillows and curse the disease that had reduced his mother to such anguish. And then there was the grotesque scald of flesh on Uncle Osuakwu's abdomen. He'd seen it years ago, on a day Osuakwu entertained an audience at the shrine with stories of his experiences in Burma during World War II.

"Look at this," his uncle had said, pulling up his undershirt to expose a gash in his belly. Osuakwu paused, running his fingers along the singed, darkened scar. "First, the white man forced me to go to Burma to fight in a war that had nothing to do with me. It was a quarrel between different white brothers. And then the white man gave me this as payment."

Ike's spell of sleeplessness left him feeling haggard. He was so fatigued that he drifted off to sleep shortly after KLM's Boeing 767 taxied down the runway at Schipol Airport and lifted itself into the air, bound for Murtala Muhammed Airport in Lagos.

The last scene he remembered was the clarity of the dawn sky in Amsterdam, a wide blue dome with no cloud puffs in sight. As the plane ascended, he looked out the window at the immensity of the sky. Then, casting his eyes down, he saw the vast mat of the landscape, the streets of Amsterdam marked off by geometric patterns amid marshes and expanses of green. Seen from the heights, the rugged beauty of the unfurled scene seemed unbearable, and he shut his eyes.

His mind lolled, unable to cleave to anything, ideas or images. Then it slowly began to focus on the last time he sat down with Uncle Osuakwu at the shrine of Ngene. Something about their discussion struck him as significant, but the details of it remained vague, even foggy.

As Ike hovered between sleep and wakefulness, a startling idea seized him. He had the sensation that Queen Bee had somehow gotten on the same flight. And that she had sneaked up and sat right behind him, staring at the back of his head. He unglued his eyes and swung back. His severe eyes met the stare of a red-haired white woman. She gave an apologetic grin, then sharply looked away.

Moments later, he was asleep. It was a restless, fitful sleep, troubled by a churn of unwelcome images. First was Queen Bee the day their divorce was finalized, her face exultant and mocking. Then Cadilla floated into the picture, his face signed with a terrible smirk, he and Queen Bee wantonly commingled, heaving on the couch until, exhausted, they lay in a heap, panting. Soon the raucous habitués who gathered outside Cadilla's store took their turn to menace his half-formed, sad dreams.

It was a long, torturous affair. Hardly rested, he heard, as if somebody had leaned into his ear and pressed wind in it, the whir of the public-address system announcing commencement of the descent into Lagos.

He stretched himself, relieved to expel the languor of a tormented sleep. Looking out the window, he saw the patternless crisscross of lines and tangents that marked the landscape of Lagos. His stomach tightened at the vision of the city's marred, ugly layout.

He must have dozed off again briefly, for he awoke as the plane glided, hovered as if in fleeting hesitancy, before its tires made smooth contact with the tarmac. The passengers went into a tizzy of clapping. One woman yelled, "Jesus is Lord!" Another woman replied, "Satan is a liar!" Shouts rang out all around: "God is great!" "Praise him!" As the plane sped fiendishly on the tarmac, rattling, several passengers stood up, opened the overhead compartments, and began to tug at their hand luggage.

A woman's high-pitched voice came over the public-address system. "Sit down! Sit down!" it ordered shrilly. "Ladies and gentlemen, you're to remain seated until the aircraft has come to a final stop and the FASTEN SEAT BELT sign is turned off. Keep your seat belts fastened!"

More passengers stood up and began to pull their bags. Among the second batch was a flabby woman who sat across the aisle to Ike's right. As she wrestled with her luggage, her buttocks filled the aisle, brushing against him. He made a disgusted face, hissed and drew away from her.

The big-bottomed woman brought down one bag. She panted as she tried to pry a second one, wedged between two heavier bags.

Ike waited until every passenger had left before he retrieved his hand luggage and made for the exit. A splash of sizzling, humid air stung his skin once he stepped onto the covered tunnel that led to the airport building. It was a harsh heat, but he found it oddly comforting. Soon sweat tickled the small of his back. He breathed deep, grinned to himself, and thought: *This is the air of Lagos, clingy and muggy.*

His watch read 5:51 P.M.

He completed immigration formalities, lifted his suitcases onto a trolley, and then beckoned one of the uniformed porters to push it.

"*Oga*, bring money to settle customs," the porter said in pidgin, gesticulating wildly, eyes averted.

"What do you mean by *settle customs*?" Ike asked, feigning ignorance.

The porter flashed a rogue, wry smile. "Ah, *oga,* you no be Nigerian?" he quizzed, pushing the trolley.

"I'm a Nigerian," Ike said stiffly, walking beside him. "So?"

"Customs no go let your luggages pass unless you settle them," the porter said in a tone of starchy finality.

"Wait." Ike pulled at the trolley to force the porter to stop. He stared at the porter's face. "You're asking me to hand you money to bribe customs, or they won't let me go. Is that it?"

The porter looked away, a nervous grin on his face. "*Oga*, dis no be matter of big grammar. If you blow grammar, customs go vex for you."

"I don't have anything illegal in my suitcases. So don't worry about any trouble with customs." He removed his restraining hand to let the porter continue his push.

The porter shook his head in a sad, bemused way. "Customs go delay you, *oga.*"

"It's okay. I have time."

As they neared the customs post, Ike thought he saw the porter's lips move in some secret communication with a man dressed in a pair of dark blue pants and a light brown shirt.

"Hey, this way," the uniformed man commanded.

"I been warn you, you no hear," the porter muttered in a tone of triumph and vindication. "Okay, make you go blow grammar to customs." He stopped the trolley in front of the officer and stalked off.

"Who owns this?" the officer said in a loud voice, as if the prospect of Ike's ownership was doubtful.

"If you mean these two suitcases, they are mine," Ike said, trying not to stare at the toothpick hanging from the officer's lips, his sweat-sodden armpit, or the belly that sagged beneath a belt.

The officer pulled the toothpick. "What do you have inside this?" He kicked the top suitcase with his dusty black shoe.

Ike checked his rage. "Personal effects."

"Personal effects? Open de thing."

Ike unlocked and lifted the cover of the suitcase. Bent over, his drooped belly swaying like a free, soft weight, the officer rummaged through the suitcase, taking out clothes and setting them down on a raised platform. Then he stood up, panting, his eyes red.

"You have twenty-two packet shirts, twelve dresses, many, many trinkets and sixteen deodorants."

Ike nodded.

"That na commercial quantity. You have to pay duty."

"What do you mean by commercial quantity?"

"Na buying and selling."

"It's not true." Ike looked him straight in the face. "They're gifts."

The officer sneered. "Gifts?" He sharply turned away.

"Don't you have family members? And don't you buy them gifts?"

The man turned and gave him a harsh look.

"These are gifts for my mother, my sister, her husband, their children—and my friends."

The officer shrugged, unimpressed. "I done tell you. This na commercial quantity."

"Show me where it's written that somebody who lives abroad can't bring in twenty, thirty shirts as gifts."

"Are you trying to teach me my job?" he asked, raising his voice. He pointed to his sodden shirt. "Are you saying the government that gave me this uniform is stupid?"

Even though he'd not visited Nigeria for more than ten years, Ike was quite familiar with the Nigerian customs' ritual, a huffing game designed to browbeat tired, cowering passengers into parting with a bribe. He was determined not to be bamboozled or terrorized, dead set against backing down.

"Did you hear me mention the government?" he fought back. "Did I once say the word stupid? All I said is, show me any law that says I can't bring in shirts and dresses as gifts."

Another officer, tall and sinewy, strolled to the scene.

"Wetin dey happen?" he asked his colleague.

"Na dis rat," the big-bellied officer rasped, sweeping his arm in Ike's direction. "He thinks coming from America gives him right to teach me my job. He thinks he can blow grammar." In a moment, two other customs officers, one of them a woman, swooped in. "Common rat!" the first officer cursed, sticking the toothpick in his mouth.

"He has no right to insult me," Ike protested, alternately seeking eye contact with the three officers. Each gave him a hostile, sideward glance. "He can't call me a rat."

"If he calls you, what can you do?" said the woman. "You think you're somebody because you come from America?"

"America my nyash!" cried another officer.

"You shouldn't insult me," Ike shouted. He panned about for any sympathetic passengers. Three passengers briefly made eye contact and then looked away, trudging after porters pushing their luggage. One of the porters made as if to shake a customs officer's outstretched hand. Instead, the porter dropped some folded dollar notes into the officer's palm, which immediately clenched. Ike felt something like a pebble wedged in his throat. Another female officer shambled to the scene.

It suddenly dawned on Ike that he risked overplaying his indignation. With nothing incriminating in his suitcase, he could bluff and—with luck—get away with it. But if the feud escalated, the officers could remark him—and, on his day of departure, with Ngene tucked inside his suitcase, they could single him out for particular torment. Despite that chastening thought, he found no easy salve for his fury.

"Why should he insult me for bringing gifts?" he asked in an even, temperate voice, seeking a path from anger to some dignified amicability. "Ask him whether I said one insulting word to him."

"See his yeye mouth," the big-bellied officer said.

"Suffer-head," the lanky officer derided. "He washes plates for a white woman in America and thinks he can come here and make mouth."

The officers broke into peals of belly-quaking laughter.

"De man na proper church rat," the other female officer said. "Leave am to carry him poverty dey go."

"Carry your rubbish dey go, foolish idiot!" the big-bellied one said, a pugilist sneaking in a punch after the bell.

Ike glanced at his watch, his temper near the boiling point. The officers had wasted more than forty minutes of his time. Yet, he silently prayed that none of them would be around the day of his departure. If they detected him, they'd be like a pack of hyenas. They would chew through his bones.

Outside the airport, he landed in a swarm of bodies, a riot of voices, and a rich harvest of smells.

A man in a flowing white gown grabbed the handle of the trolley. "Yellow, make I push for you," he offered.

"Take your hands off!" Ike barked, and gave a ferocious push.

"Welcome sir," chirruped a man with a gnarled stump for a right hand. "I prayed God to give you safe journey, sir. Please, sir, spare me one dollar."

"Taxi? You want clean taxi?" asked another man.

Ike waded through the crush of people, passengers, mendicants, peddlers, and idlers. It was as if he kicked and pushed his way to the taxi stand.

"Stopoff Hotel," he announced to the first driver in line.

The hotel was only a mile and a half down the major road leading from the airport. Twice the cab was stopped at police checkpoints. At the first, a man sporting an unbuttoned shirt, an ugly, antiquated gun in one hand, peered into the front seat and asked, "Where from?"

"Airport," the driver answered.

The officer beamed a flashlight in the backseat. He saw Ike's stony face and gave a sluggish, buffoonish salute.

"I dey your side, sir," he said.

"I'm tired," Ike replied.

With a lazy wave of the hand, the officer granted passage to the taxi. A quarter of a mile later, they ran into another checkpoint. From the back, Ike hissed.

"If criminal come so, they run," said the driver. "Na to collect money be their business."

Another gun-wielding officer lowered his face close to the front passenger window. "Wetin you carry?" he asked.

"Luggage," said the driver.

The officer turned to Ike. "Na you be de owner of de luggage?"

Seething still from the encounter with the customs officers, Ike folded his hands, threw his head back in a sign of weariness, and answered, "Yes."

"Come and open," the officer said.

"What exactly are you looking for? The luggage has been checked at the airport. That should be enough."

"Open for him, sir," the driver whispered.

Ike got out, followed by the driver. The driver lifted the two suitcases to the ground, and Ike unlocked them. The police officer stood there gazing at the suitcases for what seemed a full minute. Then he asked, "You live in America?"

"Yes."

He tarried as if time was needed to digest the information. Then he said, "What's the purpose of your visit?"

"I'm a Nigerian," Ike said. "Do I need a special reason to come to my country?" He saw the driver shift uncomfortably. "I'm here to bury somebody," he lied.

"Anything for the boys?" the officer asked in a wheedling tone.

Ike realized that the façade of his motel could be seen down the road. "Funerals are expensive," he said, pushing further into his lie. "I have nothing to spare."

The officer regarded him. At last he said, "Next time?"

"Next time," Ike echoed.

As they drove away, Ike reflected that he had not foreseen this form of ordeal. Had Nigeria changed so much since he was last here, or had he grown in innocence in the years he'd lived in America?

The lobby of Stopoff Hotel was dank and dimly lit. Fuji music blared from a hall to the left of the lobby.

"What's going on?" he asked the receptionist, a young man named Segun.

"Na de nightclub. Today na fuji night."

"When does it close?"

"Till morin," Segun said in mangled pronunciation.

"Morning?"

"Yes. And you can fit to go in."

"But how do people sleep?"

Segun gave a shy smile. "They sleep."

"Do you have a bar?"

"For inside de nightclub."

Segun cupped hands over his mouth and shouted, "Tolu!" A young man lying supine on a frayed leather couch in the lobby sprang up, wiped his eyes, and approached the desk.

"Help *oga* take him bags to room four-oh-seven," Segun instructed.

The hotel's elevator had been broken down for Segun couldn't remember how long. Ike, with Tolu dragging his two suitcases, scuffed up several flights of stairs. Alone at last, he sat on the edge of his bed for several minutes. Then he decided to go back downstairs and look in at the nightclub.

It was a dark hall with dull strobe lights. The music deafened. Cigarette smoke and the reek of beer regaled the air. Clustered around tables, the customers shouted in order to be heard. Women and men flooded the dance floor. The women shook their buttocks. The men rocked their shoulders from side to side in a controlled sway, but encouraged the women's frenetic gyrations by pasting naira notes on their backsides.

Ike picked out one of the frenzied dancers. She had Queen Bee's stature: a flat belly, wavy breasts, and the kind of curved can favored by sculptors. As he watched her, he was transported by transferred desire. His loin stiffened. He resolved to offer her a drink and strike up a conversation. That instant, his mind exhumed the word "Zulu," a rich and respectable noun that his ex-wife had turned into an execrable epithet. His body shook as if a bucket of ice-cold water had been dumped on him.

It was as if Queen Bee herself had materialized in a fuji-playing nightclub in a seedy hotel in Lagos. He detested the sound. The writhing, drinking habitués reminded him of the rowdy youngsters outside Cadilla's store. As outside Cadilla's, the air turned oppressive, suffused with the smell of alcohol and cigarettes.

He wanted to flee and ensconce himself in his room. He'd retire with some drinks, in case sleep eluded him. He had a flight to catch the next day to Enugu, on his way to Utonki. He'd been told there was only that one flight to Enugu. It was scheduled for departure at 2:25 P.M., but he had been advised to arrive at the local wing of the airport no later than 11:00 A.M.

He walked up to the bar and ordered two bottles of Guinness. As he paid, a voice said to him, "Nothing for me?"

He swirled around to the smiling face of the woman who had reminded him of his ex-wife. He struggled to find words that seemed to scamper away. She said, "If you want, I fit come your room. My name na Bimpe, but my friends dey call me Princess Bimpe. I can do you fine."

"Thank you," he said, "but I'm going to rest."

"You no like me?" She cocked her head in Queen Bee's fashion.

"I'm traveling in the morning."

"I go help you relax well, well. You do me well, I do you well."

Ike's loin went berserk. He pictured her naked, her nipples in his mouth, her head thrown back in ecstasy, her fingernails—he gaped at her fingernails, just like Queen Bee's!—digging into the soft flesh of his back, scratching, clawing, kneading. Her voice, if she didn't speak in pidgin, could have been interchangeable with his ex-wife's.

"Thanks." He sounded frantic. "Good night."

A bottle in each hand, he ran up the stairs, his chest threatening to burst. Pursued by the canter of his own shoes, he ran as if

Queen Bee were on his heels. Then, breathlessly opening his door, he looked behind, ready to shriek at his sex-crazed pursuer. There was nobody.

He waited until his panting eased off, then used his teeth to pry off the cover of one bottle. He raised the bottle to his lip and let the liquid surge into his mouth. Fleetingly startled by the sharp bitterness, he drank until his nostrils filled up with heat. He belched away the fume.

CHAPTER NINE

The flight from Lagos took off close to forty minutes behind schedule and arrived in Enugu at 4:35 P.M.

Somebody yelled "Satchmo Americano!" as Ike stepped into the cramped baggage claims section at the airport. It was his nickname in secondary school, earned because he idolized Louis Armstrong. He made a quick scan of the room, but saw no familiar face. Then somebody gripped him from behind.

Turning round, Ike's mouth dropped open in disbelief. His hailer was Donatus Adi, a classmate in secondary school, but better known as De Don.

"Satchmo Americano!" the man cried.

"De Don Oblangata!" Ike replied in like spirit. The man's paunchy, filled-out physique advertised prosperity. Ike had heard that De Don had made a fortune after an uncle of his was elected governor. "It has been—how many years?"

"Please don't count!" De Don said, embracing him. "I don't want people to know that I'm an old man."

De Don was at the airport to welcome his wife, who had flown to London to give birth to their second child, a daughter. He asked

where Ike was headed and then summoned a rheumy-eyed cabdriver named Gabriel. He handed a wad of crisp naira notes to the
man and instructed him to drive Ike to Utonki.

Holding Ike by the shoulder, De Don addressed the driver. "This
man you see here is a VIP. That's why I have paid you extra. He's
not just any VIP, an American VIP. If anything happens to him, the
CIA of America will come and ask you about it. Do you know who
the CIA is?"

Gabriel shook his head.

"They kill people like you who mess Americans up."

"God will not allow," said the driver.

"So drive carefully."

"Yes, sir," Gabriel said, stealing sidelong glances at Ike.

"And here," De Don said, handing more twenty naira notes to
Gabriel. "This is to settle police."

"Thanks, sir," said the driver.

The commute to Utonki took an hour and forty-five minutes. The
car squeaked and groaned through long stretches of the highway
that were rutted and gutted. Ike counted seven police checkpoints
before he stopped keeping count. At each one, the driver wound
down his window and held out a twenty-naira note. A police officer
would palm the money then say, "All correct!" or "Correct, man,"
waving the driver on.

Ike remained serene through it all, deep in thought. He tried to
focus on his mother, but images of his uncle and the shrine continued to flutter at the edge of his mind. Unable to ward them off, he
asked the driver if he had any music.

"Assorted, sir!" the driver answered. "Which kin' you like, sir?"

"Do you have Uwaifo?"

"Victor Uwaifo?"

"Yes. 'Joromi.'"

The air-conditioned interior pulsated with the song's thrilling rhythm, its alternation between slow and soaring notes, and Uwaifo's dexterous fingers strumming the guitar until its strings seemed to weep for mercy. Stirred by the melody, Ike shut his eyes. The music entered his body, rendered him insensate. Then he startled awake as the music ceased, his mind racing from some dark depths.

"You think I be twenty-naira police? Ejoo bring correct money. Otherwise come down!" barked a burly man in a police uniform.

Ike made to speak, but held back.

"De passenger na VIP," the driver said, his voice a veiled caution to the officer.

"Which kin' VIP no get him own Mercedes-Benz? VIP dey take taxi? Don't waste my time. Oya, multiply by two and go."

The driver added another twenty-naira note, and they were waved on. Ike hissed. The driver restarted the music.

"Shut it off," Ike said with a tinge of testiness he had not intended.

"No problem, sir."

In the silence, disquieting thoughts buffeted Ike's mind. What if his nerves failed him? Or, on the night he was supposed to take Ngene, what if some nocturnal prowler caught him in the act? And what would he do if it turned out that Osuakwu had built a new shrine for the deity, complete with a heavy metal door, a lock and key? He contemplated telling the driver to put in another CD, but couldn't bring himself to ask.

Gabriel said, "Very soon, we go reach, sir."

Ahead of them was a concrete bridge.

"Is that the bridge over River Utonki?" he asked.

"Yes, sir."

Something came over Ike as they drove on the bridge, a sense of entrancement. The bridge seemed to concretize a theme of change.

The last time he was home, the bridge did not exist. Boats powered by small engines ferried people, residents of Utonki as well as visitors, from one bank to the other.

The bridge! His sister had told him all about it five, six years ago in one of the occasional telephone conversations they used to have.

For years, the people of Utonki had importuned government after government to build a bridge over the river. Successive governments either gave a deaf ear or made excuses. They pleaded financial constraints or made promises that went unmet.

It happened that the big man who was then the country's minister of works had an eye for a dazzling belle from Utonki. When the minister, famous for his harem, proposed to take her as his third wife, the audacious young woman made a request: "Build a bridge for *my* people." The minister agreed, for he too loved to bask in pomp and pageantry. He wanted to have his friends (from home and abroad) descend on Utonki to witness the spectacle of his third traditional wedding. So he ordered the contractor to complete the job in record time. The love-struck minister also threw in a new "ultramodern" dispensary to replace the dilapidated structure where a traveling nurse used to stop twice a week to inject anti-malarial prophylactics into the bottoms of wailing children and cringing, snarl-faced adults.

The people of Utonki gave the bridge a fitting name: Path to a Pot of Sweetness.

THE CAB IDLED OUTSIDE the old, moss-pocked walls of his mother's home. Sharp-edged shards of broken bottles, meant to deter burglars, rimmed the wall. Dusk had cast a pall, but a vestige of orange clung to the sky's western flank. Ike's heart skittered as he glanced up at the electronic clock on the dashboard. It flashed 6:55.

He sat stonily, gripping the sides of his seat, a faraway expression on his face. He felt the car's soft quiver and scarcely noticed the driver.

"*Oga*, we don' reach," Gabriel said.

Ike drew a deep breath and gasped. He clasped his hands underneath his chin, like a supplicant.

The driver whistled in a tuneless, distracted manner, tapping lightly on the steering wheel. When Ike gave no sign of stirring, Gabriel spoke in a piercing voice: "*Oga*, no be here?"

Ike silenced him with a glare. A moment later, he unbuckled his seat belt, as if he had been meditating and had just been vouchsafed some insight. Rather than open the door, he sank deeper into the seat. As he gazed out at the landscape, something quickened inside him. He felt overcome by sadness—but for what? Slowly, the mist that enveloped him lifted, and he realized that two tiny teardrops were wriggling down his face.

Utonki! This was the village that had steeped him in the magic of the earth's redness and rich scents. Ah, *Utonki of the red earth*! A surreal redness, as if long ago the soil had wept blood. It was here that his tongue had learned the art of discrimination, able to tell the sweet from the tart, delicacies from bitter recipes. It was in Utonki that his ear had first picked up the sundry sounds of the world, the songs of the wind, the pitchy chirp of birds, the very earth heaving under the sun's rage. It was here that, on moonlit nights, he had played hide-and-seek with other children or sat on raffia mats, again with other dreamy children, to listen to some elder tell tales about cunning Tortoise and sinister Chameleon and about the irreconcilable feud between Mosquito and Ear. It was here that he had made his first forays into the woods, his first plunges into the river, thrashing against the current until he learned, on his own, to swim. He'd traversed the landscape as an adventurous youth, mastering the smells and secrets of flowers, the stinks and secretions of various insects. It was here that he had mastered the different techniques for climbing a guava or mango tree. It was here he had learned how to aim a sturdy stick at hanging ripe mangoes, *ube* or *udala*.

From inside the idling car, Ike noted the changes. Electric poles dotted the landscape. New houses had sprung up where he remembered farmlands. His mother's residence, a modest bungalow his parents had finished building in 1964, was now hemmed in and dwarfed by three gigantic three-story buildings, two on either side and an even taller one behind. The house behind seemed to stand on heels and peer into his mother's backyard. Zinc-roofed concrete houses stood where mud houses used to be. Several buildings sported satellite dishes or television antennas.

A clicking startled him. He turned in time to see Gabriel the driver alight from the car. The door gave a soft thud as it shut. Gabriel hastened to the back, opened the trunk, and brought out the two suitcases. Then, a suitcase in each hand, he stood outside, staring at Ike.

The people of Utonki often ululated on sighting a long-gone visitor. The first person to see you would ask, "Is it Ikechukwu, the son of Uzondu, that my eyes are beholding?" The rhetorical question would be followed by a short song: "What have my eyes seen? They have seen Ikechukwu Uzondu! Ikechukwu, the traveler, is back!" The refrain would be taken up by others. Before long, a crowd would gather, just as it had happened years ago, on the banks of River Utonki, when he had returned for his father's funeral.

Ike was too tired to face crowds now. He saw only a scrawny dog stretched out in the dust under a shadow cast by a fruitless orange tree. He stepped out. The air was mildly warm, the retreating afternoon heat tamed by the waft of breeze from the river. The sun had tucked itself in under a fluffy, lolling mass of clouds.

The evening had the same charmed, eerie feel to it that he remembered from years ago.

He inhaled until his lungs ached, his nostrils picking out the faintest whiff of something—like grass—burnt. Slowly, deliberately, he exhaled—and walked with long, quick strides toward his mother's home. A blustery breeze started up as if to stall him. It swept up dead leaves and whipped up a small twirl of dust and seemed intent on crashing into him. He turned away from it as it gathered speed, twirled and twisted with fiercer force. He covered his eyes, smiling. As granules of sand blew into his mouth, he spat and grimaced.

His grandmother, Nne Ochie, floated into his mind. She who held Wind and Sun in conversation, who discerned the spirit of things—she would have described the vigorous wind as a dance of welcome.

Once inside the walled compound, Ike looked right, to the grave where his father lay, the white marble now tarnished, spattered with sand. He felt a longing to stand beside the grave, lower his head in sorrow, and make the sign of the cross. But some part of him knew the act would not be solemn enough without his mother there to witness it. He walked toward the door but stopped outside, on the veranda with its peeled blue paint and smudges, slightly trembling.

The last time he had seen his mother was at his father's funeral. One image of her stood out among many: her face disfigured by rivulets of tears, mucus dripping from her nose, unwiped. What was the chance that joy, some measure of joy, had found its way back to that face mauled by grief?

He shoved aside the blinds, brown and frayed, their once-colorful embroidery tamed by dirt. He peered into a dusky living room.

"Mama?" he said in a choked, muffled voice. Nothing but the

muted echo of his own voice answered him. He batted his eyelids, but the room remained wreathed in darkness.

"Is Mama in?" he asked in Igbo, half expecting an answer from the void. He raised his voice a notch. A tangle of smells hung about the room. Unable to recoil, he sniffed deeply, seeking to draw out each individual smell. He detected the liquid smell of sweat, the cloying aroma of crayfish, *dawadawa*, *ogili*, and other condiments, the awful pungency of sour food, the fester of fish offal, the clingy tang of goat meat, the stink of unwashed laundry, and sheer fetid air. There was something else, a faint, elusive odor, hard for the nose to grasp.

Ike shifted his head from side to side, sniffing the air, seeking to discern the inscrutable smell. As he was sniffing, he had a sudden intuition that somebody had sidled up and stood behind him. He swung around. A gangly girl stood in the veranda, her face smeared with perspiration. She wore a checked olive-colored school uniform.

"Good evening, sah," she said in a shy, high tone.

"*Kedu?*" he asked, stepping away from the living room. She giggled, as though surprised that he spoke Igbo.

"*Odi nma.*"

"What's your name?"

"Alice."

He gasped in surprise; she was his niece, his sister's daughter. The last time he saw her, during his father's funeral, she was a tiny, suckling baby.

"Alice? You've grown so big."

She nodded, wringing her hands, eyes averted.

He took in the compound's cemented grounds where he and his friends used to kick around balls, their skins glistening with sweat. Thin metal clotheslines ran between three rusted steel posts that formed an indifferent triangle, the dry clothes swaying in the modest breeze. A hen waddled in through the gate, trailed by four chicks.

"God almighty!" Ike said, fixing his attention back on his niece. "The last time I saw you, you were like this." His hands defined a small, curved shape. "Do you know who I am?"

"Yessah," she said, without raising her eyes.

"Tell me."

"Uncle Ike."

"Wonderful! Where's your mother?"

"At Onitsha, sah. She will come next tomorrow."

"You mean the day after tomorrow?"

"Yes, next tomorrow."

"You know," he said, then resisted the impulse to correct her. "I haven't seen your mother in eleven years," he said, changing direction.

"She sent me to stay with Mama for a few days."

"Are you not in school?"

"We breaked, sah."

"You're on break?"

"Yessah."

"What grade are you in?"

She stared straight ahead, confused. Quickly recalling that Nigerians used class, not grade, he rephrased his question.

"Class four, sah."

"Where's Mama?"

"She go to church, sah."

"She went?"

"Yessah, to church. It is not long since she went," she said, finally catching on. "They're having Thursday Harvest. I'm coming from there; I carried Mama's basket of yams for her. Should I went to tell her that you came? The church is just there." She pointed.

He smiled, entertained by her misused tense. "Don't bother. Is it a long service?"

"Sometimes it's lesser than two hours, sometimes more. If you want me to—"

"No, no point," he interrupted. "I'll see her when she returns."

"Your room is ready, sah. I will on a lamp for you."

His smile became broader. "How about the electricity?"

"It has reached more than one week that NEPA took light, sah."

Ike pointed to the building to the right. "Their bulb is lit."

"They use generator to on their own light, sah."

His ears picked up the spastic whine of a generator.

Alice darted into the house and opened two rear and two front windows. The sun, trolling westward to its rest, threw tepid light. Once he stepped inside, he felt the sensation of being in a place that was at once familiar and strange. The furniture was the same from his youth, the cloth-covered dark green sofas in which, years ago, he would lounge and daydream. He could now see that the sofas were discolored, dirty and torn in places. There was the old center table on which his father was served his meals. Its top had bad scratches, and one of its legs had come unhinged, buckled in. The same familiar pictures hung on the walls: two of his father, dapper in a suit and tie, hand underneath his jaw; two of the entire family, his sister hoisted on their father's lap, Ike on their mother's; one each of Ike and his sister, taken on their respective tenth birthdays. But the pictures had accumulated so much dust and so many cobwebs that, rather than kindle fond memories in Ike, they stirred a desultory feeling in him. It was as if he'd walked into a gallery and gazed on disturbing alien figures from a time and place remote and different. Once again, he was bathed by commingled smells. He stopped outside the door of his bedroom, then veered toward a bookshelf. The shelf wobbled at his touch; his hand was smeared with dust. He peered at the tightly stacked books, then his pulse quickened when he saw Manfredi's *Ngene: The God That Owns Rain*. He felt resistance pulling at the booklet; humidity had matted the covers of several books. When he finally extricated the booklet, part of its cover was peeled off. He slapped it lightly against the edge of the shelf and then ambled toward his room.

The room remained astonishingly familiar, as if its bareness had been assiduously preserved. His room at Stopoff Hotel was splurgy by comparison. There was the same wooden desk on which he used to do his homework. Two of its legs had come loose, leaving it unsteady, a hazard. There was the old wooden clothesline that now held a handful of plastic hangers. There was a smoky standing mirror. Many years ago, when he was three or four, he would stand before the mirror making faces and sudden jerky movements, amazed that his every gesture or lurch was faithfully repeated by his double in the mirror. That object of childhood fascination was now a blemished relic, broken neatly in mid-spine, held precariously in place with a thick, ugly pad of tape. Another fixture was an oaken prie-dieu which the Irish priest who officiated at his parents' wedding had given them as a gift. On its scratched shelf sat the old transistor radio on which his father used to monitor the BBC World Service. The radio was now a carcass, its knobs long lost, its voice forever stilled.

Then there was his old bed, its coiled springs bereft of elasticity.

"I dey go, sir," said the driver, who had lumbered in with Ike's suitcases and stood pat, as if awaiting further instructions.

"Drive safely," Ike said with spirit, even though he suspected the man had loitered in expectation of a tip.

"Should I boil water for your bath?" Alice asked.

"No. I just want to lie down and rest," Ike said. The bed sagged with his weight; its springs creaked, tensionless.

"I can bring you a lamp, sah," she offered.

"Don't bother."

"There's *egusi* soup. Should I make you *gari?*"

His mouth watered at the thought of his mother's delicious *egusi*. But he had a more pressing need to take a nap. He needed to rest, to be braced for the encounter with his mother.

After Alice left the room, Ike unzipped one of his suitcases and pulled out a bottle of Hennessy, VSOP. He uncorked it and drew its nipple to his lips. He sucked a mouthful, gurgled, and swallowed. Serenity, or an impression of it, spread through his nerves. He flipped off his shoes and half lay on the bed, his upper body propped on his elbow. He took another swig, rolled the liquid in his mouth, and let it drain down his gullet. Then he stretched out on the bed, his nostrils saturated with the sheet's smell of bar soap and camphor. Dug into the pillow, his head swarmed with images. The room swirled, seemed to twist into grotesque shapes and odd, disorienting angles. It was as if some manic force had seized control of things and had violently shaken him and his surroundings. Sleep, desperately needed, eluded him.

Instead, he felt light, a floating, fragile speck whipped around by a capricious breeze. The speck glided in the sheer, swift air for a while before he realized that he was being swept to a destination that was at once mysterious and enchantingly intimate. Then, suddenly, the violent force was spent. The wind became motionless; the speck ceased its gyration.

Ike, his senses keener than ever, was gripped by a spectacular sensation. He gazed out over a landscape where a familiar story unhurriedly unfurled itself. And then he realized it was the story of Reverend Walter Stanton, a tempestuous Anglican prelate, a man who, until his astonishing doom, had seemed like an indomitable, fearless foe to Ngene—and came close to sacking the war deity from its shrine. The good old English preacher was the first missionary to burst upon Utonki, arriving in grand style in the year 1898.

Years ago—Ike was then a secondary-school student who loved to dawdle at the shrine of Ngene, eating peppered goat meat and quaffing milk-colored frothy palm wine to his heart's content— he'd been obsessed with the missionary's story. Ensconced in his favorite corner in the shrine, a shadowed spot that gave him the anonymity to flip his roving eyes from one man to another, Ike soaked up the stories and tales that his uncle and other elders told about the white preacher. Sometimes, in the midst of an account, Ike would drift off, only to awake to another part of the story. He wanted to ask questions but always suppressed the urge, afraid that his intrusion would still the story. His patience and silence paid off, for any question would finally be answered, any gap filled in, that day or later, by the same storyteller or another. It was as if Stanton's story were woven into the fabric of the very air in the shrine.

Osuakwu and the elders called the legendary missionary a man of the river. They said the Utonki River had belched one day and spat out the Englishman—and his coterie—onto the soil of Utonki.

CHAPTER TEN

*R*everend Walter Stanton appeared in Utonki on a day the sun had cast its evil eye on the world, leaving every living thing in a state of stupor, groaning. He came with a retinue of soldiers whose guns spoke from two mouths at once, two missionary underlings the people of Utonki described as his shadows, and an interpreter whose skin was as black as the blackest person in Utonki.

The spectacle of the strange visitors drew the elders and people of Utonki to the square where the community celebrated its festivities. Then, speaking through his interpreter, Reverend Stanton announced that he had come to bring salvation to a people in darkness.

The first few days, he stood in the shade of an ukpaka tree to declaim his message. Stanton sweated monstrously, for the shade could not keep the sweltering tropical heat at bay. At first, the missionary's talk provoked laughter, derision, and a harmless, muted indignation. For more than a week, he cajoled and entreated without scoring even one convert. He harangued them, "Abandon your wooden phantom and embrace the living God."

One day, Stanton led his men deep into a mangrove sacred to Ngene to cut down tree limbs for use in building a shrine for his deity. The warriors of Utonki gathered together at the shrine of Ngene, armed with machetes and guns, determined to chase off the impertinent band of missionaries. Instead, Reverend Stanton and his soldiers handed the warriors of Utonki their most crushing defeat in living memory, felling their head warrior in the first moments of battle.

The next day, Stanton got one convert. Then, in the days that followed, a few others joined. The converts began to chant the name of the pale man's deity.

In the end, it was Stanton's display of strength that lent power to his message and won him a steady trickle of converts.

Stanton's soldiers, some of them recruits from other parts of Africa, came armed with contraptions nobody in Utonki had seen before: guns that simultaneously reported from two mouths, letting out a torrent of fire from both barrels. True, the warriors of Utonki had guns, too. But theirs were rather slow and labored; they spat fire only after inconvenient pauses for more gunpowder. Such sputtering guns, founded and soldered by the blacksmiths of Awka, were no match for the invaders' weapons.

Unaccustomed to defeat, the warriors of Utonki were disheartened. When Stanton ordered them to turn in their guns, only three resisted. One was an ocher-colored childless widow. Cradling her gun as one might a newborn baby, she waded into Utonki River. Without ever varying its purl, the river drew her down into its belly, and she disappeared forever. Another warrior was a hermit known for the power of his amulets. One morning, he climbed the ukpaka tree that used to afford Stanton some shade. After shooting four rounds of gunpowder in different directions, like a general saluting air, he aimed the fifth at his own heart. He tumbled from the tree like a prehistoric man-bird, thudded against the hard, red earth, twitched, and died. Another male warrior swallowed a leafy emetic in a quantity large enough to fell a horse. As his horrified friends and relatives looked on, he retched, dredged up a copious quantity of some greenish, viscous liquid, and then lay supine.

Overwhelmed by the missionary's armed ensemble, many in Utonki *became believers. As one of the converts explained to his neighbor, "The white man's guns outspeak the guns of Utonki. Who can argue that the white God isn't stronger than Ngene?"*

Still, Reverend Stanton was often grieved by the converts' heresies and ways. In turn, the converts were vexed by aspects of the new religion that sounded contentious, if not outright nonsensical.

During one session, Reverend Stanton's interpreter told the converts that the founder of the white man's religion was a bearded Man-God born in Bethlehem by a virgin. The converts didn't find the idea of a born god hard to swallow; after all, the deities in Utonki were carved by sculptors and then infused by men or women powerful in ogwu. *"But born by a virgin?" one new convert whispered to another. Both men shrugged, bemused. "The white man knows many things," the other whispered back, "but he doesn't know how to tell a good lie."*

SOMETIMES, THE CONVERTS VOICED *their doubts. One day, the interpreter said the new God's Father lived up in the sky, far beyond the clouds, beyond the reach of eyes. He said this divine Father was so huge his feet lolled all the way down the sky to rest on the earth. He then claimed that the missionaries' God was present everywhere.*

"Our people, too, have Chukwu, the great god who lives in the sky," one baffled convert said. "Everywhere, we see the signs of his work. The drifting clouds are smoke from his pipe. Rainfall is his sneeze. All great rivers were born from his spittle. Wherever he scuffed his feet, mountains arose. Valleys were formed wherever he stamped his feet. Chukwu is mighty, but we never say that he's everywhere. His home is in the sky, and he hardly leaves his hearth to visit the earth. He comes down to peer around only when something big happens in the world. And when he comes, nobody waits to be told. New mountains, valleys, and rivers are born. The earth shakes with rain the like of which is seen once in ages. If your own God lives everywhere, then why haven't my two eyes seen him?"

The interpreter explained the parley to the chief missionary.

"It's because the true and living God is invisible," Stanton explained.

For a moment, the curious convert was silent, but his face wore an incredulous expression.

"How can something be everywhere and yet invisible?" he asked finally.

"He's creator and maker of everything. With him, everything is possible. He can do and undo," came Stanton's retort.

"Then he should do to make himself visible," the convert suggested. "Why not tell him to appear to us in his body. Then all our brothers and sisters will leave their ways and come and follow him."

"We can't tell God what to do."

"I'm not saying tell him. Take a sacrifice to him and beg him," said the convert. "It is through sacrifice that gods are deceived."

"Our God cannot be deceived," Stanton explained with visible impatience. "He knows everything, including the secrets of our hearts. You deceive your own so-called gods because they're not gods at all, only phantoms. True Christians accept God's wisdom. It's not given to us to behold God in body, only as spirit."

"Ngene, too, is a spirit, but he also has a body," insisted the convert. "Its spirit is buried in the river. But you can see its body at the shrine."

Stanton scratched at his neck, leaving splotches of reddened skin. His words tumbled out fast.

"What you call Ngene is nothing. It's a lie with which you've imprisoned yourself. It doesn't live in the river. Nor does it own the river. Our God owns everything. He made your river and also the wood Ngene was carved from."

The convert's face showed confusion.

"All these years, our fathers and forefathers made sacrifices to Ngene. They gave it cocoyam and yam. They offered it chicken and goat. In fact, when their hands were strong with wealth, they brought cows to its shrine. When their wives had new babies, or when their farms had increase, they went to the shrine to say daalu *to Ngene. We, too, learned to do like our*

fathers and forefathers. Mother goat chews yam peelings; her offspring watch her mouth and learn. As soon as we stopped suckling our mothers' breast, we were taught the secrets of the river. We learned that the river belongs to Ngene, that the god's spirit lives in the river. Are you saying, then, that Ngene stole the river from your deity? If the river belonged to your God all along, why didn't he send a diviner to tell our forefathers and us about it?"

"That's why we're here. We've come to tell you about the God who made all things. We've brought you the good news of the one true, indivisible God. We're here to spread the word about he who alone sits on the mantle of glory."

"I still have one question that scratches my inside," the inquisitive convert said with a mischievous glint in his eye.

"Ask it," the missionary invited eagerly.

"Does your God owe money to another god?"

Perplexed, Stanton asked, "What do you mean?"

"I still don't understand why your God likes to be invisible. Around here, those who take to hiding are men who don't wish to pay their debts."

An edge of exasperation nudged away Stanton's eager mien. Fixing the interpreter with a glare, he spoke in a slow, halting manner.

"Tell them to get it out of their thick heads, once and for all, that there aren't other gods besides the one we worship. Tell them that our God can't owe anybody because he owns everything in heaven and on earth. Tell them that he's invisible because he's holy. Tell them that we're all tainted sinners, corrupted by the original sin of our first parents, Adam and Eve, who ate the forbidden fruit in the Garden of Eden. Tell them that, because all have sinned and come short, our eyes can't see God in flesh and blood. Tell them that nobody who beholds God can live to tell about it. Tell them, finally, that there will be no more questions for today."

DESPITE THEIR MANY QUESTIONS *and doubts, most converts did not wander off. Instead, they returned day after day to the makeshift church*

Stanton and his retinue had built on the outskirts of the village, near the river.

The church building was made of bamboo stems and a roof thatched with palm fronds. The roof had chinks through which the sun thrust shafts of light. One day, Stanton told the converts the story of Pentecost: about the tongues, as of fire, that rested on the head of each apostle. He said the apostles, filled with the spirit, began to speak in strange tongues.

Many converts were moved. Pentecost, they surmised, was a form of agwu, the spirit of possession. Agwu inflicted madness on those it possessed. But it also gave them hawk eyes that saw in the dark and far, far into the future, tongues that spoke prophecies, and hands that knew which leaves, barks, and roots healed what sickness. Some converts thought the shafts of sunlight that stabbed through holes in the raffia and rested on their fellows were the same intoxicating spirits that descended at Pentecost. But when one of them, a woman who used to lead village women in songs, flung herself on the ground and began to speak in a strange, frenzied tongue, the missionary's face turned red. He rushed at her, kicking and stamping. She writhed and trembled on the dirt floor, indifferent to his kicks. The other converts looked on, terrified and confused. Clearly, the woman was seized by a force neither she nor Stanton could call to order. Huffing and puffing, the missionary shouted, "No madness here! I wouldn't stand for it! Carry the mad woman away!"

ONE DAY, STANTON TOLD how the Great God sent his Son to die hanging on a cross, flanked on either side by robbers. One of the robbers, thanks to his penitence, was bestowed with mercy; he ascended with Christ straight into God's palace in the sky. The other, a proud, loquacious oaf, was cast into a cauldron.

Listening, one convert named Okafor was both consoled and scandalized. Okafor was a shiftless man and drunkard. The people of Utonki said of him that whenever he walked past, something was bound to get lost. He was moved by the story of a thief who, on his last day, had enough sense to speak kindly to God's Son—and thus earned an eerie flight to the sky.

Yet, an aspect or two of the narrative rattled his fledging faith. He raised a hand and addressed the interpreter.

"Tell the white man not to think that I drink a horn or two of palm wine, and my head fills with questions. Explain to him that our elders have said that he who asks never gets lost. There's a kernel I'd like the white man to crack for me. Ask him to explain what God's Son did to deserve such great punishment. We know that a son's skull is sometimes too hard to absorb his father's word. Perhaps that's what happened with God's Son. If so, I, Okafor, will still say that death was too strong a punishment. I don't know what the white man knows, but I know that a son who shuts his ears to his father should not be killed. In truth, to hear it jangles the ear! Why bind your son's hands and feet and put him in the midst of efulefu? And this was an only son.

"I have three sons. Sometimes, they don't hear any word I say. But even when their heads become hard, I never snatch a machete and cut their heads! No, I fetch a cane and let it speak to their buttocks! That's what a father does. So why did your God hand over His own Son to be made a jest of? Why allow efulefu to shred his Son's clothes and kill him on a tree? Why do I call them efulefu? Because no sensible man would kill a god's son, even if the god asked him. Tell the white man that I, Okafor—this is what I've said."

Okafor grinned, self-satisfied. The interpreter tightened his lips, like a man ashamed of baring rotten teeth, and glared at Okafor. In his career as interpreter, he'd seen and loathed many like Okafor. Okafor was just another native heretic who fancied himself clever. A drunk who was out, without question, to make a fool of the white man—and of God.

"Wild animal," the interpreter muttered under his breath. He peeled his gaze off of Okafor, but his irritation was hard to conceal.

"Are you bloody mute?" demanded Stanton, impatient to know what Okafor had said at such length.

The interpreter made to speak but instead fidgeted, stuttered, and stopped.

Unlike the people of Utonki who only knew Stanton on the surface—as a splotchy-faced, hairy-chested man who spoke nasally—the interpreter knew the ease with which the missionary could fly into a rage. And the sting of that rage!

"I can understand pagans uttering profane thoughts about God," Stanton would scold as he made a sport of thrashing the interpreter. "They're yet to know God. But you! You ought to know better! You know better than to repeat their idolatrous language. Does it count for nothing that we've shown you the light? Bloody hell, you're even baptized! We've washed off your original sin! We've even given you a first-rate Christian name! Is all that wasted on you? Must you return to the path of the infidel?"

"Jacob," Stanton called, taking note of the wavering interpreter.

"Sah!" the interpreter blurted out.

"Don't stand there shaking like a hag! Tell me what the fellow said." He glowered at the interpreter. "And don't waste my time!"

"Yes, sah!"

But, no, Jacob the interpreter wasn't going to bear the brunt of Okafor's drink-induced silliness. Not today. He had to find an innocuous translation, words that would spare him Stanton's thundering slaps. The trick was to buy more time. In an imploring tone, he said, "Sah, na think I dey think. The man ask question which hard well, well."

"Your job's not to think," Stanton said in a harsh tone. "I do the thinking around here. Your job is just to tell them"—he swept his hand to indicate the gathered converts—"whatever I ask you to tell them. And when they have questions, you tell me what the questions are. It's that simple. Is that clear to you?"

"All clear, sah! Sorry for me to think at all at all. I know is against law for me to think, sah. No more thinking. I can't make law vex, sah."

"Bloody buffoon," Stanton said. "Who talked about the law? No, I'm not about to send you off to prison for thinking. It's a matter of, shall we

say, convenience. I happen to be the one who knows about the true living God. That's why it's best that I be the one doing the thinking, the one to answer any questions. Your own place is clear. You know the tongue of your fellow Negroes and possess a smattering of English. You're to help me to convey the good news. Do that, Jacob, and there won't be any problems. But try to think too much and you might find yourself in a little bit of trouble. Not in jail, hell no. But trouble you wouldn't like. So, tell me what the man said."

"The questioner man humblily want to know . . . No, he ask to know . . . Sah, he appeal that you use your wiseness to educate himself as to pertains to one matter . . . In short, what can make him happy, reverend sah, is to want know why the Almighty . . ." He hesitated, hedged, lost in the maze of words.

"The question hard, sah," he said finally. Then he began to laugh. It was an awkward, high-pitched laughter. He laughed so hard he folded into a crouch, like a man just fallen under the cloud of madness.

A growl formed on Stanton's face. Shoulders bunched, he reached Jacob before the man, consumed by a peculiar laughter, could collect himself to duck. A pummeling ensued.

As the villagers remembered it later, Stanton seemed to fly through the air before landing on Jacob. So ferocious was the rush that the Bible loosened from his grip, flew in the air, somersaulted, and then landed, bang, on a female convert's head. His knuckles, knees, and chest smacked into Jacob's bent body. The interpreter reeled backward and then collapsed onto the floor. Unable to check his own fall, Stanton pitched forward and landed on top of the spare-bodied interpreter. The converts let out a collective gasp and then looked on in hushed shock. Stanton gathered himself up and sat astride the interpreter's splayed legs. Eyes narrowed, he fixed his prone foe as a famished predator might a prey. His chest heaved violently as he breathed in and out of his mouth. Helpless, the interpreter glanced up at his assailant in a morose, stunned stare. There was a hint of blood at the ridge of Jacob's nostril.

A few moments passed, and then Stanton slowly rose.

"Don't make an animal of me, Jacob," he said in an even, almost entreating voice. "Christ enjoins us to forgive our brother seventy times seven times. In the Christian spirit, I forgive you. This time. Now get up and get to your job."

Jacob picked himself up with effort, dazed still by the force and surprise of the attack. As he flipped dirt and dust off his shirt, Stanton asked, "So what was the man's question?" There was impatience in his voice.

Three dribbles of blood dropped in quick succession from Jacob's nose onto his shirt. He stanched the flow with his left cuff. Then he began to speak.

"De man want to know what offense your God Son commit? What he do for his papa to let sinner people kill him? He ask, Which kind of papa be that? Daz what the man want know the answer for."

Filled with rage, Jacob didn't mind risking another attack. He stood with his legs apart, firmly planted, poised to ward off his assailant. "Tell the questioner," Stanton said in a quavering voice, then paused. "What's his name?"

"Okafor," said the interpreter.

"Tell Okafor that God sent his Son to die for our sake. To wash us of our sins. Tell him that God didn't act out of wickedness—God is all good and all loving. Tell him that a good Christian must trust God. Faith is at the center of a Christian's life. As the holy book tells us, faith is the evidence of things not seen."

Stanton then told the story of Thomas and his doubt. At the end, he said, "Tell Okafor not to be a doubting Thomas. For the sake of his soul."

EACH MORNING, EVEN BEFORE *the women had stirred from sleep to go to the banks of River Utonki to fetch water, Stanton was at the river. He swam with less skill than most other people, but his glee matched theirs. He was at home in the river, even though he was less a smooth swimmer than a splasher.*

By the time the women and children arrived to fetch water, he was done swimming. He lay on his back on a wooden ledge, his imposing torso sheathed by a pair of slim white underwear, hands raised to his eyes to shield them from the sun, biting even at that early hour.

It was his contemplative ritual. Lying there, Jacob had told some converts, the white man communed with God. Ideas took root in his mind; he grasped germs of the message he must give to the unsaved souls of Utonki. Some water fetchers stared at his bared body, the folds of his belly that sagged like pouches on either side of him. Children chortled at this massy scoop of flesh. The naughtier women fastened their gaze on the slight rise in his wet underwear, the stump of his penis that was the man's only modest part.

"Such a big man with a baby's stick!" some cheeky woman would say in a low, puzzled tone.

Other women would giggle in conspiracy.

"Indeed, it's like a child's."

"What do you expect? Don't you know the thing shrivels from hunger? The man wandered far away from hearth and wife. His thing has been hungry. A starved penis coils up, ready to die."

"But nobody knows if he has a wife or not."

"You think a grown man like him can be without a wife? Then there must be madness in his eyes."

"Who would marry a man with that sickly stick? Rather than pleasure a woman, it must cause annoyance."

"Yes, what can that one do?"

More giggles.

"Make you pregnant!" one woman would interject, snickering.

"Tufia!" the teased woman would swear. "That thing can never find its way to my thighs."

If Stanton was aware of their ogling and salacious comments, he did not let on.

Each evening, after dismissing the converts, he returned to the river. He stripped himself to his underwear. Then, standing near the shallow banks, he washed himself the same way the villagers did. Bent at the knee, he scooped water with both hands and then threw it on his upper body and over his back. He bathed unhurriedly, as if the water were a balm that soothed the pain of his desultory labors, a palliative for the many frustrations of a man fishing for souls, an antidote for a spurned bearer of light in Darkest Africa. After bathing, he lowered himself in the water and then swam out to the river's deeper parts. For an hour or so, he'd thrash about in the river. Sometimes he'd submerge himself beneath the surface, a twisty ripple indicating his zigzagging path. He often lingered for a long time, then shot up to the surface, exhaling air and water.

Many in Utonki watched Stanton at his awkward maneuvers. Unlike his morning routine, seen only by women and children, men formed the bulk of the spectators in the evenings. Until Stanton's arrival in their midst, the people of Utonki had believed that no person born outside their community could swim the river without drowning. Or without being snatched up and eaten by aguiyi, the crocodile believed to inhabit the river's depths. Once Stanton defied that belief, the men of Utonki said that the white man was a long-lost son of the river. He was, they said, an albino who'd been captured by Abia warriors when Utonki was still young. Now he had returned to life, but he spoke a strange tongue. The story added to Stanton's mystique.

Stanton's feet were always shod in a mammoth pair of sandals that he left unstrapped, so that they dangled about, awkwardly, as he walked at a brisk, hurried pace. He wore white khaki shorts and a brown khaki shirt. By the time he came out to preach each morning, the shirt would be wet, discolored by two huge rings of sweat under both armpits. Then he perspired more as the day wore on and he worked himself into a holy frenzy. Sweat formed on his brow and snaked down to his chin. Sometimes it dripped to the floor, like dew sliding from the deep receptacle of ede leaf. Sometimes, it would start raining as Stanton preached. He stayed under the downpour, unfazed.

But on the seventh day, he shut himself up in the hut the new believers

built for him. All day long, nobody would see him. Once, some curious villagers tiptoed close to the hut. They reported hearing his voice, raised and
fevered, like a madman apostrophizing unseen demons. One day, some men
searched out Jacob and asked why the white man shouted in the solitude of
his hut.

The interpreter seized the opportunity both to enlighten them and to hurl
insults at them.

"Vile heathens," he said. "Blind pagans! Why do you call prayer shouting? Your heads are so full of shit you don't know prayer when you hear it.
If you were not snakeheads, you'd know that the white man was not barking but praying. What you heard was the white man praying to the true
God. And it's your blackened souls he's praying for, too!"

The men were not impressed. Among them was a former convert, a slacker
back to paganism.

"Rump of a man," he said to Jacob. "How dare you insult us, you whom
the white man uses to wipe his anus? If his God is everywhere, then why
does the man need to shout to be heard? Or is his God deaf?"

The other men chuckled, impressed by the slacker's repartee.

On occasion, the people of Utonki poked fun at Jacob. Sometimes, their
barbs targeted the white man himself. Still, they saw Stanton as an extraordinary being, a man who was in some ways like a spirit. Who but a spirit
could have uprooted himself from his land and arrived in Utonki to speak
tremulously about a deity nobody had before seen or heard about? They
marveled at his book, his ability to decipher secrets concealed in contorted
symbols that crawled all over his book.

"Only a strong medicine man would hear things said by leaves," one man
said, shrugging with wonder.

"He has spirit eyes," another said. "Spirits can look into air and see
things in it. They can see portents in smoke. They can gape at sand and
discover the secrets of the gods. They can peer into vapor and, by studying it,
know what's going on at distant markets."

"*True talk,*" said another.

"*False talk!*" bellowed another man. "*He's not a spirit but a wizard. Wizards see as spirits see, but wizards are not spirits. He's a man like you and me, but he's eaten the meal of wizardry.*"

Stanton did not understand their language, but he sensed that there was some verbal skirmish—and guessed that he was at the center of it. He squelched the temptation to ask the interpreter to explain what the ruckus was about. There was something alluring about the cadence of their language, he thought. A time would come, he told himself, when he would converse with ease in Igbo.

Aside from his pastoral calling, Stanton was also a polyglot—fluent in Latin, French, Finnish, Swedish, Spanish, and Italian. There was also Flemish: a language he adored but spoke imperfectly.

Given his dexterous flair, Stanton developed certain quirky theories about languages. One was that a language achieved its height of musicality when deployed in a fight. "The sad paradox of language," he once wrote to a friend who was a fellow linguist, "is that men beat it, twist it, bend it to convey emotions of love. Yet, language displays its innermost archaism and flaunts the fullness of its odd beauty when at war. It's at its sweetest, most natural eloquence when deployed at the pitch of battle. War, I daresay, brings out the best in poetry. Milton's poetry proved it. Words at war embody the passion and pizzazz that love strains, at great cost and often futilely, to approach."

"*A wizard!*" repeated the man. "*That's why he sees what he sees.*"

From their facial countenances, Stanton could divine that a quarrel was brewing.

"*But wizards see only at night,*" a woman said.

Several eyes fixed her, filled with agitation and suspicion.

"*How do you know?*" challenged a woman.

"*Only a witch would know how her kind see,*" sneered a man.

"*Your wives and mothers are witches!*" the woman retorted, defiant.

Stanton, his face aglow, observed the quickening feud.

"Brothers and sisters!" shouted Jacob, borrowing Saint Paul's chastening formula. His intervention dampened the escalating row. Stanton cast an angry glance at the interpreter, as one might a zany idiot, but Jacob remained oblivious of his master's displeasure. "Why give yourselves stomachaches when I'm here? I know the things of the white man. I can explain everything to you."

A few converts gave him doubtful looks, as if they regarded him as an impostor.

"If you know the white man as much as you claim, then tell us how come he can peer into a book and the book talks to him."

"You must give me something before I break the secret," Jacob demanded. "A mask doesn't dance before it's given what it eats."

"If you think yourself to be a mask, you will eat shit!" hissed a burly man, the village carrier of Ijele, a grand, lavishly decorated masquerade. "Did you hear me? Shit is what we feed masks like you!"

"Easy, Nwafo," cautioned an older man. "You're a young man and your blood is too hot. A wise man doesn't walk to a market and ask where he can buy a fight. How has the man wronged you? He said he knows what we want to know, but he won't tell us until we deceive him with a little gift. Is that an offense? If a man asks for something and you don't want to give it, tell him so. If the man said he was looking for shit to eat, then you would be right to send him where he can find enough to fill his belly—and more to take home to his wife. But why send the man to the bush when he didn't ask for shit?" Having scolded Nwafo, the old man turned to the interpreter. "Don't take offense at words spoken by a young man. I'll take care of what your stomach will eat. If you know how the white man hears from the book, please tell us."

The interpreter paused to allow his pent-up anger to seep away. Then he said, "If it were only for that fool, I wouldn't open my mouth." He cast a haughty, condescending look in Nwafo's direction. "What I'm going to tell *you is the truth. The book doesn't talk to the white man. He reads what's written in the book."*

"Don't we have eyes like the white man? So why can't we read the same thing?"

"Because you haven't gone to the white man's school. That's where people learn how to read. If you went to the school, you'd be able to read."

"We're saying the same thing," insisted the man who had called Stanton a wizard. "Wizards go to a place where they are initiated into wizardry. That's what you call school."

"Don't speak what passes your understanding," Jacob chided.

"It doesn't pass my understanding. It's you whose mouth says what it doesn't know."

The interpreter stood silent, askance. There was little profit, he felt, in arguing with village know-nothings. Stanton read the stalemate.

"What's the ruckus about?" he asked Jacob.

"Huh?"

"I mean, what's the matter?"

Jacob explained that the villagers wondered how a book talked to the white man. On that account, they insisted that Stanton was some kind of wizard or spirit. Stanton's lips parted in a suppressed smile.

"Tell that man to come to me," he instructed Jacob, pointing to Nwafo, the young man who'd asked the interpreter to hop off and eat shit. "And him, him, her, him, and her," he added, pointing to more of the vocal participants in the argument. The chosen, their faces apprehensive, drew gingerly close to the Englishman. They arranged themselves, the six of them, on either side of him. Stanton grasped a bunch of pages from the Bible. He held out a random page for their perusal, passing the script from eye to baffled eye. They peered at the page, at its strange inert symbols that told them nothing, symbols that resembled half-formed crawly creatures. How, they wondered, could anybody decipher these symbols? Only a man who communed with spirits could do it.

Stanton flipped through some pages and then stopped. He read, "For God so loved the world that he gave his only Son, that whosoever believeth in Him might not perish but might have eternal life." His finger traced the text, as if the words might peel off the page and evaporate without that act of vigilance. His eyes darted from the page to the converts' astonished eyes. His listeners understood nothing, grasping only that sonorous mystique of an unfamiliar language. "Jacob," said Stanton, "tell them that if they stand fast, if they embrace the living God, they too will soon be able to read the Good Book. Tell them."

EACH DAY, STANTON ASKED those who wished to be baptized and to know the one true God to raise their hands. Those who did were led to Utonki River, huddled behind Stanton's broad, imposing back. The rite of baptism, the interpreter explained to initiates, literally meant "dipping in God's water." It made them new creatures, he proclaimed. (One day, an outraged woman stormed the church. She addressed Jacob: "Ask your white dibia why my husband still can't do what other men do at night—even after he'd been dipped in the water and made a new man." The interpreter was vexed. He would ask the white man no such question, he said. Then, in a caustic tongue, he asked the woman to go home and look between her thighs. "The witchcraft you put there, that's what killed your husband's manhood!")

Each day, a few men and women joined the Christians. They hungered to experience what it meant to be born anew. The rank of converts swelled daily.

Still, each night, in the secrecy of his hut near the river, Stanton raved, his anger aimed mostly at himself. He sat at his scruffy desk and made agonized entries in his diaries, his hut dully lit with a paraffin lamp. Outside, the darkness engorged everything. The river rumbled, its sound a preternatural beast's gag after swallowing a huge prey. Goats bleated. Cocks crowed, as if startled awake by terrible dreams. Dogs growled and

barked. Crickets buzzed their monotonous trill. The two sentries outside his
hut snored like overfed gorillas—as if they were paid to sleep.

Stanton felt himself tainted by the African night, smudged with Africa's
darkness. His mind, alert and rational in the day, strayed at night into
superstition. He had wide-eyed dreams that teemed with chimeras, goblins,
ghosts, and orgiastic spectacles. Africa afflicted him with insomnia. He'd
sit for hours gaping at the lamp's feeble, flickering tongue of fire. He'd chomp
on his nails, paring them until there was only raw flesh, his mind held captive by half-formed, faraway thoughts. Sometimes his gaze wandered from
one part of the hut to another. Then he'd fix it again on the lamp. Compelled
by the breeze, its light swayed now this way, now that. Shadows filled the
hut. Some had thin, oblong shapes, like giant fingers. Other shapes were
denser. He watched the shadows twist in the wavering light, their wavy
forms giving an illusion of movement. Stanton followed their contortions,
riveted. Sometimes he'd mistake or imagine their spry, gossamery shadows as
living things, restless, peripatetic, and sinister. It was as if some malevolent
presences shared his hut. Other times, he felt that they owned the hut, with
him a mere intruder. His heart fluttered, pounded.

After a spell of gazing, Stanton would pick up his quill. He would dip
it in ink and begin to scribble. He'd lose himself in long spells of writing, an
exercise in self-flagellation and atonement. He confided his frustrations to
his diary, transferred his unwept tears to it. He detailed his fears, his faith,
the hopes that lifted spirits, and the doubts that weakened his will. He
penned sketches of some of his converts and also of some of those he'd failed to
draw into Christ's fold. He wrote copious instructions for those who would
succeed him in the vineyard of evangelism. He quivered over his health,
which he felt failing, slipping. Gripped by foreboding, he was racked by a
sense of death lurking.

Most of all, he grieved over his failures as a missionary. Why hadn't
all of Utonki abandoned its false god and come into God's fold? Why were
the chief priest and his acolytes still holding out, embracers of darkness?

Stanton assumed all the guilt. He saw himself as an inept fisher of men. Reluctant to measure himself in the currency of success, he fixated on all the missed opportunities, untaken roads, and forsaken paths. It didn't matter that his number of converts grew by the day.

The more converts he won, the more viciously doubt stabbed his heart. He was convinced that he'd not done enough for the Lord. When he pondered his life and mission, he glimpsed little glory. In his mind, everything about him hurtled toward darkness and oblivion. When he imagined his future, the dominant image was the end of all light.

Each night, he'd write until his hands became numb. Then he'd collapse on his knees in petrified prayer. "Lord, lift this yoke of sickness from your humble servant," he'd implore. If only God would spare him, he'd try harder to save all the souls in Utonki.

Stanton sometimes wondered if he had set unreasonable standards for himself.

Upon arrival in Utonki, he had made a solemn pledge to God and Queen. That promise was that, as part of his personal sacrifice in the effort to bring souls to Christ, he would brave the perils and pestilences of Africa, endure the mercilessness of mosquitoes, brook the sun's tropical blast, and subsist on the native's spicy and strange menu that gave him recurrent bouts of diarrhea. He would mortify his flesh in any way that was asked of him, and he would persist until Ngene was vanquished, until the true God triumphed. To God and Queen he vowed that, until the last pagan turned away from the blighted path and trod the Way of Light, he would not count his mission fulfilled.

Eight months later, Stanton had a lot to show for his fervor. Many natives had abandoned their deity and embraced the Way. Yet, in the secrecy of his heart, Stanton chafed. He could never forgive himself for falling short of banishing Ngene. His denunciation of Ngene as a powerless, inert idol had struck a chord with many villagers, but he'd fallen short of dethroning the deity. Daily, on his way to the makeshift structure that served as a church, he crossed paths with many villagers headed for the deity's shrine. How could he be happy? How avoid the pain that tore at his insides, the pangs that wrenched his soul and mangled his spirits?

Two months after his arrival in Utonki, his interpreter approached him wearing a toothy, satisfied smile. "What's the matter?" Stanton asked, his face stern. He'd learned to keep Jacob—and other Africans for that matter—at arm's length. To their sly smiles, he'd learned to return a disinterested expression.

"Our God magic is working," Jacob said excitedly, in his faltering English.

"What do you mean by that, Jacob?" Stanton asked.

"Many pagans falling, sah. Our Jesus doing excellent magic, sah."

The statement filled Stanton with rage. He couldn't decide what riled him more. Was it Jacob's proprietary claim to a God he had yet to understand? He had a problem with a bloody African, who beneath the skin was probably as benighted as any other pagan, laying a claim to the same God. And in a cavalier, offhand sort of way, too! Or was the offense in Jacob's devaluation of God as a weaver of magic spells? The implication that the converts had fallen under some spell cast by Jesus galled him. He knew that Jacob was a victim of his grave deficiencies in English. Even so, Stanton believed that the devil could sneak in and speak in different guises.

Unleashing two quick slaps on Jacob's face, Stanton barked, "Never, ever call my God a magician! And never, ever mention the name Jesus in vain! Vile, heathen pig!" The smile drained away from Jacob's face.

Later that day, as he sat down to reflect on the incident, Stanton felt that he'd probably overreacted. He even entertained the idea of apologizing to his interpreter, but the temptation passed. What was the injustice of slapping a man unjustly compared with the heresy of reducing God to a magician? And what if Lucifer himself had planted the heretical speech in Jacob's tongue? It was better, he decided, to err on the side of injustice to man.

Besides, Stanton was in no mood to encourage premature celebration.

Arduous labor lay ahead; there were still too many people to evangelize, and too many of the converts seemed in danger still of sliding back into darkness. He was not a man to make peace with failure. Utter failure.

What if his Creator chose, in the midst of his ineptitude, to call him home? With such an unfulfilled task on his plate, he dreaded the prospect of standing before God's mighty, judgment throne. Why, God would cast him into the dungeon of eternal damnation.

So each evening he bruised his knees in prayer. He beseeched God to show him how to defeat Satan, his works and his idol. He was disconsolate, unable to sleep. In the day, he became a sulking man, prone to outbursts of fury. He took to slapping Jacob more and more. The converts were bewildered. In one breath, their missionary talked to them about peace and love and Christian charity. Then in another he flew into a rage, frothing at the sides of his mouth, slapping thunder into Jacob's eyes.

In the ninth month of his career as a soul saver in Utonki, Stanton's inner demons finally crept out to the surface. The converts saw that he'd been left a shell of a man. Pimples rigged his face and formed a mass of ripe pustules. His eyes became puffy, ringed with dark lines. There was a dull discoloration to his skin, as if his body had been emptied of blood.

"What sickness has wrestled the white man to the ground?" a convert asked Jacob one evening. Stanton had sent a message that he couldn't make it to lead evening prayers.

The interpreter shrugged. He was no encourager when it came to exchanging confidences with converts. He often feigned possession of some succulent bit of information but made it clear he was in no haste to share it with scum like them. He would boast that anybody who spoke the white man's tongue knew what the white man knew. His design was that the converts would view him as some sort of honorary white man, that they would approach him with the same deference and awe they showed for Stanton. Jacob was confident that he would have carried it off, and with ease, too, if Stanton did not so carelessly berate him and frequently slap him.

"*The sickness that would leave a man in such poor shape has come to kill him,*" *another convert chimed in.*

Jacob smirked, then turned away. The expression on his face suggested that he knew some intimate details about Stanton's health he was not about to divulge.

The next day, Stanton showed up for morning devotions and baptisms. It was as if he'd aged in the hours since the converts last saw him. One among them espied one of the white man's toenails, hideously swollen. The convert advised that the agnail should be treated with the sap of a certain herb mixed with pepper and honey. When Jacob translated the therapy, Stanton smiled sadly.

"*Tell him I'm touched, but that God will take care of his own,*" *he said coolly.*

"*The white man said I should warn you and pigs like you,*" *Jacob said in Igbo.* "*He said you must keep your stinking foolishness to yourself.*"

A murmur of disapprobation swept through the throng.

By the next day, the toe had bloated like a sun-cooked pear. Its size forced Stanton to discard his sandals. He trudged on in an unusually labored gait. The converts were used to him flouncing, walking in short, brisk steps. Now, his heels touched the earth tentatively, lightly. He shambled like a man beset by acute arthritis, each step accompanied by a grimace. One of the converts made him a shabby walking stick. To their surprise, he accepted it. As he lumbered about, he used the stick to balance his weight. It steadied him somewhat but also made his motion awkward. He was no longer able to lunge at Jacob, but the stick came in handy when he wanted to beat the interpreter.

His face became sadder and more swollen. He spat a lot, like a pregnant woman. His skin became a flaxen, wilted flab, sallow and pale. His early morning swims ceased. Tangled knots appeared in his beard and scurf covered his hair.

The physical devastation was not the worst of it. He seemed distracted;

often he gazed vacantly ahead, his sight set at nothing. When he spoke, his voice had the faintness of a man in terribly low spirits. Often, he lisped inaudibly. As he couldn't hear his words, the interpreter began to take liberties. He made up answers to converts' questions. He heaped abuse on converts, ascribing his venom to Stanton.

Stanton began to skip meals, and his eyes sunk deeper into their sockets. When he looked at people, he gave the impression of moping in a distant, unseeing way, as if his eyes could find no grip. When the converts asked why he didn't eat, he drew apart his cheeks, revealing stained teeth.

Speculations swarmed among the converts. Was Ngene behind the man's malaise? Or had he offended the spirits that taught him to hear the speech of wormy symbols in a book? Had he defied a summons back to the land whence he came?

Some converts who knew how to foretell things said that Stanton's shadow had become leaner, paler on the ground. "It means the silencer of dogs is on his heels," one of them said lugubriously. "The silencer of dogs" was their polite expression for "death."

One evening, Stanton finished baptizing five new converts. The cloud of faithlessness had lifted, and his spirits seemed buoyed. Two or three dry days, and then the Holy Spirit had touched three women and two men. They'd raised their hands and asked to be lifted from the yoke of darkness and admitted into the splendor of light. It was a day the Lord had made.

As Stanton turned to retire to his hut, it began to rain. The rain poured down in huge, slanting sheets. Within seconds, he was drenched. The sheets pelted his brow with a heaviness he found altogether new. It was as if the knots of rain were beads flung at his head. He was filled with the oppressive sense that something was terribly wrong.

He walked on. The rain gathered strength. Pools formed everywhere. Small sluices disappeared into larger, speeding pools. Walking in the downpour, he had the impression that he was engaged in futile animation, as if each step he took landed on the same spot. Suddenly, his path darkened. Whether he was nearing his hut, or getting farther away from it, he could not tell.

Then his mind became a whorl, awhirl with a parade of images, faces intimate and shadowy. His parents were the first to amble across the flickering screen in his mind, ghostly in their bone-weary gait. Then his wife and their two boys, their eyes set downward. He desperately wanted to shout out to them, to beckon them to him, but some invisible force gripped his throat in a vice. As he opened his mouth and closed it, wordless, he became aware of murmurs intruding. His family dissolved into oblivion. Next, images from his seminary days flicked past. He saw many of his teachers and fellow seminarians turned out in clerical habits. Their faces radiated holy purpose, something he found himself increasingly unable to summon. Then a succession of fuzzy figures, their faces covered with filmy matter. Finally, a wooden statue, hands spread out as if to embrace him, mouth shaped into an O, strode past, headed in the direction of the river.

"Satan!" Stanton cursed. "Accursed!"

The murmurs became louder. Their sorrowful notes wafted, like smoke, into his consciousness. The rain ceased. He awoke from his spell.

He felt drained. He half expected to see the images still. But Ngene was gone, along with the other images. All around him, he saw eyes. They stabbed him, those eyes. They belonged to his converts, including the five he had just baptized. They stood staring at him. He detected consternation, shame, confusion, and pity in their gazes. His throat tightened. A hint of tears rose in his eyelids. It was indistinguishable from the rainwater that still trickled down his body. He smothered the tears with the back of his hand. He wished he could as easily swipe away the memories of his shame.

Stanton felt an urge to swing the walking stick straight at his own skull. If he could shatter his skull in two, perhaps then God would see his P-A-I-N. The converts, especially the five brand-new ones, would see the tragic majesty of faith. They would have the uncommon luck of starting off their Christian journeys with a martyr as their guardian. They would have stories to tell, witness to bear about a man of God and the blood he shed and the death he died for God. His self-immolation in order to give God all he had. Smash this skull, he commanded his hand. His hand defied his heart. He limped away to his hut.

That night, Stanton sat at his desk and wrote with fury. His body ached. A terrible fever boiled inside him. His stomach felt queasy, as if awaiting the slightest provocation to convulse and heave. But vomiting would be a futility. His belly was filled with air. A persistent pain droned in its walls. It would be horrible, he thought, to vomit one's innards.

He wrote in a delirious state. Air stood stagnant in his hut. The hut was dizzy with effluvia. The stink of his armpit lay thick as sin. The lamplight lent a dull, ghoulish glow to the hut. It was difficult to see, but he flung his sorrows onto the diary. Sweat poured from his brows, fell freely, and smudged his entries. He wrote about his terrifying visions, about his betrayal of God and Queen, about his wife and two sons training their eyes on the ground, about the terror of Ngene mocking him, about his hopes unraveled. His heart had a jumble of thoughts, and he wrote whatever it dictated to him. He scribbled until his hands began to ache. His last words were a desperate plea: "Lord, bid me incinerate the heathen god! Command and it shall be done! Let your faithful prove themselves worthy soldiers."

He put the quill aside and lay in his bamboo bed. Sweaty and sleepless, he soaked up the voices of night. Crickets dinned at his ears. Toads croaked their dirges. The equatorial forest swayed and swooned in time to the wind. Mosquitoes swarmed about him. They bit without mercy. Distraught and terrified, he didn't bother to swat them away.

Then he began to have another wide-eyed dream. A white-shrouded figure dominated the dream. It materialized out of the fabric of darkness, a towering giant. Stanton batted his eyes. He swiped across his eyes with the back of his hand. The figure did not disappear. It stood immobile. It was a perverse patch of whiteness in a massive black quilt. He gazed at the *apparition, larger than life. He saw that its mouth was agape, the portrait of anguish. Or hunger. The roundness of it was filled with darkness. It imparted a grotesque quality to the apparition's face, as if the mouth opened up to a bottomless pit.*

Stanton wanted to shout at the pasty apparition. Perhaps, he could cast away the vile anomalous presence with holy words. He tried but seemed to contend with a force that was indifferent to his power. He cast his gaze sharply to the right. The pagan apparition refused to be shirked off. As if it had anticipated Stanton, the figure re-formed right in front of his eyes. He turned left. His nemesis stood there, too. He set his eyes on the floor; the apparition stared up at him. He shut his eyes, and the incubus glowed in the darkness beneath the pupils. Whatever Stanton did, it was there to haunt him.

Sweat poured from his pores. It was partly the doing of hot, humid weather but partly the result of a night rife with terrifying presences. His head throbbed with a searing pain. His body wafted a stench. It was, he believed, the contagious stink of Africa. Prior to blundering into this accursed continent, he'd never known himself to stink this way. He was loath to mention the name of this strange, intimate smell; he was too afraid to call fear by its name.

He saw his mission imperiled. He tossed and turned, wasted by despair. He heard the bark of some wild animal, a series of long, ravenous blasts punctuated by bloodcurdling growls. Then he heard the persistent nervous mooing of cows. His heart beat riotously, as if he were present at the carnage.

His mind fastened on the ferocious barking and the dread-drenched mooing. He pictured the scene. For all he knew, it could be happening some distance away—a good two or three miles away, perhaps. Yet, the night always created the illusion of nearness, as if the encounter between prey and predator were being staged just outside the threshold of his hut.

Africa at night held great charms and unpredictable terrors. Like the cows that mooed their agony, faced with who knew what foe. Or the night's ceaseless commotions that filled his ears. The tears that flooded his eyes each time he beheld the moon's terrible luminousness. The stars, iridescent against the sky's pitch-dark backcloth, that made him swoon. Add to these images a poisonous, slithering snake rustling in and out of a barn to claim eggs or a clucking chicken for a prize, or the upturned tail of a scorpion hidden among the rocks, ready to deliver a vicious sting. Or his particular nightly pestilence, the armada of mosquitoes that sang awfully in his ears and bit with unforgiving fierceness.

A fog seemed to dissipate; Stanton came to understand that a Christian was nothing if he was estranged from the cross. He fell to his knees, thankful that his mind was awakening to clear visions. If he must salvage things and save his imperiled soul, he had to come up with a heroic gesture.

There was no doubt in Stanton's mind what action God was calling him to take. It was to physically annihilate Ngene. That was what God sent him to Utonki to do. That he hadn't accomplished that task so far was the reason sleep had been emptied from his eyes. The reason his nights were besieged. He'd challenge the converts to an ultimate test of faith. He'd order them to prove the mettle of their faith by vanquishing Ngene. He'd goad them to seize the deity and set it on fire. But what if the converts demurred? Or, worse, renounced their faith?

Stanton was in this cauldron of thoughts when the cocks crowed the dawn. Their notes startled him. He pitched himself from the bed and wiped his eyes with palms slick with wetness. His eyes twitched, weary. The hut's dimness disoriented him. He surveyed the room, eager to master the hut. Despite the upheaval of the night, he relished the calmness that came from the simple magic of finding everything in its place.

His gaze fell, lethargically, on the paraffin lamp on the table. Its light long extinguished, the lamp was like a forlorn contraption that had served its purpose and fallen into disuse. It evoked no emotion in him, only indifference. In the wake of the night's torment, he found it hard to connect the lamp to his scribbles, the many secrets and yearnings he had confided in his diary.

Next to the lamp was his notebook, its spine mangled and fragile. It was open to the last sheet of his writing, a page filled halfway with his squiggly, unsteady longhand. Stanton picked up the diary. He held it close to his face, but inclined at an awkward angle, exposing it toward the mercenary and feeble shafts of light that seeped into the hut. His brows furrowed, he tried for a few moments to discern the blotchy writing in the rogue light. Struck by the futility of his effort, his mood darkened. With the nonchalance of a child disowning a worthless toy, he opened his hand and let the diary loosen from his grip. It spiraled and hit the table with a thump, then slipped to the dirt floor.

He was groggy from the lack of sleep but relieved that another day had dawned. He had not swum for several days, but decided he must swim that day. The jaunt to the river sapped his energy. He'd seen the villagers bathe naked, even though men and women never bathed together. For no reason he could articulate, he decided to swim naked. He removed his underwear and tossed it on the grass. He stood on the shallow banks, the water knee-deep. He was flabbier by far than any man in the village. Two sideward sags accentuated his paunch, leaving the impression of a three-sided pot.

He bent down, scooped water in cupped hands, and threw it over his shoulder. The sands, soft as sludge, yielded under the gentle pressure of his feet. He dug his heels in, entranced by the sensation of himself slowly sinking into the river's silty softness. Bathing, he muttered to himself in an unintelligible tongue.

He was still throwing water on his body and over his shoulder when some women and children arrived to fetch water. They were astounded to find him naked. They were shocked to find his penis even smaller than they had imagined. The children directed sly glances at him until the women hushed them away. With the children gone, the women began to make heckling sounds. They sneered and leered. They groaned and moaned. They grunted and gasped in mock-amorous hunger. Stanton appeared oblivious. At any rate, he ignored them.

"*A child he is where a man should be a man!*"

"*I said it before: a stick that small irritates a woman's thighs!*"

"*No wonder,*" *another exclaimed knowingly,* "*his wife drove him from the house!*"

"*Who would blame her?*"

The women talked excitedly, but their eyes remained trained on Stanton. Their looks ate him with fascination and disgust, the fascination and disgust with which a hawk stalks a sumptuous prey before swooping. A look of curiosity intermixed with pity. As they watched, he began to wade deeper. He stopped when the water rose to his waist. He crouched until the river's undulating tug lapped gently around his shoulders. He shut his eyes, readied, and plunged.

The women raised their voices in excitement, like mothers calling out to their sons at the fall of dusk. They saw the arch of his back before it disappeared in the muddy depths. They kept vigil, waiting for that moment when he would come up for air.

IKE STIRRED AWAKE TO the shuffle of feet outside his door. He heard a few timid taps, and then the door opened. His mother, a silhouette, filled the doorframe, obscuring the wicker lamp that dangled from Alice's hand.

"Ike. Is my son awake?" she whispered. Behind her, Alice swayed the lamp from side to side, and his mother's long shadow moved in the darkness.

He stretched, letting off sleepy grunts.

"Ike, are you awake?"

She rushed toward him, her shadow lengthening and contracting. They met in an embrace. He clasped her tightly, then loosened his grip, startled by how frail she felt to the touch. In the darkness he felt a twinge of gratitude that he could neither see her visage nor be seen by her. Yet, his sight unavailing, his other senses were acute. He smelled her sweat, her frowzy hair. He *saw* her through the unfaltering language of the hands. She was bonier, skinnier, feebler, than he could have ever imagined. Her flesh seemed sheared.

"Mama, how are you?" he asked.

"The way you left me," she said in a voice drained of emotion.

He felt the wash of her against his shoulder, the pound of her heart against his body. "Is your health fine?"

She sighed. "Are you talking about health? Your mother has only one breath left to her and you're talking about health." Each jut of her bones stood out, like an accusation. It had been four years since he had sent her any money. In his mind, he tried to farm the blame to Queen Bee. But he couldn't convince himself that his ex-wife was altogether to blame.

For all the harm Queen Bee had done, gambling, undeniably, had done more. It was partly because of his mother that he'd chanced gambling. Through his sister, she had sent one of those occasional heartrending letters, filled with entreaties and recriminations, chiding him for abandoning his own mother. He remembered the question that inflicted the deepest cut: *Do you have another mother I don't know about, a different mother you love and care for?*

He'd had some cash on hand then, a little more than three thousand dollars. But there were bills waiting to be paid. And Queen Bee had demanded a thousand dollars to shop for clothes.

Caught in a bind, Ike had dropped his guard of cautiousness. He had set off on his first trip to Atlantic City. He'd meant merely to dabble. He had been confident of hitting it big quickly, using the winning to provide for his mother. That first outing had proved a fiasco. His loss had been so brisk and big that, for the first time, he had drawn two thousand dollars on a credit card to pay some bills and gratify Queen Bee's shopping mania.

He was not deterred by that inaugural misstep. Instead, the

appalling adventure had lent him a strange form of determination. Not even the ensuing streak of losses could extinguish the spark of hope that spurred him. As he sneaked back to the casinos again and again and the losses mounted, the superior force of desire mastered each moment of hesitancy. He was sustained by the sheer force of hope; he was led, helpless, into gambling's firm, merciless grip.

"Welcome home," his mother said, unsettling his thoughts. "When your sister told me you were finally coming, I wondered if I would be alive to see you."

"Mama, you will be alive for a long time," he said.

"You forgot me, Ike." Her voice quavered. He squeezed her a little tighter, almost imperceptibly. "You forgot your mother. If anybody had told me the one son of my womb would ever toss me aside like a rag, I would have said it was a lie. But you did."

"Mama, please don't speak like that. I never forgot you."

"Words, words, words, that's all I hear from you. That's all I've heard for years now. Does a hungry woman live on words? When at night the stomach rumbles with hunger, do words calm it? You have left me a thing to be laughed at. Yes, Ike. I've tried to pretend to have no ear, but the ear hears things. People laugh at me. *Her son is in America*, they say, *yet she's left to chew sand for food.*" Her body shook, her voice hardly more audible than a whisper.

Ike felt the sharp slice of her words and clenched his jaws. He wanted to console her, to make pledges of redemption, but each word that scratched the inside of his throat died there.

He unclasped her. She retreated from his embrace and silently, blindly, regarded him. Alice had withdrawn with the lamp. A patch of darkness stood between them. A mosquito sang close to his ear, but he dared not slap the air. He could hear her quiet sobs, the faint chatter of teeth. What look was etched on her face, masked by darkness? A scowl? He felt scoured by her unseen, grief-stricken eyes.

It was better when they were clasped in an embrace, no dark gulf between them. In the darkness, Ike slowly clenched and unclenched his fist.

"But for God, I would have been long dead," she moaned. "Only God knows why I've been left here, to be neglected by my own son. You've let my enemies laugh at me, Ike. You should have married a good Christian wife, Ike. She would not have let me suffer. A Christian woman would have set your eyes in the direction of home. She would have reminded you of me, even if you had wanted to forget."

Ike's mind raced to the cash Usman Wai had given him, crisp notes in fifty-dollar denominations. He felt tempted to fumble in his wallet for that roll of cash and hand her six notes. Give her the cash there and then and silence this storm of sorrowful words. He restrained the urge, not because he was struck by the silliness of the gesture, but out of fear that she might disdain the gift, open her palm, and let the spurned cash flutter to the floor.

"Nobody will laugh at you," he said. "Not anymore, Mama."

She hacked out a cough; her body convulsed in the darkness. "Ikechukwu, are you asking me to cook and eat your words?"

"I'll leave you money before I travel."

His original plan was to keep all of Wai's cash. Just in case things came up. He'd need some of it, for sure, to bribe his way past the customs post on the day of departure. The statue of Ngene packed in his suitcase, he would have to tread gingerly, at once meek and quick witted. He must know the right moment to sneak a roll of cash, a persuasive amount of it, into some customs officer's hand.

In the dark, he groped for his mother's arm. She trembled in his grip.

"Mama, nobody will laugh at you anymore," Ike said, feeling an awful tightness in his chest.

She gasped and broke into a soft wail, as if his words wounded. "My son, do words fill an empty stomach? Do promises put a plate of food on my table?"

"Mama, I'm *not* making promises. I'm telling you what I'll do. I've said I'll leave you some money before I go."

"And once the money is finished, then what? I'll be back to eating sand?"

"I'll take care of you. Once I get back to America, I'll look after you."

"You spoke the same words before, Ikechukwu. Remember, in a letter after your father died? You wrote words with your hand, but your mind wiped me away."

"Things were hard for me for some time—"

"Do you tell me things were hard for you? Is there any language to describe what I've been through? Days and days in which the stomach saw no food; the mouth found no words to tell its woes. Are you telling me of hard times? If I had words, I would tell you stories that would make the wind weep. I've died many times, only the grave shunned the bag of bones I've become."

A stealth tear tickled Ike's right eye, then slipped down his face. In the silence of his heart, he recited, *Hail Mary, full of grace,* but got distracted and lost his way. He settled for the grace of the darkness that stood between them.

The silence swelled grotesquely, as terrifying as the words.

"How's Nne?" he asked, scrambling to steer the discussion to safer ground. He couldn't believe his grandmother was still alive. The last time he saw her, she was wiry and shrunken, her skin wrinkled like corn tassel, her eyes all but conquered by darkness. Yet she'd been steely, her love of talk undimmed, her spirits irrepressible. She still trudged to the village stream, her pot of water balanced on a leafy wedge placed on her head. Nne lived nearby, in a hut. "I wanted to wait and see you before going over to Nne's."

Even before his mother spoke, Ike felt something fiery pass in the darkness. "Did you hear she sent for you?" his mother asked.

"She did?" Ike said in surprise. "How did she find out I came home?"

His mother clucked her tongue. "You don't know she's a witch?" She paused, as if allowing him room to voice his mind. He stayed silent, too astonished to raise a protest. Her words swirled in the air, hard to absorb.

When he did not fill the silence, she continued. "Yes, I'm talking about your grandmother. You're not to see her."

"Mama, I don't like these words you speak."

"Still I must speak them. You're not to set foot in her hut. And you're not to see that *one* who sits and drinks all day."

That one. *That one?* "Who's that one?"

"The servant of Lucifer."

"Somebody I know?"

"The one who serves a deity."

"My uncle? Osuakwu?"

"Yes."

"I'm not to see Papa's brother?"

"He's Satan's biggest agent in these parts."

Ike shook his head in disbelief. He was certain that his father, were he alive, would have been outraged by the words that tumbled from his wife's mouth. His father and Osuakwu had always been close. Years ago, when Ike was still in secondary school, he was spiritually torn. He was a devoted mass server but also felt drawn to the shrine of Ngene, a space dominated by his uncle. Daily, he frequented the shrine, keen to observe his uncle at work and to soak up the atmosphere: the divination rituals, the easy banter traded by men gifted with words, the aroma of roasted meats, beer, and spirits. One day, somebody told the catechist that

Ike hovered around the shrine. The catechist in turn reported the matter to the parish priest, who summoned Ike and his parents to a meeting.

The priest began to chastise Ike for eating, drinking, and consorting with devil worshippers, when his father interjected.

"My son goes to the shrine, not to eat and drink with idolaters. He goes to see his uncle, my older brother. My son has my permission to visit his uncle as many times as he wishes."

That had ended the matter.

Ike swallowed hard. "Mama," he said, then fell silent, grasping for words that slunk away. Finally, he said, "You're talking about Papa's mother and Papa's only brother."

Her tone was unyielding. "They're of darkness. Light and darkness don't mix."

People of darkness. Darkness. Said in the dark, the words swirled, echoed, in the air. "I don't want to hear this. I don't want to hear you say that Nne and Osuakwu will harm me."

She sighed. "You talk like the child that you are."

"I'm no child."

"You talk because I've prayed and fasted to keep you alive. But for my prayers, where do you think you would be now?"

He didn't answer.

"Yes, where?" she pursued, sensing victory. "Dead. Yes, you would have been finished. Dead. That was their plan. My fasting and prayers alone thwarted them." She paused. He waited, too incensed to utter a word. "Yes, I fasted and prayed daily," she continued. "Otherwise you wouldn't be here to doubt my words."

"Mama," he said, then, like a slow, small rebuke.

"You use your mouth to call them Grandmother and Uncle. Yet they both had a hand in your father's death."

A sharp ache shot through his head. Her cavalcade of accusing words had turned the air leaden and blue-tinted, toxic. He stepped back and sat on the edge of the bed, which squeaked.

"Ike," she said, "I carried you nine months in my womb. I can never deceive you."

"But you're saying things that don't make sense."

"Are you calling me a madwoman?"

"I never mentioned madness, Mama. But you're saying strange things."

"Strange only because you see with human eyes."

"And you, Mama, do you now see with spirit eyes?"

Silence. For a moment, mother and son glared at the darkness that separated them. Then he said, "If anybody told you Nne killed my father, her own son, you should have told that person to go and eat shit. Same with Osuakwu. What did Nne and Osuakwu stand to gain from Papa's death?"

"You don't understand occult ways. Is Osuakwu not older than your father?"

"Yes."

"Then ask yourself a simple question: how come your father died eleven years ago while Osuakwu and Nne are still alive?"

"Mama, you know that death doesn't come according to age. You know that Papa was sick, that he suffered for many years from diabetes. You know that."

"How did he get the sickness, eh? Where did his diabetes come from? You who claim to be wiser than your own mother, answer me: who put the disease in your father?"

"Papa's mother and brother concocted diabetes and used some remote control to put the sickness in him. Isn't that what you want to believe?"

"It's what I know. A disease can be caused by spiritual means, don't you know? Don't you know that evil people can put yokes of sickness on others?"

His crown itched. Did his father's death deal such a savage blow to his mother's psyche, making her susceptible to a trickster garbed in the visor of a religious seer? Or was the blame his? Perhaps she had slipped into a state of utter abandonment known only by true orphans. Her mind, adrift, battered, and distrustful of old truths, had latched on to this poisonous notion.

He couldn't deal with this confoundedness mixed with guilt. Try as he might, there was no easy way out.

"This is—" he began in a sharp, exasperated tone. He quickly collected himself, determined to draw away from fierce words. Eyes trained on the dark patch between them, he envisioned her in a combative pose, arms folded across her breast. Suddenly, he felt an old tenderness toward her. The feeling was borne of memories of those long-ago days when she was the center of his world, the person who suckled him, bathed him, the one who stooped to dress the many bruises, cuts, and scrapes he brought home from playgrounds, the one who, on fear-filled nights, sang lullabies that gave him the gift of sleep and dreams. He groped about in the chaotic groove where words lived, until his tongue fastened on tamer language. "Mama, I want you to remember one person always. And that is Papa. Remember how sad the words you speak now would have made him. Papa would have been wounded to hear you accuse his mother and brother of playing a part in his death. He loved them, and he knew that they loved him in return. You know that Papa didn't believe in all this superstition."

"It's spiritual vision; it's not superstition. If your father had been covered with the blood of Jesus, his enemies wouldn't have been able to get to him. He would be alive today."

"Please!" he shouted, slapping his hands, tenderness slipping from his grip. "People die when they die. A friend of mine, my age, just died in the US of cancer. Both his parents and grandparents are still alive. Next thing, you'll tell me that his cancer came from diabolical means."

She let out a spurt of laughter, as if amazed by his innocence.

"You know what?" he pursued, his patience wearing thin. "All this talk of witches and wizards upsets me. Where is it coming from? Who's been telling you that Nne and Osuakwu killed Papa?"

She breathed with relief. "That's the first thing you should have asked. Instead, you started screaming as if I now visit the dirty shrines of a *dibia*. I'm born again and will never set foot in a *dibia*'s homestead. Everything I've told you came straight from a man of God, Pastor Uka. It's God who revealed everything to him."

He sprang up from the bed. "A man of God indeed! He's more like a man of fraud. Mama, this is—I'm sorry—nonsense."

In the darkness he heard her gasp. "They have got you!" she cried. "God revealed to Pastor that they were plotting to get you."

"Your pastor must be deluded."

"Son, don't argue with God!"

"So your pastor is now God?"

"He's a man of God. When you see him you'll know. Ike, my son, he's anointed, a real man of God."

"An anointed liar, that's who he is. A shameless exploiter of people."

She exhaled sharply and then followed up with a sigh. "You'll see him tomorrow. Then everything will be clear to you."

"I'm not planning to see him. I can't stand con men."

"Ike, ask God for forgiveness. Pray that God's wrath may not be unleashed on you. You call Pastor a liar? You insult a man of God. How many times did I go to the pastor crying about you— and he prayed. He prayed and fasted for your safety. He prayed and fasted for your prosperity. When I dreamed about you and went to him with grief in my heart, he prayed and fasted for your deliverance from the yoke. This man you insult, my son, he has prophetic gifts." She paused. Her words floated in the silence, permeated the air, and filled the darkness. She lowered her voice to a conspiratorial pitch. "Do you know that they're planning to make you the next chief priest of Ngene?"

His heart skipped a beat, and he sat back down. "*They?* Who exactly is planning?"

"Pastor Uka will explain everything."

"I've said I'm not seeing him."

"You're not worried that they're plotting to make you chief priest of Ngene? Tell me, is that what you want to do with your life? You're not worried that when people gather every day at the shrine, your name is mentioned as the next carrier of a false god? You don't mind losing your salvation?"

"Mama, there's no morsel of truth in all this nonsense. Nobody can talk about the next chief priest. You seem to forget that Osuakwu hasn't died. And that there's no vacancy for chief priest."

"You call me Mama, Mama, but you throw away my words, Ike. Do you forget that Osuakwu's time is running short, that he doesn't have long to live?"

"Is that also direct from God? Has God revealed to you—or the pastor—that Osuakwu is about to drop dead? That my uncle is staring into his grave?" In the darkness, he shook his head sorrowfully.

She began to say something, but her voice got choked up. She coughed to clear her throat.

"Are you okay?" he asked.

"They're trying to choke me, but Satan is a liar."

"Mama, stop worrying about me. Even if Osuakwu died tonight, there are many people who're hungry for his job. Nwoye the

Hunchback would like to become chief priest. Or has God told you that Nwoye's death is also pretty close?"

"Don't mention that name in this house! He's the devil's son."

Ike sat up, provoking the bed to a squeaky whine. "I'm going out," he said.

"Out? Into this dark night?"

"Yes."

"Out to where?"

"To see Nne."

"I told you—" she began.

"I know what you told me," he interrupted. "I heard all, but no pastor will stop me from seeing my grandmother. If she's a witch, let her cast her spell over me."

She swallowed hard. "Ike," she called.

"If she kills her own, I want her to kill me tonight."

"Ike, has madness come over you? I said you're not to see that shriveled witch."

He pushed past her. She stood still, exuding fear. He groped his way to the door, his steps guided by the flickering light of the wicker lamp Alice had left on in the living room.

"Ike, you have been drinking," she said, just as he reached the door. "It smells all over this room. Surrender your life to Christ. Submit to the Almighty and be covered by the blood of salvation. Don't let the devil lead you astray."

A loathing of the pastor he hadn't seen, but somehow pictured, welled up inside him. "I'm going to see Nne," he said stubbornly.

"You have not eaten."

When he didn't respond, she gave a resigned gasp.

DARKNESS DOMINATED A STARLESS sky. The generator in the house next door had fallen silent, leaving the house in pitch darkness. He felt wrapped by this endless dark fabric. It was the kind of night he was no longer accustomed to, resident in a city of scintillating lights. Frogs, crickets, and other nocturnal denizens filled the air with their steady din. A goat bleated in sleepy stupor. He heard the faint swell of drums floating in from a far, uncertain distance.

Witches, wizards, and demonic forces—a strange susceptibility overtook him. What if those ineffable forces had taken on flesh, real and menacing? A shudder rocked his spine. He considered returning to the house to fetch a lamp, but a lamp's paltry light was no match for the darkness. In fact, a lamp's flicker was likely to awaken ghostly shadows in the night.

He made his way toward his grandmother's hut, raising and dropping his legs with an awkwardness that, in a blind man, would be regarded as a necessary caution. His mouth open, he tried to mute his breath, but heard his heart pounding. It was only when he figured that he was a few feet away from Nne's hut that his fear began, gradually, to drain away.

Just then he heard a rustle. His heart leapt and clogged his throat. Some bird flew overhead, twittering, wings whipping the air.

Then he heard Nne's voice, sharp, riding the air.

"A son braves the night to search out his mother," she sang. "No darkness is dark enough to bar the son's path to the hearth."

His fear uncoiled and seeped away. He hastened toward his grandmother's voice. He swung his arms with abandon and strode fearlessly, as if he owned the night.

CHAPTER ELEVEN

Ike's sleep was sweet, deep, and swift. It was not the kind of restless, nasty night he was used to back in New York, nor the night of uneasy sleep he'd had at Stopoff Hotel in Lagos, dreaming of Bimpe cradled in his arm. It was as if he had shut his eyes one moment and, opening them a moment later, had beheld a room bathed with the sun's radiance. Having enjoyed a night without the burden of dreams, he awoke with none of the fatigue or languor that dreams bequeath. As happened whenever his night was dreamless, his body exuded a sense of vigor he had not felt in years. His mood, touched with the sense of a world in sync, had a generous cast.

Even so, he lounged in bed, his reverie broken by interludes of anxiety—about his mother and about his mission to steal Ngene. He turned and twisted, taking odd delight in the bed's whiny creaks.

Suddenly he heard the clank of the *ogene*. The sound was familiar and intimate. He turned his ear as if the gong would transmit a private message to him. *Kpom gem, kpom gem, kpom gem* sounded the metal gong. The beater was his uncle, Osuakwu, and this was both a ritual of salutation to the war deity and the herald of a new day. The gong clanged twice more with the familiar melody. Then Osuakwu's voice, transported on the staid air of dawn, rang clear in greeting to Ngene.

Ike's heart pounded. It was as if his uncle had issued a summons—and then left it up to Ike to choose when to answer. He resolved to make contact as soon as possible—in fact, that day. He recalled the spat with his mother. It had served its purpose; it had established the ground rules; it had served notice that he wasn't about to let himself be leashed, forbidden contact with his uncle and grandmother. As long as his mother respected those terms, he didn't foresee any more bickering or rancor during the week he planned to stay in Utonki.

He attributed the glow of generosity he felt to the two hours he'd spent with his grandmother the night before. Nne's talk and banter always reinvigorated him. When he had walked back home, his steps firmer, more assured in the darkness, he'd been surprised to find his mother curled up on the sofa, waiting.

"The service is at nine A.M. prompt," she had said, then stood and hurried away to her room. Her haste bespoke fear of a refusal, but he called out that he would be there. After his conversation with Nne, he was ready, even eager, to meet the pastor.

THREE KNOCKS SHOOK THE door. A pause, then Alice peeped in.

"Good morning, Uncle," she said. "Your breakfast is ready."

"I'll take a bath first."

"Grandma asked me to give you breakfast first. Then I'll go and boil water for your bath."

Breakfast consisted of *akamu*, pap made from fermented corn, and *akara*, fried bean cakes. As he savored the delicacies, his mother appeared, dressed in a bluish flowered lace wrapper, a white blouse, and a blue head tie. She appeared spirited, her face far from the drab, wilted look he'd expected.

"Church starts at nine prompt," she said. "We must not be late."

"There's a lot of time," he said. "It's only seven forty-five. And I've never seen anything in Nigeria start at any time *prompt*."

"It's not about Nigeria; it's about God. You can't keep God waiting." She folded her arms, but her tone was surprisingly mild.

"I think Nigerians will try," he said. "Yes, if any people will attempt to keep God waiting, it has to be Nigerians. And since God created us that way, he's likely to show understanding."

Her face darkened. "If you don't arrive on time, others might snatch away your anointing."

"God has more than enough anointing for everybody," he said. "There won't be any need to scramble. No reason for anybody to snatch the anointing reserved for somebody else."

She gave him a sharp look. "Everything to you is logic. Even when you were small enough to fit in the arm, you considered yourself a logician. But remember that God is greater than all our logic. Human wisdom is foolishness to God."

Ike paused from eating. He regarded her with an expression that hovered between defiance and sadness. "I hope God is not half as angry as you look—otherwise I'm doomed to hell." He thought he saw the hint of a smile on her face. "Don't worry, Mama, we're not going to be late. No way am I going to forfeit the anointing reserved for me."

THE CHURCH WAS HOUSED in the village's abandoned kindergarten. Ike still remembered going there as a child. The building had been shut down after the local government awarded an inflated contract to erect another school at a different site. The new school was hardly different from the old one. It was, like the old school, a sloppy, dingy structure of brick and zinc. But since so much money had been squandered on its construction, government officials dubbed it ultramodern.

Ike couldn't believe the building's dilapidated state. Its walls were pockmarked, its once-bright aluminum zinc a dirty brown, sun-charred.

This, Ike thought, was the place his mother frequented for her daily dose of divine anointing! The idea struck him as ludicrous. He stopped to read words scrawled on a broad wooden board. The script was uneven, wavy. In bold letters: MAITY DEEDS WORLD INTENATIONAL REDEAMERS CHURCH. Then in smaller print: COME TO BE PROSPARED, RELEACED FROM YOKES AND SATANIC ATTACKS, WUMBS OPENED, MIRACLOUS DELIVARANCE, DEVINE WANDERS!!! IN JESUS MAITY NAME!!!!

A bellow of laughter stirred inside him. He struggled to hold it back but let out a gush of breath. His mother gave him a severe look.

"Who wrote this?" he asked.

"Our pastor, why?"

"Why? The man's spelling is terrible. He needs a divine editor."

She flinched as if he had spoken bawdy words. "God forgive you!" she muttered.

Ike was astounded by the number of congregants crammed inside the building. On seeing Ike, many of them sprang from their long wooden benches and rushed toward him. They wore wide grins and wider eyes.

"Is this your son from America?" one man asked. "Praise the Lord!" exclaimed another man. "Our Lord is in control," a woman shouted. "Satan is a liar," somebody declared. "Come and see what the Lord has done." A woman broke out in song. The rest of the congregation picked it up. A man shouted "Alleluia!" and there was a deafening response of "Amen." "Does he still speak Igbo?" a woman asked. The question provoked a chorus of laughter. "How can?" another woman replied. "I bet he now speaks through the nose, like *oyibo* people. He even looks like *oyibo*!" More laughter. "Look at his skin, shiny like the sun." "I hope he's not married," cried one woman. "Why?" asked a man. "You ask why?" the woman chided. "You have forgotten we have many sisters in Christ praying for a good husband?" There was a burst of laughter. "Look at his teeth," gushed a brown-skinned, toothy woman. "Clear like water." "White as milk," said another woman.

When the excitement abated, Ike's mother began a round of formal introductions. She prefixed each man's name with "Brother," each woman's with "Sister." There was gaiety in her carriage; Ike, on the other hand, was pensive and tight.

"This is Sister Theresa," his mother said, putting her hand lightly on a tall young woman with dimpled cheeks, her hair parted neatly in the middle, the two locks clipped to either side of her head. "Sister Theresa Nma is a teacher." She paused for a moment, her eyes roving searchingly between her son and Theresa. "She's also a very, very good Christian girl."

Theresa held out her hand. Ike took it, surprised by its soft, limp feel. Oddly stirred, he fixed on her finely sculpted face with large, mellow eyes. She turned her head slightly away, as if she couldn't bear his attention.

"I thank God for your safe journey," she said, then executed a quick genuflection.

Ike caught his mother looking up at his face, her hand still perched on Theresa's shoulder.

"Thank you," Ike said. Then conscious that her hand was still in his, sweaty, he let go.

"Sister Vero," he heard his mother say. "She's a nurse and a good Christian girl."

Ike faced another outstretched hand. He found the new face markedly less attractive, or perhaps just less distinguished, than Theresa's. But this one was more at ease. She grinned and met his gaze, her eyes ardent and expectant.

Suddenly, Ike's mood soured. Why had he allowed his mother to drag him out to this shabby, ramshackle establishment and to peddle him to a lineup of women driven to insane distraction by dreams of American matrimony and dollars?

He shook the last hand, another good Christian girl, and then walked off to the last row of benches. No sooner had he sat down than a grizzly-haired man who'd been introduced as an elder appeared.

"No, no, sir," the man protested in a tinny, grating voice. "You must sit in front. It's not easy to come all the way from America. The front seat belongs to you. You and your mother."

Ike sat firm. "Here's okay for me," he said.

A few more people harangued him. They pointed out that a man who'd traveled from across the big sea should not be consigned to the back of any gathering. If they didn't offer him the front seat, their pastor would unleash wrath on them. God, too, would be vexed.

"I'm fine," he insisted.

"He who humbles himself shall be exalted. It's in the Bible," intoned the elder, baring teeth the color of snuff. "Since you have humbled yourself, God wants us to exalt you."

Ike shook his head adamantly.

"We're sitting in front," his mother snapped.

He was reluctant to defy her openly. The fight in him had to be reserved for the pastor. The congregants clapped and cheered as he followed her to the front pews.

His skin sizzled with the humid heat. The air reeked of a mixture of sweat, scented pomade, and talcum powder. More worshippers trickled in. His mother introduced each arrival—a "brother" or "sister" in Christ.

Each man or woman fussed over him, but Ike quietly chafed. The man he'd come to see was nowhere in sight, and his patience was wearing. After shaking another member's hand, he glanced at his wristwatch. Nine twenty-two.

He leaned toward his mother. "You said nine prompt."

Her face betrayed no apologies. "If God tells him to say extra prayers before he leaves his house, he has to obey. He can't say no to God. We have to be patient. A man of God must do what God commands."

The sun, stirring from slumber, shot shafts of light into the room. Ike focused on the motes of dust that skittered and tumbled in the ropy beams. The room was sweltering; the heat drilled holes in his skin. He sat steady and tense, his ears picking up bits of the excited chatter.

Three or so young-sounding women giggled, muttered, whispered behind him. They talked in Igbo about his fetching looks. He strained his ears, eavesdropping. "He's as handsome as a white man," one extolled. Another asked, "Do you *hear* his smell? He smells sweeter than the red flower in the mist of dawn." Another: "Did you see his eyes? Quiet as Lake Utonki, but deeper. A man with such eyes—he can kill with love." Each woman argued, unabashed, that she was the one he was going to marry. "He'll take me to the white man's land," cooed one. "An illiterate like you, he won't even bear to give you a second look," challenged another. "I'm the one for him." A snicker, then: "You call somebody else illiterate, but I bet you don't know how white people love. Do you know how a man touches his lips to a woman's?" "Who hasn't seen it in cinemas?" said one. "I've seen it, and I can do it," boasted another. "I'll welcome his lips to mine."

Ike panned his head to the side, as if he were about to look at the chatterers. They immediately hushed up. He was not quite flattered. He was never good at aimless waiting. It grated on his nerves. He showed his watch to his mother: 9:46.

"He'll be here soon," she said. "Be patient."

Just then he heard the rev of a car and the sharp cut of the engine.

A man clanged a bell. The congregation shook with excitement. They stampeded to meet the pastor at the entrance. "Daddy! Daddy!" they sang, young and old alike. They massed around the man, enveloped him. They bawled, hands upraised, like fans at a soccer game. Some uttered inaudible supplications, speaking with diarrheic rapidity. Others just droned, emitting sounds that were a cross between a quiet wail and a crazed groan.

Ike coldly observed the babble. Had God descended through the clouds and into the shaggy church, the frenzy could scarcely have been more delirious.

For a minute or two, Ike could not see the pastor, nor did the pastor notice him. As the pastor was lost in the crowd, Ike surmised that the man had to be short. His mother was in a state of possessed stupor. Eyes shut, she flailed her arms, stamped her feet, stomped an invisible beast. Her lips trembled all the while, a torrent of undecipherable words tumbling from them. At that moment, a chink opened in the crowd. Through it Pastor Godson Uka spied Ike's seated form. With a ferocious, two-handed shove the pastor sent the mob reeling. "Yankee man!" he exclaimed, cheeks stretched in a wide smile. He grabbed Ike's hand and pulled him up. He spread out arms, an avuncular figure inviting a hug. Ike plunged his hands into his pants pockets. His lip tucked between his teeth, he conveyed an expression of demure distance. Recognizing the futility of holding out for a hug, the pastor thrust out a hand. Ike took it, studying the man before him.

Pastor Uka had a high, arched pate and a boxer's flattened nose. His eyelids were swollen, the rest of his face ravaged by pimples. A smile decorated his face, but Ike remained tight-lipped, almost placid. They stood, face-to-face, like mismatched wrestlers sizing each other up. Ike towered over the pastor, a short man, no taller than five feet seven inches—even wearing shoes. His eyes glowed from pinched, narrowed slits. They darted about, transmitting a hunger whose exact nature Ike was determined to unmask.

Ike maintained his closed expression for a good minute and then cracked a grin. The pastor's visage relaxed.

"God has set you aside for great things," he proclaimed. From the backcloth of worshippers came chimes of "Amen" and "Alleluia." Ike's noncommittal nod encouraged the pastor. "He wants to use you in a big way. He wants to bless you. God has given me a mighty message for you."

Ike's mother piped up in praise. Ike erased the grin from his face.

Pastor Uka's eyes twitched. He was a study in gaudiness. He sported a dark jacket over a yellow shirt and a maroon dotted tie. A large gold chain with a wrought-gold crucifix bedecked his neck. All five fingers of his left hand and three of the right were bedeckled with glitzy rings. His hair dropped in slick curls, slaked with oil. *Peacock pastor,* Ike silently named him.

Yet, for all his dramatic sense of color, it was the pastor's face that kept Ike riveted. His eyelids blinked constantly. That, combined with a roguish smile, created the impression of a man bemused at the gullibility of the crowd he'd duped, his fleshy round countenance contrasting with gaunt faces that surrounded him, his python-skin shoes were burnished to a glitter.

"Praise God!" Pastor Uka shouted.

"Alleluia!" shouted the rallied congregation.

"Praise God!"

"Alleluia!"

Uka leapt into the air several times, his belly a bobbing, heaving sag, the energy in his short frame parlayed into combustible fuel. As he jumped and spun around, he cried: "Everybody praise God!"

The congregation responded with a series of shrill affirmations.

The pastor spun around, again facing Ike. He stretched his broad lips in a smile. "Fear not, brother," he entreated in a quiet voice. "God says he's in control. Powerful anointing is flowing around you."

Ike's mother let out a paroxysm of affirmation.

The pastor looked around the room, his body shuddering like one in the throes of malaria. He raised his head, then announced: "God has a spectacular message for his people today. God told me to tell you . . ." He paused for dramatic effect. An attentive silence swelled in the room. "You can't imagine the things that God told me to tell his people!"

"Tell us, Pastor!" pleaded the audience.

"I don't have the mouth to tell it. It's too awesome."

More cries of encouragement rent the air.

Pastor Uka began to strut about the room. Circling and circling, he randomly threw punches at the air. His bulgy body quivered, as if some kinetic force had crept into it. The congregants pressed forward, expectant. They formed an ever-tightening circle within which the pastor moved. Boisterous prayers erupted.

Anger welled up inside Ike. *What* had he gotten himself into? He had begun to perspire, his hands sweaty. Much as he regretted coming, he knew it was too late to escape. The chaos before his eyes was the very substance of the event. It was already in progress. There had been no preamble, no overture, just a swift transition from quietude to tumult. There was no distance between pulpit and pew. Nothing was choreographed. Yet, he conjectured that there was a peculiar brand of logic to this madness.

The pastor suddenly stopped short. "God told me," he bellowed, "that he has not forgotten the promise he made to Abraham, to give his descendants great increase and prosperity."

The congregation ramped up its excitement.

"God told me to tell you that, under the new covenant, you're the descendants of Abraham."

Cries of exultation.

"Abraham's increase shall be yours."

"We claim it!"

"Abraham's prosperity is your prosperity."

"Thank God! Alleluia!"

Uka began to speak but paused in midsentence. Removing his jacket, he swung it several times over his head, then sent it sailing. A spry young man jumped and wrested it from the others. He folded it up neatly and draped it over a chair. The pastor's shirt revealed swaths of sweat that ran from his armpits down to the belt line.

"God told me . . ." The pastor took a backward step, as if the burden of divine revelation had made him stagger. Something hard to define swept through the crowd. "God woke me up at five thirty-five A.M.," he continued. "He called me Godson, and I answered. He said, 'Go and brush your teeth and take your bath because I have a lot to reveal to you today.' I did what God told me. After bathing, I sat down to listen. God told me to tell his people that his abundant anointing will flow for believers. He told me that this is the week of double portions and triple blessings."

The congregation exploded in fits of praise.

Maintaining a dramatic silence, the pastor hoisted himself on his toes, then rhythmically rose and fell, swaying from side to side.

"The Lord is great!" shouted one man. He began to clap and then the rest of the congregation took it up, as if the pastor had pulled off some amazing feat.

Uka's routine ceased all of a sudden. His hands cut the air as he spoke. "God told me to tell you that His people who want children will receive them this week."

"Alleluia!"

"Ah, He told me to tell you that Satan is a liar."

"Satan is a liar!" echoed the congregation.

"I said, if you've been praying for children, God has answered your prayer."

The congregation sang its cackle of gratitude.

"God said that any believer who is now pregnant with one baby is going to receive twins. Amen?"

"Amen!"

"He asked me to tell those of you looking for a husband that you will receive husbands who count their money in dollars and pounds sterling."

Several young women rattled out: "I claim it in Jesus's name!"

Ike felt trapped in the disorienting swirl. Slowly, amazement replaced anger. It'd been a long time, several years at least, since he'd been at a church service. And then it was a Catholic mass, with its solemn air, its sober, near-somber rituals. True, he had sneaked into St. Stephen's from time to time, but usually when there had been no congregants, his thoughts alone providing the sensation of communion. The idea of clapping and stamping in church had a ring of illicitness. In America, he had only ever seen such a holy ruckus on television. It was on TV, too, that he'd first seen bodies freeze and flip backward from a pastor's touch. It was also on TV that he first heard people make strange utterances in stranger tongues.

Sweat glistened on the pastor's brow. Tiny streaks of it coursed down the sides of his face. "God told me to tell you that those looking for a job will find it this week. Those who already have jobs will receive double promotion."

"Praise God!" cried the congregants.

"But God said only those who tithe will be blessed."

A muted, deflated response.

"Have you been praying for prosperity?" asked the pastor.

"Yeah!" answered the congregation.

"God said you'll be prospered."

"Are you trapped by water spirit? God says you'll be set free."

"Amen!"

"How about those harassed by witchcraft? God said your deliverance is at hand."

"Amen!"

The pastor pulled a red handkerchief from his pants pocket and wiped his sweaty face. He then launched into an esoteric tongue, a staccato succession of sounds. "I'm burning with anointing," he blared, like a man truly on fire. He swung around, blowing breath at a group of worshippers. Staggering like drunks, they collapsed on the floor. Uka darted to another cluster. He swept his arm in a dramatic arc. The worshippers' legs seemed to turn to jelly. They became groggy, then tumbled to the ground. If his mother weren't part of the madness, if she weren't on the floor, Ike might have found the scene entertaining. She had spun around for a few seconds before pitching sideways. She was spread-eagled. She tossed and writhed in induced ecstasy. The wantonness of her posture nudged his mind in the direction of ideas he was loathe to visit.

How had she come to this *thing*? What desperation had driven her to the bosom of an experience at odds with everything she'd been and done in the past? As Ike thought these thoughts, his throat clamped up with bile.

He caught the pastor casting an intense glare at him. He glared back, forcing the pastor to blink and retreat.

"Get up!" the pastor barked. Instantly, the fallen bodies lumbered back to their feet. Uka sought out Ike's eye and smiled.

For the next half hour, the pastor rambled. He flitted from one anecdote to another, all the while riffing on the theme of prosperity. His voice would rise to the level of a tirade, then fall to a languid pitch. Suddenly he pointed at Ike. "God gave me a special message for Madam Uzondu's son," he announced. "And the message is for the gentleman's ears only."

He called for a collection to be taken, admonishing the congregation to remember that God blessed the generous giver. Then, for the first time since the service began, he sat down. His eyes latched on to Ike, who waved off the elder who held out the offertory basket before him.

As the worshippers filed out, Ike saw expressions of hope etched on their faces. It was a hope worn thin, Ike surmised, by repeated disappointment. The thought brought him to the edge of feverish anger. The idea of battling Uka suddenly took on greater urgency. It was so intense that, for a fleeting moment, it seemed as if that battle—not the snagging of a deity—was the main reason he'd returned to Nigeria.

CHAPTER TWELVE

"We're going to my house," Pastor Uka said in the imperative words of a man afraid of contradiction.

"Is my mother coming?" Ike asked.

The pastor scratched his cheeks, seemed to weigh the pros and cons. "No, let it be the two of us," he said finally, without meeting Ike's eye.

"The two of you should talk alone," said his mother, wringing her hands.

"Yes," agreed the pastor in a distracted manner. "God told me we should talk alone."

His mother nodded at Ike vigorously. "I'm going home to prepare your lunch," she said, then walked away.

The path to the village stream grazed the left side of Uka's church. Three women were returning from the stream, water jugs balanced on their heads. They stopped on seeing Ike and the pastor.

"Is it Ike that I see?" asked one of the women.

"Don't talk to her," Uka muttered under his breath. "Not a word."

Ike squinted against the sun's glare. Recognizing Masiolu, his uncle Osuakwu's youngest wife, he said, "Masiolu, it's me."

"May the eye with which I see you not grow a boil," she said. "When did you arrive?"

"Don't talk to her!" Uka commanded in a rasping, commanding voice.

"I arrived last night," Ike said.

"Wind brought us news of your arrival," Osuakwu's wife said. "We heard, but we said we hadn't seen. The ear hears things true and false, but the eye sees only what is true. Except when the eye is deceived by shadows. I hope it's not your shadow I'm seeing."

"No more word to the heathen," Uka muttered.

"It's me indeed. It's not my shadow."

"Will you come to see your father's brother, or are you forbidden to visit his house?"

The pastor scowled. "I said stop talking to her!" he shouted in a more brusque voice.

"Tell Osuakwu I'll visit this afternoon," Ike said, ignoring the pastor. "And I'll come hungry."

"Come anytime. Osuakwu can still afford food that will fill your belly. Should I then tell him to save some palm wine for you?"

Pastor Uka stood askance, glum, his face wrinkled with consternation.

"Or something stronger. I'll also come thirsty."

The women laughed and continued on their way.

Ike and Uka entered the pastor's Peugeot 504, an old but spiffy, dustless car. It lurched forward, moody as the pastor. Ike luxuriated in his defiance, leaning back into the soft, faux leather seat. Uka gripped the steering wheel as a TV wrestler might the neck of an opponent.

Uka's residence was a brick bungalow about three hundred meters from the church. Outside was the buzz of a power generator. The pastor led the way into a living room dominated by three black leather couches and an entertainment center that held a large plasma TV, a DVD player, and a stereo system. An air conditioner hummed, chilling the air, which was scented with air freshener and cologne.

"Take a seat, take a seat," the pastor said. He waved his hands in a sweeping gesture. "Take any seat of your choice." Ike plunked down on a two-seater couch. Uka took time to loosen his tie and unbutton the top of his shirt. Then he sat across from Ike, kicking off his shoes.

His phone rang. Peering at the phone, he said, "Let me take this call." He flipped open the cell phone and soon launched into a brief barking contest with the caller.

"Sorry o," he sighed to Ike as he put the phone away. "Our people can be very annoying."

"You have a cell phone," Ike said, a question that came across merely as a statement. "I didn't know cell phones worked here."

"In Utonki? Cell phones are common here," said the pastor. He saw Ike's doubtful look. "True, everybody has one."

"It can't be everybody. My mother doesn't have one."

"Then what are you doing? She can't have a son in America and yet not have a phone."

Vexed by the chastising tone, Ike fixed the pastor with a hostile stare. Uka's eyes withdrew. He looked discomfited, mildly confused. In quick succession he gaped at the carpet, then Ike, then the ceiling.

They sat in silence punctured only by the generator's rattle and the drone of the air conditioner.

"A nice house," Ike finally offered.

"To God be the glory."

Another spell of silence followed.

"What can I offer you?" Uka asked.

"Nothing. I came to talk."

"That doesn't mean you can't cool off with something."

"Nothing for me. Thanks for offering."

Uka entwined his fingers, then pressed them against his chest, cracking them. In a curt, unceremonious tone, he asked, "Didn't you hear me say you shouldn't talk to that woman?"

"Masiolu, you mean? Osuakwu's wife?"

"Yes."

"Yes."

"So why did you talk to her?"

"She's my aunt, married to my father's only brother," Ike said.

"So? I told you not to talk to her." He shut his eyes, scratching his face.

"I don't understand why it troubles you that I spoke to my uncle's wife."

Uka shook his head, glaring at Ike. "It's not me it troubles, it's God."

"Why would God be worried that I exchanged greetings with my aunt?"

"Don't you know I'm a man of God?"

"You say so."

"You think I just open my mouth and say whatever comes into my mind?"

Ike shrugged. "I presume you speak from your mind, yes."

The pastor wiped his right cuff against his brow. "Well, that's not how it happens." He tossed a distracted sidelong glance at the pane of his window, bright with sunlight. "It was God who told me to warn you," he said, his voice unsteady. "God ordered me to warn you not to talk to her."

He looked at Ike's face as if figuring out some mystery. "Listen to me," he exhorted. "You have to trust me. God had a reason for warning you about that woman. But Satan stepped in—and you listened to the deceiver's voice."

Ike smothered a chuckle. "Sorry," he said. "God didn't speak to me."

"He did, through me."

"I didn't realize you were speaking for God." He paused briefly. "Don't blame me, Pastor. God has never talked to me directly. I haven't learned any divine language. Perhaps I'm still too young, or too poor in spirit. I guess that's why I'm here: to hear the message God gave for me."

Their eyes met, but Pastor Uka quickly looked away. He pulled at his chin, then at the edge of his tufts of mustache. Ike studied the averted face. Uka cut the image of a cheap trickster, unmasked. The pastor seemed to have lost his touch.

That instant, Ike would have liked to have clapped his hands together and laughed. As the thought flashed into his mind, he realized that, in a way, he'd done precisely that. And he had the urge to laugh, again.

Uka glanced up, startled. He stood, muttered inaudibly, and scuffed away in the direction of a curtain that demarcated the living room from the rest of the house. He stopped in front of the curtain, half turned, and said, "Excuse me."

Ike nodded. A tall refrigerator dominated the room's left-hand corner. There was a mahogany dining table set against the wall to the right. Around it were six white chairs, above it wooden cabinets with sliding glass doors. The cabinets held crystal chinaware and wineglasses with deep-groove patterns. There was a wide-screened TV, and beside it a rack filled with black and burgundy shoes. He counted thirteen pairs before the rumble of a flushed toilet distracted him. He composed his face to await his host's entrance.

As soon as he parted the curtain and reentered the room, Pastor Uka said, "You need to be born again."

"How do you mean?"

"You should be spirit-filled, tongues-speaking, hands-laying, devil-binding born again."

Ike said nothing.

"Do you believe in God?" Uka asked.

"Is this a question God asked you to put to me?"

The pastor wrinkled his face. "I'm a man of God. I can't open my mouth and ask careless questions."

"God knows everything, and God speaks to you."

An indeterminate expression overcame Uka's face; he seemed to waver between a smile and a snarl. He sucked in long drafts of air and exhaled in gusts, his lips producing a soft, whistling sound.

Ike did not want the man to wilt too soon. His plan was to thoroughly trounce Uka. Yet, he had no interest in delivering a swift punch and securing a knockout. His game plan was to dance around the ring, reaching in intermittently to pelt the target with jabs, softening the man with a barrage of body blows. Then, once the con artist displayed weakness, Ike would move in with a flurry of vicious, pulverizing blows.

Flushed with a perverse graciousness, he flashed the pastor a warm, reassuring smile. "I'm a believer," he said. His voice was slow and soft, a confider's. "God knows."

Uka walked to the couch and sat down. "God already told me," he said, practically exhaling the words. Hand placed underneath his chin, his head cocked sideways, he gazed out in front of him, as if tuned to some inaudible voice in the air. "Do you know it's God who brought you home?"

Ike waited for his next words.

"Yes," the pastor affirmed. "Satan had planned how to finish you. It's God that canceled the plan. Look, a divine decree has declared you a millionaire. Your divine millions have been looking for you, but Satan kept confusing you." He raised his head, exposing eyes narrowed in desperate concentration, like a stage actor whose line had suddenly taken wings and fled.

"My millions are looking for me?"

"Yes. But you must be divinely prepared so that the divine millions can find you."

"What kind of preparation?"

"You need a wife, a nice Christian lady."

"My mother already told me," Ike said.

Pastor Uka smiled in a vacant, mechanical way. "There are many God-fearing ladies in our church."

Ike nodded. "I found out. My mother introduced me."

The pastor beamed and then shifted in his chair to adopt a relaxed posture. "You see, Satan is so wicked. He used sweet lies to lead you astray. He made you turn away from your mother, turn away from your sister, turn away from God. Satan stopped you from sowing your seeds. That's why your millions did not flow. That's why your harvest has not been as mighty as God intended. But God said I should tell you, Satan is a liar. He asked me to tell you it's time. It's your time for fulfillment. It's time for your harvest. It's time for your redemption; time for your breakthroughs. It's time for you to shine!"

Ike leaned forward.

"You must listen," said Uka in a raised voice, "and you must obey the word of God, for he holds the world in his hand. My friend, God wants to bless you with a mighty harvest. He has commanded that you'll start counting your harvest in millions. And he wants to bless you this year, not next year." He paused, cocked his head, and asked, "Does God lie?"

Ike shook his head.

"That's right, you've found divine favor. The God who owns all the seas and lands, all the gold and diamonds, wants to prosper you. He wants all your enemies to die of envy and shame. He wants to lift you above them. And God doesn't lie."

Ike corroborated with a nod.

"The only person standing between you and your divine harvest is—*you.*"

"Me?" Ike asked.

"Yes, you!" Uka let the mystery of his words linger for a moment. He intertwined his fingers as if in supplication and stared into blankness. Ike waited. "God told me to tell you this: your wealth would have been released a long time ago, but you were not ready. For the longest time, God has had your millions in his hand, ready to release it. All he wanted was for you to sow the seed. Divine law says that we must sow in order to reap. Out of jealousy, Satan blocked your way and blinded you. The evil one knew about your divine provision—and it made him mad. Satan wanted you to continue counting in thousands when the divine plan said you should count in millions. Everything has been revealed to me." He peered into Ike's eyes and thrust his head forward. "Do you want me to tell you the truth?"

"I thought that's what you've been doing all this time," Ike said.

Uka's right fist pounded the palm of his left. "Satan has used two agents to work against you. They're your uncle and grandmother."

A sneeze shook Ike, short-circuiting his reaction. Pastor Uka pressed his advantage.

"Oh yes, God showed me how they killed your father. And these satanic agents were planning your own death. That's when God revealed their plans to me. Without me, they would have finished you off. A long time ago," he said, his left arm swiping the air to demonstrate the ease of his demise. "I fasted and prayed for forty days straight. That's why you're alive today. Then God told me he would send you to me. I'm giving you divine revelations, so listen carefully."

Ike pursed his lips, then exploded with a whole trill of sneezes. Pastor Uka paused, waiting.

"My father died of complications from diabetes," Ike said, drawing the back of his hand across the tip of his nose. "It was in the doctor's report."

Pastor Uka snickered. "Don't you know that doctors see only the things of the flesh? But I've been divinely commissioned to reveal the deep realities of the spirit." He smiled confidently. "Who caused your father's diabetes?"

"Are you saying such things are caused by humans?"

Uka held steady the smile. "My friend," he said, "you're still young in this world. You're even younger in the things of the spirit."

"Diabetes can't be inflicted by people," Ike said.

"Alleluia!" exulted the pastor. "Do you know that the Lord even told me that you're going to doubt?"

"Tell me why Osuakwu and Nne would want to kill my father?"

Uka crinkled his forehead and turned sharply away, as if Ike's doubt had crossed the line into unforgivable heresy. Then he seemed to reconsider, speaking in a slow, emphatic manner. "I'm telling you what the Almighty revealed to me. Your uncle and grandmother are grandmasters in the demonic world. Your uncle is like Ahab, your grandmother like Jezebel. Both of them are worshippers of Baal. God has given me the prophetic powers of Elijah. A ball of fire will descend from on high and consume Baal and all its worshippers. That's why Osuakwu and your grandma are terrified of me."

"You have confronted them, then?"

"You mean spiritual confrontation?" the pastor sought clarification.

Ike affirmed with a nod.

"Every night!" cried Uka. "We're talking about spiritual, not physical, confrontation. Since God planted me here, they've been grounded. When they attempt to fly to do their witchcraft, I'm there to crash them. When they and other witches and wizards gather under the banana tree at midnight, I go and disperse them. I'm awake every night. I pray. I call down Holy Ghost fire. I break spells and yokes. I unbind the bound. Without me, this village wouldn't know peace at night. You wouldn't have been able to sleep at night."

Lower lip clipped between his teeth, Ike swayed his head slowly from side to side in a simulation of rapt attention.

"God wants you to sow in His church," the pastor said, returning to his script. He brought together the tips of his fingers, forming a triangle. He lowered his voice: "God wants you to sow here in Utonki. He has commanded that a temple should be built here to His eternal glory." He paused to gauge Ike's receptivity. Satisfied, he changed tacks. "Do you agree that He who owns heaven and earth, the sole giver of life, the source of all health and wealth, deserves a befitting place of worship?"

Ike's slight nod indicated assent.

"God is asking you to sow fifty thousand dollars to build him a church here. If you obey, you'll become a millionaire. As simple as that."

Ike leaned back on the sofa, jaw in cupped hands. Pastor Uka's eyes darted. Inside Ike, a peal of laughter began to well up. Then it burst out of him, a surge of laughter. "So God wants to make me a millionaire?" Ike asked. "But first, I have to give you fifty thousand dollars?"

"You're not giving me, you're sowing," Uka corrected.

"But I'm to hand you the money."

"Yes, to build a temple for our Redeemer."

"I want to do more." Ike paused, and then affected a contemplative face. When he glanced at Pastor Uka, he saw that the man's expression was bright, expectant. "If God wants me to be a millionaire, I'm going to do more. But I want to be assured that you've given me God's word."

"I'm a man of God," Uka swore. "Why should I lie?"

"Do you talk to God often?"

"Every single day."

"And I must not visit my uncle or my grandmother?"

"If you go to see either of them, you'll die. I received that message this morning. If not for my fasting and prayer, you would have been finished months ago."

"You're saying my uncle and grandmother wanted to kill me?"

"Totally! They would have used demonic means to finish you. Thank God that your mother came to me at the right time. I began to pray and fast, seeking God's favor for you. Then God told me that the devil is a liar."

"Wonderful!" Ike enthused. "And you said I'm about to receive a million dollars?"

"Not just a million, millions."

"Where's the money coming from?"

"Just trust. God works in mysterious ways, and he never lies."

As if sensing doubt, Uka became more animated. "Look, when God called me to serve, he promised to use me in mighty ways. He has used me to release thousands from bondage. He has used me to heal hundreds of sick people. When I hold crusades, the blind see, the lame walk, the deaf hear, the dumb talk. Barren women have children. Cancer disappears. Diabetes is canceled. In his mighty name, I've raised people from the dead. And he's used me to prosper a lot of people."

"Fine, then," Ike said, "here's my deal." He leaned forward.

Pastor Uka followed suit, face aglow. "When next you speak to God, report back that I've decided to triple the amount I'm supposed to sow. I'll sow a hundred and fifty thousand. In fact, I'll sow that amount for every million I make—"

"Praise the Lord!" Uka exclaimed. His belly flapped up and down as he sprang from the sofa, clapping hands, a wide smile stretching his cheeks.

Ike waited for the pastor's excitement to run its course. Then he said, "My little request is that God should first give me an advance of one million."

Uka dropped back to the sofa, momentarily speechless.

"I think it's a fair deal. I'm tripling the seed."

Uka's response came in a weary voice. "You can't change how God works. First you sow, then you reap. I told you that."

"What happens when the seed is not there?"

"You can't tell me you don't have fifty thousand dollars."

"I *can* tell you," Ike said sharply. "If God ever spoke to you, he would have told you that. You seem to believe that American streets are littered with dollars."

"You can always take a loan."

"Of fifty thousand?"

"Yes."

"Did God just suggest that?" There was a dash of mockery in Ike's tone.

Uka sat biting his lower lip, silent. Ike's ire rose. He stood up and straightened his back. He walked over to the pastor.

"You've been exploiting my mother," he said, his hand jabbing the air as he spoke. "She gave you her meager feeding money. She bombarded me with letters. *Come home, come home,* she cried. *Come and meet this powerful pastor. Come,* she begged, *and be saved from your uncle and grandmother.* My poor mother! You're not satisfied with stealing her feeding money. You dreamed up a scheme to get your filthy hands in her son's pocket. You call yourself a man of God, but you're rotten. Rotten inside and out! You say your God wants me to sow fifty thousand dollars. But fifty thousand, in truth, is the size of your greed."

Ike paused. His mouth was dry; his chest puffed. Uka sat gravely, immobile, hands clasped, with an impression of detachment in his posture, as if Ike's fiery words were directed at another man. He stared blankly, as though he saw nothing and yet everything. At irregular intervals, his toes rubbed against the carpet.

"I went to visit my grandmother last night," Ike continued. "Yes, I was with her for more than two hours. We talked and joked. She didn't eat me. This is the woman you just warned me not to see—or I'd die. The birds in your dreams, do they tell you such pathetic lies?"

The pastor's face twitched, but no words passed through his lips.

"Tell me," Ike pursued. "After all the lies you tell, how do you lie down and sleep? I would spit on you—but I don't want to dirty my spit!"

Turning sharply, Ike scudded toward the door. He twisted the knob and stepped outside. Then, peeping in just before he banged the door, he saw Uka look up. "I want you to know I'm going to see my uncle. Today, not tomorrow."

CHAPTER THIRTEEN

Ike stepped out into a breezeless, sweltering afternoon. The sun was overhead. Its rays singed, its heat sizzled on his skin.

He'd intended to walk home and tell his mother all about his spat with Pastor Uka but decided to call on his uncle right away.

Ike's shadow was a squat, disfigured thing on the ground. He walked briskly through the heat. His legs seemed powered by some strange energy. Having blitzed Pastor Uka, he was in a buoyant mood, free of resentment. Drums of victory beat in his head, but he cautioned himself against over-celebrating. From the outset, he'd known that the pastor would be the weaker of the foes he would have to engage and dominate. His uncle, Osuakwu, was bound to be far tougher.

In planning the operation in the comfort of his apartment in New York, Ike had not foreseen any obstacles. But now, his two feet planted in Utonki, his mother's home within shouting distance of the shrine, he found himself increasingly powerless against the fear-tinged breeze that lashed him when he least expected.

Ike knew this much: that until he entered the shrine and sat among other men and looked his uncle in the face and spoke words that would shake off the nervousness in his voice and dislodge the doubt in his heart, until he peered at the statue itself and remained steely, he could afford no sense of victory.

The twin emotions of elation and terror tussled within him as he walked. He was aware of the irony of hastening to see an uncle he would betray in a matter of days.

Betray! The word stung. But Ngene was no longer what it used to be, a war deity. The warriors of Utonki had not fought a war in more than a hundred years. In fact, there were no warriors to speak of.

Years ago, before he traveled to America, Ike had listened, captivated, as a frail old man recounted the story of Utonki's last war—a short-lived campaign to punish the people of Amanuke whose fishermen had encroached on the Utonki River.

"The fight lasted only a day," the bent warrior recalled through fits of coughing. "Our warriors were so fierce that we wasted the enemy's blood." He exposed yellowed teeth in a sly nostalgic smile. "The next day, we gathered at the glade of Ngene to gird ourselves for another battle. We found ourselves suddenly surrounded by soldiers in peak hats, their guns trained on us. Then a white man stepped forward and asked for our leader. Ataa, our greatest warrior, stood up. In battle, pellets bounced off his body. Machetes grazed him, but they could never scathe him. A warrior of his stature had not been seen in Utonki for many, many moons. The white man took him away, and he never returned, alive or dead, to Utonki. The white man also gathered and hauled away our guns and machetes. He said the queen who ruled his country was now also our ruler. This woman we'd never seen—and who had never seen us—had declared that the river no longer belonged to us. She'd ruled that any stranger who wished could come and fish in it." He bared his teeth again. This time, the smile was baleful, a thing born by pain.

As Ike recalled that story, he felt that Ngene was now no more than a retired god, a slumberous deity, in limbo. Its decline began on that day when the white man burst upon Utonki's warriors and showed his superior hand.

Or perhaps Ngene was always a shirker, a dozer at his duty post, except that the warriors of Utonki did not know it. Else, how could it have failed to sniff out the white man's ambush? On its watch, how could the white man's army have crept upon the spears and guns of Utonki and crippled them?

He calculated the uncertain cost of spiriting off Ngene against the certain advantage of an assured windfall. True, the deity's disappearance would propel Osuakwu into a state of shattering grief, but what of it? He thought about the once-upon-a-time when every living soul in Utonki, man, woman, and child, paid obeisance to Ngene. That time was now a vanished memory. Today, most of the people had become Christians. They had traded in their war deity for the one whose love was so overpowering that He assented to being impaled. Ike pictured Ngene as a deity staring with dejection at the backs of its former followers flocking to churches—and to charlatans like Uka.

Mark Gruels had argued that, in a postmodern world, a god that didn't travel was dead. There was a ring of truth to it, perhaps a chic kind of ring, but he found it comforting enough. In an age when gods must travel or die, he, Ike, would become the instrument to refuel Ngene. It had fallen to him to show the world to Ngene, stuck too long in Utonki, and Ngene to the world. He pictured a party that would be thrown on the marvelous lawns of some swanky home to celebrate the acquisition of Ngene. It would be an extraordinary affair, the biggest debut party, graced by all the big collectors. They'd cast killing eyes of envy at the lucky new owner of Ngene, an African god of war.

A film of sweat spread over Ike's face. He searched in the pockets of his pants for a handkerchief. Finding none, he ran a palm across his slick forehead and then rubbed the sweat between his hands.

He looked at the lump of his shadow, then remembered a game he used to play as a child, trying to outwit his shadow. He would stand stock-still until he was certain his shadow had been lulled to inattentiveness. Then he'd suddenly sprint, feint, or bob. Like the game with the mirror, it amazed him that, whatever his gambit, he never was able to shake off his shadow. It clung to him with tenacity, impossible to elude.

"Who do I greet?" asked a woman in a high-pitched voice.

Squinting against the glare, Ike made out a woman with a woven basket delicately balanced on her head. He acknowledged her greeting with a smile.

"I bet you don't remember me," said the woman.

He didn't remember her name, but he *knew* her story. She was the widow of a truck driver who'd died years ago in an accident the week before she gave birth to their first child, a son. The baby had been born a spitting image of his father, complete with a scar above his left eyebrow, an exact copy of a scar on his father's face. People marveled at the resemblance. It meant, they said, that the man's death was premature, it had not been cleared in the spirit world; the accident that claimed his life was the work of some spiteful, malevolent *dibia*. His son's uncanny resemblance meant that the man had reincarnated.

As the story played out in Ike's mind, he suddenly remembered her son's name. "You're Obiajulu's mother," he said.

"You know me," she said exultantly, smiling. Then the smile disappeared. "You must have heard," the woman said, as if the words themselves bore light. "Obiajulu left me."

"Ah-ah!" was all he could say, as if a ballast of heat had hit him.

It was then that he noticed the funereal blackness of the woman's wrapper.

"Obiajulu became a truck driver, just like his father. *They've* taken him away from me. The truck he was driving ran into a ditch. He was thrown out, and the truck fell on him. I saw my son's body, crushed like pulp. It's less than two months ago that we put him in the earth."

Sorrow swelled his head. "*Ndo,*" he said, hurrying away.

"Ooh." She sighed in acknowledgment.

Death seized his thoughts. Dead, dreary things flickered into his eyes. The caked, clayey earth bespoke death. A hardy slab, untouched by rain, the earth seemed baked in some radial oven. Death presented its awful face in the charred bark of trees. It loomed in the scalding rage of the very air. Its scent laced the air, giving it the reek of turned earth and dead, rotted leaves.

CHAPTER FOURTEEN

Something twisted inside Ike's heart the moment he faced Osuakwu's homestead and the detached oval structure to the left that was the shrine. Freshly polished, the shrine's earthen wall glowed. Much of the wall was decorated with *uli* drawings, a labyrinth of wriggly lines and loopy geometric patterns. Ike made out a river, two sacred pythons—one curled up, in repose, the other stretched out, in motion—a swarm of fish, and numerous portraits of cheery people standing or squatting in canoes afloat on the river.

Two cars were parked outside the grounds. Both cars gleamed in their white exterior and ash interior. One was a Mercedes-Benz, the other a Toyota 4Runner. Ike walked so close that his arm grazed the Mercedes. In the front seats of both cars sat a driver and a police officer, their seats reclined, eyes shut in indolent slumber.

Ike crouched and entered the low open eaves that served as the shrine's entrance. The transition from the glare of sunlight to the shadowy dimness of the shrine left him unseeing. A twinkle of motes swarmed before his eyes, tinted gray. There were several men in the shrine—their voices and silences touched him—but he was too blind to tell them apart.

"Osuakwu!" he hailed, looking in the direction of a figure in a reclining chair.

"Who am I greeting?" asked the man. The voice was unmistakable, a raunchy baritone he immediately recognized as his uncle's.

"Who are we greeting?" the other voices echoed.

Osuakwu's voice was warm, the others' genial. Reassuring voices. Ike had been wound tight by fear, but now he had to let that fear uncoil and seep away.

"Osuakwu!" he greeted again.

"Eeh!" his uncle replied. "Who greets me?"

The air reeked of gin and palm wine. Ike's sight had been restored; the fuzziness dispelled. In a furtive move, he flashed his eye to the right-hand corner where stood the wooden statue of Ngene. Then he hastily looked away. He looked about him, relieved to be able to make out the human forms.

"Does your own son have to announce his name?" he teased. "It's Ike. Ikechukwu."

Osuakwu was splayed out in a cane chair. He sprang awake as Ike announced himself, then made an exaggerated motion of wiping at his eyes. "Who am I seeing?" he said. "Did you say Ikechukwu?"

"Osuakwu," Ike greeted.

In silence the other men observed the re-acclimatization between the chief priest and his nephew.

"My eyes are not lying to me, then?" Osuakwu asked. He wiped at his eyes again. "It's not a dream I'm dreaming?" He extended a hand.

Ike chuckled, then rushed forward to take the hand.

Osuakwu's hand was frayed and wrinkled, like worn leather. His grip was strong, his hand scabby. He held on, swinging Ike's hand from side to side, in no hurry to let go. He muttered, "My son, my son," as if in time to the rhythm of the swinging hand.

The old man still boasted a full head of hair, cut evenly low, lush in its absolute whiteness. His exposed torso was chafed and scaly but seemed otherwise sinewy and invigorated.

"Osuakwu, are you going to eat that hand?" teased one of the men.

"It's as if he doesn't know that our hands are also itching to be shaken," another said.

"Release the hand," another admonished lightheartedly.

There was an uproar of laughter.

"I see you're all about to die of envy," Osuakwu said. "You're all threatening to die if I don't let you touch my son's hand. Yes, all of you are hungry to touch this hand softened by the air in the white man's country. Will you all die if I say you won't shake this hand? Well, then, start digging your graves. This son of mine won't shake your shitty hands. Not today. If you're dying to shake hands, then seek out *efulefu* like yourselves. Go shake fellows whose hands are dry and withered, like yours."

The men cackled with laughter. Osuakwu said to Ike, "Better shake their hands, Son, or an owl's chilling hoot will not let me sleep a wink tonight. If you don't shake them, they'll send their witch-wives to suck my blood tonight."

Laughter resounded within the shrine.

"Don't mind Osuakwu," one of the men said to Ike. "He speaks so easily about witches because he knows no witch dare fly near his house. Any witch that dares, dies."

"You've spoken the truth," Osuakwu concurred. "But that doesn't mean you won't poison my drink if I deny you my son's hand. Or use *nsi* to blind my eyes."

Four of the nine men were about the chief priest's age. The rest were much younger. The older men's faces were rife with wrinkles, their teeth crusted with yellow plaque. Each man asked if Ike knew him. He remembered most of them by face and knew five by name. There was Iji, the sharp-tongued old jester who specialized in mongering scandal. There was Akwuniko, the sinewy middle-aged man with vein-lined hands who carried the Ijele masquerade. There was Man Mountain Polycarp, a spry, bearded mini-giant of a man, a retired driver for a department store in Port Harcourt. A fiery labor unionist, Polycarp used to dazzle youngsters with tales of heroic worker strikes. He also relished telling stories about a man called Karl Marx, a name he pronounced as *Kalu Mazi*. "He was the greatest friend of workers and poor people in the world," the driver would say. His face set in awe, he added: "And you've never seen a beard as bushy as Kalu Mazi's. His beard is in the *Guinness Book of World Records* because it was proved that he had the biggest beard in world history." There was Agbusi, Osuakwu's assistant in priestly duties. Agbusi was a gourmand of legendary status; his waking hours were occupied with eating and drinking, punctuated only by the intermittent moments when he talked. There was Jideofo, a willowy, light-skinned man whose red Volvo Ike vividly remembered. Jideofo passed himself off as a diviner, but others in the community had unflattering things to say about that claim. They dubbed him a failed trader turned scam artist. Some said he was an outright fraudster. There was a story that he'd fleeced a well-heeled Hausa businessman in the northern city of Jalingo and then fled the city in time as the fuming dupe closed in on him both with police and a private hit squad. Such was Jideofo's guile that he easily evaded the hunters hot on his heels. Some said he was the boss of a gang of armed robbers who menaced highways, far and near. It was rumored that he was impotent. This, despite—or indeed because of—his succession of wives and harem of paramours. His public fondness for women, his detractors said, was a mask, meant to leave the impression that he was a virile lecher. There was even a story that he'd been an affluent widow's gigolo. The woman had pampered him, taking care of his material needs in expectation of his devoted amorous attention. Jideofo had cheated on her for several years before she finally found out. Discovering his plan to marry a glamorous young woman, the distraught widow had cast a spell of impotence on him. Some claimed that Jideofo was a womb swindler. He'd procured some charm from an Indian mystic for his malevolent purpose. He married a woman long enough to raid her womb, scouring it for all its ova. He mystically turned the harvested ova into a wealth-generating magic. He then sent his hapless victims away, barren for life.

"Sit down," Jideofo said, flashing a disarming smile. He slid aside, pressing his body against the wall, to make room on the raised platform. Ike felt a brief fear, but calm quickly returned. He accepted the offered spot, sandwiched between Jideofo and Agbusi.

"*Nno*," Osuakwu said.

"*Nno. Nno*," the others chorused, welcoming Ike.

Eyes bathed Ike. Beads of sweat rolled from his armpits. A croaky note pierced the silence. Ike craned his neck, searching for the source of the sound. Jideofo stood up and rifled through his trousers, producing two sleek cell phones. Brow creased, he inclined the ringing phone to the light. Finally pressing the phone against his ears, he shouted, "Chief Jideofo here." As he carried on a loud conversation, the other men talked in muted tones.

"A great friend of mine," Jideofo said with a flourish when he was done talking. "He's interested in running for the Senate and wants me to *see* if the road is clear."

"They are all rogues, these politicians," said one of the men.

"All they know is grab, grab, grab," said another. "They grab whatever is within sight."

"And a lot of what's not in sight," the first man added.

"Let's not deceive ourselves," Jideofo said in a magisterial tone. "Who among us will spit out the sugar that is put on our tongue?"

His challenge was met by a spattering of inarticulate grunts and muttered protests.

"Let's not lie to ourselves," he insisted, slipping the two phones back in his trouser pockets. "Everybody likes his sugar."

"But the thing that is sweet also kills," one of the men said.

"We have to break a kola nut," Osuakwu announced, stilling the argument.

He washed his hands in an earthen ewer, then selected a kola nut from a wooden bowl. He shifted in his chair, his gaze focused on the statue. The nut cradled in his fingers, he began to make invocations, fluidly moving from ritual language to proverbial statement.

"Ngene, you're the hand of splendor, the hand of riches! You're the breast that suckles the baby! Crab's head that baffles the world! Ngene, you said you prefer scrambling to sharing. It's that scrambling that we've started already. When it comes to talk, any man can boast he's the equal of another. It's in the test of strength that we know the man of valor from the weakling. Ngene, you're the one who swallowed the thing that swallowed an elephant. You're the one who pried off game from the lion's jaws. The majesty of the lion and the majesty of the man of wealth are of a kind. You're the lion that guards the hearth. The lion may be alive or it may be dead, but may no man pull its tail. Do we scold a lion to his face? We throw words at a lion asleep in his lair; when the lion awakens, his slanderer must fall silent. The brave man goes to war, but the coward owns the story. A brave warrior is saluted twice, once in life and once in death. Ngene, you're the chief warrior among deities. The hunter may be brave, but can he bare his eyes to the porcupine's quills? The mouth said the head should be cut; when the head is cut, the mouth goes with it. Ngene, you're the *ukwa* pod, full of amazements. At birth, the pod is as small as a baby's thumb. Mature, it's heavier than a man's head. Falling from a tree, the pod smashes the tortoise; rolling, it squashes the python; the old woman stoops to heave it up and falls squat on her bottom; speared open, it smears the hand with sticky, slippery sap. Ngene, you said if your enemy sues for peace, then you become a dove; provoked, you become a hawk. Pushed to fight, you spare no foe. You said if your foe stands in front, you will afflict his front; if he stands behind, you will menace his back. You said it's not good when a man eats *igbagwu* and eyes *akpu*. Ngene, you're that flood that defies swimming. You're the deluge that razes ramparts. Your rage sweeps away the homestead."

Osuakwu paused, his face set in the cast of a man in the throes of deep mysteries. His rib cage swelled and contracted from the exertion of an invocation spoken with force and rapidity. The torrent of words had struck Ike with a mixture of awe and an oppressive sense of terror. It was as if Osuakwu had sloughed off a familiar identity to become a different being, human still, but only barely. The transformation was most evident in Osuakwu's eyes.

Ike shook with fear at his uncle's eyes. They'd assumed a vapid, strangely distracted quality. They seemed able to pierce the membrane of secrets concealed in Ike's heart. They could penetrate his remotest thoughts and grasp his invisible schemes. It was as if they could discern the invisible hieroglyphics of desire embossed in his soul. They seemed no longer capable of functioning like ordinary eyes. It was as if they no longer focused on things with fixity and solidity.

Sweat ringed Osuakwu's eyes. Streaks of it coursed down his face, then dropped onto his shoulder and bare chest. He surveyed the room. His frightful, vapid eyes settled briefly on each man's face. Their blank gaze seemed at once unseeing and all seeing. Eyes that plumbed beyond the surface, drilled past the superficiality of concreteness. Ike felt dazed as those eyes gazed at him. He could hear the sound of his chest exploding inside him. He began to feel drowsy.

Another phone began to ring, the tone a vaguely familiar melody. Osuakwu grabbed a sleek, black phone from a low bamboo table. "Allo!" he barked, a disconcerted look on his face. He told the caller to call back, he was in the midst of breaking a kola nut, and then hung up.

The intruder dismissed, Osuakwu held the kola nut to his face, his eyes trained on it. He spoke in a less fevered voice, his tone calmer. "Ngene," he said, "when the sun blazes, we know it's time to offer you the nut of noon. The palm of a hand cannot conceal a pregnancy. The palm does not conceal the sun. We beg you to come and eat this nut. May other deities of Utonki come and take their share. Our fathers, your nut is here. May the powers embedded in the earth come and take their seat. The mysteries that inhabit the rivers, come for your due. A good cheek should never be slapped."

"*Isee!*" chorused the men.

Osuakwu continued: "It is no trouble to hand a gourd to a monkey. The question is, how do you get the gourd back?"

"The truth!"

"He who wants to be like an eagle should not fly with turkeys."

"*Isee!*" the men punctuated.

"The sighting of a deer surpasses the killing of it. The doe and her offspring wear the same skin. A masked spirit always sets its sight on sunset."

"It's as you say!"

"Surprise is what defeats a warrior, yet surprise is the test of a warrior."

"Eh!"

"Our meal is cooked. We're only waiting for it to be taken down from the fire."

"*Isee!*"

"May our eyes not see what has never been seen. And may we never have a story we can't find words with which to tell."

"*Isee!*"

"May we be like the sun, shining on friend and foe alike. May we be like wind, traveling the world without any foe to bar the door."

"*Isee!*"

"May we be like truth because truth is like noon."

"*Isee!*"

"Truth is naked."

Lifting his face, Osuakwu cast his eyes at the rafters. Then he continued: "Chukwu, you who hold the sky, we offer baskets filled with thanks. You who nestle your head on the clouds and use the earth for a footstool, we offer you kola nut. You created the coconut and gave it water to drink. We pray that you may give us the luck of the coconut. The tree whose breaking crack we hear, may it not fall on our heads."

"*Isee!*"

"You have looked after our son here," he said, motioning in Ike's direction. "You guided him as he traveled through seven seas and seven hills to return to us. You made sure that his toes struck no stone or stump. We thank you for being awake when we sleep."

"*Isee!*"

"May we not die premature deaths; instead, may our troubles be limited to pangs of hunger. A man with life will find food to put in the stomach. If death doesn't kill the penis, it soon eats bearded meat."

"*Isee!*" the men exclaimed, chuckling.

"May we never be afflicted by ten malefactors at once."

"*Isee!*"

"Chukwu, we look up to you in the clouds, and we show you the nut in our hand. You should eat in wholes that we may eat in bits."

"*Isee!*"

"May we not be like yesterday, for yesterday shrivels and dies. May we be like tomorrow, because tomorrow is never exhausted."

"*Isee!*"

"May we not resemble the path to the firewood den; the path is abandoned as soon as the den boasts no wood. Instead, may we be like the path to the spring; the path is forever trod by human feet because a spring never dries up."

"*Isee!*"

"When I chew and spit on a neighbor's chest, may he not chew and spit into my eye."

"*Isee!*"

"May fish have life and may the river have life."

"*Isee!*"

"He who pollutes a stream must remember that he drinks from the same stream."

"*Isee!*"

"Our people, may this nut bring us the good things we dream about. And may it chase off the evil things our enemies dream for us."

"*Isee!*"

"May my guest not stifle me; when he leaves, may he not have a hump."

"*Isee.*"

"Our people, we shall live."

"*Isee!*"

Osuakwu broke the nut. He spliced two tiny pieces and threw one at the statue, the other outside. He put the other lobes in a wooden bowl. Suddenly, his eyes widened in excitement. Gazing at the lobes, he wore an expression of intense fascination. "Look," he said, leaning forward so that Ike could see the bowl. "They've given us four lobes! Four, for the four market days—*Eke, Oye, Afo, Nkwo.* Four, the sign of prosperity. It means that hunger will never dog you; your journey will always be filled with success."

Ike's eyes flitted toward the statue, and he quickly withdrew them. He smiled wanly at his uncle, struck by the cold irony in the old man's prophecy.

A puff-faced man called Don Pedro was the youngest in the circle. Standing up, he spliced the four lobes into smaller pieces. He held out the bowl to Osuakwu. The priest pinched a piece and began to chew slowly. When it came his turn, Ike pitched a piece of kola nut in his mouth and crunched it down. Its sharp bitterness made him smart.

"So you still know how to eat kola nut?" Iji asked.

"Why not?" Osuakwu said, frowning. "If Ikechukwu has forgotten how to eat kola nut, do you think he would have found his way back home? Next thing, you're going to ask if he still eats *akpu* and *ofe onugbu.* That a man lives among white people doesn't mean he's become a white man."

"Osuakwu, let's thank Chukwu that our son here is not like *ofeke* who flies away to any new song," said Agbusi. "I tell you: some of our sons and daughters, once their feet touch the white man's soil, forget their hearth. One of them came home recently and told his mother that he no longer ate *akpu.* It smells, he said, forgetting that the sweetness of *akpu* is in its smell. And he said he no longer liked *ofe onugbu*—it was too bitter. When his father offered him palm wine, the rump turned up his nose. The wine was dirty, he said. For food, he ate uncooked leaves! Uncooked leaves, as if white people had turned him into a goat. He even took to speaking to his parents in the white man's tongue, even though neither his father nor his mother ever broke a slate or learned ABC. He spoke through his nose, too, just like the white man! That's why I say, let's thank Chukwu that our son here still knows the ways of his people."

"The man you described is *efulefu*," said Osuakwu. "Mark my words, *efulefu*. He's the type who would sell a parcel of land and buy a mat. There's a difference between *efulefu* and *nwa afo*. My son here came from good loins; he's *nwa afo*. He may go from here to the moon, but he won't ever forget the path back to his home. Where he stands, no *efulefu* can stand beside him."

Ike sat with a strained smile as his uncle and the shrine's habitués praised him and castigated mimics of white ways. Seizing on a lull in the seesaw, Ike said, "Osuakwu, I didn't know you had a cell phone."

His uncle laughed. "I have two. A man must dance the dance that reigns in his time. The dance of today is cell phone." He pronounced the words as *cellu phony*. "Every puppy now carries one. That's the latest thing *oyibo* brought."

"I would have been calling you from America."

"It's not too late to start. *Tabu gboo*," Osuakwu replied. "I'll give you my numbers. and you can start calling." He paused and rubbed his palms together, producing a soft chafing sound. "Masiolu told me that you'd like something to eat. They say that surprise is the doom of the warrior. Still, I think both Masiolu and her mates can scrape up something to fill your stomach."

The mention of food triggered long-forgotten memories of prandial delights at his uncle's. In his younger days, Ike used to salivate at the prospect of eating at his uncle's. Osuakwu's wives—there were four of them, the youngest younger than Ike—spoiled him. The four women were such excellent cooks that Ike used to marvel at his uncle's culinary luck. When Ike ate at his uncle's, each wife brought a cuisine, sometimes two. Primed by the aroma, Ike's appetite always roared, keen as parched earth. He'd fall to with gusto, his shoulder looped over the variety of steaming meals, head fixed on the mini-banquet. He looked up only after his belly was bloated, stretched to a bursting tautness, so that the least movement was agony.

One part of him yearned for that, but a different part of him demurred. Nostalgic memories imperiled his mission and had to be kept at bay.

"I'm not hungry," he said. He clasped his hand, steeling himself against the quest that agitated within.

"But you told Masiolu you were going to eat."

"I spoke in jest."

"In jest?" Osuakwu quizzed. "Is that what your white hosts have taught you, not to eat food but to make jokes about it?" He scrunched up his face and regarded his nephew. "That little tummy of yours looks unfed to me. Have your white hosts been starving you?"

"I eat," Ike protested playfully, rubbing his unprepossessing paunch with wide exaggerated arcs of the hand.

"Well, I know that Masiolu was putting a few things together for you. You have to go into the house and see what she's prepared. Even if you're not hungry, dip a finger in the soup and lick it. We have all kinds of drinks here, but it's better to have oil in your stomach first. Go and see Masiolu."

Ike rose, relieved that the decision had been made for him, and headed for Osuakwu's homestead.

CHAPTER FIFTEEN

ke returned to the shrine forty minutes later. He had overindulged in a delicious meal of pounded *akpu* and *ora* soup. "Did Masiolu find something for you to eat," Osuakwu asked, "or did she send you away hungry?"

Ike gasped and rubbed his taut stomach.

Osuakwu and the other men laughed at the gesture. "*Odi nma,*" Osuakwu said, "now you're ready to drink. Don Pedro, give him what he wants to drink. We have gin, we have beer, and we have palm wine."

"Gin," Ike said.

Osuakwu reached to the left of his cane chair and picked up a bottle of Schnapps. He used his hand to wipe off a thin film of dust from the green bottle. He twisted its cap, and the muscle in his arm tautened until it came open. He rose, holding his waist at a slightly bent angle, then walked to the statue.

"Ngene, we come with something to drink," he said. He tipped the bottle and let three drops fall on the statue's head. Straightening himself, he walked to the shrine's wide entrance. "Our fathers, we have something to drink." Then he allowed a tiny stream of gin to drop to the earth. Osuakwu handed the bottle to Don Pedro, then reclaimed his chair.

Pedro picked out a large glass tumbler from a clutter on a carved table. He raised the tumbler, blew twice into it, and then flipped it. He handed the cup to Ike and readied the bottle, pouring until the tumbler was nearly full.

Ike brought the glass to his lips and braced himself. The gin's fiery power exploded in his mouth. He winced, then sucked in air.

Osuakwu burst out in laughter, slapping his thighs. "Has it woken you up?"

Ike nodded.

"That's why it's called you-push-me, I-push-you," Jideofo said.

"Hot water that only strong heads can carry," Osuakwu said. "Don Pedro, pour me some wine—or did I throw a stone at your father?"

Pedro laughed, then obliged.

Ike gathered himself and downed another helping. His tongue, better prepared, was less scalded. Impressed, Osuakwu said, "Now, you've shown yourself a match for it." The other men spoke their praises.

They fussed over Ike for a while, then drifted to other topics. One man talked about a land dispute that had wound through the courts for nine years. And then the judge, having accepted a bribe, had ruled for the impostor. Another man related the scandal of a young woman from a neighboring town who had eloped with a man, an osu. The young woman's grief-stricken mother had drowned herself in a well.

"The young man must know a special way to pleasure her thighs," Don Pedro suggested. "A *dibia* must have given him a powerful love potion."

"Yes," Iji concurred. "I know a *dibia* whose potion has never failed. Not once! Touch-and-follow, that's what it's called. Touch a woman with it, and she'll cling to you as a snail clings to a leaf."

"Would this charm work on white women?" asked one of the younger men, casting a mischievous glance in Ike's direction.

"*Kpom kwem!*" Iji said, as if affronted by the very question. "Are white women not women? Let me tell you, a woman, whether black or white, carries the same thing between her thighs." He looked at Ike, seeking corroboration. Ike kept a straight face, as if oblivious. Osuakwu began to laugh, and the others joined as well.

Ike leaned back, his head pressed against the cool earthen wall. The glass of gin held in both hands, he sipped intermittently and squirmed as the men traded ever-edgier stories. Sometimes a verbal fight would break out between two or more of the men. The antagonists trumpeted each other's scandals. How long, Ike wondered, before one of them went past the point of restraint and threw a fist? But it never got to fisticuffs.

A dull pain sat in Ike's lower belly. He'd made a mistake, he realized, by drinking such strong stuff after eating spicy *ora* soup and a bowl of pounded yam. He felt giddy; the edges of things seemed to shift, testing his sight. Gin fumes now wafted from within him, the air in his nostrils leaden.

"There's nothing worse than a man who buries his senses in drink," Jideofo said.

"Except a man who raids wombs," Iji riposted.

The two men seemed experts at needling each other, their taunts acerbic and casual at once. Were they, Ike wondered, as tipsy as he? Did alcohol beat a conga in their full, sated palates? He drank again. Then he stole a glance at his uncle. If Osuakwu was worried, he hid it well, his face imperturbable. He was sunk in his cane chair, hands twined behind his head, eyes slightly shut. He wore a wistful, incurious expression, as though indifferent to the bitter propulsion of stories and insults.

Iji was about to talk, but Osuakwu's voice interjected. "Ikechukwu, the journey that brought you home, is it a good one?"

Osuakwu sat up, hands clasped close to his body, his shoulders hunched. A tremor rocked Ike's body. He felt drowsy, like a man shaken awake as he tottered over a gorge. He opened his mouth but remained mute. The words welling up his throat were a lump he could neither swallow nor emit. He nodded.

An odd silence descended on the shrine. The silence was eerie and pregnant, as if the air in the shrine stood still, straining. Ike heard his heart beating, leaping for his throat.

"*Nno,*" Osuakwu said, once again welcoming his nephew.

"*Da alu,*" Ike said.

"*Nno. Nno,*" the rest of the company echoed.

Ike nodded to his right and left.

"I welcomed you once, and I welcomed you again," Osuakwu continued. "Yet, you're a son to me—your father's mouth followed mine to suck from the same breast. You're my son and this *obi* is yours. You can walk in and out of here at will, and there won't be anybody in the world to throw a suspicious eye in your direction. Why then do I persist in welcoming you with the anxiety of words I should reserve only for strangers? One reason is that you have come from a long, long distance. You've crossed wilds and seas to arrive in Utonki. So we must tell you *nno.* But there's another reason." He paused and raised his eye to Ike, as if it was up to the younger man to unravel the mystery. "Did you tell Nwanyi Eke you were coming to see me?"

Nwanyi Eke was the name Osuakwu called Ike's mother. "No," Ike said.

"Aha," Osuakwu said, throwing up his hands in vindication. "If you had told her you were coming here, she would have thrown herself in your path. Tell me, am I lying?"

Ike gazed silently.

"Your mother is my wife. I accompanied your father to go and talk about her. I was there—at the head—the day we asked her people to let her live among us. If I had uttered one word of doubt, just one word, your father would not have proceeded. That's how close we were, your father and I. Did your father not tell you that he and I were not the only fruits of our mother's womb?"

Ike shook his head.

"He didn't?" Osuakwu asked again.

"No."

"Well, you're hearing it today. If your father didn't tell you, I can tell you because you're also my son. Nne had had two daughters and one son before I was born. Each of those children went back to the spirit world soon after birth. I came next and lived. Four years after I suckled Nne's breast, your father came. Your father and I were close. You should know that. Even after your father joined the church of Father and I answered the call to serve Ngene, we remained close. True, your father tried to talk me into abandoning Ngene, but it was all the talk of brothers. I would ask him if he didn't see that Ngene fed me well. I told him Ngene fed me yams and cocoyams, chicken and turkey, goats and cows. I teased him about the tiny wafer Father pasted on his tongue. How could such a wafer feed a grown man like me? My brother and I were like Teeth and Tongue, inseparable. Yes, sometimes Teeth leaves Tongue bloodied. Sometimes they would quarrel, but nobody ever heard that Teeth and Tongue went their separate ways. No!

"Ten and one years ago, Death sneaked in at night and took my brother. I don't think there was anybody more grieved by his death than I. I rolled myself on the ground and cried. I cried in a way that a man doesn't cry unless his world has been broken in two. If it was possible to fight Death, I would have girded myself and tried. But I know the story of the king who hired two medicine men to ward off Death. What happened? Death killed the two healers and struck terror in the king's heart! Do we frown at Death? If we screw up our face at Death, it poaches another. Do we flee from Death? If we try to flee, Death strikes down another and leaves us with two funerals. If I could have sacrificed myself to Death in order to retrieve my brother from its clutch, I would have done that. I had to check my grief only because I realized it fell to me to help Nwanyi Eke to hold herself together. For several years, I tried to help your mother mend her broken life. Every morning, after beating the gong in greeting to Ngene, I went to see Nwanyi Eke, to inquire after her health. Each night, right after eating, I visited her again to make sure her day had gone well. She seemed pleased with my visits. Once, when *iba* had beaten me down with its fever and I couldn't go, she hastened here, her face scarred with fear. For the three days I was flattened by *iba*, Nwanyi Eke joined my wives to prepare me meals filled with sharp leaves.

"Everything changed three years ago. I went one morning to inquire after your mother's health, but found the doors and windows barred. I knocked and knocked, but the door remained shut. I went away, thinking she must have left early for the farm. I returned that night, but there was nobody to open the door. I feared that something dreadful might have happened, but a passing neighbor assured me he'd seen her, hale and hearty, earlier that evening. I went home. The next morning, I went back to see Nwanyi Eke. I met a shock that I've never shared with any breathing person. When I knocked on the door and said my name, Nwanyi Eke began to howl from inside the house. She called me the very devil. She said

Nne and I had killed her husband, and now I wanted to kill her
as well. She shrieked that Nne and I should stop attacking her at
night or her God would clip our wings. She shouted that I should
take my demons and go home. She cried that she was now covered
with the blood of Jesu Christi."

Osuakwu paused, his voice nearly broken. Ike glanced up. His
uncle's hands, clasped together, trembled. The old man's chest
heaved. Ike lowered his head and sniffed the gin, his emotions chaotic, anger mingled with shame. His eyes had misted up; the gin in
his hand transformed into a small pool of tears.

"Ikechukwu, my ears heard words no mouth should ever utter.
For a man to be accused before the world of killing his own
brother, a mother blamed for the death of her own son—no words
can be more bitter to the ear! I left your mother's home and ran
as fast as my bones could carry me to tell Nne what my ears had
heard. Before I could open my mouth, Nne began to tell me her
own horrors. The evening before, your mother had stood at Nne's
threshold and called her all manner of names. She called Nne a
sucker of blood and devourer of her son's flesh. She told Nne—the
mother of her husband—that death stalked her door. Are such
words spoken? Are they spoken even to one's enemy? *Tufia!*

"It was shortly after that I heard that a man had come to Utonki
and set up a mad church. And I learned that Nwanyi Eke had left
the church of Father and thrown herself, body and mind, into the
madness. She began to dance to the tune played by the *efulefu* who
said he was a man of God. Every mad thing the man said, she took
with two hands and put inside her bag. He told her that death was
on its way to call Nne home, but that Nne and I had used magic
to deflect the cold-fingered one to her husband. Are such things
heard? He told her, this *efulefu*, that we were now planning to kill
you as well as your sister. Does it not bite the ear to hear such

madness? Yet your mother opened her ears and let the madman pour it all in."

Suddenly silent, Osuakwu rocked himself forward and backward.

A lump blocked Ike's throat. His uncle's face was a portrait of pain. In the silence Ike could hear the sound of men breathing, waiting.

"Pour me more wine," Osuakwu said. Don Pedro rose to the task. Osuakwu drank lustily, head tipping ever backward until he had finished off the drink. He belched and wiped his lips. His features softened.

"I'm glad you came to see me. If news had reached me that you, my son, had come home and then went away without coming here, it would have killed my spirit. Listen, let me give you a message you must carry to Nwanyi Eke. Tell your mother you came to my *obi*. Tell her you tasted Masiolu's cooking, that you ate kola nut and drank gin—but your stomach didn't churn nor did your head ache. Tell her I didn't kill you." He paused and glanced around the roomful of faces. "Does a sane man kill somebody he must bury and mourn?" he asked.

"*Mba!*" chorused the others.

"*Mba!*" Osuakwu echoed. Shoulder raised, he filliped his fingers in a gesture of abhorrence. "But the madman who brought the church of dancers must be from a clan where mothers kill their own babies, where brothers slaughter brothers."

"Osuakwu!" a voice hailed from outside.

"Ogbuefi Okwuego," Osuakwu saluted in return.

All eyes turned to the shrine's entrance. A man shuffled in, old and stooped, steadying himself on a walking cane. He exchanged pleasantries with Osuakwu and the shrine's habitués.

"How were the people of the white country when you left them?" the man asked, turning to Ike.

"They were fine," Ike said.

Stabbing the floor for emphasis, the old man said, "You must wipe your eyes with two cuffs when you're dealing with white people. They're slippery as fish. They can kill you while smiling at you."

"Mind your words," Iji teased, "or Jideofo will soon ask why you speak as if white men were your drinking pals."

The old man stamped his walking stick on the floor. He scanned the room, then spoke to Iji. "There's nothing I don't know about white men. Don't forget, I met many of them in Burma. There's no trick a white man will bring today that will bewilder me. I've studied them front and back." He fixed his eyes once again on Ike. "What I tell you is this: look at a white man with the same eye a flutist casts toward a masquerade wielding a machete. Smile with him, play the flute for him—but never take your eye off him. Be alert so that when he brandishes the machete, you can flee! *Nno.*" He shook Ike's hand, then grunted as he lowered himself onto the sitting platform.

"*Da alu,*" Ike said, wincing from the fierce pressure of gas in his belly.

"I was talking to my son about the new church—"

The old man hissed, cutting into Osuakwu's speech. "Why not leave talk about the insane to the insane?"

Osuakwu smiled sadly. He addressed Ike in the reestablished silence.

"There's no wrong your mother hasn't heaped on my head. She said I was planning to make you the priest of Ngene after my bones have danced their last dance. I had to laugh at that one. A rump like me to choose for Ngene the man who will serve him? When the time comes that they look for me but I can't be found, Ngene will speak his mind about a new carrier. If he wants you, you must come home to serve him—or you'll fall into madness. That you're in the white man's country does not mean you can reject the call. When Ngene winks at a man, the man has no choice but to serve. When I was called, did I want to answer? No! Ask Ogbuefi Okwuego who just came in. He and I had just come back from Burma. Like other young men, my dream was to snatch one of the white man's jobs. Then I started fainting when the sky opened up and wept its waters. When they told me Ngene had called me, I told them to go and put their ears back on the ground, that I had other things I wanted to do with my life. They laughed and went away. My son, when I began to see the things I saw at night, I needed nobody to tell me to answer the summons. Ngene chooses his own carrier. If he wants you, you must leave everything else. If he doesn't, nobody can sneak you into the priest's chair. I, Osuakwu, won't dare. I can't!"

"Only a man who courts death would dare usurp a deity's voice," said the newly arrived old man.

Osuakwu ran a hand across his brow, sweeping up a pool of perspiration that dripped onto his thigh. Grabbing a raffia fan, he cooled himself with wide, strong arcs of the hand. He spoke while fanning, his speech set to the rhythm of his hand's wide motions. "My son, a stranger arrived in our midst with a basket of stories he plucked from the air—and he has used these to drive many apart. Nwanyi Eke gave her head to this bringer of mad tales. The man put poisonous seeds in her head. He told her that I, Osuakwu, am a wizard, that I suck the blood of my own brood. The seed of that tale germinated and tarred your mother's heart. It was as if she too had become a stranger.

"At first, I laughed it off. I was sure your mother would return to her senses; she would come to know that the stranger's stories were madness. I thought that the stranger would be found out, that one day we'd wake up to hear he'd fled from our midst. Our people say that if a profane act marks a year, it becomes part of custom. I've waited for your mother to come to my compound and say that what she said before she no longer says. It's been three years and Osuakwu is still waiting.

"Has the stranger tucked in his tail and fled? No. He's still here, his gut swelling by the day. More and more of our people are joining his madhouse. More and more are accusing their blood brethren of being killers and suckers of blood. They go to the stranger in droves—gorging on the very air he fouls with lies. Our noses have been rubbed in feces, but what are we to do? When a goat enters a homestead and urinates as well as defecates, why, it's already too late to shoo it off.

"Each day, this stranger tells his followers that Ngene is a fallen god. He boasts that his own God will come down one day in a ball of fire and consume Ngene."

"He told me that," Ike said.

"Oh, he did?" Osuakwu asked. "Then you know I haven't told a single lie. He wants to destroy Ngene. He doesn't know what happened to the first white man who dared fart in Ngene's face."

"You're talking about Sutanteeny?" the old man asked, his thick accent burdening "Stanton" with extra syllables.

"Yes. Ngene flicked him as one flicks a fly."

"That's the fate that awaits that rump that calls himself Uka," Iji said.

Osuakwu turned to Ike. "You're telling me that that grandson of an abductor has carried his madness to your ears as well?"

"Yes," Ike said. "He invited me over to his house. I came straight from his house to here."

"He speaks the words of a madman!" cried Don Pedro. "The swollen phallus boasts about teaching the thigh a lesson. But once discharged of its seeds, it collapses in a heap."

The men chuckled at the analogy. Ike felt a string of sweat tickle his spine. He took another swig.

Osuakwu sat erect in his chair, brow furrowed. Then he said to Ike, "Go outside and bring me a stone. The first stone you see."

A stone? Ike was mystified but in no mood to ask questions. As he struggled to stand, he noticed that his right leg had been deadened by a cramp. Worse, the gin combined with the heat had rendered him lightheaded. He stood up with effort, favoring his left leg. As he scuffed outside, his gait was unsteady, his head disoriented. The world spun madly about him. When he saw a stone, he steadied himself before bending over to dislodge and lift it from the soil.

"I have a question for you," Osuakwu said once Ike handed him the stone. "This stone you just fetched, is it alive or is it dead?" His face wore an earnest, expectant look.

Ike peered at his uncle, lost for words.

"You've gone to school, and you know more than all of us here. That's why I ask, that you may explain to us: is the stone dead or is it alive?"

Ike was tempted to launch into an exposition of the principles of animation and inanimateness, but held back. After a weighty pause, he said, "I'd say dead."

"You've answered well. You've spoken like the man of great learning that you are. But now, I have another question: If the stone is dead, how come it doesn't smell? And how come it isn't decaying?" He regarded Ike with a fixed look.

Ike swigged his gin, staring. After a while, he asked his uncle, "Are you saying the stone is alive, then?"

"Did you see me open my mouth? I asked you because you're the one with learning."

Ike had the sensation of drowning in a river of gin. It was as if, starting with his ankles, the drink had slowly risen to his knees, then his thighs, his waist, past his chest, and pressing to submerge the crown of his head. He said, "Maybe it's alive."

"Then why does it not breathe? Why does it not rise and flee when human feet are about to step on it? Why does it lie there, indifferent to storms and the punishing blasts of the sun?"

"I don't know," Ike said. It was less a confession than a plea to be spared further interrogation.

Osuakwu smiled. "Ngene and I are like this stone. If you guess we're dead, your guess is wrong. Yet, if you guess we're alive, your guess may also be wrong." He pointed at the statue. "That madman thinks Ngene is this carving from a tree. Ngene is a mystery deeper than what any man can understand. That mystery lives in the river itself that coils around Utonki. It is a river that provided our ancestors with both life and protection. That river is still doing its work today, even though the *oyibo* has come and turned today into yesterday, making a lion into a lamb. Can any man carry off a river in a basket?"

Ike shook his head.

"No," Osuakwu verbalized. "A river far surpasses the strength of a basket. Does fire consume a river?"

"No," Jideofo answered, speaking as Ike's uninvited proxy.

"No," Osuakwu echoed. "However fiery a fire, a river easily drenches it and snuffs out its rage. That's why Ngene and I are not a bit worried when a madman talks about a ball of fire."

"The only fire the crazed churchman knows is the heat of his own fart," said the old man.

The comment provoked an explosion of laughter. Ike, too, laughed, grateful.

Osuakwu waited until the laughter died down, then he addressed Ike: "Let me ask you, my son. This man who calls himself Pastor Uka, do you know anything about his God?"

Ike, drawing the glass of gin to his lips, shook his head.

"Well, I'll tell you. You see, when I first heard what the rump was telling his followers about Ngene, I said I would go and visit his God to lodge a complaint. But when I asked where his God was, I was told that it was invisible. My son, it's not good to have dealings with a god that is not visible. The spirit of Ngene is in the river, but its body is here, in this statue. Why did our ancestors insist that each god must have its wooden body in a shrine?"

"Tell me," Ike said.

"Open your ears and I will. In the days of old, when lizards were still in ones and twos, our ancestors knew that gods are not far from humans in kind. Like us, gods can fall asleep, shirking their responsibilities. Their heads can swell with pride. Filled with bitterness, they can turn against the very one who feeds them. Full of spite, gods can bite both foe and friend alike. Our ancestors knew this; that's why they insisted that gods must have bodies. You should ask me, why bodies?"

"Why bodies?" Ike asked.

"Because bodies die. Did you know that our people sometimes kill off a recalcitrant god?"

Ike had a vague sense of this practice, but he wanted to hear his uncle flesh it out. "They do?" he asked.

"Yes. When a deity leaves what it was asked to do and starts doing something else, when it turns on the community it's supposed to protect, or when it begins to thirst for too much human blood, the people snatch up its body—its wooden body—and set it afire at the boundary of the clan. That's one way of killing a god."

"So there's a second way?" Ike asked.

"Yes, in fact there's a simpler way. A deity is like you and me; it needs to eat and drink to live. That's why we offer sacrifices to deities. When a deity doesn't receive the kind of sacrifice it needs, it dies."

"These things are deep mysteries," said Iji.

"Yes," Ike said.

Osuakwu ran his wrist against his forehead, smudging the drop-lets of sweat. "My son, that's why, when they told me that your mother now belongs to a church whose god is invisible, I knew that there was trouble. I put my ears to the ground, curious about the madman who brought in this church. What I found out almost deafened my ears." Seeing two of the men whispering, he paused. He resumed when the whisperers ceased their muttering. "I found out that the man was born in Amanuke. I also found out Uka was not his real name."

"It isn't?" Ike asked with awakened curiosity.

"No. He chose that name, and he chose it to hide something. Listen and I'll peel it open for you. This madman's grandfather was a feared robber whose name was Okaa Dike—"

"Okaa Dike?" exclaimed the old man.

"He's Okaa Dike's grandson?" Iji asked, whistling his amazement.

"Yes, Okaa Dike," Osuakwu confirmed. "Most of you hear the name today, and it means nothing to you. That's because you're too young. But there was a time when you didn't mention the name Okaa Dike unless you were well fortified with *ogwu*. In his time, Okaa Dike struck terror in the hearts even of brave men. There was no barricade he could not breach, no fence he could not sneak through. He had one *ogwu* that was called Ikuku, because he could turn himself at will into wind. That way, he entered any barn and squeezed under-neath any barred doors. If Okaa Dike wanted to steal from you, you tried to stop him in vain. In his heyday, he was better known as Efi Epeka, for he could hoist a stolen cow on his shoulder and carry it a long distance to his home. Nor did he hide his nocturnal activities. Okaa Dike was known to send a message to his victims that he was in possession of their property. If you wanted your goods back, he gave you the option of trading in something else of value, or giving him the price he named. He openly boasted about his thieving. It was said that, once, a fellow robber challenged him to a contest to decide who had the superior prowess. The two decided to visit each other's home and steal whatever they could. Okaa Dike asked the other man to start. That night, while Okaa Dike slept, his adversary sneaked into his barn and stole two goats and some tubers of yam. The next morning, the successful robber thumped his chest, showed off his loot, and made a mockery of Okaa Dike. Okaa Dike thundered out in laughter at the other robber's boasts. 'My friend,' he asked in genuine surprise, 'this is the best you could do? You still steal goats and yams? Shows that your stealing arts are those of an infant.' That night, the other robber made certain that his cows, goats, yams, and other possessions were taken inside his hut. He then bolted down his door. Satisfied that Okaa Dike would be a frustrated prowler, the man went to sleep. When he awoke the next morning, he found himself in Okaa Dike's home! And Okaa Dike had also hauled home the man's two wives and all his children. That day, the whole world knew Okaa Dike was a robber without equal." Osuakwu paused again. A wicked grin lit up his face.

"Tell me how he ended up," Ike said. "How did he die?"

Osuakwu thrust his gaze at vacant space, his face screwed to an expression of unyielding nonchalance.

"Did he die a normal death?" Ike prodded.

Turning sharply, Osuakwu looked at his nephew. "A normal death?" he muttered, his forehead creased. "A man who didn't live normally, how could he die normally? But I haven't finished telling how he lived. When Captain Park, the white conqueror, arrived in these parts with his new ways and laws, Okaa Dike recognized him as a threat. It is said that he tried to rob the white man, but Captain Park proved that he knew what the old rogue knew. Okaa Dike thought hard and long and then decided it was best to befriend the white man. Their friendship paid off, for Okaa Dike was soon made a warrant chief, with power to judge cases among his people. Imagine making a thief into a judge—that's one of the ways *oyibo* muddied our water. Captain Park was like a man who doesn't know how a corpse was buried; such a man exhumes a corpse from the leg. You can guess what kind of judge the rogue became. He could make right wrong or wrong right. In his mouth, white became black; black turned white. You won only if you stuffed his pocket. If you depended on the straightness of your case—if you thought your case to be as clear as noon—then disappointment awaited you in this man's court. Two men appeared before Okaa Dike feuding over a bewitching damsel. The judge dismissed their claims, then forced the woman into his harem. In one land case, neither party saw fit to grease Okaa Dike's palm. He denied both claims and took the disputed land for himself! Once, he ambushed another beautiful woman on her way to the stream. He carried her home and ravished her. He swore to jail her husband if she let out a scream. That ambush became his undoing. The woman's husband knew everything there was to know about spells and malevolent charms. He pronounced a terrible curse on Okaa Dike. His male offspring would ever be wifeless. If they had children, it would be with women of the road, women who spread their thighs to the manhood of strangers."

Osuakwu's lips parted in a malicious smile. A whirl of thoughts crisscrossed Ike's mind. Head cradled in one hand, he secured his depleted glass in the other. He remembered how he'd been struck by the oddity of finding the pastor's home bereft of a wife's presence.

"You have seen the pastor?" Osuakwu asked.

Ike nodded.

"Then you've seen how old he is. A man his age without a wife—tell me that something isn't wrong there."

Iji cleared his throat fussily. "The man has changed his name, but he can't shake off his curse."

"And he can't," added Osuakwu with finality. "I don't care how much he bleats." To Ike, he asked, "Do you know he's been to jail?"

"Jail? No. What for?"

"Well, anything born of a snake will never fail to resemble a rope. He used to live and work in Lagos. He sneaked in at night and stole the money kept for the salary of fellow workers. He went to jail for five years. He fled the city after his discharge—too many people knew him there. He landed here and began his church of madness."

For a minute or two, Ike quietly digested the welter of information about the man he knew as Pastor Uka. Unable to decipher what was true, what concocted, he tottered between acceptance and doubt, illumination and lingering darkness. As he harvested heaps of details about the pastor's past, dim as well as remote, he was riled by an awareness of a decided slipperiness, an elusive quality to it all. The more stories he heard, the more questions were agitated in him. Some of the questions were fragmentary, unformed, impossible to articulate; others he chose not to ask. As his thoughts swelled and ran in disparate directions, he remembered a simpler question. "You haven't told me how Okaa Dike ended up," he said.

"How else? Dead!" Osuakwu said. "And at the hands of the white man."

"They quarreled?"

His uncle's tone was at once deadpan and oblique. "Captain Park found the rogue on top of his wife. Okaa Dike's charms could not still the fire from the white man's gun."

"And today, his snout of a grandson takes insane aim at Ngene,"

Jideofo said. "You can heal a madman, but you can never take away that occasional mutter from him."

Don Pedro took the bait. "Indeed it takes an insane man to threaten Ngene with fire. A child sees two fighters who're separated, and he hungers to fight."

Osuakwu's words scalded, but he spoke in a flat voice, free of bile. "The madman's mouth may crackle like the *ukpaka* pod, but when his eyes see something greater than madness, nobody need warn him to take to his heels. A child becomes sleepy only after he eats the thing that keeps him awake. Okaa Dike's grandson is a man blown about by the wind. An *efulefu*."

For some time, the old man seemed to drift in and out of sleep. Suddenly, his head snapped forward. He jerked awake, yawned, and began to speak.

"If *oyibo* had not spoiled the day, a man like him would never dare utter one word in the face of Ngene. He would not live to see another sunrise; his anus would have been sealed up for him."

"Do you think he's got away scot-free?" Osuakwu asked, a frown darkening his face.

"How can?" answered the old man. He took a moment and looked around the shrine. "Let me ask the young men here a question. Can any of you tell me the story of the village of Hiho?" He looked around, his gaze pausing questioningly on each younger person's face. "I didn't think you'd know," said the old man. "Do you know why? Because the story is older than you. Only Osuakwu and one or two others here can tell it. So listen.

"Once upon a time, there was a small, remote village in a patch where nothing remarkable ever happened. One day, the young men of the village met to talk about their village. Speaker after speaker said he was tired of living in a village where nothing grand ever happened. They resolved to do something dramatic, something that would put salt into their tasteless lives, something that would make the rest of the world hear about their small village. So they decided that all the villagers, men, women, and children, old and young, must gather to cut down an iroko tree. Once the tree began to topple over, all the villagers must line up and catch its massive trunk with their bare hands. At first, the village elders balked at this insane plan. The iroko, the mightiest of the mighty trees, was not to be caught by bare hands, they warned. But the young men were not about to accept the defeat of their dream. They insulted the elders, calling them corpses on stilts. Day and night, they taunted the oldies until, finally, each one of the elders agreed to queue up. Hearing about the plan, the village children were seized by fright. The iroko tree, they cried, would crush them into the dust. Again, the young men were not going to accept no from anybody. Puppies, they called the children. Puppy, puppy, puppy. Tired of being insulted, the children agreed to line up. The women wailed and said they were not up to catching an iroko tree with bare hands. They, too, were teased until they agreed to the plan. The appointed day came. The entire village, men, women, and children, old and young, stood in line. From early morning to late afternoon, sweat poured out of the young men who sawed at the majestic iroko. Finally, a crack warned that the tree had begun to fall. A shout went out to catch it. In unison, everybody in the village of Hiho raised a hand. As if rejecting their handshakes, the tree smashed their bodies and crushed their bones into the earth. Since then, no human voice has ever been heard in Hiho. But the village had given the world one big story. A big, cautionary story."

"That's what will happen to the madman who calls himself pastor," Osuakwu said. "He has thrust out a hand of challenge—and Ngene never shies away from a fight. If an adult lizard doesn't show what makes him an adult, children will roast him for their meal.

Uka may think his madness has fetched him profit, but let's wait. A house constructed with spittle is always demolished by dew."

Falling silent, he gazed vacantly, gnashing his teeth. He looked in time to see Ike draining off his gin.

"Give him more," Osuakwu said.

Ike made to protest, but Don Pedro was quick to the task, pouring until Ike made a motion of ducking his glass.

Ike cast a resentful eye at his refilled glass, as one might an intractable task. His stomach growled. As each moment passed, his body seemed to grow denser, and yet he was a man blanketed by a cloud.

If he was going to drink the gin, he had to drink it like a flagellant. He readied himself and threw back his heavy, swirling head. He twirled the liquid around in his mouth, letting it scald his gums. Then he swallowed in one brisk gulp. It was akin to pouring liquid fire down his gullet.

His legs chafed with the stiffness of cramps. Sitting still, he gently kneaded his thighs and calves. Gradually, the cramps lost their sizzling power. He rose to take his leave. For the first time, he looked fixedly at the statue, for inebriation had scuttled his scruples, emboldened his gaze. The statue—its white paint smudged with sacrificial blood—returned his stare with stiff indifference.

"You must visit again before you leave," his uncle said. "Masiolu has fed you today. My other wives must also cook for you."

"Yes," Ike said. He momentarily peeled his eyes from the statue. "I'll come again, in a day or two."

"Come the day after tomorrow, in the afternoon. You'll meet a man of learning who knows everything about John Stanton."

Ike brightened. "Stanton?"

"That's the one. None of us here had been born when this man arrived on the bank of River Utonki. He was the first man to challenge Ngene to a duel. A man who teaches at our big school has written the story of what became of him. That man will visit me here in two days. He's the man who rang me on the phone as I was breaking kola nut. I'll ask him to bring you a copy of his book. You know the story of what happened to the white man who trifled with Ngene. You will now read it in a book."

A shiver lashed Ike's body. His lips parted in a weary smile. He cast a sideward glance at the statue. He saw it—he could swear—wink at him, a quick, insidious wink.

He looked at his watch. "I have to go," he announced. Then a lie: "I'm expecting somebody."

He scrambled to his feet. Alcoholic fumes floated about in his head. He tried to stand still but had the sensation that the ground shifted, spinning slowly.

"Shake my hand again," Osuakwu requested.

"And ours too," Iji said.

Ike went from person to person, pumping hands. He wore a fixed, mirthless smile. The most imperceptible gesture seemed overly exaggerated, tiresome. His feet could not coordinate well with his eyes. He misjudged the elevation of the single step that led out of the shrine. He staggered back for an instant, but rallied just in time. Then he hoisted himself over the step, sapped by the effort.

CHAPTER SIXTEEN

Ike's mother sat outside the house, a corn-filled basket between her legs. She stopped husking as he entered.

"What took you so long?" she asked. Her eyes animated her sweaty face. "I was about to send Alice to the pastor's house with food for the two of you."

"I left the man's house a long time ago," Ike said. "Mama, what do you know about this man you call pastor?"

She sat up. "He's a holy man of God. And he's going to bless you."

"How about his past?"

"How about it?"

"Do you know he's the grandson of a terrible robber?"

She sprang to her feet, clenched arms placed on her hip, a fighter's posture. "Ikechukwu, who are you talking about?"

"Pastor Uka," Ike said gruffly. "But Uka is not his real name."

"My ears won't hear your sick words." She raised both hands and plugged her ears. She sat back down, her face an expression of pained bewilderment.

Ike waited until she removed her thumbs, humming a religious song.

"I heard things today about Uka."

"Why are you listening to Satan that wants to deceive you?"

"I went to visit my uncle."

She made a swift sweeping movement as if something had stung her. "Which uncle?" she asked, drawing up her legs as if about to rise once again to her feet.

"How many do I have?" He was unfazed, his temper shortened by gin, ready for a fight. He then spelled it out: "My only uncle. My father's brother. Osuakwu."

It was as if the very devil had materialized before her. In an instant her eyes flared, filled with ire. Her face scowled up, took on a shape of menace. The air was combustible. She released a deep, disgusted sigh and a grunt. Then she hunkered back down on her husking task. A vanquished foe, she'd skulked away from a duel.

Ike felt a fleeting pity. In his younger days, he'd lived in terror of her. Cross her and he—or his sister—courted flogging. Her instrument of flagellation was a cane so sturdy it lasted for years. She hurled rebukes as the cane crashed against the flexed muscle of the buttocks. She caned like one possessed, impervious to any pleas for mercy. There was no relenting until she was drenched in sweat, her victim's buttocks on fire, raw with welts. Afterward, the beaten skin swelled so hideously that for the next few days sitting would be out of the question.

It was now years since she had last caned anybody. For all her indignation, he knew she dared not raise a hand to him. A perverse, fractured sympathy flowed out from him toward her, the sympathy of a man who still savored every bit of his victory. He was just sorry to see her wilt so easily, dominated by her child. She was a hurt, hampered lioness. His sympathy was that of a hunter taking aim at a lioness hobbled by age and injury, a cowering, feeble foe.

The gin had sickened him. Walking was as much of a chore

as standing still; the ground shifted and played pranks with his unsteady feet. The world whirled about him, left him giddy. He'd taken care of his mother; he now craved a pillow on which to nestle his head.

Stepping into the house, he threw one last glance at his mother. She'd thrown her entire being into husking. He scuffed away to answer the call of his bed.

His body was lulled into a near-tranquilized state the moment he lowered himself, shoes and all, on the bed. He lay face down. Hanging on to a fading consciousness, he began to retrace the day's events.

He replayed his encounter with Pastor Uka. As some of the episodes floated in and out of his mind, he summoned a smile.

On balance, he reckoned the day a success, if not something of a coup. The scare he'd felt moments before stepping into Osuakwu's shrine—and the way he'd quivered as Osuakwu prayed over the kola nut—seemed now distant. Distant and uncalled for. If the statue of Ngene disappeared—*when* the deity disappeared—Osuakwu would swear that one man, and one man only, was responsible. That man was Pastor Uka, who carried the burden of cause, motivation, and declared intent. Osuakwu knew that Ngene was Uka's Baal. He knew about Uka's boast that Ngene would be destroyed, decimated in a puff of smoke that would come from heaven. It suited Ike's purpose. He could plot and execute his goal in absolute anonymity, beyond the pale of suspicion.

Ike tried to shape his face into a smile but couldn't, the skin on his face set as the bark of deadwood. Above him, the ceiling spun and spun with gathering speed. He became a miniaturized being, a mere eye, encased inside a cyst. He floated, tumbled freely, in the spheres. Light as gossamer, this eye was on a journey to see. It bobbed and bumped until he attained an altitude that should have hampered scale. Surprisingly, everything could be seen in replete, complete splendor. Everything in the world and beyond spread itself out, surrendered to the gaze of the eye. He could see a sea, a shimmering, emerald sea. The sea's waves roared with laughter. The sea's froth sang of idyllic joy. Looking at the sea's rollick, Ike knew the wondrous language that linked past and present things.

CHAPTER SEVENTEEN

Thumps rattled the door. Ike bolted up, then realized he had dreamed through a downpour. Its rage spent, the storm now fell in feeble sleets on the zinc roof.

Slowly he opened his eyes. A sharp ache throbbed within his skull. He rubbed at his eyes as he clambered to sit up.

The door shook with another round of knocks.

He winced. "Who is it?" he asked in a sour tone.

"Alice, sah."

"What do you want?"

"Somebody wants to see you, sah" his niece said. "She's been waiting."

"She? Who is that?"

She whispered: "I don't know, sah. She's a mother."

"A mother? How do you know?"

"She's here with her children," she said in a hushed voice.

Ike hissed. It was not as if he didn't expect that a stream of relatives would come to "greet" him—greeting being, in this case, an excuse to lay their woes at his feet and then request some money. It was a game marked by conceits, highly interesting if you were merely an observer of it. But if you were cast in the role of inexhaustible benefactor, it could be a trying experience.

"I'll be out in five minutes," he said.

He leaned back in bed, propped on his elbows. Peering out the window at the red, soggy earth, he pressed on both sides of his head to crush the pounding pain. He felt mildly peeved at the unknown intruder who'd come to claim a first place in the game of "greeting" and "receiving."

He mentally rehearsed the game's all-too-familiar ritual. It invariably began with an eager smile, a hug, or a firm handshake. Then followed a superfluity: *"Did they say you came back?"*

You nodded.

"I was just at the market to buy a few things to make soup—the price of things these days!—and then I overheard somebody say you'd come home. Great happiness swept me away. I didn't know when I broke into dancing—such was my delight! Every day, I've been praying to God to keep you safe in the land of white people. Every day, I say to God, I'm a sooty destitute, I have nothing, but please bless Ikechukwu with health and riches. Bless Ikechukwu for me, because I know that when he has, he won't see me hungry and throw his eyes in the bush. Poverty is not bad; what's bad is to be poor in people, to have nobody. Our people say that when I lack and the person who would help me lacks, too, then death has entered and occupied a seat. That's why I've been begging God to forget me but never to forget you. To look at you—see your cheeks, surfing with sheen, your skin aglow—God has been hearing my prayers! Just to see you, happiness has filled my stomach to the brim.

Into the ear flows a catalog of privations and a litany of needs. Then silence, a deep, expectant silence.

He drew a deep breath, filling his lungs with the doughy scent of wet earth. Suddenly a radiant sun broke out. It imbued the fizzling ropes of rain with a silvery brilliance. He could not tell what day it was. Had he slept and woken up on the same day, or had he fallen into a sopor, slept through a night, and woken up the next day?

He'd taken much longer than five minutes. Cupping both hands in front of his face, he blew breath, sniffed—and recoiled. There was no time to brush now; he lobbed two cubes of peppermint in his mouth. Then, with instinctive wariness, he set out to meet his guests.

The visitors sat on a wooden stool out in the veranda, a woman flanked by five children, two daughters and three sons. They sprang to their feet as he made his way, warily, to them. He did not immediately recognize them. He squinted, looking. The odor of squalor wafted into his nostrils.

"Good evening, sir," said the woman. She had a placid look and wore a blouse of faded blue over a skirt that had come apart at the hems. Her feet were shod in a pair of thread-bare slippers.

"Good evening, sir," chimed her brood, shyly averting their eyes, their faces impassive.

"Good evening," Ike said, peering.

"You don't remember," she said, her tone half guilty, half recriminatory. "Regina. Don't you remember Regina?"

"Regina?" he said doubtfully. He was about to ask which Regina, but—jolted by recognition—held back. His mouth flew open with shock. The frumpy, reeking apparition before him was his first love, once the object of his anguished infatuation.

"You don't remember me?" she inquired in an apologetic tenor. Her voice, now familiar—the sole survivor of her ravaged body—snapped him awake from his doldrums. "I know I've changed. Life has been hard."

She'd hurt him years ago. She had dumped him for Emeka Egoigwe, a tall, mustachioed man of ostentatious habits. Egoigwe had made a vulgar display of his fortune, acquired—so it was widely whispered—by unscrupulous means. He owned more cars than anybody cared to count and had a fetish for matching the color of his clothes and wristwatch with the color of each car he drove. He—again, it was whispered—used bleaching creams to lighten his skin.

Two of Ike's friends had warned him that Emeka Egoigwe—who was called Merciless for the way he picked up, used, and dropped women—appeared to have designs on Regina, but Ike had dismissed their report. "Egoigwe is not Regina's type," Ike had told his friends. "He's an uneducated oaf. Regina doesn't care for money. She loves me because of my brains. Do you know she cries whenever I write her a poem? Does Egoigwe know how to read, much less how to spark a woman's heart with a love poem?"

"Remember that woman does not live by a poem alone," cautioned one of his friends.

"And that some women love the poetry of fresh-minted cash," said the other.

"Not my Regina!" Ike boasted, his finger slicing the air for emphasis.

A few days later, Regina broke up with him via a blithe, terse letter, written in a lackadaisical tone that lanced him. He still remembered the lines that most savaged him: *Don't think that I no longer care for you. I enjoyed your poems and stories and our visits to Uvunu. But it's time for me to graduate from childish love. It's time to grow up.*

It was as if somebody had used a sharp, serrated knife to slice his heart. It grated to read Regina consign what they had to childish distraction, to be discarded in order to graduate into a mature, cash-driven love. No, he could not recognize Regina in the words! Egoigwe, the rogue opportunist, must have offered her the sentiment even if not the language.

Ike might have skulked off to a corner to lick his wounds. Instead, he was too obsessed to let go. He had enlisted his two friends in an amateurish plot to frighten off her suitor. They composed a letter that they clipped under Egoigwe's windshield: *We, the undersigned, having constituted ourselves into a vanguard and committee in the defense and cause of genuine love, hereby give you, Mr. Emeka Egoigwe, hereinafter to be known as the putative usurper, an ultimatum to forthwith cease and desist from any form of amorous contact or advances to Regina.*

The next day, an uncle of one of the boys called the vanguard to his home. He informed them that Regina's new lover had blazed with rage over the letter. "You three boys are lucky that I talked the man out of visiting you individually at home to personally deliver his response to your letter. Are you boys mad? Is Regina the only woman in this world that you would risk provoking a man as callous as Egoigwe? Do you even know anything about the man?"

The three boys stared in silence.

"He's a killer," said the man. "He's like our police: he can kill and go."

On learning that Egoigwe's fortune came from a career as a ruthless drug pusher, Ike and his friends had decided to give him—and Regina—a wide berth.

From afar, Ike had monitored Regina's relationship with the wealthy drug pusher. He had tracked their numerous breakups and reconciliations. He knew of all the times the man took Regina on a shopping spree in Rome or London, of the black-and-blue beatings he gave her anytime he suspected that her eye had strayed in another man's direction, or whenever she dared ask questions about his escapades with other women. Through all the time he monitored the vicissitudes of their relationship, Ike's one dream was that she'd return to him one day, a teary penitent. That she'd throw herself on his mercy so that he would have the opportunity to withhold any forgiveness or mercy.

Shortly after Ike got a scholarship from the Rotary Club International to study at Amherst College, he heard that Egoigwe, after a breakup that lasted more than a year, had returned to marry Regina. From time to time, he'd draw her into his mind, his remembrances fueled by malice. He wished her marital woe. He hoped that he would abandon her for another woman. Sometimes he caught himself and recoiled, shocked that the passage of time had done little to curb the bitterness he felt toward her.

A year ago, without an effort on his part to conjure her, she had popped into his mind. In the next e-mail to his sister, Nkiru, he had inquired after her. Nkiru's reply had startled him. Emeka Egoigwe had died shortly after Regina's birth of their fifth child. Nkiru offered no further details; apparently, the accounts of the man's death were too sketchy.

Now, as Regina stood before him, Ike realized that his heart had softened, even if it still incubated a measure of resentment toward her.

"I heard you came home," she said, her voice breaking. "I brought my kids to come and greet you. It has been a long time. A lot has happened."

His ears registered the sound of her voice, but her words glided past, left no emotional print on his mind. She seemed to register his inattentiveness. She fidgeted and fell mute. He waved her and her children to a long stool on the veranda. She slouched down, then her children crowded about her, nervous. Her children wore desolation on their bodies, their eyes sunken. One of the boys, the youngest child, scratched persistently at his skin. Ike looked at the child, then flinched at his pocks of rashes.

Ike and Regina exchanged looks. There was a plaintive note to her expression, as if she trusted her eyes to plead her case. Shame, loathing, shock, seized him all at once. Her eyes—unbelievably dead! Their deadness deepened her pallor, completing her slovenly, frowzy appearance. Those eyes! How they once sparkled with life. He used to gawk at them, enraptured by their seductive power, amazed at their flirtatious glaze that drew him effortlessly into obsession. How those eyes once complemented her chiseled face that was adept at transmitting infectious joy. Her pulchritude gone, her face—marred and joyless—was a macabre advertisement of angular jutting bones.

His eyes fell to her breasts. He could remember when they were supple and firm. Now they hung flat, lifeless as rubber. He looked away with the quickness of a guilt-ridden voyeur.

The woman in front of him was woebegone, the portrait of a hag. Time and hardship had laid their merciless hand on her.

He made mighty mental efforts to recall the pristine body that had awakened his youthful desire, but the devastated body in front of him was unyielding, blocking him from the reach of that beatific memory. He tried to recall their trysts of long ago, how they would repair to their favorite hideout—a copse that was past the shallow, clayey Uvunu, off the beaten track. He worked his mind to recall how his fingers would find and knead her breasts, her lips smack against his, both of them trembling, pouring perspiration. The body before him would not cooperate. It stubbornly transposed itself in place of that former vivacious body.

"Things have been hard for me, very hard," she said. She swept both hands to indicate her children. "Feeding them is often impossible. They stay up at night, crying from hunger. When I heard you'd come home, I said let me take the children to go and see you. You have a good heart. I know you will help."

Her certitude irked. *Why,* he thought, *drag another man's children to me to feed?* He wished to be curt and dismissive, but the children's eyes gawked at him, their own voiceless pleas even more harrowing.

Suddenly, his thought zipped to Queen Bee. One day, perhaps, Queen Bee would come to him, her skin disheveled, body as ravaged as Regina's, to plead for succor. A sinister gush of compassion rushed inside him.

"I understand your husband—"

"He died four years ago," she interjected. She patted her youngest child on the head. "He died a week after Tochi was born." The rash-infested child squirmed.

"But he had money—your husband." Only after the words had tumbled out did he realize that an accusatory accent, unbidden, had crept into his voice.

She emitted a grunt and rolled her eyes.

"No, he was known to have money," he persisted. "What happened to it?"

Tears welled up in her eyes, and she turned her face away, gazing vacantly. He watched her struggle to hold tears at bay. He saw her composure weaken. A single tear streaked down her cheeks, but she wiped it before it could drop to the floor. She quickly turned to face Ike. Her two youngest children stood in front of her, staring, as if her distress were a rare form of entertainment. The three oldest clung to her side, like protectors offering an armor of comfort. They cast sneaky, accusing glances at Ike.

"Go outside with your brothers and sisters," she instructed her oldest daughter. "Take them outside and play."

"In the rain?" asked her daughter, frowning.

"The rain has stopped. Take everybody outside."

Her youngest son balked at going outside with the rest. She glared at him. Picking at his rashes, he ran to join his siblings.

"Have you heard how my husband died?" Regina asked in a dry voice.

Ike shook his head from side to side.

"In London, right at Heathrow—that's where it happened."

"At Heathrow? From what cause?"

"Just listen," she said, a sad smile parting her lips. "He'd arrived from Thailand, carrying things in his tummy."

"What do you mean?"

"I'm telling the story. Just *listen*," she admonished. "His stomach bulged with packets of heroin he'd put in condoms and swallowed. He was standing in a queue to go through customs. Then he suddenly became sick. One eyewitness said he hugged his stomach, then began to shout like a woman in labor. After a while he fell to the ground and began to roll around, still shouting."

"Did they get him medical help?"

"Medical help?" she echoed exasperatedly. "From what I was told, British officers surrounded him and began questioning him—"

"Even as he rolled on the ground?" Ike interjected.

"Am I speaking with water in my mouth? Yes, they questioned him as he rolled all over the ground, grabbing his stomach."

"That's murder!" he said heatedly.

Calmly, she said, "They were questioning him until he began to foam at the mouth. That's when they called for an ambulance. He was already a quarter to dead. Before they could get him into an ambulance, he'd become a corpse."

"You should sue," he said, his voice rising with excitement. "That's murder! They had no right to deny him medical attention. Even the worst criminal has a right to medical attention. Sue Heathrow . . . Maybe it's British immigration you should sue. Or customs. Just find a good British lawyer. It's called wrongful death."

"Wrongful death?" she sneered. "Do you write poetry with death? Is death ever wrong?"

"Yes, the British authorities were negligent. You can get money. A lot of money."

She regarded him inquisitively. "You see me in this condition and you're telling me to go to London and sue? Who'll allow a rag like me into Britain? And even if they allowed me, then what? You want me to walk into a court in England and tell them, 'You people killed my husband. Yes, my husband swallowed things a man should never put in his stomach, but it's you who killed him.' That's what you ask me to do?"

"But you, you knew he was in that line of business. Why did you marry him?"

Silent, she cast him a reproachful eye.

"No, you knew," he persisted. "Everybody knew, so you must have known."

She spoke in a tone of despair. "I pleaded with him to stop. Many times, I did. He'd made a lot of money. I begged him to start a clean business."

"You did—so?"

"The first time I suggested it, he beat me black and blue. He threatened to divorce me."

"And you backed off, scared?"

"Me?" she said with a sneer. "Have you forgotten about my stubbornness? I kept telling him, despite the beatings. One day, instead of beating me, he asked me to sit down. He wanted to talk."

"About his drug deals?"

"Yes. He asked why I wanted him to stop. I told him I was afraid for our young kids—we had two then. What if something happened to their father, how was I to raise them alone? I told him I didn't want to be widowed at a young age—or to have a husband in jail, which is the same thing."

"And what did he say?"

"He laughed for a long time. Then, beating his chest, he said, 'Me, dead? Me, go to jail? Have no fear; I'm like wind and water.

Is the wind ever caught in a trap? Does the basket hold water?'
He told me that he'd secured himself spiritually. I think his words
were: 'I'm protected by three spiritual insurance policies.'"

"What did he mean?"

"I asked the same question. He explained that, before each trip, he
first would go to see a pastor, a *malam*, and a *dibia*. He paid the pastor to fast and say *powerful* prayers for him. Then he paid the *malam*
to chant Koranic verses for his success. From the *malam*, too, he
got a protective amulet."

"A protective amulet?"

"It was supposed to confuse the eyes of anybody in uniform, customs or police."

Ike let out a chortle but quickly collected himself.

"Finally," she continued, "he told me that his *dibia* gave him the
charm called *oti n'anya afu uzo*."

"What's that?"

"You know what it is," she said, turning slightly away, a tinge
of impatience in her tone. "Have you stopped speaking Igbo? *Oti
n'anya afu uzo*. The charm does what its name says: 'look all you
want, you can't see a thing.'"

"It was meant to make him invisible?"

"Yes," she said with emphasis. She turned, glancing up at him,
her eyes dulled with sorrow. "He trusted in these three men. He
boasted that they gave him full spiritual protection. He assured me
he would never be caught."

"And you fell for that?"

"I cried. I told him that others like him had been caught in
America and sent to jail. Or in Indonesia—and beheaded. There
was this friend of his—they called him Khaki No Be Leather. An
only son, he was caught in Indonesia and beheaded. His old mother
went and hanged herself. I reminded my husband of Khaki. 'Are

you wishing me dead?' he fumed. 'You want me beheaded so you can carry my money and run to your boyfriend, eh?' Before I could speak, he slapped thunder into my eyes. Twice. *Twap! Twap!* Then he shouted, 'If you're a witch and you're planning to kill me, I'll kill you first.' I'd never seen him more mad with rage—and more scared."

"He did all this and you stayed with him," Ike said.

"You speak as if you're not from these parts, as if you don't know how difficult it is for a woman to get up and leave her husband. The scandal. The evil eyes cast at you by your own family and others. The rumors that the man must have sent you home because he caught you with a lover. I *had* to stay."

"And you must have stopped haranguing him about drug pushing, I bet."

"The day after he slapped me, he brought Pastor Uka to our house."

"Uka? Did you say Uka?"

"Yes, Pastor Uka. He was my husband's prayer warrior. He now owns a church here in Utonki."

"Go on," Ike prodded. "What happened?"

"My husband brought Pastor Uka home. Then Uka said God had told him I was possessed."

"Possessed?"

"By the marine spirit. That's what the pastor said; that I was bonded to the water mermaid. He said God also revealed to him that I would bring bad luck to my husband—unless I was delivered. I saw hell that evening. I was forced to kneel in front of the pastor while he danced all around me and barked sounds that had no meaning. Occasionally, he grabbed my head and pressed hard until I cried out in pain. Whenever I cried, he shouted that it was the marine spirit fleeing out of me. This lasted for three hours."

An ache seared his skull, a pain born the moment she mentioned Pastor Uka. A ropy pain, it stretched from his forehead to the nape of his neck. It pulled and tugged at the tense, taut line. He leaned against the wall, eyes shut.

"So you know all about Pastor Uka."

"My husband said the man was next to God. You won't believe the kind of money Uka made from my husband. And from other drug smugglers."

"They just threw money his way?"

"They believed his prayers could save them from arrest. My husband certainly did."

"The first moment I met Uka, I knew he was a bloody charlatan. Your husband must have been—pardon my bluntness—a fool."

For a moment, her eyes blazed with belligerence. She folded her arms across her chest. Twice, she opened her mouth but seemed unable to coax words.

"I didn't mean to insult him," he said. "But I don't know why—forget it."

"People believe what they believe," she said resignedly.

"But you should have put your foot down. You should have told your husband to quit trafficking drugs or else."

"Who told you I didn't? In fact, despite the beatings, I harassed him so much that he lied to me. He told me he'd stopped anything to do with drugs. For a long time, he didn't travel abroad. Life became sweet for me again; I stopped waking up at night with terrible dreams about being a widow. Then I had Tochi, my last child. A few days after Tochi's birth, my husband told me he had to travel to London. He said since Tochi was going to be our last child, we needed to throw a big party. He wanted to buy a few things in London for the big bash. He never mentioned he was first going to Thailand, for then I would have known. I would have known."

Ike felt that the story had come full circle.

"You have to sue," he said, nodding to drive home the point. "Make those British officials pay for their negligence."

Silent, she cast a vacant gaze.

He asked, "How about the man's assets in Nigeria? He must have left quite a ton of money."

"A ton, you say?" She sighed bemusedly. "I don't know about a ton. Drug dealers make a lot of money, but they throw a lot of it away. It's the nature of their business. One Christmas, my husband gave five cars—expensive, brand-new cars—as gifts to his hangers-on. He was impulsive in that way. He had lots of girlfriends—here and in other parts of the world. He paid rent for them. Money passed through his hands and went quickly to other hands. I don't know how much he left in the bank, but I know he owned three buildings."

"Uh-uh. Are they not rented?"

"They are—but his brothers collect the rent and keep all of it. My children and I don't see a kobo of the money."

"Why is that?"

"When my husband died, even before his corpse was flown home, his brothers came to the house and accused me of being a witch. They said Pastor Uka told them I had used witchcraft to cause the heroin to burst in my husband's belly. They said both the *malam* and the *dibia* had confirmed it. I was confused, didn't know what to say. To have a newborn baby on my arm and to be dealing with this sort of thing just after my husband's death—I was just confused. I told them they were talking nonsense. They gave me dirty slaps, worse than any beating I had ever received from my husband. If I denied it, they said, I should go and swear at a deity's shrine in Okija. If I was a witch, I'd die within seven days. If I lived, it meant I was innocent."

"Preposterous! Did you go?"

"Am I mad? I knew that the priests at the shrine give oath takers a concoction to drink. It's meant to test your innocence, but it's a well-known scam. Somebody who wants to get you just offers a bribe to the priests. The priests then sprinkle a slow-acting poison in your drink. Within seven days, you're dead. That's what my brothers-in-law planned for me."

"What was their reaction when you refused to go?"

"Oh," she gasped, "merciless beating. Right in front of my crying children. It was as if they meant to kill me with blows if I wasn't going to drink poison. They left bruises all over my body. Then they gave me thirty minutes—only minutes—to take the children and run from our home in Enugu. I was not permitted to take anything, only the dress on my body. Everything else, they took, including a Toyota Camry my husband had given me three months before his death. My children and I were homeless. That's why we left Enugu and returned to the village."

"How did you feed the children?"

"How else? I turned a professional beggar. Father Nduka at Saint Matthew's helps us with food and a little money here and there. He pleaded with some women to give me their used clothes." She shrugged sadly. "If anybody had told me that I, Regina, would one day be wearing secondhand clothing, I would have said, 'Never!' But such is life." She shrugged again.

Ike seethed. "That can't be done!"

"It's done," she said in an even, resigned voice. "There are many women like me in this country. A man is not supposed to die before his wife. Often, when a man dies first, his relatives accuse his widow of witchcraft. Then they drive her away and inherit everything the man owned."

"Why didn't you get a lawyer? You ought to fight these bastards in court."

She gave him a quizzical look. Then she said, "Ike, this is Nigeria."

"What's that supposed to mean?"

"Here is not America."

"I still don't get your point."

She looked away, gazing into vacancy. It was as if something about him—his innocence? his naïveté?—could no longer be stomached. After a moment, she slowly steered her eyes back to him.

"If you can help us with something, try," she said. "God will bless you. The kids can't sleep at night because their bellies are empty. When they fall asleep, they soon wake up crying for food. But what can I do? Should I cook myself for them?"

IKE SAT ON THE stool long after Regina had left with her children. His mood was wistful. The rope of ache that split his skull in half had grown, leaving raw nodes of pain all over his head. He placed thumb and two other fingers on the tautest spot. He pressed, then released, pressed and released. He kneaded his neck, varied the pressure, his fingers calming the searing sensation. When he thought his fingers had dissolved the pain, a sudden spasm jabbed at him. It reminded him that the pain's roots lay in the soul.

He thought about the paltry sum he'd given Regina. Two thousand naira—less than twenty dollars. It was all he could afford. He still had five days left to his stay in Utonki, and each day was sure to present claims on his wallet. There would be a steady retinue of "greeters." Each would be armed with rending tales and expect some monetary gift.

Regina's eyes had brightened when he'd handed her the money—plus three cheap T-shirts. As he gave her the gifts, her eyes had regained a hint of their once-accustomed sparkle. Her gratitude had gushed in a babble of words. And then, in a flush of euphoria, she'd jumped from the stool and flung herself at him. He'd stiffened at her approach, his body still as a statue as she rounded him in an embrace. Her body lay flat against his, a fleshless, quivering medley of bones. She wafted a sufferer's stink, an unwashed, sweaty smell. It swelled in his nose. He held his breath, repulsed.

Jealous of his livelier memory of her, he shut his eyes. He was desperate to expunge her present image from his mind. He wanted to imagine the days when this same body boasted softness and a welcoming fragrance. He tried all he could, but the apparition blocked all paths to a vivacious past. He was relieved when she let go. He began breathing again.

She had summoned the children and ordered them to take turns saying "Thanks, sir" to him.

Moments after her departure, he still stood on the spot, his hands folded across his chest, his thoughts entangled and grim. Then he sat down, on the same spot where she'd sat, the stool still warm with her heat.

His rage poured forth in different directions, unsure of its target. A rogue stream of self-loathing bile flowed toward himself. Why hadn't he stopped Egoigwe from stealing his girlfriend? And why was he still a struggling man after all these years of living in America? If he'd made a fortune, he would have been able to offer Regina substantive help, not the miserly gift he put in her palm—enough, by the most optimistic calculations, for four meals at the most.

There—there was a leap in his mind—was another justification to snag Ngene.

"Do you want to eat now, sah?"

He turned to Alice. "Not yet," he said. "Where's Mama?"

"She went for evening service at the church."

He pictured his mother's grimaced face as Pastor Uka related his version of their encounter earlier that day. Strangely the image did not move him in any way. Regina's visit still occupied his thoughts. He wished to take a walk in search of solitude. He needed the right space to begin untangling the clutter that filled his mind.

He decided to walk to the grove of Uvunu. There was a tinge of nostalgia to the decision, for it was at that shallow stream that Regina and he had had their first trysts.

"I'm taking a walk," he told Alice.

"You didn't eat lunch, sah," the girl said in a voice strangely inflected with maternal concern.

"When I come back."

"Then dinner will be cooked. Will you eat your lunch and dinner together?"

He quickened his steps, ignoring her.

A sand-colored grasshopper leapt from his path and landed to his right, disappearing in the underbrush. He scuffed his feet at the spot where the grasshopper had taken cover. The insect hopped. With a swift swipe of the hand, he caught it in midair. Slowly unclenching his hand, he stared at the grasshopper's dark secretion. It brought to mind one of the pastimes of his teenage years. He and his friends would spend afternoons scouring the grass and gathering a variety of grasshoppers. They'd pause as the sun began to sink, then each person would bring his harvest. The result was a great miscellany of insects in different shapes, sizes, and colors. They'd begin their games, pairing different hoppers in a macabre simulation of love and feuding. Afterward, seized by a paroxysm of violence, they'd decapitate the grasshoppers and cast their bodies in open places where chickens would peck at them.

Accompanied by memories of his grasshopper-hunting days, he arrived at the stream. To his delight, there was nobody in sight.

He hoisted himself on a ledge slick from the recent rain. The wetness licked his pants, touching his bottom with a gentle titillation.
Shutting his eyes, he breathed deep. He exhaled, opening his eyes,
taking in the tangled shrubs, willowy trees that danced to the wind,
and the unhurried pool of water.

A toad jumped frantically from underneath the brush. It jumped
and then jumped again, in desperate haste. A slim green snake slith-
ered past, giving chase. But toads made perilous dinner. Ike once
saw the carcass of a green snake, its body gashed open just beneath
its mouth where a swallowed toad had flexed and swelled itself. A
green snake was no match for a toad's genius for self-inflation. It
was a lesson little green snakes learned only too late.

Uvunu was a sliver of a stream. Its serpentine course ran along
a track of soft, clayey bed. Ike watched birds as they glided in the
openness overhead. Sometimes two birds would swoop to a collision,
belly to belly, their contact enacted with breathtaking harmoni-
ousness. From the surrounding thicket other birds twittered and
chirped, as if in encouragement of their commingling, amorous
siblings. Crickets chirred, perhaps enacting their own love rituals.

Ike was entranced by birdsong. He sat up and removed his shoes.
Unshod, he walked toward the stream, relishing the way his feet
sank in the soft, wet earth. For a moment he stood at the edge of the
stream and gazed at its liquid sparkle. He admired the tiny silvery
fish that darted about with dexterous ease.

Gingerly, he stepped in with one foot, then the other. A strange
weight seeped out of his feet and disappeared in the lazily flowing
stream. A calm washed over him. His body became open, hungry.

He knew it was time to walk home.

CHAPTER EIGHTEEN

Alice stood outside the house, hands folded, like a dawdler in the singeing heat. She gave the shy smile of a youngster with an exciting message for an older person.

"Chair came just after you left," she said. "He wanted to see you."

"Chair?" he asked. "What—*who*—is Chair?"

"Chief."

"There's somebody called chief around here? Does he have a real name?"

"Chief Tony Iba."

"Ah!" he exclaimed, surprised.

He had heard it said at Osuakwu's shrine that Tony Iba, a classmate of his from many years ago, was now a hotshot in the ruling party and had been elected as chairman of the Oliego Local Government Council. He'd learned that Iba maintained two palatial homes, one in the city of Enugu, where he spent his weekdays, the other in Utonki, his weekend retreat.

Iba was a good five years older than Ike, but they'd both been classmates in secondary school just after the war. Tony had served as a servant to a Biafran army officer during the war. He had a repertoire of dramatic war stories; he used them to convince his gullible classmates—and even some teachers—that he'd seen action as a soldier. A notorious slacker, he despised homework. But once freed from the rituals and rigors of the classroom, he exuded an ingenious charm that infected teachers and fellow students alike. He wore cologne to school and sometimes sneaked in spreads of nude women he'd torn out of *Playboy.* He had a superb talent for yarns and gave hilarious impressions of soldiers' lascivious games. Affable, he spoke a brew of English of his own invention, at once ungrammatical and alluring. He relished scandalizing his more innocent classmates with lewd pranks and salacious stories. His moniker was adopted from a movie star whose mannerisms—lines, facial expressions, and drawl—he could imitate.

Ike recalled Tony Iba's famous falling-out with a history teacher. One day, the teacher had asked the class to enumerate the factors that led to the fall of the Roman Empire. Tony had answered, "They fell, sir, consequent from their carelessness." The teacher had stared at him for a full minute, then said: "You, Tony Iba, are bound to be a failure in life." Tony was not one to concede the last word to anybody. He sat up, dwarfing the short teacher. "Sir," he said in his mock-reverential manner, a smile hovering over his face, "what you have just perorated is your personal ideology. Since you're not God, your case is appealable. I plan to elongate my life into fantabulous success."

Even in those days, most people had an instinctive sense that Tony Iba, alias Tony Curtis, would wangle his way into a measure of success. Ike was not surprised when, a year or so ago, his sister, Nkiru, wrote an e-mail with the news that Tony had struck it rich—nobody knew how—and had built a big house that was the talk of Utonki. And then, at Osuakwu's, Ike had heard that Iba was Utonki's political colossus, a man called (with an odd mixture of aspersion and affection) *onu na elili ora*, "the mouth that eats for the community."

"Yes," Alice confirmed, barely able to conceal her excitement. "He said if you didn't remember him by his real name, I should tell you it's—"

"Curtis. Tony Curtis?"

"Yes, sah. He said he just arrived from Enugu and heard you're in town. He'll be in Utonki for two or three days. He said I should tell you to come to his house this night. Or tomorrow—or anytime you want."

Ike's excursion to Uvunu had restored his nerves. A soft breeze had taken the edge off the evening heat. He decided to go directly to see Tony Iba.

FROM THE OUTSIDE, IBA'S house was as impressive as Nkiru's letter had suggested. It was a white three-story structure that towered over the trees and seemed to peer, with a sneer, at the rusted zinc and thatch roofs of surrounding buildings. A high wall rimmed with steely spikes ringed the house, obscuring its grounds from view. Ike banged on the wrought-iron gate. A shirtless young man of squat physique looked through a peephole.

"I'd like to see Tony," Ike announced.

"You mean Chair," the gateman corrected.

"Is Tony in?" Ike persisted.

"Chief went out," said the gateman. He regarded Ike with a quizzical squint, doubtless curious about this man who addressed a big man without the appellation of chief.

"When is he coming back?"

"I don't know. He went to see his friend who came back from America."

"I'm *the* one."

"You're the person from America?"

"Yes. I was away when he called at my house."

"Ah, welcome, sir," the gateman fussed, drawing the gate open. "God bless you, sir. Forgive me, sir. Sometimes I can be foolish. I didn't know you were Chief's friend, sir. You can go and wait for Chief. I'm sure that now, now—soon, sir—he'll be back."

Iba's house was set at the right-hand corner of the walled sprawl. To the left was an open six-car garage with a greenish canopy. Three cars were parked in the port, all of them covered with a tarpaulin. A fourth car, a black Mercedes sedan, was parked just outside the entrance to the house.

Ike buzzed the doorbell and was let in by a man dressed in a bow tie, white shirt, and black jacket—like a faux butler.

"This way, please," the man said.

From within, the house was even huger than Ike had imagined it. They walked past a mini-courtyard adorned with a dry water fountain and seraphic totems wrought in concrete. Ike's eyes darted into a room where a boisterous audience was huddled around a TV set. Something about their spiritedness suggested the program was a sports event.

"A moment," Ike said, drawing his escort's attention. "Let me see what's on TV."

"It's basketball," the escort explained. "There's a bigger TV in the living room. I can turn it on for you."

"Let me peek in quickly," Ike said. He stepped into the room. On the TV screen was a 1991 NBA championship game between the Chicago Bulls and the Los Angeles Lakers. The game had been played two years before Ike's arrival in the United States, but he had seen a tape of it at the apartment of a college friend who was from Chicago and fanatical about the Bulls.

Five young boys, two girls, and four adults sat in a semicircle on the carpeted floor, most of them absorbed by the game. One of the boys wore a T-shirt with TOMMY HILFIGER scrawled on it in large letters. Another sported an oversize T-shirt with the letters FUBU running down the length of its back. One of the girls faced the TV but directed her attention to a dust-brown teddy bear splotched with palm oil. The other girl was equally occupied with ministrations to a sheared twiggy Barbie.

Enrapt in the game, the watchers hardly paid attention to Ike. They hooted at a dunk and then hissed at a missed layup. They sighed and cursed when the referee made a call they disliked. When a player executed a crossover dribble, they hailed the maneuver. When another player fumbled, they chided.

Michael Jordan got a pass, dribbled past three defenders, then levitated for a dunk. Another Laker defender lifted up, the weight of his body deployed to stop the airborne Bulls star. The impact stunned Jordan and sent him reeling, earthbound, like a meteor. The ball, released awkwardly, bounced on the rim twice and then fell in just as the umpire's whistle blew for a foul. The Bulls called a time-out. Jordan got up and glared at the man who'd hit him hard. Then he stormed off to his team's huddle. The action faded to a commercial break.

"Jordan is angry," announced the Hilfiger boy with the authority of a mind reader. He added: "Jordan will kill them today." "He can't do anything," said one of the older men. "He's not a god." "He's the god of basketball," said the Hilfiger youngster, punching the air. "Well, we're seeing a god who has been tied up today."

Ike was astounded by their fervor. Before he left for America, Nigerian TV stations never showed a basketball game. It was in America that he saw his first live professional basketball game. Jonathan Falla's parents had invited him to Boston Garden to see a play-off game between the Celtics and Philadelphia 76ers. He remembered it as an ugly, physical game, replete with grunts and knuckles that came close, twice, to degenerating into an all-out brawl. The sheer spectacle of it had intrigued him, but it was not exactly the game to convert a reluctant watcher. He remained a dabbler, neither indifferent nor an avid fan. There was one exception: he'd become a devoted fan of Michael Jordan. In equal measure, he admired Jordan's breathtaking flights and his business savvy.

"You all like this game?" He broke his silence in Igbo, marveling at their concentration.

They all looked at him at once. Eyes, old and young, locked on him as if he were an irksome interloper.

The Hilfiger youngster spoke first. "I want to be like them." He spread his arms in an expression of largeness. "They're paid bags and bags of dollars. Just for throwing that ball through a hole."

"I know," Ike said. "I live in America." He saw their eyes widen. "I've actually seen them play."

"With your two eyes?" one of the older men asked.

Ike was amused. "Yes, with my two eyes. I was there, just like the people you see on TV. I could have shouted the name of one of the players, and he would have heard me."

The FUBU, silent for a while, asked, "Do you have to be as tall as two men joined together to play?"

Ike laughed. "Most of them are very tall, but not all of them. There's one man who used to play; his name is Muggsy Bogues. He's shorter than I am."

"Shorter than you?" one of the adults echoed, his tone skeptical.

"He's so short I can use my chin to give him a knock on the head."

"Then why don't you play?" the same man asked. "Does money taste bitter to you?"

"It's not a game that everybody can play," the Hilfiger boy explained.

"It's true," Ike said.

"If I ever go to America, I'll play," said another man, running a hand over his head covered with knots of gray hair. "If they pay me bags of money, I'll play."

"Nobody will pay you even *shishi*," another teased. "It's not a game for gray-haired weaklings."

"Send your wife over tonight, and I'll show her what a man with gray hair can do. Only don't blame me if she drops twins on you in nine months."

Laughter swept the room, drowning out the other man's retort.

"Tell me," asked another man. "Is it really true about the money they're paid?"

Ike nodded his assent.

"I hear it's enough money to fill a large room like this one," said the gray-haired man, his arm defining an arc.

Ike nodded again.

"And all they have to do is drop a ball in a hole?" the man asked, his tone wistful.

Ike chuckled. "It looks easy, but it's not."

"What's so difficult in it?" asked one of the boys. "I can do it."

The gray-haired man let out a dreamy gasp. "If I find my way to that America," he said, "no more trouble. I know a *dibia* or two who can arm me with the right charm. Everything I throw up will go in that hole. Even with my eyes shut, the ball falls in. After they've seen me in one game, nobody will talk anymore about that bald boy."

"Jordan," Ike said.

"He misses half his shots," the man said, his face screwed up in disdain. "Do you have his phone number?" he asked Ike.

"No, why?"

"I can take him to the best *dibia* in these parts. Then everything he throws will find the hole."

Ike bent over with laughter.

"He must have a *dibia*," suggested one of the men. "A man with so much wealth in his hand can't be without one."

"True," conceded the gray-haired man. "But his *dibia* must not know his work." Glancing up at Ike, he said, "If you bring him to see me, I will take him to a good *dibia*."

"Jordan is retired," Ike explained. "You're watching a game he played in nineteen ninety-one. He got tired of playing—so he's in his house resting. He used to be the king; the new king is a young man called Kobe Bryant."

"Eh-eh," exclaimed the man in vindication. "If he had a good *dibia*, why would he get tired? Does a living king hand his throne to another king?"

"Jordan and his team had conquered other teams six times. He decided it was enough. He wanted to rest."

"Are you telling me he got tired of making money?"

"He already has a lot of money," Ike explained. "A lot."

"Does a man ever get tired of money? Does he have as much money as Chief?"

"More," Ike said.

"How can?" one of the men said. "There's no way a man who throws a ball through a hole will have more money than Chief."

"Jordan does."

"Impossi-can't!" shouted one of the men. "Chief is a politician. You can't compare a common player with a politician."

"All I know is, I'll never get tired of money," crowed the youngster in the fake FUBU shirt. "Let my money fill a huge basket, I'll still look for more."

"Only a man with no sense runs away from money," the gray-haired man ruled.

Ike suspected that they were not moved by the spectacle of

nimble men slicing, gliding, feinting, flying. They hardly cared for the dunks, the pump fakes, the cross-over dribbles, the fade-away jump shots dropped from impossible angles. It was not the grunts and hard fouls or the fluidity of movement that astonished them. These fans in faraway Utonki seemed enthralled by the basketball players' storied wealth.

Of course, it's always about money. When Jordan peeled his feet off gravity's earth and levitated, it was about money. When millions of Jordan's fans around the world became light with him, lithe and almost free, suspended with him in sheer air, able to soar with him all the way to the big, bigger, biggest mall, there to enter the kingdom of the Jordan Shoes, it was about money. Jordan, like his fans, was buoyed by the dollar. Money generated his élan, birthed his appeal, fueled his flights, consecrated him the archangel of the green-colored god. An American columnist had written about Japanese men, women, and children weeping on the streets of Tokyo when MJ announced his retirement. Nobody had forewarned them that the flights would ever stop, that patient gravity would someday triumph over their identifiable flying object. A grounded, flapless angel is a despairing, depressing sight. For all his dexterity with the ball, Jordan was a more sagacious moneymaker, money spinner, money gobbler. Best ever, in the spectacular dunk, in buzzer beating, but also in buzz generation, in turning a buck, in spinning a dream, in dream bursting. Wanna be like Mike?

Ike fixed on the two girls. They were entranced by their toys, indifferent to the conversation.

Ike asked the men what they would do if they had as much money as Jordan.

Their excitement became palpable, as if their millions were in Ike's hands, waiting to be released once they gave the right answer.

"First, I'll never use water to wash my hands," said the gray-haired man. He saw the look of surprise on Ike's face. "If I have that kind of money, why should water still touch my hands? I'll wash my hands in beer. Or whiskey, like Chief."

Ike let out a burst of laughter. "Don't tell me Tony Curtis uses whiskey to wash hands."

"He's now Chief Iba. If God blesses you as Chief has been blessed, would you still wash hands with *common* water?"

Ike's smile prodded the man to continue.

"If I become a rich man, *nkwu* and *ngwo* will never touch my lips. I'll only drink Coors Light and Heineken." He ran his tongue over his lips. "I'll never wear knickers, only trousers. I will even wear trousers to play the game."

"It's against the rules," Ike said. "The rule is that they must wear shorts to play."

The man snickered. "Who made that rule?"

"The game has a commissioner. He makes the rules."

"The commissioner must have a lot more money than Jordan."

"No," Ike answered. "In fact, Jordan has enough money to buy the man many times over."

A confounded expression clouded the gray-haired man's face. "There's falsehood in your talk," he said accusingly. "How can a man command another who is richer? Can I go and tell Chief what to do? If I'm as wealthy as Jordan, nobody will stop me from wearing trousers."

The others echoed the sentiment, casting suspicious eyes at Ike.

"I'm not lying," he assured them.

"I'll still wear trousers to play," insisted the gray-haired man. "Nobody can stop me."

"Okay," Ike conceded. "What else do you plan to do?"

"I won't drink water anymore. If I become thirsty, my servant must bring me a Coke or Fanta. And I'll eat fried eggs each morning."

"That's all?"

"And each afternoon and night."

"Me too," exclaimed the Hilfiger boy. "I like fried eggs and plantain."

"Shut up!" one of the men chided. "Have you ever eaten fried eggs in your life?"

"I have, to God!" swore the youngster. "Chief's cook has given me fried eggs."

"Then he's teaching you to steal," griped the man. "Wait till I tell your father about it. He should know where to look when his money begins to disappear. Women and children are not to eat eggs. It teaches them to steal."

"Children eat eggs in America," Ike said. "And eggs are very cheap."

"That your America is good," said one of the men. "So you eat eggs every day?"

"I don't," Ike said.

Their eyes registered disappointment and pity. "Don't you have enough money?"

"I just told you that eggs are cheap. But they're not good for you. They sicken the heart."

They laughed doubtfully. One said, "Give me fried eggs every day. I don't care what it does to my heart."

"Fried egg is all you talk about," Ike teased. "A wealthy man must have other plans."

"My feet will never touch the ground again. Wherever I go, I'll drive. Even to visit my neighbor, I'll go in my car. Of course, I'll not *drive.* I'll be *driven* by my driver."

"Uh-huh."

Ike pointed at the boy in a Hilfiger shirt. "So you, tell me how you'll spend your millions."

A wide smile stretched the youngster's cheeks. "I'll eat only foreign food."

"Foreign food? Like what?"

"I'll start with eggs."

"Eggs?" one of the adults interjected. "Next, you'll start stealing. Eggs, you said? Your father must hear this."

"Go on," Ike urged the youngster.

"I'll also eat ice cream every day."

"And what else?"

He tugged at his shirt. "I'll buy lots of shirts like this one. Tommy
Hilfiger, FUBU, Calvin Klein. Then I'll buy four—no, ten—big
cars. Hummer, Navigator, Bentley, Mercedes, Rolls-Royce—"

"Have you seen any of those cars?" Ike asked.

"Chief Iba has a Rolls-Royce," said one of the men.

Incredulous, Ike looked over his shoulder at the man who'd
opened the door for him. "Is it true?"

"Chief is not a small man," the escort said.

Ike pointed at the carport. "Is one of those covered cars a Rolls-
Royce?"

"No way!" the man cried. "His big cars are in Enugu. The village
is dusty. Chief can't leave his expensive cars in the dust."

"Okay, you get your Rolls-Royce," Ike addressed the youngster.
"What else?"

The youngster smiled in delight. "I'll own a big house. Bigger
than this one."

"Idiot!" cursed Chief Iba's prim servant. "Get out, now, now!
You will never come here to watch TV."

"I mean as big as this one," the youngster corrected himself.

Iba's servant was unforgiving. "First, let your father build a mud
house with raffia roofs before you start talking," he berated.

"He's a child," Ike said. "Tell me more," he goaded.

The youngster fell silent.

Ike caught another youngster gazing at him. The kid was shirt-less, his bulgy stomach accentuated by a swollen belly button. "You, what's your name?"

For an instant, the lad stiffened and looked away.

"I'm talking to you."

"Me?" said the youngster. Then he answered, "Ogii."

"What's your favorite food?"

Ogii smiled, his hands coyly covering his belly button. "Did you bring home pizza?" he asked. "I like pizza."

"Which type do you like to eat?"

"I've never tasted it, but it's on TV. If I become a big man, that's what I'll eat."

"I don't like pizza," Ike said.

Ogii looked aghast. "Everybody in America likes pizza. On TV, everybody eats it. They eat it and smile."

"Watch, Jordan just killed them!" shouted the Hilfiger boy. "I knew he was angry!"

Ike joined everybody to look at the replay of Jordan's dribble, elevation, and thundering dunk.

"I will be like Jordan," Ogii cooed.

Everybody laughed. Ike waved good-bye. Then he followed the escort out to the wide, high-ceilinged living room of the main house. The air was scented, a bit too heavily, with a floral essence. The air conditioner purred, wafting a chilled air. An ebony grand piano was set to the right of the room. Two bleached-blue daven-ports were placed side by side. Black leather sofas and embroidered ottomans were arranged in two sitting areas set off on opposite ends of the oblong room. Three chandeliers hung from the ceiling. The marble floor had a waxy shine. A huge entertainment unit held a flat-screen plasma TV and other gadgets. Figurines cast in plaster dotted the room. Ike was drawn to six framed paintings signed by four Nigerian artists whose names he didn't recognize. Two of the paintings depicted nude women, one black, the other white, one big-waisted with generous, droopy breasts, the other tall and thin, her slight breasts accentuated by dark, prominent nipples. The other paintings were abstract works dominated by whorl-like patterns or sturdy strokes. He went from canvas to canvas, gazing intensely until overcome by repulsion. Each painting seemed distinguished by a certain extravagance, an excessive avidity of color, as if commissioned by a man who traded subtlety of touch for a touch of gaudiness. Dismayed by the overwrought paintings, he wandered toward a giant rosary with fist-sized emerald beads staked around a large crucifix. On the floor, next to the beads, was a life-size photograph of Tony Iba in the habit of a knight, complete with plumed visors and a sword at his right shoulder. Heftier than Ike could have imagined him, Iba wore a blue sash across his neck with the words KNIGHT OF SAINT LUMUMBA. Then there was a photograph of Iba's family taken in a studio, his wife to his left, leaning into him, bearing a sad, reluctant smile, their two daughters standing on either side of their parents, their son stooped in the middle.

In the center of the room, recessed into a wall, was a fireplace. Ike gazed at it, unable to fathom the mystery of it. After a while, he shrugged and looked away.

A home like Iba's could easily belong in one of the tony quarters of the Bronx or in the more affluent sectors of Westchester County—anywhere, better still, where money counted more than taste. As he gazed at Iba's picture, Ike had the feeling that he was being watched from behind. He turned sharply and saw Iba's face, fleshy, with exuberant eyes.

"Tony Curtis!" Ike shouted.

"American Yankee!" Iba retorted.

Ike raised a hand, but Iba rounded him in an embrace. The servant watched from a respectful distance, eyes alight.

"How long since you arrived?" Iba asked.

"In Utonki or here?"

"Here."

"Thirty, thirty-five minutes."

Iba looked at the servant with anger. Fear swept away the smile that hovered on the man's face. "I was going to offer him something to drink, sir," he said, "but he was busy looking at the paintings."

Ike confirmed the account. Iba beamed at him. "You've visualized my paintings?" He affected a weary countenance. "Each is cost me a bundle."

"They're colorful," Ike offered.

"Yes, yes," Iba said, "they're spectaculous, indeed."

"Very spectacular. Yes."

Iba put on a mask of despair. "But I shouldn't be throwing away so much hard-boiled money into such luxuriations. Where will I find money to eat?"

"You don't seem in danger of starving," Ike said. "A man with this kind of house—did I say house? A man who owns this kind of mansion won't ever have trouble looking for food." He turned to his left, then to the right, indicating a sweep of the house.

Iba glowed. "My brother, let us titrate all the praise to God. He created the bottom and the top—and he architected this humble house."

"Humble house? This is—it's a bona fide palace! A veritable palace fit for a king."

"Ike the grammarian man!" shouted Iba, impressed by the sound of Ike's words.

"I mean every word."

"We conjugate all the glory to God almighty. He tumbles down

blessings to my arena. That's why I've made it a point of fundamental principle to take care of poor people. This efidice contains a
room where poor people watch TV. Even in my absent, the facility
is available unto them."

"I saw the poor people's TV room," Ike said. "They were watching a basketball game."

Ike strode to the piano. "A beautiful grand," he said. He struck
several keys, then drew his fingers across them. A berserk clangor
issued forth. Casting a quizzical look at his host, he asked, "How
often do you play it?"

"Me, play?" He chortled. "Am I a white man?"

"I guess your children play?"

"Well, you have to probe from my wife."

"Is she home?"

"Missus? No! She and my childs habitate far, far away. In
London."

"You're alone in this big house, then?" Ike asked.

"Yes o, my brother. I am quartered here, sufferating alone. My
missus and childs say the heat is three much here. So therefore they
navigated abroad to London where God blows AC inside the air. My
own is to sufferate for them to enjoy."

"I'm sure you're not complaining. You're a virtual bachelor. And
if I know you—"

Iba winked and brought a finger to his lips, playfully hushing
Ike. "Please, my brother, don't revelation my secret o." He motioned
in the servant's direction. "Simeon likes missus three much. In fact,
four much! He is her real husband; I am only a borrowee of her.
Whenever she lands here, she always donates fine, fine designer
shirts to Simeon. As for me, nothing! So Simeon can carelessly navigate my secrecies to her earlobes. And she will vex and somersault
me inside pepper soup!"

He and Ike laughed. Then, turning to the piano, Ike said, "It looks—definitely expensive."

"All gratifications to the owner of the sky and the earth," Iba remarked. "The moment I saw the piano in a *Famous Homes* catalog, I convicted myself to purchase it."

Iba's teeth gleamed, radiating pride. "Now, I have to be a fantastic hostage by tabulating a drink in front of you." He pointed to a small bar. Ike saw a tall rack studded with wine and liquor bottles. "Just announce your likes and dislikes to Simeon. For your informations, we also have a variation of beers in the refrigerator."

"I'd like to use the bathroom first," Ike said.

"Simeon, herald our distinguished guest to bathroom," Iba bellowed.

"This way, sir," said the servant.

Ike was astonished by the bathroom's width and golden flourish. The faucet, magazine rack, towel-holder, bathtub and sauna were all gold-plated. He cast a sidelong glance at the jet of his pee streaming into the bowl with an unerring aim. *"I'll make my money,"* he mumbled to himself, *"and my bathroom will be better than this."* He blew three breaths on the mirror. Across the spread of vapor, he scrawled GOD SNATCHER. He leered at the script and then smudged it. He ran fingers lightly over his ragged stubble, sticking out a tongue as if taunting the mirror.

He froze, imagining Iba or his servant watching him from a remote monitor. Iba was just the kind of man to orchestrate such a gimmick. The fear passed quickly. He did not usually linger before a mirror; but something about the mammoth size of this one drew out the imp in him.

He leaned forward and inspected his face. His eyes were slightly puffed, ringed by vague brown lines. He turned sideways and gave himself over to self-admiration. He was lean and flat-stomached, a contrast to Iba's paunchy heft.

Washing his hands, he made weirder faces at the mirror. A basket near the basin counter was stocked with a variety of cologne and perfume bottles. He removed the cover from three of them. His nostrils approved the scent marked Givenchy Pour Homme eau de toilette. He sprayed it on his neck and shirt, then unlocked the door.

To his surprise Iba lay on a sofa, his shod feet dangling to the side. Deep, snoring breaths escaped from his recumbent body.

"Don't worry, *oga* will wake up in five minutes," Simeon assured him. "What do I get you to drink, sir? We have spirits, red and white wine, juices, and minerals. We have assorted beer. We also have palm wine."

"Nothing for now," Ike said, waving him away. He too craved sleep, but as he lowered himself onto the soft sofa, Iba awakened.

"My main man from America!" he shouted, as if he'd been alert all along. "You look sharp—what's your secrecy?"

"Yankee magic," Ike said.

Iba roared with laughter. "American Yankee!" he cried, stamping his feet on the marble floor. When Ike rose to go, his host walked him to the door. Then, giving a parting handshake, Iba slid five hundred-dollar bills in Ike's palm.

Ike stared at the cash, somewhat uneasy.

"What's this?" he asked, his voice surprisingly calm.

Iba's face bore a self-satisfied smile. "Your share."

"My share? Of what?"

"Dividends of democracy! Almightiful God is using me as a classified retributor. Even though you are located in Yankeeland, still yet you're one of my royal constituencies. Therefore you deserve to reception your own dividend."

CHAPTER NINETEEN

Two days later, Ike's sister, Nkiru, arrived from Onitsha. Her sad eyes and acne-ravaged face startled him. Only three years Ike's senior, she could have passed for ten. Her hair, plaited in stylish rows, was speckled with rushes of gray. She had the surliness of one whose former beauty had been scarred and spoiled by suffering.

Nkiru had married early, just shy of twenty, and had given birth to six children but lost the last one at birth. As she herself told it in one of her rambling e-mails to Ike, she came close to dying as well.

Her life was hard. A petty trader, she owned a roadside kiosk in Fegge, one of the slums of Onitsha. Her ware included cigarettes, chewing gums, bar soaps, a variety of mints, sachets of sugar and salt, canned sardines, roasted groundnut, and shots of *kai-kai*, the locally brewed gin. Her *kai-kai*, which she got from a supplier in Asaba, the town split from Onitsha by the great river, had the reputation among her clients as the most potent in all of Fegge. When the men drank it, the gin lacerated their tongues and walloped the gut—which was exactly how the aficionados wanted it.

Nkiru's husband was a police sergeant who invested his meager salary—and his more ample takings in bribe—in gambling, beer, and marijuana. With a husband given to such recklessness, Nkiru was saddled with fending for herself and the children. She went at the task adroitly, but the pittance from the stall could only be stretched so far. Inevitably she turned to her brother for assistance.

No week had passed since he'd given her his e-mail address when she did not send multiple e-mails detailing her woes, her hapless condition. From time to time, he sent money via Western Union but never as much as she asked for. Her tirades and pleas exhausted him, and, woeful as her marriage was, he could neither forget nor forgive the obnoxious stubbornness with which she had made the choice to enter it. He remembered their parents' outrage on discovering that Nkiru had started dating the police officer, then a constable, the year she finished secondary school. Their mother had locked the door and dealt her a merciless flogging. Then Nkiru had been forbidden ever to see the man. The next day, they eloped. She reemerged several weeks later, obstinate as ever, to announce that she was pregnant. Their parents, devout Catholics then, could contemplate neither an abortion nor the shame of their only daughter having a child out of wedlock. Yet, to compound matters, the officer had accused her of sneaking about with other lovers, even naming names. In the end, it was only after her child, a son, was born that he came around and married her.

Nkiru's rebelliousness had brought shame on the family and led her to a grim life. She sacrificed her university education to hitch up with Reuben the officer.

FOR THE TWO DAYS before Nkiru arrived in Utonki, Ike's mother had hardly spoken to him. She muttered monosyllabically. When he greeted her, she whispered a low, inaudible response. When their paths crossed, she mumbled. She used Nkiru's daughter, Alice, as a conduit to send him any messages that were unavoidable. His meals were couriered by Alice. Once, when Alice was away running an errand, his mother brought his food. She placed the plates on a table next to his bed—and then, walking backward, made a languid motion of the hand.

Ike knew that his visits to Osuakwu and Nne had cut his mother deeper than the sharpest knife. When around him, she wore a dazed look and walked in a flatfooted, plodding manner. He was worried but not sorry.

He wanted the rift mended, and he'd hoped that Nkiru would serve as an agent of reconciliation, but he was clear on one point: he would never capitulate. He would never negotiate away his right to visit Osuakwu and Nne as often as he pleased.

When the fuss of pleasantries had worn off and he had sat down with his sister to talk, Ike rushed to make a point he considered of fundamental import.

"I'm going to be blunt, Nkiru," he began, like a pugilist issuing fair warning before unleashing a killer punch. "I'm angry with you."

Nkiru sprang to her feet as if stung by a bee. Ever the fighter, she pounded her chest. "You, angry? What do you mean?" She placed clenched knuckles on her waist and glared down at Ike.

"Sit down," he said, his voice calm.

"You can't tell me what to do," she shouted. "You're not my husband. And I'm older than you." She sat down, her eyes blazing.

Ike met her glare. "You knew all along that Mama had thrown herself into the deceptive hands of Pastor Uka. You knew Uka had filled her head with crap, but you said nothing. You should have warned her about the man. You should have told her that he was a scam artist trading on her fears and sorrows. Then the situation would not have got out of hand. Instead, it's absolutely awful. Today, does Mama talk to Father's only brother? You know the answer is—no! Does she talk to Father's mother? No, too! To her, they're devils in human skin. They're wizard and witch. She has accused them of killing her husband—and of plotting to kill you and me."

"That's why you're angry?" she asked, as she drew her face away and muttered under her breath.

"You should not have let these things happen," he said, attempting a conciliatory tone. "Now it's up to you and me to open Mama's eyes. It's our duty to reconcile her with Osuakwu and Nne."

For what seemed a full minute, Nkiru glared at him. Twice she opened her lips to talk, but no words came out. Her lips twitched. She found her voice just as he started to speak further.

"These people killed our father," she said, "and you want Mama to sit down and eat with them?" She paused and momentarily regarded him with eyes that were less angry than sad and confounded. Then she continued: "Ike, you're old enough to know what's right from what's wrong. Mama has told me everything, how you brought her to shame by insulting a man of God."

"A man of scams!" he shouted.

Her expression took on a stern aspect, but her voice remained even. "Let me tell you, Ike. When Mama's pastor told you not to visit these evil people, you should have listened."

Ike felt himself temporarily immobilized. "You too," he said at last. "You too are part of this nonsense. You're superstitious. You're willing to believe any crap. You believe that Nne and Osuakwu conspired to kill Father."

"You've gone through university, Ike," she said, her tone drained of heat, "but some things are not taught in school. There is evil in the world. The answer, my brother, is to cover yourself with the blood of Jesus. When you went to see Osuakwu and Nne, did you not drink?"

Ike nodded his affirmation.

A look of alarm wreathed her face. "Did you eat?"

He affirmed again.

"Please, o, please," she said, slapping her palms in an urgent, hysterical gesture. She loosened her wrapper and retied it as market women do just before they fight. "Come with me immediately," she begged, her body shivering with anxiety. "You've eaten devilish food and drank satanic drink. Let's go, my brother. Let's go and see Pastor Uka. I know you insulted him, but I'll fall on the ground and beg him for you. As a man of God he'll forgive you for every insult. In fact, he's forgiven you already—trust me. He needs to pray to release you from all bondage. Please, let us go."

Loathing filled his chest to bursting. "You—you're mad!" he cried. He stood and stormed off. Yanking at the door, he turned and announced, "I'm going to see Osuakwu now. Then I'll visit Nne before coming home. Don't bother to leave me food; I'll return filled."

He slammed the door after him. At first, his ears picked up a whimper. Then came the explosion of a funereal wail.

CHAPTER TWENTY

Osuakwu had a kola nut in his hand and was about to say invocations when Ike stooped in through the shrine's low eaves.

"My son, the leg that brought you is fine," his uncle said, waving Ike to the raised platform. There were four other men in the shrine. Ike recognized Iji, Agbusi, and Man Mountain Polycarp, but not the fourth man who sported a groomed mustache and wore a ribbed beige T-shirt.

"Ngene," Osuakwu prayed, "we have kola nut in our hands. Take the nut and eat. Spirit of noon, we're in the crook of your loins. Take the nut and eat. Spirit of morning has carried us, and has now handed us over to your care. While the morning spirit cradled us, we never had strife nor did we hear a wail. So we ask you, spirit of noon, to emulate the morning spirit. Until you put us in the care of the evening spirit, may we not hear a cry and may our heads not hurt." He raised the nut above his head. "Chukwu who lives in the sky, take the nut and eat it. You rest your head on the cloud while your legs sweep the earth, we ask that you bless us."

He broke the nut into four lobes, took one, and then put the others in a bowl. He asked Ike, as the youngest, to cut the lobes into more pieces and serve everybody, starting with the oldest.

As each man crunched his piece, Osuakwu lowered himself onto his chair. "The den of Ngene never goes dry. There's *nkwu*, there's *ngwo*, and—for those from the white man's land—there are drinks that stuff the nostrils and touch the eye. To each man, his own."

Ike, remembering the monstrous headache from the gin, decided to go for *ngwo*, the sweet, frothy palm wine. He poured himself a cup and sat back down.

A generator buzzed steadily behind the shrine, powering a standing fan that swept from one side to another, blowing bellows of hot air. Save for the drone of the generator, the pant of the fan, and the grunts of men, the shrine was silent. Ike held the cup of palm wine to his lips, his eyes fixed on the statue of Ngene. His heart beat frenziedly. Glancing sideward, he saw the stranger watching him.

"I'm Ikechukwu Uzondu," he said, stretching a hand toward the stranger. "Osuakwu is my uncle."

"Oh-oh," Osuakwu said, as if stirring from slumber. "Age is doing things to me. Ike, my son, this man you see here is just like you. He speaks and writes the white man's words as if he was born with it. His name is Okwudili Okeke. There's no white man's country his feet have not touched. He knows so much of the white man's language that they gave him the title of doctor, even though I hear he can't cure common headache."

Everybody laughed.

"He's the man I told you to come and meet."

"You wrote a book about Stanton," Ike said.

"The white man who perished trying to poke a finger at Ngene," Osuakwu interjected.

"You're the guy from America," Dr. Okeke said, taking Ike's hand. He foraged in his bag and brought out a slim book.

Ike accepted it. He held the book away from his face and then squinted to read the title: *Rev. Dr. Stanton: A Missionary's Misadventures in Africa.*

"How much do you sell it for?" Ike asked.

"It's free to you—compliments of the author."

"Thanks," Ike said. Then, as his thought went to Foreign Gods, Inc., his heart leapt with a mixture of excitement and panic. "Wow," he said, blowing breath.

"Ngene is no puppy of a deity," Osuakwu said.

"Even the British are not in doubt about that," Dr. Okeke said in Igbo. Then, to Ike, he said in English, "I wrote my book after stumbling upon the diaries of Reverend Stanton at the British archives."

Osuakwu smiled. "We sit in this small shrine in Utonki, but the exploits of Ngene have reached the ears of the British." He smiled as his eyes lingered on the statue of Ngene. Then he began to shower the deity with praises.

"Ngene, warrior's penis that sired a warrior! Ngene, your fart is thunder, your breath fire. In the days of brave men, you led Utonki's men and women in their march to war. Ngene, whenever you appeared in the thick of battle, a shower of lightning heralded you. Ngene, you made your foe beg for the comfort of his mother's womb! Besieged by your rage, valiant men lost heart. They beckoned on their legs to run, run, run; they ran like deer from a lioness!"

Ike thumbed open the first page of Dr. Okeke's book and read.

The heyday of Ngene was many, many moons ago, before the white man came and turned the world on its head, made today into yesterday, and decreed the cohabitation of lion and lamb. These days, many an elder of Utonki, thinking back to the days of valor, would sigh and grumble that the world was no longer what it used to be. "Greatness has vanished from the world," such a man might say, depths of sadness etched on his brow.

Once upon a time, Ngene was unrivaled in the lands of Olu and Igbo.

Yet, the deity's appearance was unremarkable. Its carver seemed to have set out to achieve an odd discrepancy between reputation and appearance. Any trained eye that fell on the statue was struck by its ambiguous motifs. They were etched in the deity's every gesture—and stipulated in its size.

Rising only to an average man's thighs, the wooden statue is dominated by a stylized, androgynous figure delicately seated atop an orb. The deity's hands are spread out in a posture that suggests splayed vulnerability. Seen from a different angle, Ngene seems frozen in the pose of an embracer yearning to be embraced in return. From yet another angle, its gesture is proprietary, as if it were gathering the entire universe onto the arc of its dominion. In one hand, the deity holds a short spear; in the other, a large round object. The object's size and roundedness bring to mind a giant egg. But if food-minded villagers are to be believed, it's not an egg but a mound of pounded yam. "Look at its mouth," they'd challenge a doubter. The deity's mouth is shaped into an exaggerated gape. "A mouth like that shows a deity whose appetite roars."

In long-gone days, when lizards were in ones and twos and Utonki was the terror of its neighbors, the deity's mouth inspired dread. It belched thunder, claimed its worshippers, and flashed lightning. Those who still venerate the deity would boast that those were the days when men were men, and warriors were known for the valor of their arms. Then that world fell on its face, ruined by the rule of white men who made wimps of warriors and haughty warriors of cowards.

These days, the elders would look at the deity's mouth and tremble with sorrow. They would say the once-thunder-belching mouth has been reduced to a pout. Rather than evoking fierceness, the deity's expression now suggests archness and anguished despair. For some elders, the pout resembles a famished yawn. Others say it's a sign of boredom, or a child's bewildered wail.

The statue was hewn out of the bulk of an oji *tree. When first sawed, the* oji *tree glistens, its exposed skin aglow with whiteness. Then, as the sun beats it, the skin turns a peculiar hue, a cross between brown and red. In the pantheon of trees, nothing is sturdier and heftier than oji. Nor is any tree more steeped in folklore. In some stories, its tip is deemed to be halfway between earth and sky. It was on such a tree that the cunning Tortoise and his dupes, the overtrusting Birds, perched for their last discussion as they headed for a feast in the sky. In carving Ngene out of such a tree, the artist realized the ultimate ambiguity. The statue conveyed an impression both of solidity and dynamic energy.*

By stifling the old order, the colonizing white man robbed Ngene of its once-unchallenged perch. When he outlawed wars and disarmed warriors, the white man stripped Ngene of its offices. Had the deity been a mere puppy, instead of the former scourge of enemy cavalries, the white man might have banished it altogether.

Ike paused, sipped his *ngwo*, and exhaled. Glancing up, he saw Dr. Okeke pulling at his mustache, looking at him with interest.

"This is wonderful." Ike shook the booklet. He pictured Mark Gruels reveling in it. "Fantastic!" he cried, to calm his quickened heart.

"I went deep, deep into the British archives to dig up the story. And then I came here to interview Osuakwu and other elders."

Ike gulped down the *ngwo* and wiped off the froth from his lips. Something about the air in the shrine made him uneasy, panic stricken. He wanted to sneak away. Perhaps, in the quiet of his room, he would be at ease, able to wade into the rest of the book.

"Osuakwu," he greeted.

"Eh, my son," his uncle said.

"I meant to stop in and greet you quickly."

"It's fine, my son. Go, but always return."

Ike took his leave. He walked home in quick, long strides. Alice met him as he entered the house.

"Your food is ready, sah."

"I'm not hungry yet," he said, then swept past her to his room. He lay across the bed and opened the booklet.

Then he was lost in the story of that famed missionary named Stanton, a man who made a sport of punching and slapping his interpreter at will, a man whose fierce bouts of temper drove away some of the converts that his theatrical personality had drawn to him, a giant of a man whose small, uncircumcised penis was the object of lewd jokes, a creature of habit who trudged to the banks of the river each morning, and removed everything but his underwear, indifferent to the scandalized stares of onlookers, and dove in for a swim. One day, with his mission thriving, converts arriving in droves, Stanton took ill, his condition worsened, kept him homebound, indoors, a wrecked man gripped by fever, at night his booming voice chastising the demons only he could see. When everybody thought the man a hopeless case, he'd ventured out of his hut. The next morning, he had dragged himself to the river, stipped naked for the first time, and plunged. He neither surfaced nor was his bloated corpse ever spat out by the river. Then the people of Utonki said that the white man who came by the river had taken a trip home by the same river.

CHAPTER TWENTY—ONE

The night when Ike planned to snatch Ngene seemed to steal upon him. Yet he was steeled, ready.

His first seven days in Utonki had seemed a whirl, rapidly passing into oblivion. He'd been too involved in a flurry of activities to keep a firm grip on time as it slipped away. It was only on that decisive day, amazed at how soon it had come around, that he sat down and attempted to look back. Even so, he was able only to resurrect fragmented accounts of how he had spent his days.

He remembered the steady retinue of near and distant relatives who came to see him, their pleas for cash prefaced by grim tales of woe. He'd been at one traditional wedding, two funerals, and a child-naming ceremony. He remembered each event for its ritual and color, its dizzying sounds and movements. He recalled how each ceremony lasted long, accommodating his people's knack for talk—meandering, circumlocutory, proverb-laced talk.

The rest of his time had gone into a routine he'd set by his third day. It included daily visits to see Osuakwu, Nne, and Iba. Each evening, he walked to Uvunu, the stream where, long ago, Regina and he had made their rendezvous of youthful love. He went because the brook's sights and sounds calmed his nerves. He would sit on the ledge, shaded from the waning sun by the shadows of the trees, then sway his dangling legs while delighting in the ambience.

Uvunu offered a rich banquet of colors, varied scents, and seductive music. All around him, the scenery seemed to ooze with sensuous life. Reclined on the ledge, he opened himself. He let his eyes feast, permitted the sounds to pour into his ears and pores, and allowed the scented air to saturate his lungs. The panoply of plants filled him with wonder. He marveled at the creepers that matted the ground. His eyes traced a vine twined over the stem of a tall tree, before reaching out for one of the tree's branches and losing itself among the foliage. He saw brambles and cactuses that stood in ambush for careless wanderers. Butterflies, some radiantly colored, others less so, fluttered about or perched on flowers. The wind made a rustling sound, and the leaves swayed in a lazy dance. Toads croaked. Crickets chirred. Decayed leaves and moldered stumps diffused an oaken scent in the air while flowers countered with their intoxicating aroma.

But hard as Ike strained his ear, he could hear no echoes of the sound he came to seek, to tease back from years past. It was the sound of moans that gurgled in Regina's throat during those callow escapades in love's name, then slipped out in calibrated songs. It seemed lost forever—that cry of desire that once hushed the world's other clacks and clangs. Regina's elusive love song was a heady, sibilant displacement of air.

What a pity that Regina was now a ragged apparition. The greater pity was that the trees had forgotten how to sing her moans.

CHIEF TONY IBA, ALIAS Tony Curtis, had decided to prolong his stay in Utonki, but only after he had made Ike promise to visit every day. The arrangement suited Ike rather well. He talked with the habitués who gathered at Iba's each evening to watch reels of old American sitcoms, movies, and sports. Whenever Iba dozed off for his incessant short naps, Ike sneaked out to see the TV watchers. He nagged them with questions about their American fantasies. From them he spooled reams and reams of anecdotes.

Iba himself was the source of a particular brand of comic relief—the more poignant for all his efforts to dispel any suggestion of levity. Twice each day, at 9:00 A.M. and then at 9:00 P.M., Iba's servant rang a bell and then bellowed, "Tea is served!" Then he appeared, butler-like, in one hand two spotless, pressed cotton napkins, a tray aloft in the other, with crackers, three varieties of cheese, gold-plated teacups and spoons, and two ornate crystal containers, one for milk, the other for ground sugar.

Wherever Ike went in Utonki, he opened his ears to stories. He also opened his lips, determined to drink until he was drunk. He drank whatever was offered—*nkwu, ngwo*, or bottle after bottle of beer at Osuakwu's shrine, or, at Iba's, glass after glass of wine mixed with tall shots of cognac or liqueur. He drank until his mind became a blur, an insensate bubble afloat in a whirlpool.

The alcohol sedated his spirit. It steadied his nerves and kept him from shaking in the presence of his uncle and the deity. Inebriation enabled him to keep his mind limber, free from agitation over the mission that inspired his return. It gave him the advantage of shadowing his uncle's deity without feeling a tinge of remorse. Tipsy, he was able to circle his quarry without betraying signs of undue anxiety. He drank to lure his mind to forgetfulness. He feared that remembrance could paralyze him. It could cost him his resolve. On the other hand, forgetfulness would steel him.

Ike spent the early afternoon of the seventh day packing. Then, as the sun began its lumbering descent, he set out to make farewell visits to Osuakwu, Nne, and Tony Iba. He asked Alice to tell his mother that he would come home well after dinnertime.

He was unusually quiet and withdrawn. At each stop, he drank slowly, absentmindedly. At the shrine, he sat in pained rigidity, knees drawn close to him, clasped in place by the bow of his entwined hands. He freed his hands only to take liberal swills from his beer-filled mug. He set his head at a stiff, cocked angle, dreading to cast even a furtive glance at the statue. The compound was even more noisy than usual. When Osuakwu remarked on his unaccustomed taciturnity, he shrugged it off.

"It's the sorrow of the traveler about to leave home," his uncle pronounced with an infallible air. The other men nodded or muttered their agreement.

Nne, too, noticed his wistfulness. "My son," she said, rubbing her palms, "your spirit is quiet. Your voice also sounds mournful. Is it me you mourn?" When he said nothing, she continued: "Have you realized, as I have, that you'll never see me alive again? Is that what sags your spirits?" She paused again, raising her head to reveal a neck gnarled with wrinkles. She seemed to listen to the birds twittering from the branches of the frangipani tree to the left of her hut, next to one of the mango trees. A startled look came over her face, as if the birds had confided some secrets. "Something ails you," she said, her tone portentous.

"I'm fine, only tired from getting ready for my trip tomorrow."

Head raised, she regarded him with a blind glare. He looked away, disturbed by the intensity of her sightless stare. Her palms, rubbed slowly, penetrated his consciousness with their soft, faraway whistle.

"Something other than the weight of departure ails you," she insisted. "I know it, yet I remain blind to what it is. Tell me, my son: is it because soon you will look and not find me? If so, I say, brighten your face. Am I to sprout roots on this earth? Don't grieve for me, my son. I've lived. I've lived so long that the very ground sings me to my every destination. My feet in turn have mastered the shape of each path I walk. The earth knows the tread of my feet. Years ago, a black coat fell over my eyes. I stopped seeing as I used to. Yet, I started *seeing* in a new, deeper way. I now see even the things masked by the night. That's why it troubles me that I cannot see this thing that has darkened your voice. Is it fear for me, Son? Is it my death? Whatever it is, I beg you to sweeten your face. Remember that your heart is still young. It's too young to bear a sad weeping."

He drank the potent *nkwu* she offered him in a gourd. As he rose to leave, he slipped a wad of naira notes in her palm. She raised a cry that moved the air with its joy, momentarily silencing the birds.

Leaving her, he headed for Tony Iba's mansion. His gait was a slow, shambling roll, like a drunk's. He ambled along, dreaming of the drinks that awaited him.

By the time he left Iba's home, at 10:36 P.M., he had drunk so much that he felt ready.

KNOWING THAT OSUAKWU RETIRED each night around 10:00 P.M., Ike staggered into the open, dark shrine with the swagger and abandon of a burglar breaching a house whose occupants he had spied taking off on a long vacation.

Yet, something about the ease of his entry stirred up a rogue dread. As he fumbled toward the statue, he heard the awful dissonant sound of his uncle's snoring. It cackled to a crescendo, then snapped. As if ambushed by the sleeping chief priest, Ike stood in the shrine, unable to move a limb. His heartbeat became so cranky that he feared he was going to fall flat on his face. He was assailed by some heaviness in the air and a stink that was indefinable. The drink that had fortified him moments ago seemed to have drained away, leaving his mind lucid, a prisoner to a welter of emotions.

A persistent thought beat a conga in his mind: *What if you're caught?* He stood, transfixed by the question's awful refrain. For a moment, he was so confused that he considered exiting the shrine empty-handed, renouncing the dream that had brought him into a god's lair at 11:00 P.M. Then an idea entered his head. *Caught, I'd say that I entered the shrine to save Ngene from Pastor Uka. I'd say I had overheard Uka plotting with some shadowy men that night to steal the deity and make a bonfire of it, and I hastened to protect it.*

Preposterous as the response was, it sufficed to bolster his resolve. It was as if a force stronger than dread had come to the rescue and pried him from his fluctuating heart. That guiding force held up beatific images to his imagination. It showed him glimpses of all the pleasures to be had by a man if only he stood firm. Instantaneously, the welcoming waft of crisp dollar notes filled his nostrils. He pictured a penitent Queen B kneeling before him. Cadilla and the insolent horde that gathered at his store would be dazzled by his affluence, struck with awe. All his bills would be paid off, with lots of cash to spare. The vision took on a palpable force, and that force melted his fear and sluiced away its sediments.

His legs, which had been heavy, jerked, like a horse's, into life. His heart continued with its clamor, but its beat was now harnessed not to capitulation but to dreams of things to be possessed by the brave who stared fear down.

Hands sweeping the dark air, he touched the deity's face. His fingers felt something viscous and thick, and he knew it was sacrificial blood. He groped along the statue's wooden outline all the way to its torso. In the dark his hands could feel the sturdiness of the chiseled wood. The statue rested on a squat base that enabled the deity, in the eye of even casual beholders, to exude an air of grandeur appropriate to a god whose department was war.

He placed one hand around the statue's neck and the other on its rump, and then lifted. Finding it much heavier than he had expected, he put it down. How could something so spare and lanky prove so dense and earthbound? In the dark, he wondered whether the deity had tensed itself, made its weight leaden, bent on deadening the abductor's will.

He knew that Ngene was a mobile deity. As a youngster, he had on numerous occasions seen Osuakwu hoist it upright on his shoulder and trek to villages far and near—wherever an oath needed to be taken—and back. Yet, his uncle was not only much older, he was also a man of meager musculature. And years of overquaffing *kai-kai* had made the old man seem frailer than many men his age.

Ike flexed, but when he lifted the statue a second time its weight seemed lighter, mysteriously much lighter. He placed it on his shoulder, the same way he'd seen his uncle carry it, and turned to leave. He didn't raise his legs high enough; his sneakers scraped against the earthen floor and screeched. His heart jumped. From a nearby room Osuakwu coughed twice, muttered something dreamily, then resumed his snoring.

He gingerly stepped out of the shrine.

A soft breeze cooled the beads of sweat on his face and neck. He drew several deep breaths and prayed the night to keep his secret. The drafts of air were mixed with the deity's disgusting smell. He kicked out his legs to shake off an incipient cramp.

His head, crammed moments before with a jumble of emotions, became strangely uncluttered. The pressure of the statue's weight against his hand and shoulder kept him rooted in the present. He wondered how long he'd been in the shrine, impaled by fear. It seemed to him like hours.

As he walked with the statue toward his home, his legs felt now limber, now lifeless. Sometimes he feared that his legs had turned into wooden stilts, had the illusion of being rooted on the same spot, or even of falling backward. That illusion was heightened by the night, shrouded in a widow's dark cloth, a swirling, liquid darkness. In his mental rehearsals, he had counted on the darkness serving as a dumb ally of his scheme. Instead, it had unaccountably turned foe. The darkness cast spells, exhumed fears he never suspected he still nursed, and made his heart pound like a drum beaten by a drummer possessed.

A spasm rocked his spine as a roving owl cooed its awful anthem. Other cacophonous creatures paused fleetingly, as though wary of the owl's talon and scotopic eyes. Then they resumed their unmelodious din.

It was an awful moment. Until he encountered it, he would have sworn that he had shaken free of the dread of darkness. His heart, pounding anew, betrayed him.

His tossing, riotous mind swept him in the direction of his life in America. All he could think of was the word "accent." It was as if the very name of America could be formed with those six perilous letters. Instigated—provoked—by that word, his heart surged up in a new wave of resentment toward America.

Indeed, that one word, "accent," was the reason he was out that night, a deity's stinking statue pressed against his shoulder. Some part of him felt that America's collective will had compelled him to sneak out that night, a thief. It would also be the beginning of his revenge—if his will could hold up against the sway of fear.

He could accept that he'd failed at shedding his burdensome accent. He'd tried, but failed, to coax his tongue to roll around English words in a fashion acceptable to that strange animal called corporate America. Yet, he was, until that moment, certain of his liberation from the species of irrational fear that froze him in the shrine. If, before that traitorous moment, he had looked hard at himself, if he'd stared into his inmost heart and assessed himself as a man, he would have considered himself free of any form of superstition. At any rate, he would have judged himself beyond the spell of pagan notions that once enthralled one of his maternal aunts, his mother's older sister, now long dead.

Onu kputu kputu, this aunt was called, an onomatopoeic tribute to her diarrheic mouth, a mouth that was never dry of stories. He remembered her long-ago stories about nights so dark they gave people a perfect sense of what it must mean to be purely, horribly blind. Such nights, she would say, were favored by witches and wizards who traipsed through space, disguised as bats and owls, to do their bloody business. It was the sort of darkness, according to another lore of hers, which made malevolent spirits hungry for the road. Another of her claims was that, whether dark as charcoal or bright with the dazzle of moonlight, the night had eyes.

She was the archetypal talebearer, said to stay underneath a shade and still see the sun. She knew when any man slipped out at night to sneak into a widow's bed. She knew when a married woman took a lover among the sex-crazed youth of the village. She knew all the men and women who had eaten the malediction of witchcraft, who sailed at night to drink others' blood. She could tell who among the villagers harmed their neighbors with malignant gris-gris.

Tiny lakes of perspiration emerged from imperceptible pores and streaked Ike's forehead. The itchy dots became streams. With each step, some silent voice told him it was better to turn around and return the deity to its shrine. But, at last, he arrived home.

He gave a delicate push and the gate squeaked open. In his pocket he searched out the key to the house. He was about to insert it into the keyhole, but recoiled. What if his mother had chosen this, his last night, to brave another conversation with him? He left the statue outside the door, then entered the house. The darkness in the living room seemed even heavier than the one outside. For a moment, he stood, ears strained to pick up any sound. Hearing none, he dashed outside and hoisted the statue up, carrying it in his twinned hands. He set it down quickly to lock the door. In his bedroom, he walked cautiously, using his toes to grope, to navigate toward the suitcases. He swaddled the statue in some of his clothes and old dust-laden newspapers his late father had read and hoarded. He pushed the swaddled treasure against the back of his bigger suitcase and then arranged other clothes around it. He locked the suitcase, then felt the tug of a hideous pressure in his loin. He retrieved the bottle of cognac he had emptied and hidden under the bed. Then, kneeling, he held the bottle with unsteady hands and peed, relishing the bottle's feel of heat.

He tucked the bottle under the bed and lay down. The night air had become cooler, but he was drenched, exhausted. It was as if he'd just brawled with a strong, sinewy foe. He began to make the sign of the cross, but his maternal aunt's apparition materialized in all her taunting solidity, aborting his prayer. She stood over his bed, her ironic storyteller's face wreathed with malice. "Do you have the strength to wrestle with Night?" she teased. She rocked with a menacing laughter. Still quaking with mirth, the ghost merged into the darkness and disappeared.

He lay in bed, unable to sleep. The air in his room was dense. Breathing became a chore. Sweat beaded his forehead and poured from his armpits. He tossed and turned, ravaged by insomnia. Unable to see, he didn't know what the time was, but he was tormented by the sensation of time grinding lazily, guaranteeing a long, stretched-out night. He felt as if he were the lone solitary soul awake in a sleeping, dreaming world. His body was too racked by weariness to fend off the terrors or pray the demons away.

In the eerie swell of silence and darkness, his interior quaked with clanks and tremors. He was like a man swept along by a powerful, implacable current. He grasped after every flimsy, floating twine, aching for rescue. After a while, he reconciled with the futility of every effort.

Suddenly, he heard isolated pelts on the zinc roof. Then the beat changed into the furious clang and clatter of a tropical torrent. Would he survive the storm? Ike wondered.

Chief Tony Iba had promised to send a driver at 8:00 A.M. to give him a ride to the Enugu Airport. Until then, he would lie awake and await the dawn.

A PIERCING CRY STARTLED him awake. The cry circled and circled in his head as he struggled to rouse from a sleep that had drawn him away.

"*Aiyi! Aiyi! Aiyi! Utonki, anwuo muo! Anwuo muo! Anwuo muo! Anya afu m ifeo!*" Osuakwu's wail shook the leaden dawn.

The clarity of the cry astonished Ike. Living in several American cities, he'd forgotten how quiescent the Utonki dawn could be, so that the voices of women going to or from the village stream or of men greeting one another as they set out for their farms carried far.

The priest kept screaming that he had died, that his eyes had seen something. It was the same torrent six or seven times and then silence.

Ike's hands shook. As he held his breath, he made out other sounds and voices. He heard neighbors' doors as they were unlatched and flung open. Then there were the worried voices of men and women, stirred too early from sleep, as they hurried toward the shrine, exchanging questions. At such times, certain that something dreadful had happened, the people of Utonki were wont to speak at the top of their voices. It was as if, speaking loudly, they could shake off the tremor in their voices. That tremor was a product of deep, instinctive fear—of that yet-unknown malevolent force that seemed to hold Osuakwu to the ground, writhing. Several loud voices intruded on Ike's consciousness.

"What is it this early in the morning?" "What is this thing our ears are hearing?" "Why is Eze Ngene announcing his own death?" "Did the night grow horns to menace the chief priest?" The voices made dire assertions: "Something stronger than Cricket surely has gone after Cricket in its hole." "A toad doesn't do a noon sprint for play; something is usually after it." "There's terror in that cry." "When a woman runs and holds her breasts, it is still play. When a woman must flee, she doesn't hold down her flapping breasts." They prayed: "May our eyes never see our ears." "May all bad spirits fly off to the Evil Forest." "What we don't know, may it never know us." They made declamations to shore up their spirits: "There's nothing the eye sees that can make it cry blood." "There's nothing that can't be mended in this world, only death."

Osuakwu's fresh cry of agony drowned out the other voices. His anguished cry, like a toneless refrain, was harsh decoration for the conversations.

One man's voice struck a note of prophecy: "Perhaps Ngene has decided to change the hand that brings it food."

The suggestion shocked the drove into a momentary hush. Presently, a man's excited voice said, "You have brought out a new word! There must be a fight between Ngene and Osuakwu. Why didn't I think sooner about that instead of twisting in worry?"

Eavesdropping from his bed, Ike understood the implication of the theory. His maternal aunt had once told him that the deity was capable of acting capriciously when it wanted to dismiss an inept priest or to hire a new man to minister to it. Sometimes the deity just killed off the incompetent chief priest. Then, through divination, it revealed the name of the next man it had chosen to be his voice. But there were times when the deity made a serving chief priest go berserk, a raving lunatic.

The words of the worried whispering men suggested that Osuakwu's cries signified the onset of the priest's mental malady.

Ike started as a tap on the door disrupted his monitoring of anonymous voices. He curled up to feign sleep. Three sharper knocks thudded against the door, but he maintained silence. His mother turned the knob and stepped in. She stood near the door, as if scared of her son thundering in rage if she went closer. One eye opened, Ike looked at her, mute. Strips of light silhouetted her emaciated frame. As if he were seeing her for the first time, it dawned on him that she had lost a frightful amount of weight since her husband's death.

Against the light, she looked like a shroud, ghostly. He'd easily defied her wish that he not visit Nne and Osuakwu. His triumph was proof that she'd also shrunk from all directions, lost her vitality and voice. In the face of his open defiance, she had merely skulked off into silence. Inside, he felt a tinge of regret at the ease with which he disobeyed her.

"Are you awake? Or did I wake you?" she asked in a tentative, apologetic tone.

He rubbed his eyes with the back of his palm, thinking, *Who but a corpse could sleep through the chief priest's rumpus?* He wanted to say that he was awake, but the words died in his throat. Did she, he wondered, hear his heart's riotous beat?

She sniffed the air.

"Something smells in your room," she said.

"I smell nothing," he said quickly, reprovingly.

"Pastor would have come to sanctify your room. But you chose to dine with demons." There was an old feisty spark in her voice, as if she had equipped herself for one last, parting fight.

"Thank him for me for not bothering," he said.

"*Anwuo muo!*" the chief priest wailed again.

In the semidarkness, Ike's mother appeared to tremble. Ike sat up in bed, again wiped the sides of his eyes, and yawned. His breath smelled rotten.

"Have you heard *your* uncle's cries?" she asked. "Perhaps the devil he's been eating with now wants to eat him. Perhaps a black scorpion has stung his anus. Perhaps his youngest wife has broken his head with a pestle. People had warned him that a man his age shouldn't have married a girl young enough to be his granddaughter. But did he listen? No! He sold his ear to the devil and bought a mat with the money. Maybe the sapling has finally cut off his— rope."

Ike smiled, amused by the difficulty with which his mother said "rope." Even children freely used the word, but his mother spat it out as if it were a sin-drenched word, a poisonous word that had crawled into her mouth.

When Ike said nothing, she asked, "Are you still leaving today?"

"Yes. Chief Iba will send me a driver soon."

"I'll be praying and fasting for you. Pastor will pray even more, so that God may open your eyes."

"You don't need to fast for me, Mama. Please, please, eat. You need it. A week or two after I return to New York, I'll send you more money. You'll have enough money to eat whatever you want."

She shook her head sadly. "Pastor and I'll pray and fast until you're delivered. Go well." She sniffed the air, turned, and walked away.

Osuakwu wailed. Ike's nostrils filled with a faint, yeasty smell.

Outside, a car horn beeped. Ike dragged his suitcases out. He lifted the one with the statue and pushed it inside the trunk, waving off the driver's offer to help.

"Death has come for me at dawn!" Osuakwu wept.

Ike's legs felt wobbly. "I will be back," he said to the driver as soon as the trunk was shut. Rushing back to the house, he washed his face with his palm. Using a washcloth, he scrubbed his armpits and neck. He dressed hastily in a pair of jeans and a maroon T-shirt. Then he hastened to Osuakwu's abode.

Many people milled about, hands clasped across their chests, murmuring or silent. Ike wove his way past the small, growing crowd to the entrance into the shrine. Osuakwu sat on the bare floor, torso leaning back, eyes fixed on nothing, like a dead man's. Osuakwu had cast aside his undershirt, revealing his World War II scar, and his chest that rose and fell at uneven intervals, like a heart's throes before death.

"*Osuakwu, ogini?*" Ike asked, standing to one side of his prone uncle.

Other sympathizers hushed, as if they expected the distraught priest to gather his wits and speak reasonably to his US-based nephew.

For a while, Osuakwu did not stir. Ike felt perspiration trickling from his armpits. He folded his arms, confused, afraid to speak any more words. Suddenly, Osuakwu sat up, his lips parted as if to shriek, except that no words came.

Their eyes met. Ike saw a vacant look in Osuakwu's gaze, as if his uncle could suddenly see into time, into space, into the recesses of secret treacheries.

Ike couldn't tell how he was able to mutter, "I'm leaving this morning." Hands still folded, he edged his way out of the crush of people, his legs wobbly but miraculously holding up.

CHAPTER TWENTY–TWO

The departure lounge at Murtala Muhammed International Airport was bedlam, a stew of heat, intemperate voices and sweat-drenched passengers. Ike took his place at the rear of a line that meandered to the KLM check-in counter.

He tapped his shoes on the terrazzo floor, comforted by the tactility of the ground beneath his feet. He'd spent time rehearsing this serene pose, but his ability to pull it off surprised him.

A woman directly in front of him whipped around and cast a frowning face up at him. Sweeping her hand in an agitated manner, she griped, "Is this line moving at all?"

He shrugged in a listless gesture that stopped short of ignoring her. She was traveling with three restless, unruly children, two boys and a girl. Unaware of the crowd around them, they played tag, carelessly bumping into other passengers. Even when they knocked down somebody's luggage, they did not pause for a moment. Other passengers muttered their irritation. One woman loudly chastised them. They stopped long enough to give her a disgusted stare and then promptly resumed their rowdy games.

Ike had watched their sport with thinning patience. Their mother's aloofness galled him. Nonchalant, she uttered not a word as her children roved and roamed, unfettered. They shrieked, blithely indifferent to strangers' disapproving stares, as if the airport were first and foremost their playground.

The line nudged forward. A customs officer tramped past, using a walking stick. Ike recognized him as the man he'd had a run-in with the day of his arrival. His heart jerked. He drew a deep breath and exhaled slowly.

His real torment began to take concrete form when he finally took his turn at the counter. He faced a bony, flat-breasted woman. She spoke without lifting her face, as if her questions were directed at somebody invisible or one whose presence her eye could not countenance.

"Country of citizenship?" she asked, peering at a small screen in front of her.

"Originally Nigeria."

"Then latterly what?"

"I have dual citizenship," he said, ignoring her sarcastic tone.

"Dual citizenship?" she intoned. "Why you no triple am?"

"I have American and Nigerian citizenships."

"American and Nigerian—or do you mean Nigerian and American?"

"It doesn't matter," he said, his patience wearing thin. "Our constitution—"

She raised a hushing hand, cutting him off. "Did I ask you about *our* or *your* constitution?"

He glared at her, his temper haywire.

"Country of domicility?" she shouted.

"America," he answered in a whisper.

"Eh?"

He raised his voice. "I said America. America."

"Passport and ticket." She held out her hand, eyes fixed again on the screen. He had the freedom to inspect her facial features. She wore too much makeup for the good of her angular, pimple-ravaged face. He reached into his pocket for the documents, his eyes set on her hand, vein crossed and thin.

She took his passport and ticket without looking up.

"Point of destination?" she asked.

"New York."

"Any check-in luggage?"

"Yes. Two."

"How many pieces?"

"I just told you," he said in a bristly tone.

"How many pieces?" she repeated, stressing each word.

"I told you. Two."

For the first time, she glanced up. Their eyes met briefly, then she flung her eyes away. Her manner suggested that she found him wanting, not worth a fight.

"Aisle or window?"

Still staring at her, he didn't answer.

"I said aisle or window?" she stressed, raising one eyebrow.

He liked standing up to stretch his legs during long flights; and he hated bothering other passengers when he needed to make a run to the toilet. "Aisle," he said.

"Lift your suitcases to the scale. One after the other."

First, he heaved up the suitcase that contained the statue. She looked at the reading. Then, turning to him with a tinge of belligerence, she said, "You have to remove something. We don't carry any suitcase heavier than fifty-five pounds." She slapped at the suitcase. "This one is fifty-seven."

"It's just two pounds," he said, his tone pleading and defiant at once.

She hissed. "We don't allow it. Even one pound above, *I* won't allow it."

Queen Succubus, he thought.

They looked at each other, silent.

"Remove it and reduce the weight," she said, pounding her hand on the counter.

"How?"

"*How?*" she echoed, turning up her nose. "What do you mean by how? Remove something. And quick, quick. Passengers are waiting."

"I'm a passenger," Ike said, glancing backward. There were only four passengers. He placed his elbows on the counter and leaned forward. "Please, help me," he said.

A bitter feeling flooded him, the saliva in his mouth pasty and sour.

"You done begin beg now," she gloated in pidgin. "But before, you just dey rake."

He gritted his jaws and looked at her, determined to salvage some of his dignity.

"Okay," she said with the immodest graciousness of a false benefactor. "This one time, I go help you. But you have to *drop* something."

Ike realized with relief that her toughness was a mask. Beneath the veneer lurked that familiar desire for a little extra cash to augment her undoubtedly miserable salary. Ike recalled reading a piece by some Nigerian newspaper columnist whose name he no longer remembered. The man had written that negotiations for small-time bribes were often conducted in pidgin, but big-time corrupt deals were transacted in proper English.

"How much make I drop?" he asked, his spirits brightened. Then, realizing how inept he was in the lingo, he felt foolish.

She leaned over the counter, like a lover reaching in for a kiss. He stepped away from her as if in disgust. She looked left and right, as though searching out any eavesdroppers. Then she whispered, "Three thousand."

His lips flew open. "Three thousand naira—for a mere two pounds? Come on, sister!"

She stiffened her face. "Which kin' sister? I no be your sister o. At all, at all; God forbid! Look, no be by force. If you no 'gree, just reduce your bag. Simple."

"One," he said.

"One what?"

"One thousand naira."

"No," she said curtly. "Three thousand. Otherwise, reduce de weight." She looked away. "Quick, quick," she ordered, the old feistiness back in her voice.

"One thousand five hundred," he said.

"Two five," she said, unimpressed by his amended offer. Her voice conveyed finality.

He made to count out the notes, but she interrupted him.

"Make we weigh your other suitcase first."

She looked at the scale. "Good," she said. "Fifty-four."

She extended her hand, and he pasted twenty-five hundred naira in her palm.

She pointed at a huddle of men and women in light brown uniforms. "Make you go get customs clearance. When dem clear you, then you bring the suitcases here for check-in."

Ike rolled the two suitcases toward the customs officers. There were three passengers ahead of him, waiting to be attended—which meant to be harassed or harangued for a bribe.

His head felt hot, his forehead covered by a light sweat. There was a growl in his belly. Perspiration trickled down from his armpits. His recent calm had taken flight. He felt groggy, his legs heavy, leaden.

He'd heard that Nigerian customs officers could detect fear, however faint. They could look at a man's eyes, glazed red, shifting this way and that, or tightened jaws, or clenched lips, or incessant yawning, or a cocked face, or the spray of perspiration on the nose or forehead, or the sweaty stain around the armpits, or at arms folded across the chest, or at hands restlessly going in and out of pockets, or the quickened rise and fall of the chest—and tell. They could fairly guess which passengers had some concealed, illicit goods in their suitcases. They had a nose for detecting whom to target for the juiciest bribe.

A woman in a long denim skirt slid a roll of cash into the hand of an officer. She was waved on. The woman traveling with three rambunctious kids now stood between Ike and the customs desk.

A fear gnawed at Ike. The cash from Wai's gift and loan had dwindled. Moved to pity by his mother's woeful condition, he'd finally handed her two hundred and fifty dollars. He gave a hundred to his sister. He had thirteen hundred dollars left on him, which would be plenty or paltry depending on how the game turned out. And he held none of the aces. He also had four or five thousand naira, but that would be virtually useless in such negotiations.

He overheard the woman ahead of him pleading that she didn't have three hundred dollars on her; she had come to bury her mother. Her children, oblivious, danced atop and around a pile of suitcases.

"Wetin dey inside?"

"Wetin you carry?"

Shaken from his reverie, Ike found himself face-to-face with his nemeses. The same question asked simultaneously by two customs officers. One, his voice harshly stentorian, had a boxer's tubular forearms and a thick, dyed mustache. The other was wide girthed, shirt sodden under the arms. He held a toothpick in one hand, a walking stick in the other. Ike recognized him as the main officer he had battled the day of his arrival. His heart cranked. Other customs officers stood aside but eyed him predatorily.

He had rehearsed a charm offensive, but now his confidence had seeped away. He rubbed his palm against the sides of his shirt. He made to speak, but no words came out.

"You dey deaf?" barked the flabby officer. He raised his walking stick and stabbed at Ike's suitcases.

"Personal effects," Ike managed to say, clutching at that fast-disappearing vine of courage. His right leg seemed in danger of buckling. Inside him, a dead weight threatened to snap and drop.

"Always personal effects!" grumbled the officer.

"Which kin' personal effects?" prodded the mustachioed officer.

"Clothes and so on," Ike said.

"Clothes and so on," a female officer snapped. "Dis one wan' blow grammar o." She screwed up her face at Ike. "You think say you be Americano? Which one be *personal* effects?" She pronounced "personal" as if it were a lurid, seedy word. Her mimicry provoked laughter from her colleagues.

"Oya," commanded the stick wielder, "put the bags here." He struck his stick at an oblong desk. "Then, quick, quick, open dem. Make we see dat your personal effects."

A sharp pain shot through Ike's stomach as he lifted both suitcases onto the inspection slab. He first opened the less heavy one. Several officers rushed forward to look. Shut off by taller men, the woman stood on tiptoe and craned her neck.

Hidden within folds of shirts and trousers were plastic bags filled with *gari*, *egusi*, *ukwa*, and ground crayfish.

"You call dese personal effects?" sneered the paunchy officer. "Who give you license to export food?"

"I'm sorry," Ike said, seizing an opening, hoping his tone conveyed the right mix of meekness and fearlessness. It was best to negotiate with the ravenous pack on account of the spurious charge of exporting food. If he could keep them from prying into the suitcase with the statue of Ngene, then things would not careen out of control.

"You no fit talk grammar again?" jeered the woman. "Oya, bring your export license make we see am."

He would have played the bereaved card, but the passenger before him had snatched it up.

"I came home to see my mother. She was so sick we thought she was going to die. God spared her life. She's the one who gave me the foodstuff."

The officers' collective gaze burned like red coals. Had they smelled him out, Ike wondered. Were they readying to pounce?

"I'm sorry, officers," he said in his most conciliatory tone, playing a wounded, submissive foe. "I didn't know that a license was needed to take food away. I'm sure my mother did not know, too, or she would not have gone to the trouble."

The taunting woman piped, "Dis one still dey talk big, big grammar and logic." She began to remove the packs of food from the suitcase.

Ike scanned different faces but nowhere found a hint of sympathy. He turned to the flabby officer and smiled. "My *oga*, don't you want me to enjoy the same food you eat? See how your skin shines. My mama wants me to have the same kind of shine, shine skin. That's why she gave me the food, to be like you."

Some of the officers laughed, but not the man Ike addressed. "Is against the law," he pronounced, stiffly.

Ike thought it was the right moment to broach a settlement. So far, he had managed to appear reasonably at ease. He had joked, he had shared an obligatory narrative of woe, and he had cajoled.

"Next time my mama gives me food, I won't make the mistake," he said. "But how can you help me today?"

"Open de second bag," ordered the female officer.

The words were like the slice of a sharp serrated knife. Ike felt faint, feared he'd reel and fall.

"Madam, why do you hate me so much?" he asked in a mellow, beseeching voice. "Was it wrong of my mama to give me food? God had saved her from a terrible sickness. Should I have rejected the food she went out and bought for me?"

"You dey waste time, jare!" the woman said in a brusque, impatient tone. "I say, open de other suitcase."

He considered reaching inside his pocket to signal a readiness to offer a generous bribe. But they'd sense he had something he was dying to hide—and they would go for the kill.

In his informal research, he had worked out how to negotiate a bribe and the ideal moment to pull out the cash. He had learned that customs officers fell harder for bribes offered in dollars than in naira. In that regard, he was ready. But timing, he knew, was critical. To offer a bribe too early in the game could prove as dangerous as dithering. The trick was, the briber should neither seem overhasty nor vacillate.

The woman held him in a fierce, flattening glare. "Quick, open!" she urged.

He rolled the numbers on the lock until three zeroes aligned horizontally. He then lifted the cover of the suitcase.

Two officers dug their hands into the suitcase. Suddenly, their eyes widened in excitement. Ike felt close to tears.

"Wetin be this?" asked one of the officers, holding up the heavily padded object.

A lump choked Ike's throat. "A sculpture I bought," he said. A few times, he'd imagined some crazed customs officer unwrapping the statue at the airport, in the full glare of astonished onlookers. He'd always shuddered at the prospect. He had even entertained the scenario of the statue being seized. What would he do then? He recoiled from considering that dire outcome. It would be as death. His head swooned and his legs were rubbery.

"Ah, antiquity!" one of the officers shouted, hardly able to contain his excitement. The cry attracted a huddle of officers.

"No, no," Ike said, shaking his head vigorously. "It's just a simple carving." His mouth felt dry, his heart pounded, and his vision became suddenly hazy and unfocused.

"Okay, unwrap de ting," the woman ordered. "We wan' see."

Ike stood pat, as if transfixed.

"You no hear? Don't waste our time o," shouted the woman.

Several officers spoke at once, a commotion of voices. Their dissonant sounds assaulted Ike. He felt the airport begin to turn, twist, whirl. Faces began to dissolve, morphing into indistinct shapes. He had the sensation of sinking in a soupy, brackish river, the choppiness of its surface presaging the wild pulsations of its undertows. He was about to be swept off by the river's churning eddies when he felt the grip of a rough, charred hand. He turned quickly to his left.

"Come!" The summons came from the mustachioed officer. Taken by the hand, Ike followed, as if without volition. Once they were outside of earshot of the huddle, the officer stopped. His eyes burrowed into Ike's, his lips thick, lined with a film of oil.

"Trus' me, I be friendly force," the officer said, gesticulating wildly. "God just touch me with milk of human kindness toward you. Das why I go help you. As I look you, I see say you be gentleman. Das why I wan' help. You see, is against law to smuggle food out without license. And is against law to smuggle antiquity out. Even if the carving no be antiquity, we get power to charge you as smuggler. Las' week, we detain one man overnight. De nex' day, we charge 'im to magistrate court. So na big trouble you dey so, but I go help you." He paused, and the dreadfulness of his words seeped into Ike's every pore. Then he asked, "How much you fit drop?"

Drop. Drop. In the mouth of the woman at the check-in counter, Ike had despised the word. This time, the word spelled sweet relief.

Something about the man—the char of his palm, the swell of his lips, the reek of gin on his breath, the sweaty stink of his shirt, the dyed blackness of his mustache—left Ike with no illusions. The man was no friendly force, only the most ruthless negotiator among the pack.

Rather than name a price they could haggle and negotiate around, the man had asked him, in effect, to come up with an offer. It was a bribe taker's coup, a brilliant strategy. If Ike's offer was paltry, the man could reject it out of hand. But Ike could also make an offer that exceeded the man's expectations. In that event, the man would still act dissatisfied—in order to coax an even handsomer sum.

Head raised, Ike considered what opening offer to make.

"You dey lucky say I dey your side," the officer said, breaking into Ike's thought. "If you no be gentleman, I go jus' leave you and that wench." He pointed to the quarrelsome woman. "As you see am so, she wicked pass wicked." He peered into Ike's eyes. "So, how much?"

"Tell me," Ike said, and met the man's gaze.

The officer gave a nervous smile and averted his eyes. "I dey inside your pocket?" he asked. "Na you go say. But de offenses fit land you for serious trouble o."

"Remember I came home because my mama was very sick," Ike said, determined to mine his earlier lie for what he could get from it.

No trace of sympathy registered on the officer's face. Instead, the man said, "Two thousand dollars."

Ike cringed. "Where can I find two thousand dollars? My mother was in the hospital."

"Das why I no talk big money. I mercy you."

Ike knew that the gale had swept past, and he'd survived it, even if barely—even if by a stroke of luck that now needed to be perfected. His shot nerves had repaired themselves, and he could affect a becalmed state. He felt steeled enough to pursue another emotive line.

"The worst thing is I lost my job in New York just before I traveled."

The officer turned away, a vexed look on his face. "Look, my friend, I done tell you say your palava big o. Trus' me, thank your God say no be that wench dey handle you. Two thousand dollars no be anything for dis kin' case."

"I didn't even finish paying my mother's hospital bills."

The officer turned sharply. His face bore the expression of a man with no time to kill. "Oya," he said, in a tone of reasonableness, "bring one thousand five."

"A thousand five hundred?" Ike asked.

The officer nodded.

"Dollars?"

The officer puffed up his chest. "A thousand five hundred dollars," he said, chopping at the air. "Last."

Ike cadged. He appealed to the officer to remember that he'd returned home to see to the care of a hospitalized mother, and that he'd just lost his job prior to the trip.

"Oya, bring one thousand," the man officer said. He frowned up. "I no wan' waste more time."

Ike cast a sideward glance at the huddle of officers and saw the "wench" wagging her fingers at the statue.

"Five hundred," he offered.

The mustachioed officer glowered at him. "You tink say na joke I come here joke?" He made an exaggerated motion of turning away.

"Please," Ike pleaded. "I'll make it six hundred."

The officer would not budge. Irritable, he threatened to hand Ike back to the hound. "You wan' make dat woman put you for cell?" he asked. "As you see am so, she can castrate any man. Just like dat, no mercy! If she vex, na inside detention you dey go. Straight! Mosquito and bedbug go take you do Christmas. Den tomorrow, we take you to go see magistrate."

Ike felt touched by anger. Yet, through the fog of that emotion, he was able to glimpse the fortune that awaited him once the statue made it to New York City. He turned aside, pulled his wallet, counted seven hundred dollars, and then handed the bills to the officer.

The officer touched three middle fingers to his tongue and counted the cash. "Add hundred," he ordered. Weary of the haggling, Ike complied. A wild, nervous smile lit up the man's face. "Oya, no more problem. Come, you fit take your bags now."

As they walked back to the customs desk, the officer lifted his shirt and tucked the cash underneath his belt.

CHAPTER TWENTY-THREE

A sally of stench hit Ike's nostrils the moment he opened the door to his apartment. It left a ghoulish impression, reminded him of feculent silt. He jerked his head back in a flinching gesture.

Had something—a rat perhaps—burrowed its way into his apartment and met its death? Had he forgotten to flush the toilet? Had he left dirty dishes in the sink? Or was it some food, carelessly left out, that had gone moldy and festered?

Holding his breath, he pulled his suitcases into the room. He then slammed the door behind him, for he did not want the smell to slip out his door and menace other tenants. As the hallway light shut out, he found the apartment wrapped in a gooey darkness.

His right hand groped the wall, searching for the switch. He flicked it, but light did not flood the room. A chill zipped down his spine. Bumps erupted on his skin. He flicked the switch again. And then again and again.

Fear compounded his anger. Why had the bulb chosen now to die? He was sure he didn't have an extra bulb in the house.

Then he remembered the disconnection notice from the light

company three days before his trip. His light bill was then delinquent by three weeks. He'd scrawled the power company's customer service number on a piece of paper and tacked it on the wall beside the refrigerator. But, swamped with errands, he had forgotten to call and make the payment.

He whacked the side of his head.

"Idiot!" he cursed.

Teeth gritted, he gave the switch a sharp, upward chop. Scraped, his finger sizzled with pain. He sucked in air, wincing. He ran the hurt finger across his lips, probing for a cut, for blood.

Something seemed to stir in the darkness. He crouched, then ducked to the right, like a karate maven evading a punch. Who, what, was this thing appareled by the night? Was it the source of the terrible smell? Was the stink this being's rancid breath?

His eyes roved and scoured the darkness. For a while, there was nothing but an eerie stillness, the sinister stillness of a night-draped terror. His eyes began to water from the intensity of gazing into darkness. His eyelids began to twitch, blinking uncontrollably. A misshapen figure formed and unformed before his teary eyes. This image wiggled, feinted, danced like a waif.

Ike opened his mouth to shriek, but his vocal cord was bereft of sound, lifeless. He wanted to pirouette, grab the doorknob, and yank the door open. The hallway light would flood the room, revealing the prowler. But his limbs remained frozen. If he turned, he would expose his flank to attack. Why, the fearsome foe in the dark might then fell him with a vicious blow.

There was a scurrying. He started and jumped. Landing, he stamped his feet furiously. He swung his arms wildly. Heels dug in, he bent his knees, flexed his biceps, and raised his hands, pivoting from side to side, ready.

Gradually, doubt settled in. Was there really somebody

—something—enfolded in the darkness, ready to do him harm? Was there anything more than an illusion?

Next came shame. Surely, if people could see him now, they'd think him deranged. What shame to be caught in a fighter's springy posture, flailing against an illusory antagonist.

Next—dread swept him. It came back with the thought that there was indeed a presence in the darkness. It was no less real for its invisibility. If he pitched his hand forward, he'd touch this *thing*. Its skin would be horrid to the touch, a feral foe's furry skin, or hard, like something hewn from bark.

The thought of it made his skin crawl with bumps.

He stood pat, shivering.

The smell came at him in waves. Sometimes faint, sometimes overpowering, it made him dizzy. He was trapped between the liquidity of the odor and the horror of the darkness.

He wiped his eyes. The traipsing figure seemed to fall instantly quiet.

He sniffed lightly, seeking to detect the stink's particular character. He ruled out a dead rodent. The odor didn't have the stark smell of decayed flesh. He had a hunch that it wasn't food either.

Did the stink emanate from trapped, soured air? Was it because he'd shut up everything before he traveled; every window latched, a pad of newspapers squeezed in to cover a small hole where the air conditioner was installed. Had the trapped air fermented and turned acrid?

Could a smell so foul be birthed by sheer air?

The phone rang. Heart heaving, he sprang for it but blindly crashed against his suitcase, which toppled over with a thud. He heard its lock spring free, its contents spilling. His left leg caught the fallen suitcase. Doing his blind best to regain his balance, he was instead propelled forward, an awkward flying object. For a moment he had the sensation of being suspended in midair; he couldn't tell where was up, where down. Then his right rib cage slammed against the edge of the shaky-legged center table his ex-wife had spitefully left behind when she cleaned out the rest of the furniture. The table gave a cracking whine as it shattered. He crumpled to the ground, sideways, bunching up his body as actors do in movies when shot. The pain took its time sharpening, spreading. Ripples of it tore through his body. He gasped, grabbed his rib cage, and slowly rolled over to settle on his back.

As if from a dreamy fog, he heard the phone ring two more times. He let out a mirthless smile as his voice announced, *I am not here to take your call. Please leave a message, thank you.* Three beeps—then:

"Chief Ike, this is Usman Wai," announced the caller in a familiar raspy voice. "Just calling to find out if you made it back today as planned. Please call me as soon as you come in; I'll be up till midnight. Even later. Don't fail to call—it's extremely important. Hope you had a terrific trip. Bye for now."

A click. Silence.

The pulsing pain concentrated his mind. For a while, nothing else mattered. Not fear. Not the stink-touched air. Not a girl's string of curses that reached him from the street. Not the smattering of jeers and cheers that answered her. Not the indolent chatter of the adult congregants gathered in front of Cadilla's package store to dawdle, dream, and flirt. Not the sound of a car screeching to a halt in front of Cadilla's. Not the boom of merengue music that followed.

Nothing mattered but the spasms of pain.

Lying on the floor, curled up in the fetal posture, the darkness seemed cushiony. Bottomless.

The pain spent its edge, abating gradually.

Afterward, he lay on the floor, from comfort less than necessity. He was in a half daze, floating in and out of a state that was neither sleep nor wakefulness.

CHAPTER TWENTY—FOUR

Throughout the night voices crowded his head. They were of the night, born of the dark coming from somewhere beyond his reach, muted, inaudible, insistent. His head was the echo chamber for their inarticulate, inchoate musings.

He lay down where he fell, captive to the strange autogenous sounds that whirred inside his head. And to the hurly-burly that floated up from Cadilla's store.

After a while, he felt pressure build up around his groin, an urgent summons to pee. A groping trip to the bathroom was out of the question. For a while, then, he simply ignored the tightening sensation. Finally, he swept the floor until he touched the fallen, yawning suitcase. He dug his hand into it and probed. His fingers touched a heavily wrapped sturdy object. He shivered with foreboding, hoping the statue had not cracked with the suitcase's crash.

He drew out a cotton shirt and rolled it up into a ball. Urine seeped out in treacherous spurts as he struggled to unzip his pants. He placed the balled shirt against his groin and allowed himself to go. The shirt quickly soaked up, warm to the touch, but turning cold. He let the wet shirt fall off his hand, and then he yanked his waist away.

He tried to draw a deep breath but stopped when his expanding lungs instigated a shooting pain.

The stink! It now oversaturated his lungs. It wasn't, he now realized, the smell of something dead. It was neither rotten food nor air bottled up in a locked, dank space. The ooze had an implacable quality to it. Indecipherable. The closest he came to fathoming it was that it was not one thing but an awful miscellany.

He rocked with a shudder as a rogue word flashed through his mind. Haunted. His apartment was haunted.

He'd expected to gain a sense of relief once he returned to the staid familiarity of his residence. Instead it had come to this: fear. It'd come to a terrible heaviness of spirit—and to a mind encumbered by a palpable gloom.

HE WAS STILL SUPINE when strips of light began to sneak into the room. Rising slowly, he staggered toward the windows, his body tilted rightward to contain the still-raw pain. He parted the gauzy, see-through blinds and then drew apart the satiny folds of the curtain. He opened the window, and air rushed in through the metal security grille.

He looked out on the streets, milling with people. The young waltzed in that shoulder-swaying, weave-legged fashion that was a simulated dance. The old trotted to a slower rhythm. Streets abundant with sounds, swagger, colors. Cars zipped past. Buses stopped and shuttled. There was an odd robustness in this multitude of solitary beings.

For the first time he felt he'd truly returned from Utonki. The city was *there* before his eyes. It was there in more than one sense. There—for him. Strangely—considering all his old grouse against the city—he felt comforted to be back. His heart swelled with the satiety of a man about to reach out and touch his dreams.

It was magnificent to have his sight back. He turned away from the window, fixing his eyes on the familiar contours of the room. Shafts of sunlight swept the room. Everything that fell under his gaze brought him a flush of delight. The smashed center table that he now saw as a blow struck against Queen B. He looked at the fallen, open suitcase, its lock severed, the wrapped statue of Ngene lying atop a disheveled mess of clothes. Even the flowered shirt wet with his piss. He smiled bemusedly, the terrors that had seized him in darkness gone with the light.

A sudden spasm stabbed his side. He bent sharply. A whiff of stink floated to his nostrils. Quickening, he sniffed. To his dismay, the smell had grown even stronger, as if the light had fermented it.

He panned around, searching for any visible source. He looked under his couch and inside the refrigerator, but found nothing. Dipping his head first in his bedroom and then the bathroom he detected nothing.

He returned to the living room and sniffed again. Once again, the smell seemed ranker.

He balled himself up on the couch, in no mood or shape to continue the futile detective work. His entire body was racked by weariness. *Sleep,* he thought, remembering how the terrifying darkness had wrung sleep from his eyes. If he slept, he would awake refreshed. With some luck, he'd discover that the odor had lifted and crept away.

He shut his eyes. For a moment, a drowsy sensation overwhelmed him. Limb by limb, it claimed him. The sounds of the streets became muted, and the world gyrated slowly in whorls. His body sloughed off layer after layer of weight until it was ready to float away, doze off.

The air felt suddenly heavy and still. Something opaque, mildly menacing, stirred in the air, stretched in the stillness. This thing had a presence oblique as mist, and a voice that croaked from an indeterminate distance, muffled. It struggled, turned, twisted, and tossed. It then became a word being born in the dense air, a fetus of a name that had been here before, a name straining to be exhumed, born again. Slowly, assuredly, some disembodied force whispered the sound. The sound seemed to emanate from the womb of time, to ride the air, until it became a veritable howl birthing a name, a name that belonged to the past but was now insistent on inhabiting the present. For a moment, the sound seemed emblazoned in the very air. Then it groaned and moaned its way into the open, slid and slipped out into the world, this name that was both not his and his.

Su-tan-tee-ny. Su-tan-tee-ny! Stanton!

Ike was about to answer to the name when he clambered into consciousness, his body hot, beads of sweat smudging his brow. His heart, like the name that pounded in his head, jumped like an animal snagged by a trap, startled.

The unclaimed name swelled the air, swirled and prowled, howled intermittently. *Su-tan-tee-ny. Stanton!*

For a moment, its echoes lured Ike back into sleep. Then, as if from nowhere, a muddy flood rushed down the side of a mountain. It turned into a crashing river, a howling river powered by rage, as it sped toward him. Catatonic, he was the river's for the taking. He wanted to shriek. If he could shriek, rend the air with his agony, perhaps something, somebody, might save him. The river might even show mercy. But something smothered his throat, stilled his voice. Suddenly, his frozen body received some residual animation. He arched, ready to take a plunge, to lose himself in the rushing wave. Then, just before the final moment, the turbulent flood about to smash into him, he harnessed everything within him and—jerked awake!

CHAPTER TWENTY-FIVE

ke's brow boiled, the room topsy-turvy. In the distance, he glimpsed a parade of specks floating toward him, growing larger, clearer, as they approached. Then, in quick, whirling succession, he saw his mother's whitlow-ravaged thumb, his uncle's war-earned belly gash, and those eyes deadened by grief.

He didn't know how to fend them off. He sat helpless before their menace. Light sweat slicked his forehead. A nervy pain pounded inside his head. Slumped on the couch, he panted, unnerved by the nightmare that had startled him awake and by the grotesque images that came with waking.

Relax, he coaxed himself, but his inner voice carried little conviction. *Relax. Think of other things.*

Sleep was impossible under the circumstances. To regain quietude, he had to master his mind, to rein in its many flights. The trick, he felt sure, was to shepherd his thoughts toward more practical matters. And there were quite a few.

It was paramount to pay his electric bill, to have his power restored as soon as possible. Sleeping in darkness—*being awake in darkness*—was no joy. He had to pick up his mail, buy some food, and, once power was restored, check his e-mails.

The trouble with focusing on practical problems was that he had little money. He didn't have a dime left of the five hundred dollars Tony Iba had given him. All of it—and more—had gone to the customs officers in Lagos. Then he had spent forty dollars on transportation back to his apartment. There was nothing in his checking account. And he had used up his credit card limit buying the ticket.

Despite his money woes, he decided not to rush into selling the deity. He'd wait for a week, even up to ten days. With Ngene in his possession, he could afford to tarry. He had a hunch that the deity's value would appreciate if he waited. Yet, he had to arrange to pay the electric bill. Several other bills, ignored before his trip, would have fallen overdue. Thinking about it all seemed to take too much of his energy. For want of something to occupy his mind, he reached for his cordless phone. He pressed the button for voice messages and—prompted—entered his password. Then he pressed the phone to his ear. An automated voice announced: *You have nine new messages and four saved messages.* Two messages were from Usman Wai, including the one that had sent him crashing to the floor. Three were from the rental management office. Of those, one was a gentle reminder that his March rent was a month past due and that he had yet to respond to two letters from the office. The second message, left three days later, was a terse request to call the office immediately. The third informed him that another letter had been dispatched to him demanding immediate payment of overdue rent along with assessed late fees. Three callers had failed to leave any message.

Afterward, he lay down on the couch and thought about his friend Jonathan Falla. The last time they had spoken, Jonathan had raved about the home he and his partner, Chelsea, had just built on the hills of Leverett, Massachusetts. He had insisted that Ike come spend a weekend. "Man, let's eat, drink, and tell stories about our yesterdays," Jonathan had said in his exuberant manner. Ike thought about it. Perhaps it would do him good to take up the invitation. Just for a few days, to clear his head, which had fallen prey to a ceaseless churn of memories and sounds, the worst being the constant whir of silence.

He picked up the phone to call Jonathan. That instant, a dreadful idea flicked through his mind. The notion was this: *The reek in his apartment came from him! He'd tracked it in, lugged it all the way from Utonki.* And there was a chance that the stink would dog his every step, accompany him wherever he went. He put the phone away.

It was at first a brush of an idea, something fleeting. The thought irritated him more than it disturbed him. When all was said and done, it was preposterous. But then it stuck, made it impossible to free himself from its snare. The harder he tried, the more entrenched the idea became. His power of resistance was failing him.

A drink, a drink! Caught in a warp, he knew that the answer was to sedate himself. He needed to run out and pick up a bottle of Jack Daniel's whiskey or Grey Goose vodka along with some soda. Or he could grab one or two six-packs of Guinness. He realized the need to act urgently, for the odor appeared sinister. Ike sensed it swelling, thrashing about the room.

A fierce ache beat inside his skull. His eyes shivered with unbearable pain. He placed a thumb on one side of his face, the rest of his fingers on the other, and then pressed. Kneading his flesh, he worked from the chin slowly up to the crown. The pressure in his fingers sought to reach the pain, to mollify it.

Another thought slipped into his mind: *The stink was wafting from the wrapped deity.* He sprang up, picked up the swaddled statue, and raised it to his nostrils. One quick sniff was all he needed. His stomach quickened. He threw his head back, repelled by the horrid stink. He propped the statue against the wall.

"I've become a chief priest," he muttered, sinking in the couch.

His heart began to pound. He had to stave off the intruding thought.

Relax.

Other dreadful thoughts sneaked past each barricade he sought to erect. His head felt light, buffeted both by the odd stink and the fear that gnawed at him.

Relax!

It pierced him like shrapnel, this sense of toxicity in the air. His mind zigzagged, contorted by a dizzying flurry of ideas. The befouled air threatened to suffocate him.

He decided, in desperation, to go to Cadilla's to buy a drink or two. Standing up, he panned around, looking for his bunch of keys. It was nowhere to be seen. *Saw it a moment ago,* he bitterly reminded himself. *And it was in full view!* He rifled through the two suitcases, patted down his pockets, and then dug fingers underneath the crevices of the couch. No luck. He scanned the bathroom and bedroom. Panting, he decided to take a break. He stood still, trying to collect himself, to let his rage subside, to think. Then he threw himself into the same ritual, looking over the spots he'd searched before. It was futile. Frustration.

After he'd turned over the room more than five times, he sat down and shut his eyes. He drew deep breaths and exhaled through his mouth. Then, opening his eyes, he looked at his feet—and there was the bunch of keys!

"Ah-ah!" he exclaimed, worn out by his exertions. He lay down and put the keys on his brow, relishing their steel-cold feel. Head dug into the leathery softness of the armrest, he let his legs dangle off the sofa, neither on it nor on the ground.

Be still, he cajoled himself. *Too late to fret.* Then a terrible, comforting idea flitted across the mazy screen of his mind. He remembered that his uncle Osuakwu had said that a starved deity was apt to turn dangerous.

"I've become a chief priest," he said again. Shutting the door behind him, he hurried down the stairs, aware—a realization he embraced calmly, with no fuss—that he was going to buy food and drinks for two. From now on, he'd have to sate the deity's hunger and slake its thirst. He'd need to keep it in good humor.

He'd become a chief priest with no apprenticeship, no induction into the god's protocols.

I've become a chief priest. The thought brought him to the edge of an ironic smile.

When he came back, he dropped drumsticks of Jamaican jerk chicken and grains of rice on the floor next to the statue. Then he spilled drops of whiskey on the floor as well.

CHAPTER TWENTY—SIX

Four days later—three days sooner than he'd planned—Ike arrived again at 19 Vance Street in Greenwich Village. Unlike his first visit to the gallery, when he had fretted outside for a while, he strode in, this time—a portrait of calm and confidence. There was something bouncy inside him.

The difference was that the statue of Ngene weighed against his arm.

But his stride was checked momentarily by the stink in the gallery. It seemed more pungent than during his first visit, just days before his trip. It was certainly punchier than the smell in his apartment. He paused only for a moment or two, sniffing the air. Then he walked past the spiral staircase, hardly looking at the content of the showcases as he made for the counter.

Part of the reason he'd come to the gallery early was that he could no longer stand the stench in his apartment.

To compound matters, it was a mobile, restless stink. His first night home, it'd stayed in his living room. The next day, it had wandered into his bathroom. By the third day, it had completed its conquest by overpowering his bedroom. The more it spread, the more it took on a palpable character, as if some blacksmith's bellows were blowing its fumes. The smell had kept gathering strength, at once penetrating everything and pulling everything into itself, until it seemed to waft out of the wall's invisible pores.

The smell was unbearable, but that was not the sole reason he'd decided to make an early trip to the gallery.

There was the menace of insomnia, the nightmare that drove sleep away. Whenever he shut his eyes, his body drowsy with sleep, he'd visualize himself trapped in a valley, a raging flood plunging down a hillside, sweeping up rocks, and heading for him. He would awake with a start, drenched in sweat, too scared to fall back asleep.

But even that was not the main reason.

Then there was the question of his bills. The day after his return, he'd picked up his mail. It was a litany of bills.

He tore open one of three letters from the rental office. The word URGENT was printed in red ink at the top of the page. The letter reminded him of the delinquency of his rent for the months of March and April. It instructed him to immediately pay the sum of $3,000 plus $300 in late administrative fees. Another letter from the power company threatened disruption of his service if he didn't pay a balance of $277.59 within five days of the notice. Next, he slit open an envelope from Visa. His credit card had a debit balance of $2,682. He gazed at it, brow knitted in a frown.

But those debts weren't the main reason, either.

There was Usman Wai, his old friend who'd made him a loan of more than $1,250. He'd finally returned Wai's repeated calls that had taken on the quality of a harangue. "It's about the money I loaned you," Usman had said after asking a few polite questions about his trip. "I have an emergency—and need it immediately. In fact, like yesterday."

But paying Usman back was hardly the reason he hurried to Foreign Gods, Inc.

The major reason was a phone call just before 6:00 P.M. from his sister, Nkiru.

"THEY HAVE KILLED MAMA o," his sister cried as soon as he took the call.

"*Who* have killed Mama?" he asked, impatient with her hysterical manner.

"Osuakwu the devil and his fellow worshippers of Satan. They have broken Mama's legs o. She's in the hospital."

Shocked, he nearly dropped the phone. "Mama is in the hospital? What happened?"

Ike weathered Nkiru's tears and tangents of holy denunciations to grasp what had happened.

On finding out that Ngene had disappeared, Pastor Uka had proclaimed it an act of the God he served. He had then scheduled a special all-night service to praise the true God that had vanquished a false idol. Uka and his congregants were in the delirium of celebration when, just after midnight, an army of idol worshippers stormed in. Pastor Uka was beaten to a near-comatose state. Ike's mother, after taking several blows and slaps to the face, had dashed to the low-lying window and lifted herself over. She had broken a leg and badly bruised her hip in the jump.

"It's the same Osuakwu you love who did this!" Nkiru shrieked in remonstration.

"Was Osuakwu one of the attackers?"

"Did he have to be?" she asked. Then she cried, "He arranged it!"

Ike grew dizzy. "So, how's Mama?"

"How is she? As *your* uncle's people left her! And now the hospital says they won't treat her unless I pay a deposit of two hundred fifty thousand naira. Look at me, where will I find that kind of money?"

"I'll send it," Ike said. "I'll wire two thousand dollars."

"When?" Nkiru demanded.

"Tomorrow. Latest, the day after."

"Don't let Mama die o!" the sister implored, and then hung up.

THE NEXT DAY DAWNED with a dazzling face. The radiant sun lent a comforting warmth to the air, moved by the slightest breeze. Encouraged by the weather, Ike's spirits were buoyant as he descended the steps of the subway at the juncture of Lafayette Street and Flatbush Avenue.

He entered a packed subway car. Legs spread apart, he leaned into a handrail, two women on either side of him, and in front a man with a silvery beard who continually nodded his head as if the very air supplied music. Ike held tight to the heavily padded statue as if to hoard its horrid waft to himself. Besides, he wasn't about to risk slackened vigilance. Some daring thief might pry the quarry from his grip and dash away.

He stepped out at his final stop, ascended to the street, and beheld a rainstorm. For a moment, he thought to tarry under a shelter to wait it out. But he didn't want to risk becoming agitated and fainting away under the storm's spell. The gallery, two blocks away, seemed a safer bet.

He stepped out, the waddled statue clasped to his chest, and walked in long, hurried steps, as if it were possible to outstrip the storm. That instant, the storm seemed to change gears. Its roar deafened, muted every other sound. Ike felt lured out, entrapped by the storm's sparking fury. Pelts burrowed down his hair, turned into crawly worms on his scalp, dribbled over his eyebrows and then down his face.

Halfway to the gallery, he realized that he'd become hopelessly drenched. Worse, water had soaked through the paper wrap that concealed the statue. His steps were brisk, no question. Yet he felt bogged down, like a man attempting a race in a pool. After a while, he had the sensation that something viscous, dark red, and warm seeped through the paper and dripped down his belly and arms. He raised his arms and peered at his shirt, completely wet and matted to his chest. There was no discoloration at all. But for that ever-present, dreadful fear of a capricious spell, he was fine.

As he adjusted the statue and extended a hand to push open the gallery's door, it seemed to pull away from him. A woman stood on the inside, beaming.

"Gosh, you're drenched!" she said.

"Thank you," he said, and quickly stepped through the entrance.

He walked with deliberate slowness, as if it had become necessary to atone for his quickened pace out in the rain. With each step, his sneakers squeaked, leaving a track of wetness on the floor. His shirt and pants clung to his body, made him itch. He made circuitous loops, pausing to inspect other deities, his ears tuned to the rain's *doowah, doowah.*

It took several minutes before he loitered near the checkout counter and stood, favoring now this leg, now that. A tall, slightly stooped man in a light green pullover shirt strolled toward him, eyes dully set on the gods in their glass-enclosed cocoons. There was about the man an air of inbred self-assurance, and he seemed familiar in a way that was at once vague and insistent. If he had to guess, Ike might have said he'd seen the fellow on TV or in one or another of those entertainment magazines whose star-studded covers stared at you from grocery store racks. Yet, the more he struggled to place the man, the deeper the impression of an encounter that was more intimate.

Well, Ike thought, giving up, freeing his mind to focus on the hope that burdened his arm.

Ike heard the crunch of shoes and looked up. Mark Gruels came into view, holding up a statue. A white woman with a roundish, confident face followed closely behind him. The statue blocked Gruels's view, so that he brushed past Ike with no acknowledgment. The woman met Ike's stare but showed little curiosity, her face tinted with rouge, thin lips softened by red lipstick. A curl of silvery hair hung over her left eye. As she walked past Ike, he saw, buried beneath her veneer of makeup, wrinkles that grooved the sides of her eyes. For a moment, her waft of perfume broke the gallery's clingy stench.

"Peggy!" shouted the man whose face Ike had given up trying to place.

"Giles!" the woman shouted back. "I didn't think you shopped here."

"Well, because you didn't bother to tell me there was such a great store. I had to find out by accident—literally days ago."

"I fear you're now going to raid all the good gods. It's like you, isn't it?"

The moment the man spoke, Ike's consciousness had been jolted into recognition.

Gruels turned slightly and smiled at both the man and the woman. "Mr. Karefelis went on a binge the first time he showed up. Two weeks ago. He's slowed down a bit."

Karefelis grinned. He leaned forward and pecked the woman on both cheeks. "And how's Mr. Lauter?"

"Paul's in Paris."

"I like the poetry of it. Paul in Paris!"

"He's back in three days actually, and we're having Charles Rosen and Cynthia Fisher over to dinner on Saturday. Would you care to join us—if you're still in town?"

"Not on Saturday, I'm afraid. Some clients will be over from

Japan, and dinner is planned with them. But so great to see you. You look dazzling as always. Paul—"

"No, Paul has nothing to do with nothing."

"You're full of poetry tonight."

"And you're the usual Giles, dependable dean of flattery."

"And of bullshit!" Gruels added.

The trio's laughter shook the air.

Gruels stood the statue on the counter and slapped his palms. Then he walked around the corner and positioned himself inside the enclosure that marked out the counter. Brows furrowed, his eyes concentrated on the cash register.

Ike stared at the statue, rotund and gargoyle-like, ocher in color, its face frozen in an expression of infantile glee. It flaunted a swollen belly, large hollowed-out eyes, and a stiff, massive phallus held up in two hands.

Standing on the same side as Ike, the woman unslung a brown handbag from her shoulder. She exhaled. "All right, Mark," she said, "let's go for it."

Gruels lifted up a tag hanging from the statue's neckless head and marked ON SALE. He raised his pair of glasses to his forehead, bent forward, and squinted at the back of the tag. He then punched in numbers.

"Four hundred thirty-five thousand six eighty—even," he said.

The woman unclipped her handbag and brought out a checkbook. Gruels handed her a golden pen. Watching her from behind, Ike felt momentarily woozy. He'd known in some abstract way of the existence of the breed the woman belonged to, the rich who could write a check for half-a-million dollars or more without flinching. Now, he was witnessing such a transaction at close quarters! It was as if something was drawing him into a dreamlike state, as if he was being transported by sheer proximity to the magic. He imagined the incandescence of the life lived by this woman and by the likes of Gruels. And then he imagined himself living that life, albeit on a much smaller scale.

She tore out the check. As she held it out to Gruels, Ike felt his knees threaten to buckle. His body swayed, but he rallied and stood firm, anchored by the weighty bundle in his hand.

"Reminds me," Gruels said, palming the check. "Can you look in early next week? Say, Tuesday? Are you in town?"

"I bet I am. Why?"

"I'm expecting a hot new deity. Something you'd like. It'd be here in three days. I expect it to go fast, too."

"I'll definitely stop by. See you Tuesday, then."

"It's a stunner. You'll be rapturous."

"And where's it coming from?"

"I wanted it to be a surprise, but I can tell you. It's a mountain deity from one of the indigenous peoples of the Philippines. Take my word: you're going to be blown away. Absolutely!"

A young man in a pair of shorts and a T-shirt with slightly wet armpits emerged from behind Ike, picked up the deity, and followed the woman outside.

"Can I help you?" Gruels asked.

Ike had turned to look at the departing woman, and so Gruel's attention caught him off guard. Inside him hope and fear warred, constricting his throat. He smiled.

"Yes?" Gruels said, eyes sharp. His elbows rested on the counter, his shoulder thrust forward. His voice was now joyless, tinged with impatience. It was as if he'd observed Ike's dawdling presence with mounting irritation, and now, his customer gone, he could vent.

For an instant, Ike was startled dumb. Could the man have forgotten meeting him just a few weeks ago? There was nobody else in sight. Even so, Ike looked about him, as if to make sure he was the addressee.

"Yes, can I help you?" the man said.

Ike took three steps toward the counter. "You remember me?" he asked. Then, noting a frown on Gruels's face, realized he'd said the wrong first words. A fire, a pressure, assailed his groin, but he knew it was out of the question to interject an inquiry for the toilet at that point in time.

"I've met you?" Gruels said, raising his eyebrows.

"Yes, I came two—three weeks ago."

"Here?"

Ike nodded.

"Well, I talk to an awful lot of people. I can't help forgetting a few faces now and then. Anyway, how can I help you?"

"It's this," Ike stuttered, lifting up the bundle. He heard the door to the gallery open, the crunch of shoes announcing an entrant. His bladder threatened to burst with pressure. "I brought this."

Gruels frowned up again, eyes narrowed to small quizzical squints. "And what exactly is *this*?" He spoke hesitantly, each word momentarily imprisoned in his mouth, rolled around, before being uttered.

"It's a god. We spoke about it. A god of war." The words welled from an icy pit within him. He was surprised that his throat ferried words at all, for each word left a bruise as it thawed and tore out of him. "It's called Ngene."

Gruels scratched the side of his face with an expression of agitated lack of interest. For a moment, he sized Ike up.

"It's a war deity," Ike said again, filling the silence.

"A war deity," Gruels echoed dubiously. "From where?"

"Utonki."

"Otoonki," he sneered, deliberately massacring the pronunciation. "Where's that?"

"Nigeria. Southeastern Nigeria."

Gruels hissed. Ike felt a violent pulse in his groin, then the private shame of a rogue drip of pee.

A few moments passed in utter silence. Then Gruels straightened and walked toward Ike.

"Another African god," he said, then tightened his jaw. He wistfully shook his head from side to side. "Don't know that I'm interested in another African god." Ike was riveted by a sleek of sweat that ran from his armpit down the side of his body. He pressed his right arm against his body and let his shirt mop up the sweat. Gruels's voice sounded peremptory: "Unwrap it—let's see."

Ike moved with haste. His shaky hands ripped the newsprint until the bare statue was revealed. He held it up. A vaporous whiff slapped his face. His nose itched, and he shuddered with a sneezing spell. Gruels approached to look but suddenly flinched, frozen in his tracks.

"Wow! Stinky!" he exclaimed, covering his nose. He colored and let out three massive sneezes. "Where again did you get this?" he asked, between eruptions.

"Utonki. My hometown."

"This mother fumes!" he said. He held Ike in a suspicious stare. Ike felt hope yield place to fear. What if the man spurned the deity? What if he ended up stuck with Ngene—what would he do with it?

"Before I even talk to you, I need some documentation. Some literature about the deity."

"I've got two," Ike said brightly, thankful for the booklets by Manfredi and Okwudili Okeke.

"For this kind of product," Gruels said, "I'd require three—three documents that authenticate the god."

"I brought two," Ike said again.

"Forget it, then. Two just won't cut it."

"It's an authentic god," Ike swore.

Gruels gave him a look that said, *Take your word for it?*

"Trust me," Ike continued, his tone more assertive. "You'll find several items on the Internet. Lots of pieces, even photographs. Just Google it. Ngene is spelled N-G-E-N-E. Utonki: U-T-O-N-K-I."

Gruels's cell phone began to ring, a chirpy tone. He pressed the phone against his ear and turned away. He said a warm "Hello!" followed by a litany of yeses, and then broke into deep laughter.

Left alone, Ike felt the grind of pressure in his groin begging to be relieved. Asking Gruels for the use of his bathroom, Ike conjectured, could prove a big mistake. Yet the pressure became fiery, nearing an unbearable stage.

His skin crawled with the touch of something like blown breath, moist and hot. A spasm racked his body. A single thought pressed on his mind, of grief-stricken gods.

The gods are bawling tears, he thought, as something as vague as the smell of tears tickled his nostrils.

"Why are you crying?" Gruels asked, intruding on Ike's reverie.

Ike felt alarmed by the wetness streaking down his face.

"Are you okay?" Gruels pursued, fixing him with a confused look.

With the back of his right hand Ike swiped off the tears. Then he gave a wan, embarrassed smile.

"Anything the matter?" Gruels persisted.

Ike touched his face.

"Fine, then," said the gallery owner, scratching at his jaw. "We better make this snappy. As a principle, I pay no attention to Internet stuff, but I'm willing to make an exception. I'd rather trust my sense of smell—and your stuff has a distinctive stink. Let's see what you got."

Ike stood the deity on the ground and pulled out the folded

booklets. Gruels unfurled the first one, Manfredi's, and then put on a pair of glasses that hung from a Velcro rope around his neck. He flipped through the pages, less reading than skimming. He opened Okeke's booklet and went through it in the same cursory fashion. Turning the last page, Gruels leaned against a shelf and gave Ike a sidelong glance. He raised his head, biting his lower lip, a man lost in thought.

"How much?" he asked. His terse tone revealed a man whose habit was to get quickly to the bottom of things.

Confused, Ike grunted, "Huh?"

"What are you asking? Give me a figure."

The abruptness knocked Ike off balance. He didn't do well under such pressure.

"It depends on you," he said. The moment the words passed his lips, he sensed their imprudence.

"Depends on me?" Gruels asked, scratching at his chin in that same irritated way. Then he looked agitatedly at his wristwatch. "You leave it up to me, I pay little for this. Or nothing." He swept an arm in the deity's direction. "Frankly, I'm not looking to add to my African inventory. Not at this time. African gods are no longer profitable. So, how much?"

"It's a powerful war deity. In olden days, it helped my people in their battles. No deity equaled its power. No warriors stood up to my ancestors. None. We—*they*—crushed all their enemies. This deity was responsible. All neighboring armies feared Ngene. It was—"

Gruels dashed up, interrupting Ike. At proximity, Ike felt dwarfed. A palpable tension sneaked into the space between them. Ike's groin burned with a bursting pressure. It worsened his fear, his dread of coming helplessly under another man's physical and emotional power. Gruels gripped him by the shoulder, he saw the profusion of hair on the man's arm, smelled the man's cologne. The gallery owner's gentle shakes belied the man's discomfiting stare.

"I don't take to a priest preaching to me about his god's great prowess. I'm not going to fall in love with Nagini—or whatever it is you call it. I'm a businessman." He paused, his grip tightening. With a stronger shake, he said, "Give me a damn figure—and let's save each other's time. If I like your price, I buy. Otherwise, I'll shake your hand and wish you luck selling it elsewhere."

"It's you I want to sell to," Ike said, and immediately rued his tactlessness, the impression of being willing to abandon other options.

"Then give me your fucking asking price."

Ike's groin pulsed with pressure. Two hundred thousand dollars? Two hundred eighty thousand? Four hundred fifty thousand? Each figure received its due of fleeting consideration before he fled from it, wary of selling short. He would be ecstatic with five hundred thousand—half a million. But what if he could get more? Obstinately, he said, "Give me an idea."

Gruels glowered at him, then said, "You're really wasting my time. Really."

"Okay, three hundred and fifty," Ike proposed.

"Three hundred and fifty what?"

"Thousand."

Gruels looked at him askance, then burst out in laughter.

"Three hundred and fifty thousand dollars for an African god? What year do you think this is? You've got to be kidding!"

Ike remained oddly calm, collected, unfazed by the tone of derision.

"I told you to make an offer," he said, his tone slightly accusing. In his mind he radically scaled back his expectation. Maybe Gruels would offer something in the region of two hundred fifty thousand.

Gruels pulled at Ike's shirt. "Come this way," he said.

They rounded a corner and faced an area with a pile of small and tall showcases, some of them with two or more statues. For a moment, they stood in silence. Ike squirmed, muscles tensed to rein in the pressure in his groin. Still silent, Gruels began to pace back and forth, his eyes roaming, looking at the deities in the vitrines as if he were seeing them for the first time. The statues seemed to follow his restless movement, staring back, films of dust visible in the hollows of their eyes. The stink seemed ranker.

"You're looking at my inventory of African gods," Gruels said at length, spreading his arm. "You can see there's hardly any room on the shelves. You know why?" He fixed Ike with hard, searing eyes. Ike looked away, irritated. "African gods are no longer in vogue, that's why. Three, four years ago, they were all the rage. Even two years ago, they were still doing decent business. Every serious collector had to have three, four, five African gods. They flew off the shelf. Then things—tastes—changed. This is like any other business—it's prone to shifts in tastes. It just happens that African gods don't excite collectors as they once did. That could change tomorrow, but I'm looking at today—and it's not pretty."

Again, Gruels made a sweep of the hand as he spoke. "See? My entire African inventory's been on sale going on three years, yet it remains slow-moving." He pointed to an oblong statue: "That's a Wolof god of fertility. It's been marked down by eighty percent—and it's still here. This one, a Bambara water goddess. Six years ago, it would have fetched half a million—easy. Now, take a look at the price tag. A mere eight thousand five, yet no buyers." He touched a toothy statue. "This, a Fanti god. Been on the shelf for four years." He touched another one, a scrawny-chested figure with shriveled scrotum and an erect phallus. "A Tiv god. Five, six years ago, collectors would have paid a handsome sum for it. Today, there are no takers, even though it's going for five thousand." He led Ike to a showcase at the end of the wall that held a rectangular object, a cornucopia of animal skeletons, bird beaks, straw ropes, chiseled bark, twigs, and raffia. "It's a ritual totem used in funerals of warriors. Four years ago, I sold one for close to two hundred thousand. This one's marked for eighteen thousand. No buyers." He thrust a finger at a case that contained a wiry, spear-like figure. "That's a Ligbi god of revelers—a deity I personally like. But guess what? Nobody's looking at it." Gazing up at a tall case with three sections, he said, "That one—on the top row, second from the right—it's an Akan warrior god. I discounted it, first fifty percent, then seventy-five, but it's still on the shelf. And it's been on sale going on two years. Here, this oval-faced statue is a Luba patron god of clairvoyants and sorcerers. There's a Malinke earth goddess, there's a Baoule god of fire, and there's a Shona mermaid." He placed a right hand on the showcases as he named each statue. "This is from Togo—an Ewe guardian of magic." He caressed the glass that held a mask with the flat horns of a buffalo, a hyena's ears, and a crocodile's huge jaws. "This is a Senufo funeral mask. Used to be I couldn't get one in before somebody bought it. Not anymore." He moved on to another, a statue that was half human, half beast. "This is a Chi Wara deity of farming. I once asked a hundred and eighty grand for one. Can you see the sale price? Twelve thousand—yet nothing doing." He glided to another set of showcases. "Look at this one, an Efik rain god; this, an Urhobo canoe to heaven; this, Shango, the Yoruba god of thunder; this, a Fon earth goddess. Look, I've got inventory from all over Africa—the Kongo, Bamana, Bembe, Baga, Xhosa, Yaka, Dogon—you name it. I wish they did as well as they used to. I've offered huge discounts, but collectors simply aren't interested. African deities are no longer in vogue."

Gruels paused, entwined his hands, and set a rueful, faraway look on the lineup of African gods. Ike felt disheartened. A storm raged inside him, left him reeling. Some icy spear pierced deep. His flesh felt minced and sheared, as if lobs of it would fall away from the bone. He was uneasy and confused. His lips puttered, but his mind couldn't fasten on any words.

"So what's my point?" Gruels asked, breaking the silence. "African gods are not the inventory they used to be. They've gone cold. You want a great payday, then go get me an Asian god. They're big, Asian gods are. There's also a huge demand for Latin American gods. But African gods—they went cold several years ago, and they're still cold. Anybody in this business knows that African deities are now at the bottom of collectors' lists."

Rolling off Gruels's tongue, the word "cold" had the sting of a well-aimed punch to Ike's gut. Cold. Cold gods!

He shifted from leg to leg. He thought about his mother lying in a hospital, broken to bits. "This is a powerful god," he said.

"You don't need to tell me. It has the stink of a great one—no question. Problem is, I have to look at market trends. And the odds are not in its favor."

"It'll sell," Ike assured in a pitiful voice. "Trust me."

"I can't trade what I know for *your* trust. You can afford to be sentimental—it's your ancestral deity, after all. But I'm not in the sentiment business. I buy and sell gods, period. Go to Asia and get me a god—any god—and I'll make you a great offer for it. Or to Latin America. That's what collectors are looking for. This one just isn't it."

Gruels shrugged, then stared at Ike with an attitude of shrewd distance. The air conditioner purred, punctuating the silence. Ike's legs were cramping up. He asked, "So how much?"

"Am I offering?"

Ike nodded.

"A thousand bucks."

Ike cringed and let out a puff of breath. His right leg buckled, and he had to grab the edge of a showcase to keep from reeling.

"It doesn't even cover my flight ticket," he said in a carping tone, his voice quaky. He knew his sister would be calling later that day, tomorrow at the latest, asking for a transfer of twenty-five hundred dollars for their mother's hospital care.

"A thousand bucks is about right," Gruels said in a flat, unyielding tone.

"My flight ticket cost fifteen hundred dollars," Ike said. "I then had to travel to my hometown. I spent more than a week there. Each day cost me a lot of money. On my way back, I was stopped by customs at the airport in Lagos. They nearly seized the god. I gave them eight hundred dollars to let me go. If they'd caught me, I would have been in big trouble. Years in jail. I would have been finished." He glanced up at Gruels. As their eyes met, Ike swallowed hard. Then he continued: "It's a powerful god, trust me. I'm sure it's worth good money."

"*I'm* the dealer here," Gruels said sharply. "I *know* something about the value of stock." The door creaked open, the sharp blast of a car horn and other street clatter slipped in. Ike and Gruels turned toward the door at the same time. A young petite woman with wavy blond hair loped in. Gruels brightened. "Amanda, thank God you're back." He glanced at his watch again, and turned to Ike. "I'm afraid I've got to run. Running behind for a meeting." He scrutinized Ike's face. "Listen, here's a deal. I give you fifteen hundred. Take it or leave it—but it'd be a mistake to say no. Trust me, it's a darn great deal. It's on the generous side of the ballpark, I assure you. You don't believe me, try other galleries. Or—this is another option. Leave the item on consignment. Tell me what you'd like to ask for it. I sell, I take my commission—twenty percent—and you get the rest." He angled his face closer to Ike's. "Matter of fact, it sounds perfect. Fair?"

"But I need money now," Ike said with artless candor.

"Up to you, then. I'm happy to write you a check right away. Fifteen hundred. Or you put it on consignment. Your choice."

CHAPTER TWENTY—SEVEN

Ike made his way up the stairs to his apartment and jiggled the key in the lock. He twisted the cold, oily doorknob and prepared to walk in. A waft of rank air arrested him. It seemed to leap at his nostrils, this stench, fierce as a wounded beast on its second—more ferocious—wind.

He stood pat, unnerved, framed against the door that was still partially ajar. Staggered by the stink, he held his breath for as long as he could manage and then exhaled sharply. Moved by curiosity, he sniffed the air. Immediately, the spiteful smell saturated his lungs. Something like an icy lump tumbled down into the pit of his stomach.

His thoughts ran to disinfectants, one of those things he should have stocked up on but never remembered to—until a pressing, repellent need arose. It would take a powerful disinfectant to dislodge this foe, to shoo off the feculence.

There was nothing to do about the reek for now, he decided, insuperable as it was. It was more urgent to search out some still, refreshing place where his ravaged spirits and fatigued body could start their recuperation.

He collapsed onto the couch. A raw pain seared through him, and his bones creaked with sadness. In his head a swarm of emotions, a mangrove seeded with a riot of thoughts that thrashed this way and that. Idea after idea teased him, flirtatious, each as elusive and capricious as a streaking meteor, incandescent one moment, erased the next. And like the meteor, each idea's combustion was doomed to peter out.

Amid the buffet of unformed thoughts, Ike felt enveloped by an eerie blankness. His mind was not cluttered but strangely arid. He was on the cusp of abjection.

He fished the check from his pocket. One edge of it pinched between two fingers, he gazed at it. On the subway, riding home, he'd had one hand in the pocket of his pants. The check was clasped in the palm of that hand. He'd clawed, folded, twirled, and rolled the check. His restless fingers had left the check creased and frayed, wrinkled and unsightly. Toward the check was now directed a full measure of his disgust.

In a snap, he recalled the sum of all he'd suffered. The heartbreak he'd inflicted. Osuakwu stirring the morning with his wails. His mother mauled, lying in a hospital unattended, perhaps even breathing her last that very moment. The paltry sum scrawled in Mark Gruels's oddly feeble hand.

Ike felt an urge to tear up the check. Shred it and throw its pieces up in the air. He gaped at the check until, powerless before a sweeping urge, he broke into laughter. He shook so much that his fingers parted. The check glided to the floor.

He slapped his hands as if to remove some invisible stain. He began to make a hasty sign of the cross, but stopped halfway. Lifting his legs onto the couch, he rested his head on the leathery arm. Then he shut his eyes.

—

ONCE AGAIN, THE FLOOD came. This time, there was no heraldry. One moment, he was safe; he luxuriated in a bed of plumes. The next instant, he was immersed in a flood. It churned and tugged and tumbled. Underneath the rage, it was airless. Afraid of asphyxiation, he lifted his head for air. Bobbing along the surface was the statue of Ngene. It gazed at him, seemed amused. Disconcerted, he ducked under. The stream's howl deafened him. The maddening siren belched from a vortex.

He clambered awake, his pounding heart reverberating in his ears. With his left cuff he swiped a streak of saliva that dribbled down one part of his cheek. A sticky substance smeared his cuff. From habit, he brought the cuff to his nostrils, then turned sharply from the rotten, sickening stink. His neck was sweaty, the collar of his shirt sodden. Gripping a fold of his shirt, he used it to dab at his neck. Then he became aware of the phone's impatient ring. He reached out for it, stretching himself from the couch.

"This is a call from A and M Rental Management. Please hold for the next available agent."

He banged the phone down. It began to ring almost immediately. *Let it ring,* he thought. Last night he'd disconnected the voice mail. A sly sinister smile formed on his face.

He placed both hands against his chest and felt every chug of the ferocious beast inside him.

His eyes remained drowsy from interrupted sleep. Yet, the moment he shut his eyes the image of Ngene appeared. Reclining against the wall at the very spot where he'd left it for several days, it looked grotesquely emaciated. There was a terrifying indeterminacy about its visage. It seemed to be weeping and laughing all at once.

IKE UZONDU NO LONGER counted time in days, only in the swarm of maggots, the buzz of flies, and depth of the stench. What went on in the streets no longer touched him. The clamor from Cadilla's had taken on a muted, faraway quality. He sat and stared at the spot where he had stood the statue before he took it away to Foreign Gods, Inc. He stared at the decayed chicken and cuts of beef he had left on the floor to feed the deity that was no longer there, even though its stink remained. He gaped at the maggots that crawled in and out of the decayed food, at their soft, squiggly bodies that seemed drunk from the beer and gin he had spattered on the floor as well.

His phone had rung innumerable times—Usman Wai, his sister, the rental office, Jonathan, strangers—but he had not picked up.

Today, whatever the day was, he knew there were more maggots than ever, more flies flying their egg-laying sorties, a stronger stench infusing the air in the room. He knew that tomorrow, whenever it arrived, there would be even more maggots, a greater clatter of flies, a deeper reach of the smell.

He couldn't tell what would come next, then next. There was the business of feeding the maggots, hosting the flies, inhaling what the air gave. The maggots and flies were not enough. He was now chief priest to Ngene. And a chief priest should know what he had to do. He was going to buy another ticket and take Ngene back to Utonki.

He picked up his phone and dialed.

Mark Gruels's unmistakable voice answered.

"I sold you a god recently," he said, unsure how many days or weeks or months ago because he now counted time in the swarm of maggots.

"Yes, Ngene," Gruels said, his pronunciation perfect. "You were here about two weeks ago. I can't forget that accent, buddy."

"I haven't cashed your check. I need my deity back."

There was a burst of laughter, then a pause. "That's ridiculous. The thing's sold."

"I want it back," Ike said. "I'll bring back the check."

"It's gone," Gruels said. "Gone two days after I bought it. A Japanese guy snatched it up."

"We have to get it back. It must return to its shrine—or trouble continues."

"What do you mean trouble continues? Are you threatening me?"

"No, but I—we—need to take it back."

Gruels fell silent for a moment, as if to think. Ike's hope rose.

"Listen, this is an odd call. A buyer sometimes decides to return stuff—for any number of reasons. But you don't sell stuff and then ask the buyer to return it. I bought that deity. You can't ask me to hand it back to you—any more than I can ask the man who bought from me. Besides, the guy who took it wasn't really a collector, just happened to stroll in. And he was flying out that night, I believe. Back to Japan."

"You must have his address. I have to have it back."

"No, I don't. No, you don't. You don't sell stuff and then ask for it back. That's not business; that's some crazy children's game. Even if I knew the buyer's address—which I don't—I don't play that game."

Ike saw three flies land atop a mound of maggots that wiggled over a greenish, rotted piece of chicken. He winced. "Please," he said in a choked voice, "check for the man's address."

"Are you for real?" Gruels said. "I don't keep a bank of my customers' addresses."

"He must have left credit card records," Ike said.

"As a matter of fact, he didn't. He paid cash." After a pause, his tone impatient, Gruels asked, "Why are we even holding this conversation? Where's this leading?"

"I need the deity back. Maggots are crawling all over here."

"Maggots? This is crazy. What have maggots got to do with anything?"

"It has to go back to Utonki."

"No, it doesn't. Its new home is somewhere in Japan. You should be proud that a deity that once lived in your village has traveled to Asia."

"Please," Ike said, like a child asking for candy.

"Listen," Gruels said. "I'm going to make you a deal because the deity you sold me happened to be a class act—as far as my African inventory goes. By the way, did you know that Ngene farted storms from its rump? We sprayed perfume on it every day—and it still stank up the store. It has character, an audacious personality—I grant you that. So, here's the deal. I paid you what, fifteen hundred dollars, right."

"I haven't cashed it," Ike said.

"I've never done this, but you brought me a great god—and I like your accent and all. So let's say I throw in another thousand bucks."

"I want Ngene back," Ike said. A clump of maggots toppled from the edge of a stripped chicken bone. He gasped. "I don't want the—" He swallowed the rest of his words, startled by the sound of voices outside his door, followed by four sharp knocks. The phone clicked and then died in his hand.

ACKNOWLEDGMENTS

IN WRITING THIS BOOK, I benefited from the kindness, encouragement and goodwill of numerous friends, relatives, colleagues, students, publishers, and acquaintances. Many simply listened to my incessant stories. Their attentiveness made the solitude bearable and lightened the occasional sense of lonesomeness.

My deepest affection belongs to Sheri. I still marvel at my incredible luck, how I crashed your birthday party and stole you away! To my siblings John, J.C., Ifeoma, and Ogii: How extraordinary to be the children of "C" and "E." Fond regards to Doris Fafunwa and her late husband, Aliu Babatunde Fafunwa, for the gift of a magnificent wife; and also to Lola Jackson (sister-in-law), Tunde Fafunwa and Tani Fafunwa (brothers-in-law). I'm in awe of Huguette Njemanze-Fafunwa's insatiable appetite for books, and by Ifeoma Obianwu-Fafunwa's amazing creative flair.

The best thing that happened to this novel was its landing in the lap of Soho Press. I'm indebted to E.C. Osondu, a fine writer and genial spirit, for pointing me in Soho's direction. My editor, Mark Doten, proved a writer's dream. His grace, persistence, and attuned instincts guided me through the maze of revisions. Paul Oliver and his publicity/marketing team exude such palpable passion. And to Bronwen Hruska, the publisher at Soho, I say—*Daalu*! Kudos to the marketing staff at Random House for getting this book in the hands of readers.

I celebrate Wole Soyinka for his peerless generosity. Chinua Achebe, John Edgar Wideman, Ngugi wa Thiong'o, Ekwueme Michael Thelwell, and Kofi Awoonor have taught me much about life and literature. I hail Stephen Clingman, a patient guide. Michael Archer and Joel Whitney published an early excerpt on guernicamag.com. Several readers enriched this novel with their incisive critiques: Ma Phebean Ogundipe (whose textbook sparked my fascination with the English language), Karen Fritsche, Olu Oguibe, Kitty Axelson, Paul Nnodim, Nina Ryan, Nitor Egbarin, Holly Williams, Scott Myers, Rudolf Okonkwo, and Willie Nwokoye (a co-explorer of language and rites).

I salute Okey and Hadiza Anueyiagu, for their love for my family and me; Ikhide Ikheloa, for all the hell he raises because he believes that literature matters; Okezie Nwoka, for his bristling intelligence; Obiora Udechukwu, *Odogwu nwoke*! I've been sustained by many friends and relatives: Ian Mayo-Smith and Krishna Sondhi, Vijay Prashad, Nana Becky Clarke, Greg and Deirdre Falla and my Greene family, David and Chinwe Iloanya, Victor Manfredi, Sowore Omoyele, Okwy Okeke, Chenjerai Hove, Chika Okeke-Agulu, Cyril Obi, Abioseh Porter, Chuks Odikpo, William Wallis, Michael Peel, Kaye Whiteman, C. Don Adinuba, Bayo Okelana, Niyi Osundare, Victor Ehikhamenor, Chika Ezeanya, Bankole Olayebi, E.C. Ejiogu, Okwui Enwezor, Obiwu Iwuanyanwu, Nduka Otiono, Ndaeyo Uko, Mukoma Ngugi, Richard Dowden, Chika Unigwe, James Nagenda, Onyekachi Wambu, Maik Nwosu, and Paul Ezigbo.

I thank Reverends Damian Eze, Richard Fineo, and Efeturi Ojakaminor for the constancy of their prayers. I'm grateful to my former colleagues at Simon's Rock College and Trinity College and my colleagues in Africana Studies at Brown—for making me feel at home.